The Stelladaur Series

Book 2

Fading Heart

The Stelladaur Series

Coming Soon:

Stelladaur
Book 2

Fading Heart

S. L. Whyte

The Stelladaur Series, Book 2
Fading Heart by S. L. Whyte

ISBN: 978-0-9857523-3-0 (paperback)
ISBN: 978-0-9857523-4-7 (hardcover)
ISBN: 978-0-9857523-5-4 (ebook)
Library of Congress Control Number: 2014920096

info@fireglasspublishing.com
www.stelladaur.com

Interior art and Stelladaur Academy logo by Konohiki Place
Book interior and cover text design by Jill Ronsley, suneditwrite.com
Cover art design by Alicia Lockwood, ALimages
Author's photo by Garrett Wesley Gibbons, Aderyn Productions

Summary: Reilly travels through another portal, this time back to Ireland in 1896, in his continuing quest to find his father and to discover more secrets of the Stelladaur. He must face the Deceptors of Black Castle—the demons of Hell—in his attempt to rescue the one he loves.

Printed and bound in the USA

How far away the stars seem,
and how far is our first kiss,
and ah, how old my heart.

—William Butler Yeats

For Larry

Your kindness sustains me
Your laughter inspires my curiosity
Your wit enchants me
Your love reaches my soul in the seemingly mundane

Contents

Gratitude

To those who inspire me with ideas and encourage me in my work, I thank you sincerely. Most importantly, to:

My readers, young and old alike, for your enthusiasm for The Stelladaur Series. Your genuine support brings deeper purpose to my writing.

My dear friend, Regina, for believing in my work. Without you the journey would be much longer.

My daughters-in-law, Annie, Mary, and Traci, for the countless ways you inspire me, even when you don't know it.

My nieces and nephews: Megan, Heather, Courtney, Hunter, Nathan, Matthew, Kristin, Joshua, Caleb, Aimee, Malauri, Makayla, Malachi, MariAna, Addison, Avery, Ada, Logan, Ellie, Wyatt, Shay, Clint, Cole, Aleena, Bailee, and Cutler. I love each of you. I think of you when I write, and I wonder if you have found your Stelladaur. Thanks for just being you!

My amazingly talented editor and book designer, Jill Ronsley, for your committed efforts, honesty, expertise, and encouragement. I cannot say enough. You are simply irreplaceable!

My truly gifted artist, Konohiki Place. Thank you for sticking with me for the long haul! You are undeniably talented, gracious, and good. Your work adds an intriguing and inspiring dimension to *The Stelladaur Series*.

Chapter One

Vantage Post

Reilly tried to move, but the weight of the beam pressing on his thigh and across his chest pinned him to the ground. Inhaling was difficult. A searing pain in his upper left leg intensified with each shallow breath. The euphoric melody he had heard as he went through the portal in the reading room only moments before vanished, replaced by the screeching and screaming of people running past him. The haunting wails sounded familiar, though he did not know why. Great wooden beams crashed to the ground. His body wanted to jump to his feet and run, but he could only cover his ears in an attempt to keep the cacophony from breaking his eardrums.

His nose twitched from a thick, spicy smell that added to the queasy feeling in his gut. It certainly wasn't the university library's invigorating aroma of leather, plank floors, and oiled hardwood. Reilly wondered if he had tripped going through the portal and banged his head … or maybe he hadn't made it through at all. Maybe the paneled door he had stepped through was just the entrance to a storage closet. Maybe a massive earthquake had hit at that moment. Another beam crashed to the ground, only feet away. He flinched and grunted as he pulled himself up on his elbows and felt the wood slide down his chest a few inches. He strained to lift it off his legs, but it barely budged, and he fell back, panting with pain.

"It's coming down! We're going to die!" someone yelled. "Hurry, before another tree falls!"

"No!" another protested. "Run!"

Turning in the direction of the voices, Reilly saw a throng of people racing towards him, but they passed as if he didn't exist.

"Hey! Somebody help!" he shouted, but no one seemed to hear him above the clamor of frantic people, shaking earth, and falling debris. Blinking to clear his blurred vision, Reilly spotted a clump of spiky red mushrooms poking up from a cluster of ferns. Despite the pain, he strained to lift himself up on one elbow and grip the beam lying across his legs with the other hand. His fingers slipped on damp, mossy wood, and he realized it wasn't a beam, but a large tree branch. Panicking, and now fully aware that he was neither in the old library nor in the portal, he called out for his dog.

"Tuma! Tuma, where are you?" The albino dog, who had arrived mysteriously at the worst time in Reilly's life, did not appear. Another thick branch crashed down, landed crisscrossed over the one on his leg, and rolled off. It shifted the branch that had pinned him, which scraped down his shin with mighty force. He screamed in pain, but barely heard himself above the chaos.

Slowly, Reilly sat up and took a deep breath, relieved to be able to do both. He looked at his leg and felt nauseous. A piece of wood had pierced his thigh like a giant sliver. He yanked it out and yelled even louder. The thick smell of blood permeated his nostrils as it began to gush through his torn pant leg, and he covered his mouth to keep from retching. Feeling dizzy, he hung his head to his chest, letting his tangled hair cover his eyes. It was difficult to breathe again, and he could not tell if the reeling motion came from inside his body, or from the moving ground. Still trapped at the ankle, he fell back again and closed his eyes, slipping out of and back into consciousness.

It's so much easier to close my eyes. Everything's quiet and still … Where's Tuma? She was with me when I left in the reading room … I wonder if Chantal and James are still there … and when I walked through the portal.

Massive branches continued to crash to the ground. If Tir Na Nog was anything like what he imagined, this was not it.

It was supposed to be a beautiful place. I thought my dad would be here.

It was difficult for him to know if he was thinking clearly, not only because he had no idea of where he was, but also because he wasn't sure if he was alive.

Can I think if I'm dead? Can I bleed? Reilly groaned and barely opened his eyes. Then his eyes closed.

I'll just lie here … in my kayak … and glide across Eagle Harbor to Eilam's Hut.

Eilam's been my best friend since I was really young … he doesn't even have an age … people think he's crazy … but he knows stuff they never even consider … stuff about portals … talking trees … Tir Na Nog … and he knows where we go after we die.

Reilly groaned softly again.

Tuma … She showed up at the kayak hut after my dad drowned in the sailing accident. Eilam said he sent her to me … Dad! Where are you? … Tuma?…

There's the dock. Eilam doesn't seem to be around! Has he gone, too …?

Something warm and wet touched Reilly's lips.

I've got to get out of here! Now!

Reilly opened his eyes wide.

"What was the last portal?" he blurted, as if he was answering a question on *Jeopardy*.

"Shhh. Drink this." A girl pressed a cup to his mouth. "Quickly, there isn't much time." She held the back of his neck and poured warm liquid between his parted lips. It trickled down his throat like a thick cough suppressant, leaving a salty, black-licorice taste on his tongue.

"Good!" She pushed hard on the branch that still trapped Reilly at his ankle. "Now, let's get this off of you." He looked down at the gash in his leg but leaned forward to help her.

"Can you get up?" The girl pulled gently on Reilly's arm without waiting for a response.

"Yeah, I think so." The pain receded to a dull throb. He struggled to stand, still tasting licorice. "Am I dead?"

"Not yet." She almost laughed. "But we will be, if we don't hurry. Come with me!" Reilly took a few limping steps, but he began to walk more confidently as, to his surprise, his legs regained strength. He clicked his tongue and glanced back at the cup the girl had tossed on the ground. "Keep your eyes open for more falling branches, and be ready to jump over big limbs," the girl warned. She led the way as they ran.

The forest looked as though someone had been playing with Pick Up Sticks. Hurdling debris, Reilly heard the thunderous noises quiet to a soft rumble, and the ground beneath his feet no longer shook. Within a few minutes, they reached a giant willow tree. The girl released her tight grip on Reilly's hand, and pushed her fingers against the trunk.

"The lift was originally designed to hold all five of our family members, but it's smaller now, so it's a tight fit." There was a grinding noise and the trunk opened.

"Why is it smaller than it used to be?" Reilly asked as they stepped inside.

"See these nicks in the walls? We don't know how it happens but whenever there is a new nick, the lift shrinks. Besides, not all of our family is with us now."

Reilly nodded and poked a finger through one of the larger nicks.

"I saw you from our Vantage Post and figured you must be new to the Great Forest. I mean … well, it was obvious, the way you somersaulted right in front of that huge falling tree. Were you *trying* to get yourself killed?"

"No … I, uh, I just came through the closet at the library," he said, looking around as he realized he was *inside a tree*.

"The Library?" she whispered. "How did you escape without being captured?"

She pushed a brass button on the control panel, and a gust of air whooshed through the cracks in the wooden walls. They began to move upward. "We've got to hide you before they find out you're here, or my whole family will be in danger," she whispered more softly.

"I'm sorry. I didn't know—"

"Shhh!" She interrupted, her silver eyes glaring at him. "They may already have seen you coming, and besides, our lift has been synched!"

"Who synched it?" Reilly whispered. "And what does that mean?"

"Shhh!" She shook her head and put her finger to her mouth.

They rode in silence for half a minute, long enough for Reilly to assess his surroundings. Rough lumber lined the walls of the hollow trunk. There were big gaps between the planks, and splinters protruded in spots. The lift rose so fast that everything beyond the cracks was a blur. Reilly glanced up to see that the ceiling, covered with dripping moss, was alive with insects, bugs, and worms. He stepped closer to the girl, wondering what creatures lived in the dirt floor beneath them.

The lift lurched to a stop and their feet sank into the soft floor, leaving footprints as they stepped out. Reilly followed the girl down a narrow hallway lined with high, sunlit windows. As they approached another door, he saw a green woodpecker on a perch above the doorknob.

"Katell, this man escaped from The Library," the girl said to the bird. "We've got to get him inside, fast."

Man? I'm just a kid! Reilly thought.

"Stalwart 59," the girl commanded. The bird uttered a shrill staccato sound and flapped its wings as it gripped the perch. Then Katell faced the door. He hammered a series of long-short-long pecks with his beak, and the door opened.

Reilly and the girl entered and walked up a spiral staircase made of twisted tree branches, with a chartreuse handrail as smooth as polished jade. When they reached the landing, the space opened into an inviting room. Chairs, a couch, a piano, and end tables sat in a cozy arrangement on top of a green and blue woolen rug. Beautiful paintings hung on the walls—pictures of the sea and coastal cliffs—and reminded Reilly of home.

"Please have a seat," the girl said. "I'll find my mother." She flipped her long, white-blonde hair over her shoulders as she left him.

Exhausted, Reilly sat down on the couch and scanned the room. Leaves draping the high ceilings, ivy framing the windows, and oddly-shaped doorways made of intertwined branches dispelled any question in Reilly's mind about where the lift had stopped. He was sitting in an enormous tree house.

"Welcome to our home." The woman rolled her *r* and tightened her vowels in a strong Irish accent.

Reilly rose to his feet. The mother looked like the girl's twin, with shorter hair and a few wrinkles curved around the corners of her mouth.

"My name is Brigid," the woman said, with a warm smile. "My

daughter, Lottie, tells me you have escaped from The Library. Please, sit down."

Brigid sat next to Reilly on the couch, and Lottie took the nearest chair.

"Aye, you must have had quite a fright," Brigid said, taking Reilly's hands in hers. "You are safe here, at least for now. How did you get here?"

Her hands felt warm and firm, and Reilly did not resist her grasp. But his mouth had the stuffed-with-cotton feeling he had felt when his father died, and he could not find the words to make sense of any of this.

"Uh … I …"

"Take a deep breath, lad. You'll be just fine." Brigid patted Reilly's hand. "Why don't you start with your name?"

He took her advice and breathed in slowly and deeply, then exhaled long and loud.

"My name is Reilly. Reilly McNamara." The girl's eyes shot to her mother, but Brigid remained focused on Reilly without the slightest change in expression. "I have no idea where I am or how I got here."

"How did you escape after the Deceptors began to torture you with their lies?" Lottie asked.

"Deceptors? What's a Deceptor?"

"Oh, dearie me," Brigid said, shaking her head and squeezing his hand. "This is worse than I thought. They have completely erased their identities from his mind."

"No one has erased anything from my mind!" Reilly declared, pulling his hand away. "The portal was supposed to take me to Tir Na Nog. Am I in Tir Na Nog?"

Brigid looked at her daughter. They both sighed.

"No, my dear, you are in Ireland," the woman said. "Tir Na Nog is but an ancient legend. Though we like to believe it exists, no one knows for sure that it does."

Reilly glanced around the room, looking for anything familiar.

"Other Stalwarts have had experiences with portals," Lottie said. Reilly assumed she meant to sound encouraging, but then her voice lowered. "Our family has not been so lucky."

Nothing was making sense, but he pushed on. "Lottie said your family could be in more danger with me here. I don't know what's going on, but I don't want to cause any trouble to your family."

"You're no trouble, dearie." Brigid replied. "Now where did you say you come from?"

"I live near Seattle. In Washington."

"Aye, the coastal settlement discovered just before the turn of the century." Brigid leaned in a bit closer. "That's such a long way to travel—and through a portal, you say?"

"The turn of the century?" Reilly said, his voice cracking. "What year *is* it?"

"It's 1896." Lottie frowned. "What year do you think it is?"

Reilly breathed in deeply and closed his eyes. He released the air slowly before he looked at Lottie again. "It's 2015. As I said, I found a portal in the library. My dog came with me, but I can't find her." Without warning, his breathing became shallow and he began to hyperventilate. "My dad died … in a sailing accident a few months ago … I thought I'd find him here … this can't be happening."

The room started spinning. He saw Lottie leave and then return with a mug in her hand. "Take a sip of water," she said. He took the cup and gulped down the cool liquid.

"My friend, Eilam, left for no reason …" His dizziness increased. "And my dog is lost. I don't know … what to do." His head drooped to his chin and he blinked rapidly, trying to stay awake.

Reilly drifted off as he heard Brigid's soothing voice. "Poor thing." Then she added with conviction, "The Deceptors have already begun the Detachment Process."

Chapter Two

Prince Ukobach

Reilly lay in the oversized hammock enjoying the warmth of a soft blanket spread over his legs and feet. He remembered the weight of the tree branch the last time he woke up, and he reached for his thigh. He touched a bandage but felt no pain. Reilly missed the pain and wondered why. But, he reasoned, it was pointless to try to probe his conscious self for answers. On the other hand, without help from Eilam or Tuma, he doubted he would know what questions to ask anyway. His stomached growled, and he figured it must be a good sign. At least he was alive.

He stretched and reached his hands behind his head to scrunch the pillow. The suspended bed rocked like his kayak on a slightly breezy day. But this wasn't Eagle Harbor near his home. Uncertain in his new surroundings, Reilly touched his chest and fumbled for his Stelladaur on its cord around his neck. Then he recalled he had lost the jewel somewhere last week. Eilam had told Reilly he wouldn't need it anymore and that what he needed was inside himself. It all sounded good then. But this was now; and now, none of it made sense.

He put his hand inside his shirt, hoping by a twist of fate—a miracle even—that his Stelladaur *had* returned and he had missed it. His skin felt warm. He rested his palm on his heart, as if to pledge allegiance to something—perhaps his own thumping heart—but no precious stone lay in its brilliant form at his chest.

There was a knock at the door.

"Come in," Reilly said, pulling his hand out from under his shirt.

"Good morning!" Lottie chimed as she stepped into the room. "Did you sleep well?"

"Yes, thank you."

"I brought you a bit of breakfast." She carried in a silver tray and placed it on a stand beside the hammock. "Do you like cream on your berries?"

"Sure."

Reilly thought she meant whipped cream, but watched her lift the small pitcher and pour thick white liquid over a bowl of dark red and blue berries. She did it gracefully, like a dance.

"A little sugar?" she asked.

"Please."

She picked up a small spoon and sprinkled the sugar with a gentle rhythm, watching it land over the berries. Her obvious attentiveness seemed strangely recognizable to Reilly.

Sitting up to swing his legs over the side of the rocking hammock, Reilly lost his balance slightly.

"Careful." Lottie dropped the spoon on the tray and grabbed the edge of the hammock. "You may still be a bit dizzy." Her silver eyes met Reilly's. They reminded him of the color of the harbor on an overcast day.

"No, I feel great," he insisted, blinking as he looked away. "Thanks for the food." He reached for the bowl and spoon, and enjoyed the tang of berries on his tongue.

"You slept for two days," Lottie said as she sat down on a nearby chair. "I've been checking on you."

"Oh … thank you." Reilly wasn't sure what else to say. "Did I snore?"

"Not at all," she laughed. "You slept calmly and looked peaceful, and … and fine."

He swallowed a mouthful of berries. Looking into her silver eyes again, Reilly felt a blossoming connection, equaled by awkwardness. "You've been awfully kind."

"My pleasure." Lottie smiled shyly. "We were surprised you didn't wake during the Crumble yesterday."

"The Crumble?"

"Yes, another home was destroyed, this time in our neighborhood. We weren't able to help them salvage any of it. The mother and two small children took cover in the Undertunnels, but the oldest boy was captured. Their father was taken years ago."

Reilly puckered at a mouthful of sour berries.

"Do you need a drink?" she asked, handing him a mug.

He peered into the mug. "What is it?"

"Water, silly. We save the tea for emergencies."

"Tea? Is that what you gave me before?"

"Yes. That was Arbutus tea, and it was definitely an emergency." Lottie reached behind her neck and gathered her long hair in her hand, pulling it over her shoulder. "Drink."

Reilly cupped his hands around the mug and took a few sips. "So your homes are being destroyed?"

"Yes."

"Who is destroying them?"

"The Deceptors, of course, though they are dreadfully subtle, and we rarely see them coming."

"You keep talking about Deceptors." He put the mug on the tray and picked up a piece of bread. "Remember, I'm not from around here."

"Surely … having come from The Library … you must know."

"But I don't."

"Yes, of course." Lottie shook her head with a look of pity, like Brigid's when she had mumbled something about a Detachment Process. Lottie pulled her chair closer to Reilly and looked directly into his eyes. "Deceptors destroy homes, villages, towns, even entire countries. As far as we know, they've been around for centuries. Every generation, they feed on their prey in different ways, so people are caught off guard and don't realize what's happening … until it's too late. The Detachment Process happens gradually."

"You keep talking about that. Detachment from what?"

"First from your own sense of self—the real you. Then from your roots—your family. The Deceptors have endless ways to do this to people and they use them, one at a time. That's why it's a process."

"Why?"

"Deceptors obey Prince Ukobach. He teaches them to believe they are entitled to do as they please—and destruction, in whatever form they conjure, is all they please. The more destruction they create, and the more homes or families they destroy, the more powerful they become. It's as if their billowing fire cannot be extinguished."

"Has anyone confronted this Ukobach?"

"A part of Prince Ukobach lives in every Deceptor. We don't know how he became their master, only that his powers were once as great as the Gods'."

"The Gods? What Gods?"

"The Gods of Ifreann, or Hell."

In all the portals Reilly had been through, there was never a mention of any Gods; it was new and confusing information. *It could be another Irish myth or superstition*, he tried to reason.

"Are there no laws here in Wicklow?" His voice rose with frustration.

"Laws? Surely where you come from there are laws, but does that mean homes are not destroyed, or that there is no crime?"

"Well, no, not everywhere. It's relatively safe where I live, but there are other dangerous areas. And yes, many homes are destroyed by crime, or by war."

"Always wars." Lottie shook her head and lowered her eyes. "Even by 2015, has humanity still not discovered how to live peacefully? Have they not yet learned the key to understanding the connections to eternity within themselves?"

Reilly stared at Lottie. Her last statement brought a tingle of déjà vu. "What did you say?" he asked, as he put the last chunk of bread back on the tray and stood up.

"I said, I hope by your time people would have finally realized the key to peace lies within themselves."

He stared at Lottie as she raked the last six inches of her white-blonde hair with her fingers. Although he no longer felt dizzy, something about this girl made his head spin. She smiled at him. Reilly turned and began to pace the floor as he looked at the items in the small room: the hammock, a nightstand, the chair Lottie sat on, and a branch protruding from the wall, where his sweatshirt hung.

"Thanks for rescuing me," he said, as he turned back around. "And for bandaging my leg. It feels much better." Holding his thigh for a moment, he walked toward her.

"Yes, the Arbutus tea heals wounds quickly." She continued to stroke her hair as she held his gaze.

"How old are you, Lottie?" Reilly began to walk again, hoping it wasn't obvious how taken he was by her silver-grey eyes.

"Fourteen. And you?"

"I'm sixteen. Do you have any brothers or sisters?"

"I have a younger brother named Dillon. He's twelve. My sister, Sorcha, is seventeen. The Deceptors took her three years ago."

"I'm sorry." He still didn't know what she meant, but let it go. "I have a sister, too. Chantal. She's ten years older, but we're good friends."

"Sorcha and I used to be close, too." Lottie stopped combing her hair and Reilly stopped pacing. "I really miss her."

"Do you think you'll ever see her again?" He tried to sound sincere, but worried that he didn't. "I'm sorry, I don't mean to pry. It's just that my dad was taken from me, too, and … well, I know how awful it is."

"You said he drowned, right?" Lottie did sound sincere, and Reilly decided it was without even trying.

"Yeah. We were sailing, and a storm came in unexpectedly." He walked toward his sweatshirt, hanging on the branch, and absent-mindedly fumbled with the zipper. "Sometimes I think I'll go crazy trying to erase it from my mind."

"Me, too. I keep wondering if I could have done something, if I'd known the Deceptors were targeting Sorcha."

Reilly lowered himself into the hammock. "Lottie, sometimes there isn't anything you can do." Reilly looked deeply into her eyes. "Sometimes it's just the way it is."

She kept her eyes on his without saying anything, and Reilly entertained the strange feeling that Lottie could look right into his soul—as if she knew his thoughts, or even his heart.

"Maybe." She paused, then added, "But I believe Sorcha is still alive. Somewhere."

He could see the topic was distressing, so he decided not to press for more information. "So when do I get to meet Dillon and your dad?"

"Dillon is helping my mother and father at the Embassy. My father is up for re-election at the end of the month, but with so many Crumbles lately, he's hardly been able to campaign."

"Oh." Reilly was sure he sounded like an idiot. Fortunately, she continued before he could ask more stupid questions.

"Now that you're rested, I'll find you clean clothes and we'll go to meet them. If you dress in something more appropriate, maybe you won't look so conspicuous to the Deceptors. You look like one of their escapees."

"Escapee?" his voiced cracked.

"From The Library … remember?" Lottie sighed and shook her head as she walked toward the door. "I'll be right back."

Pacing the floor again, Reilly stopped at his sweatshirt and put his hand in a pocket. The Fireglass! Eilam had given it to Reilly, and he and Norah used it to help them go through one of the portals together.

The Fireglass resembled a cylindrical magnifying glass. Reilly ran his fingers across the etching of a crudely shaped star—a Stelladaur—on the outer surface. The first time he did so, he felt a strange surge pulsate through his body, but this time there was nothing. When he and Norah looked through the Fireglass and her Stelladaur at the same moment, they warped through a fireworks display, and the Stelladaur etched on the outside of the Fireglass spun around the device until it blurred with motion. Now it seemed lifeless.

Reilly checked the other pocket and pulled out a small ruby. He rolled it in his fingers, remembering walking on a beach of rubies with Norah in a portal-land called Bozka. He replaced the ruby and discovered the red flower he had tucked behind Norah's ear after they watched the fireworks on the Fourth of July. He found it again the day she had disappeared. But the flower was still perfect, undamaged, as if it had just been picked from its stem. He sniffed the soft petals deeply. Breathing in the exotic aroma filled his senses with a bitter torture. *Where are you, Norah?* he whispered. Pain scorched inside his chest … not just the sadness of missing her, but burning, throbbing pain! It faded as quickly as it had come, and he dismissed it.

The sound of footsteps coming down the hallway intruded on Reilly's thoughts. He quickly put the flower back into his sweatshirt pocket, and dug his hands into his pants pockets to search for other treasures. Empty. The knife Eilam had given him on his birthday over two months ago, and which he had kept with him since, was not there. The key he used to open the portal door in the library was gone. Reilly vaguely remembered hearing something drop to the ground with a *clink* as the euphoric music started to fade when he and Tuma went through the portal.

Lottie entered the room, juggling a few items of clothing in her arms. "Dillon is tall for his age, so these trousers should work fine. If you roll up the sleeves, no one will know the shirt is too small." She handed Reilly the pants and held the shirt up to his chest.

"What if I borrowed one of your dad's shirts?"

"Are you complaining, Mr. McNamara?" Lottie said mockingly. "Or simply disappointed with our fashion trends?"

"Neither," he chuckled. "This reminds me of a time when I had to wear a tuxedo, one with tails, and I looked like a penguin. It can't be that bad. Thanks."

Lottie raised her eyebrows. "Very well. I'll meet you in the sitting room in a few minutes. It's down the stairs to the right." She left the room, closing the door behind her.

The pants were too short, and the shirt fit tightly across his torso. "I feel like a duck," he whined to himself, loading the baggy pockets with the Fireglass, ruby, and red flower. "I hope I don't start quacking. And what if my tennis shoes give me away? Nobody here has Nikes—that's for sure." When he found Lottie in the sitting room, she handed him a pair of brown leather shoes that looked as if they had been pulled from a museum shelf.

"My uncle forgot them after his last visit. I'm afraid they're a tad dusty," she said, blowing on the shoes as she handed them to him. "He's about your size, so I hope they're a good fit."

Smiling, Reilly kicked off his own shoes and slipped into the loafers. "Perfect."

"All right, then," Lottie said. "Let's go to the Embassy. There's a chance the Deceptors heard us speaking in the lift the other day, and if they did, they'll be keeping a closer watch on our house. Lifts are synched by the Deceptors soon after they capture a family member. The lift is their first point of attack, and the Deceptors become particularly aware of any outsiders that may be a strength to the remaining family members."

"But I thought your mom said I'd be safe here."

"She only meant you'd be safe from the Crumble, not from the Deceptors themselves." She walked into the hallway and opened the front door. As they stopped outside, Lottie said, "Katell, please signal me if you sense any danger." The bird blinked twice and gave a slight nod.

Reilly silently followed Lottie to the lift. This time he noticed a red button with the letter "U" next to the brass one Lottie had pushed before they descended. Insects still drooped from the ceiling, and the floor was thick with pine needles and undergrowth—so soft that Reilly thought they might sink through to the ground below. Looking more closely at the crevices in the walls, Reilly noticed they were covered with jagged nicks, as if struck or attacked with an ax. Within a minute they landed on solid ground, the door opened, and they stepped into the forest.

"Is it okay to talk now?" Reilly asked.

"Yes. We've just come through one of the Undertunnels and there is less chance of being noticed here. The Deceptors' first point of attack is our homes. Some of the city buildings are synched, too, but to our knowledge they haven't bothered with the country roads."

"This is a road?" He looked ahead at the pathway, which reminded him of the forest trails near his home. After a few minutes, they rounded a corner and stepped onto a path that opened into a lush clearing of rolling hills as green as those he had seen in pictures and movies of Ireland. A horse-drawn buggy was headed in their direction. They stepped to the side and let the carriage pass.

"Weird," Reilly whispered to himself.

"Pardon me?" Lottie said. "Did you say something?"

"Nothing. This is all so much different than what I thought it would be."

Lottie smiled as she smoothed the wrinkles of her long skirt and adjusted the satchel hanging over her shoulder. "I'm a good listener." She tucked her hand through Reilly's left arm as they began to walk.

Reilly immediately thought of Norah. He felt a split second of searing pain in his chest, longing to protect her.

With his hands tucked into the pockets of his baggy pants, he felt the ruby and red flower on one side, and the Fireglass on the other. He wondered why he was glad Lottie was at his side. She seemed older than fourteen.

Reilly could feel Lottie look up at him with her mesmerizing eyes, but he looked straight ahead. "I don't know why, but going through this portal—the one to Ireland in 1896—is much more difficult for me to grasp than going through any of the other ones," he began. "And I've been through seven. It all started a few weeks after my dad drowned. I found a star-shaped stone called a Stelladaur and learned how to use it to go through portals to other places. Usually, if the stone was wet and I held it up to the light at a certain angle, I could open a portal. Sometimes a portal opened from the place where a rainbow met with the ocean. One time it opened through an ice cube. And the last one—before I came through the library—was in a fireworks display."

He glanced down at Lottie from the corner of his eye. She seemed to be taking it in well, so he continued. "Anyway, each place I went, I discovered more about the Stelladaur and what it can do. There's a Stelladaur for each person ever born, but many never find theirs. If they do find it, their Stelladaur can bring them whatever they want most, if they learn how to access its power. You probably think this is a joke, huh?"

"Not at all," she said softly. "I've always believed other realms exist beyond here, and I've wished I could find one. But I've never felt comfortable telling anyone that before … until you, Reilly."

"I … uh …" He fumbled in his pocket for the ruby and the flower as his mind raced with thoughts of Norah and his heart beat rapidly. "I have—had—a couple of friends I could talk to about the Stelladaur. But they seem to have all left me."

"I'm sorry." She patted his arm. "Who?"

"There's Eilam. He's been around longer than either of us. Until a few days ago, I saw him just about every day of my life. Then he left me a note that said he had to go away for a while, and to remember the things I'd learned from my Stelladaur."

"Where is your Stelladaur now?"

"Also gone."

"And you don't know where?"

"No. I always kept it hung around my neck on a cord. Then one day it was just gone. Eilam told me I wouldn't need it anymore … that if I listened to my heart, I'd always know what to do."

He wanted to stop walking and to take the flower from his pocket, to look at it and touch it carefully, to see if by magic Norah would appear at his side. But it felt good to have Lottie's hand rest on his arm, and he was comfortable talking with her. What was it about warping through time zones and parallel worlds that compelled him to connect with these two girls? He ached for Norah, but being with Lottie lifted his melancholy mood.

"And do you believe that?" Lottie asked. "Do you believe that if you listen to your heart, you'll know what to do?"

"I think so," he said, though he knew he was trying to convince himself.

"Tell me about your other friends. Is there a young lady in your life?" Lottie asked with a lilt in her voice, clasping both hands around Reilly's arm.

Reilly couldn't bring himself to be completely honest with her. "I have my dog, Tuma. I guess she's my girl."

"You mentioned her the other day. Tell me more about Tuma."

"She showed up one day at Eilam's hut. He said my dad sent her to me."

"I see."

"She helped me find the portals. She came with me through the one in the library, but now I have no idea where she is." Reilly looked down at the thick grass as they walked along.

"Perhaps she's nearby and you just don't know it."

Reilly took his hands out of his pocket and placed one over Lottie's. "Are you always so optimistic?"

She looked up, and this time he looked back at her. Her silver eyes looked right through him again, and reminded him of the first time his eyes met Norah's. This moment felt different, and he couldn't make sense of it. Reilly missed Norah so badly that the bones in his body hurt; yet he was shivering with confusing excitement.

Excitement was replaced with distraction, though, as they walked around a bend. They had arrived.

Chapter Three

The Embassy

The cobblestoned streets and red brick buildings of the town looked like something he had seen in a recent movie … or had he been here before? Zipping through portals to parallel worlds had left his brain reeling in an attempt to understand reality-then and reality-now. A warm breeze blowing against his face caught Reilly's attention. He strained to listen and thought he heard the wind whisper, "All is now." Reilly shook his head, wondering where the sound had come from. The tingling sensation that pervaded his chest reminded him of the assurance he had felt when the Stelladaur hung by its cord around his neck, so for the moment, he stopped questioning.

"The Embassy is just around that corner," Lottie said, pointing to the far right. He nodded, and increased his pace to keep up with her.

A shimmering green building, conspicuously different than the others, came into view as they rounded the corner. "Is that it?" Reilly asked, though it was obvious. "What's it made of?"

"Jade," Lottie said. "The town hall was originally built centuries ago by an earl who inherited his father's fortune at a young age. Among other things, the earl studied foreign trade, and became the chief importer of jade from Asia."

"Wow!"

"It took nearly thirty years to build this palace, but then he and his family lived here until their deaths."

"How did they die?"

"We think Deceptors tortured and murdered them. There are stories about ghosts who still live in the great hall. It used to be a fortress but was refurbished nearly a century ago. It's been the Embassy Headquarters for all of Ireland ever since."

They approached the wide steps leading to the main entrance and stopped as Lottie removed her shoes. "The bodies of the earl and his family are entombed somewhere within the walls—though we don't know where—so we enter the doors with respect and honor."

Nodding, Reilly took off his shoes and followed Lottie up the steps to the main door. It, too, was made of jade, streaked with yellow and brown. A massive brass door handle was positioned in the center of the door so big Reilly could not fit his hand completely around it. Once inside, they paused to put their shoes back on.

"First, we check in at the registry, and then I'll take you to meet my father," Lottie began. "He'll need our help." They walked a few steps to a desk where a white-haired woman sat, knitting with red yarn.

"Good morning, Lottie," the woman began. "Where have you been the past day or so?"

"Tending to our houseguest, ma'am," Lottie said. "Flynn, I'm pleased to introduce you to Mr. Reilly McNamara."

The woman rested her knitting on her lap and reached a hand over the desk.

"Hello," Reilly said, shaking her fragile hand.

"Aye, what a fine young fellow, Lottie." The woman winked at Lottie and turned back to Reilly. "And where do you come from, Mr. McNamara? That name typically comes from the west part of Ireland. Haven't heard it in a while."

Lottie interrupted. "That's right. He *is* from west of here. On the far coast, actually." Lottie glanced at Reilly, who nodded in agreement. She picked up a quill and wrote in the registry. Reilly peered at the book and noted that Lottie had signed both of their names, and written in the date and time—18 July 1896, 11:15 a.m.

So I went back in time over a hundred years, but not exactly to the day, Reilly thought as he computed the dates. *I came through the portal in the Suzzallo Library on July 5th, the day after Norah and I watched the fireworks ... Maybe time speeds up after a person goes back that far.*

"Welcome to Wicklow!" The woman paused, then picked up her needles and continued to knit. "It's too bad your visit is at a time when our village is under attack. And yet, the Deceptors are always near." She shook her head and murmured something under her breath.

Lottie reached into a basket at the edge of the table and pulled out something red. "Here, put these wristbands on," she said, handing Reilly two knitted bands the size of a dress-shirt cuff. She looped one around each of her hands, and nodded for Reilly to follow her. He placed a band on his right wrist. Then he slid his left hand through the knitted band and placed it a little higher on his arm, so it wouldn't cover the golden Thread of Gratitude he had received from Flavio Xanthipee in Zora.

The old woman mumbled about Deceptors as they walked away. Reilly tugged at the golden thread.

The building was not as magnificent on the inside as the jade exterior. They walked down a long, windowless corridor with many closed doors on both sides. Reilly presumed they must be offices, but he didn't ask. A pungent odor he almost recognized made his nose twitch. It reminded him of the Arbutus tea Lottie had given him, but also a mixture of other unusual plants or herbs. At the end of the hallway, they came to a steeply ascending stairwell with steps made of uneven granite rocks.

"The magistrate's office is on the second floor," Lottie said. "My father will be pleased to meet you, I'm sure."

"Uh … great," Reilly said hesitantly.

They climbed the stone steps, one hundred in all, which switch-backed four times until they opened into a cavernous room. Dozens of people worked busily at long tables, shuffling papers or stuffing envelopes. Every person wore red knitted wristbands.

"What are these for?" Reilly asked Lottie, tugging slightly at one of his bands.

"It's my dad's campaign color." She scanned the room and nodded at red banners and posters draped on the walls to make her point. "And we wear them for protection from Deceptors."

"Okay, but …" He still didn't understand the purpose of the knitted wristbands, but she interrupted him.

"When a magistrate is up for re-election, his color is always red. It's the color of victory."

"Hmm …" He remembered going through another portal, to Bozka, where Aka-ula told him red was the color of love, but also the color of war. He decided to not press her further about the wristbands. He would ask her about them later. "How long has your dad been a magistrate?"

"Each term is for five years, and he's served three terms already."

"Since you were a baby?"

"It's been his profession my entire life. I don't know anything different." Lottie waved and smiled at people as she and Reilly walked toward the end of the room. "When the Deceptors are in full force, and when Crumbles happen frequently—and during election time—it's vital that we protect our wrists."

Reilly raised his brow. Lottie stopped to look directly at him.

"During campaign time, anyone at the Embassy could be at risk of being taken by the Deceptors from *here*. People tend to become divided rather than united when they differ on policy or strategy. So while we're here, we wear the bands as a reminder to be on guard." Reilly watched Lottie crisscross her hands to clasp both wrists. *Why do the wrists need to be protected*? He wondered, but shuddered at the possibilities and decided he didn't really want to know the answer—at least not now.

"My parents and Dillon are over there, at the main Vantage Post." Lottie grabbed Reilly's hand and pulled him forward. They walked quickly to the far end of the room, where a wall of open-air windows revealed a panoramic view of the rustic countryside. Six white marble pedestals, each with a brass telescope securely anchored to it, lined the giant windows like miniature cannons. Three of them were in use.

"We're here," Lottie announced.

Lottie's mom turned around first. "Oh, yes, my dears!" She walked toward Reilly with outstretched arms and hugged him tightly. "You look much better after your long rest." She released him and turned to her husband. "Quin, here is the lad."

"Lad? I should say not," Quin said, shaking Reilly's hand vigorously. "He's nearly a man, no doubt."

"Nice to meet you, sir."

"Aye. And this is my son, Dillon." Dillon barely stepped away from his telescope and nodded briefly, pulling a strand of oily reddish hair from his cheek.

"What's it like in The Library?" Dillon blurted, with a warm smile that revealed two buckteeth.

"Dillon!" scolded Brigid. "Not now!"

Dillon's smile vanished.

"Yes," Quin agreed. "The man surely does not want to remember his suffering more than is necessary."

"Well, actually, I didn't really—"

"No, no. Not here, not now," Quin insisted. "But if you're willing, we could use your help. With so many details of the campaign still underway, it's difficult to keep the Vantage Post fully staffed."

"Of course, I'd be happy to help. What are we looking for?" Reilly stepped to one of the telescopes and ran his fingers across the smooth brass.

"Patterns. Any pattern that would indicate a Crumble is beginning," Quin said. He stepped up to the telescope Reilly was touching. "From the Vantage Post, we have a complete view of Wicklow, and all the roads coming in and going out. We survey for unwelcome intruders entering our territory."

"Like Deceptors?" Reilly asked.

"Yes, but they usually appear in disguise. They rarely reveal their truest self." Quin adjusted the focus. "In any event, the most effective way to prevent Deceptors from attacking, and avoid an imminent Crumble, is to strengthen the homes' aura."

Still not understanding, Reilly barely smiled, then shook his head.

"A Crumble is when a tree home is completely destroyed by the Deceptors, ususally in disguise," Lottie tried to explain. "They chop away a little at a time with their silent saws and axes, often without the family members even knowing. The trunk gets so weak and narrow from all the chopping that it can't support the home, and it crumbles to the ground. Anyone in the home who has not already been captured must run for his life and find shelter elsewhere. The Deceptors take the fallen wood from the Crumbles and burn it at their great bonfire. Or make their prisoners carry it."

"Why?" Reilly asked. "Where?"

"The bonfire burns on the Cliffs of Black Castle of Wicklow, just beyond the far glen. We can see the flames from our scopes, but we can't get close enough to save those who are led into captivity," Quin continued. "As I said, the best way to prevent a Crumble is to strengthen the aura above each home. Look here." He stepped to the nearest telescope, adjusted the focus bar as he peered into it, and motioned for Reilly to take a look. "Notice the patterns in the aura above that home. There's a lot of white and soft yellow, indicating stability. But see the deep orange on the outer edges? That means someone in the home is at risk. It begins with some form of disrespect for others or with dishonesty. When the colors blend to crimson, a Crumble has already begun. We keep a close watch on every home, making notations in the log of any changes or patterns."

Reilly stepped back from the telescope and looked first at Quin, then at Lottie. His mind raced with possible conditions that might put one of their homes at risk of a Crumble: lying, cheating, stealing, abuse, or other secrets. He wondered if homes in the twenty-first century had auras, too, considering the fact that with a click of a button or a tap on an electronic device, filth and violence invades almost every home. He realized millions of people might be living secret lives of deception and despair. Reilly could not imagine a force or shield of any kind that would be strong enough to protect against human dysfunction like that.

"When the colors get muddy and you can't distinguish one from another, it's too late," Lottie said. "By then, the best we can do is to warn the family to get out safely, if they choose. Some refuse to believe the strength of their aura has diminished, and they get captured."

"Stubbornness runs deep," Quin added, shaking his head.

"Where are they taken?" Reilly held his hands to his stomach.

"To the bonfire, carrying the tree limbs from their own homes. Every Crumble contributes fuel to the Deceptors' black, billowing aura," Lottie continued. "It's a dreadful sight from the Vantage Post."

"But why would anyone give up their home to join the Deceptors? That doesn't make sense." Reilly looked to Quin and Brigid, then back to Lottie.

"Now, now, dearie, remember you've been through quite an ordeal yourself." Brigid stepped closer to Reilly and patted his arm.

"The fact that you escaped from The Library is more than commendable." Then she lowered her voice to a whisper. "We've never personally known anyone who has done so, and lived to tell about it."

"But I—"

"Enough!" Quin asserted. "This is not the time or place. Meanwhile the telescopes are unattended to."

Why won't anyone let me talk about the library? Reilly wondered.

Lottie stepped to her father's side and tucked her hands through his crossed arms. "Yes, Father. We are here to help. We'll monitor things while you tend to your other responsibilities."

Brigid blinked quickly to clear away tears, and Reilly wondered if she believed, as Lottie did, that her daughter, Sorcha, was still alive. A penetrating glance from Lottie confirmed his thoughts.

Quin exited the Vantage Post as Reilly, Lottie, and Brigid stepped up to a telescope. For three hours, they scanned homes throughout Wicklow. Reilly identified homes beyond the town's borders through his scope, but the aura readings were less accurate at further distances.

"You're a natural at aurology," Lottie insisted as she smiled at Reilly.

"Hmpf!" Dillon snorted. "He's just lucky."

Lottie ignored her brother, and showed Reilly how to make notations in the log for each home he scanned.

"A laptop and Google Maps would sure be helpful," Reilly muttered as he did his best to manipulate the crude pencil in his hand.

"What kind of map?" Brigid inquired.

"It's a … sort of hard to explain. It's an efficient invention that has the ability to scan just about any location on Earth, and display it on a screen."

"I'm not sure what a screen is, but it seems a laptop would work much better than our scopes." Lottie lamented. "Did you bring one with you?"

"No," Reilly laughed. He tucked his hands in his pocket and touched the Fireglass, wondering what he would see if he looked at the auras through the strange device Eilam had given him.

Herbology experts, called Infusionists, arrived every hour on the hour to thoroughly review the log before returning to their offices on the first floor, where they created healing teas from the bark of Arbutus trees, wild mushrooms, clover, and other native plants. Their priority was to prepare the Elixir, reserved for emergency conditions and offered to families at great risk.

In the mid-afternoon, someone delivered a pot of soup and plate of bread. Lottie and Reilly ate as they sat on a window seat centered on the wall of the Vantage Post.

"Wow, it feels good to sit down." Reilly stretched from side to side at his waist. "Standing for so long at one place tightened my back."

"It's not easy work, but Father insists the VP be staffed with at least three scope guards around the clock," Lottie said between sips of soup. "It's been one of the most successful elements of his career. Before he was elected, this area was simply a lookout in the magistrate's office. Father said he was elected to serve the people, and he didn't need a fancy office with a panoramic view to do that. He had the scopes installed and started studying the landscape, watching what people were doing, and discovering patterns in auras. He was first elected at a time when the influence of the Deceptors was beginning to take greater effect in many ways, and he recognized their main target was our homes. How's your soup?"

"It's good, thanks." He watched Lottie closely and could not shake the idea he had met her before.

"What?" she asked. "What are you looking at?"

"I'm sorry. I don't mean to stare. You just remind me of someone," he said. "But I'm not sure who."

"Yes, I know just what you mean." She munched on her bread, and kept her eyes on Reilly. His stomach felt oddly full and empty at the same time. "Let's ring for a replacement and take a break, shall we?"

"Sure," he said, though he was not sure what she meant.

Lottie set her soup bowl on the bench and walked to the wall, where she pulled on a hemp rope that extended through a hole in the ceiling. A bell tolled unexpectedly. Looking up, Reilly saw a large silver bell hanging from above the rafters. Within a minute, two men entered the Vantage Post and stepped to a scope.

"Thank you," Lottie said, grabbing her satchel. "We'll come back before the evening shift."

"Don't go far, Lottie," Brigid instructed. "Remember, your father will be practicing his speech for everyone at the Embassy, and he'll want your opinion, too."

"Yes, of course, Mother."

"Can I come with you?" Dillon piped up.

Lottie frowned, and her mother came to the rescue. "No, dear. The conversation won't be nearly as entertaining if you leave me here alone with *them*." She nodded at the two men and turned to wink at Lottie.

Lottie and Reilly left the Vantage Post and walked into the auditorium, still filled with dozens of people working briskly at tables. With banners, ribbons, and wristbands all in motion, the campaign posters seemed somewhat lost in a sea of red, some hanging from the ceiling and more dotting the outer walls. Reilly walked a few paces behind Lottie, reading posters: QUIN FOR THE WIN! and QUIN AGAIN! and QUIN ENDS POVERTY AND KEEPS WICKLOW SAFE!

"Come on, Reilly," Lottie said turning around to face him for a moment. "Let's get some fresh air."

Compelled to read more posters, he ignored her and fell half the distance of the room behind her. Swaying above the entrance to the room, and somewhat hidden behind a large ceiling beam, something on another poster caught Reilly's eye: the letters I-N-L-E-Y. He walked closer, trying to peer around the beams as the word came into full view. M-C-K-I-N-L-E-Y. Reilly stopped, staring up, to read the entire slogan: QUINCY MCKINLEY—THE PEOPLE'S MAGISTRATE.

"Can it be?" He whispered aloud. *Yes, it makes sense!* He reasoned silently.

Lottie turned from the entrance door of the Assembly Room to look for Reilly. Just then, Quin's voice rose above the hum of workers. "Don't be long, Charlotte. I want you to hear my speech."

"Yes, Father," she shouted, as she waved. "I won't miss it!"

Reilly walked toward her, mesmerized by the fact that the fourteen-year-old girl with silver eyes was Charlotte Louise McKinley, his fourth great-grandmother—the one who had written the book he found in the library, *Finding Tir Na Nog*. Reilly was certain that Lottie had no idea she was related to him.

Chapter Four

Echtra

"Are you all right? You look as though you just saw a ghost!" Lottie said as they strode down the stone steps to the first floor of the Embassy.

"Uh … I'm fine. I think fresh air is a great idea."

They walked down the long corridor past the offices that smelled like spicy clovers, and smiled at the old woman knitting. Lottie removed her wristbands and dropped them in the basket. Reilly did the same. The woman still mumbled about Deceptors but grinned strangely, showing two missing teeth. "And who is this with you, Lottie?"

"My house guest, Reilly McNamara," Lottie replied. "Remember, Flynn? You met him earlier today."

The woman look confused and returned to her knitting.

"She was terrorized by the Deceptors," Lottie whispered as they left the building. "Knitting is the only thing that calms her mind enough to stay on this side of insanity."

Stepping outside, Reilly took a deep breath, relieved to be in the open air again.

"There's a garden courtyard around back," Lottie said, nodding. "It's lovely. Would you like to sit there by the water fountain?" She took Reilly's arm and flashed a girlish smile. Reilly tensed at her touch—it was just plain weird to have his fourth great-grandmother flirting with him.

"Uh, great ... I mean, I like gardens," he stammered. "Uh ... flowers sort of reminds me of my friend, Norah." He wasn't sure why he blurted it out, and immediately wished he hadn't.

"I see," Lottie replied, loosening her grip on his arm.

"She's only a friend," he lied. "And I haven't known her long."

"But you do have feelings for her. You'd wish to court her?"

"Court her?"

"You would choose her to be your wife?"

"Whoa!" He stopped walking and released Lottie's hands from his arm. "That may be how things are done here, but where I come from, kids my age just go on dates when they like someone ... like that. It means a boy and a girl spend time together, to get to know each other. After a few dates, or more, then we might decide to be dating."

"Then you are *dating* Norah?"

"We hardly had time to consider if we were or not before we were separated."

"Nevertheless, you would not consider courting me because your heart is with her." Lottie turned to look away. "I saw it in your eyes when I asked you if there was a young lady in your life. You avoided the question by telling me about Tuma."

Reilly stepped closer to Lottie, taking her elbow to gently turn her towards him. "You're right, Lottie, but I also have feelings for you. More than you know."

"You cannot court or *date* two women at the same time, Reilly. Would that not confuse one's heart?"

"Lottie, please, you don't understand."

She pulled away and continued walking toward the courtyard. "I know I'm younger than you, but maybe if you stay in Wicklow for a couple of years, you'll see that I'll be a woman then, the age you are now, and then you may feel differently."

They walked in silence until they entered the courtyard.

"Wow! This is beautiful," Reilly said, trying to find common ground. "I've never seen so many flowers in such a small space."

"It's magical. And one of my favorite places to come."

"I can see why." They walked through the garden along a cobblestoned pathway that meandered among roses, azaleas, irises, orchids, lilies, and dozens of flowers Reilly could not name. Just beyond a bed of heather trailing over a small rock wall, he noticed a wooden bench. "Let's sit over there."

Lottie sat down and began to smooth the wrinkles on her dress, adjusting her position on the bench nervously, before removing the satchel from her shoulder and holding it on her lap. "My father designed the garden for my mother the first month he was elected. The only thing here at that time was the fountain in the south corner and a few flowers surrounding it. Of course anyone is welcome to wander through and enjoy it, but my parents secretly consider it their own special place." She pointed to a water feature at the opposite side of the garden. Reilly had noticed the sound of the trickling water when they entered the garden, but the fountain had been hidden from his view.

"Lottie, I need to tell you something."

"Yes, I know. Your heart belongs to Norah and you cannot open it to me."

"No … I mean, yes."

"Which is it, Reilly? You cannot have both."

He stood up and paced back and forth a few steps. "You're not making this any easier, and it's not what you think."

"I'm listening," she said in a tone that sounded too mature for her age.

"Okay, I'll try." Reilly sat on the bench beside her. "But it may be difficult for you to hear."

She furrowed her brow and pressed her lips together, but kept her hands folded in her lap, twirling her thumbs nervously. "I'll not interrupt."

Reilly took a deep breath and faced her directly. "You seem much older than fourteen. And if circumstances were different, I might want to take you on a date. But it's not your age that's the problem, not exactly. It's just that … well, I don't intend to stay in Wicklow for two years and even if I did, I couldn't think about you that way." As usual when he was frustrated, Reilly needed to move. He jumped to his feet to walk around. Lottie remained silent and looked as if she hoped he would change his mind as he talked it through. "You're right … I love Norah. I've never told anyone how I feel about her until now." He sat back down again and took Lottie's hand in his own. "But I know I can trust you with that secret because you and I have a special connection, a unique friendship, so to speak."

"I beg your pardon," she demanded as she pulled her hands away. "How dare you be so forward when you have just professed your love for another young lady!"

"You said you wouldn't interrupt. Please, let me finish."

She shook her head and lifted her nose toward the sky. "Very well."

"We can only be good friends, Charlotte Louise."

"How do you know my full name?" she demanded, turning to face Reilly.

"I heard your father call you Charlotte."

"But no one, not even my parents, calls me by my middle name!"

"I know your name because Charlotte Louise McKinley was—is—my fourth great-grandmother." He said it as calmly as he could, though the words felt as jumbled as they would have been if he had tried to speak in an unknown foreign language.

Lottie gasped and covered her mouth with both hands. Reilly stared at her, somewhat in shock himself. After holding her breath for a few seconds, she exhaled slowly and lowered her hands.

"If this is true, then you must be the one," she said quietly.

"No, I'm not—I just told you, we can only be friends."

"Yes, I understand that now, but there's something else *you* do not know."

He remained silent and waited for her to continue. After all, none of the past few days had been anything he had expected.

"You said that you believe your father is in Tir Na Nog. How is it that you came to believe this?" Lottie's eyes widened and she stepped closer to Reilly. "Have you been there?"

"No, but I've been to places just beyond its borders. Every time I go through another portal, I think I'll find Tir Na Nog. But I can't quite seem to get there."

"I know what you mean." Lottie sighed.

"You do? Have *you* been there? I thought you said it was only an old Irish legend."

"That's what my mother said, but I think she's wrong. I've been searching for this magical place since I was little, and I feel in my heart that it does exist." She opened the satchel on her lap and reached inside. "Since I have not yet found Tir Na Nog, I enjoy writing about what I imagine it to be. See?"

Lottie handed Reilly a small leather-bound book. He held it as if he had been frozen under a spell.

"Please, open it! I don't mind if you read it."

"I … uh … I've seen this before." He turned the book over in his hands, but he didn't open it. "This is the book I found in the library. I thought I had brought it with me through the portal."

"That cannot be! It's been in my possession for over a year." She snatched the book from his hands, noticeably annoyed. "Don't make light of it. A girl's journal is private, and you would *not* find it in The Library."

Reilly finally understood that the library she spoke of was not *his* library.

"I'm not making light of it. I just recognize that book," he insisted. "I'll prove it to you." He glanced away from her to concentrate on his memory of the book. "There is no title on the cover of the book, but on the first page are written the words, 'Finding Tir Na Nog, by Charlotte Louise McKinley.' And at the bottom of that page, it reads, 'An Echtra waiting for the guide to appear.' There is only writing on a few other pages."

Lottie held the book to her heart with a stunned expression.

"Then it *is* you!" she cried.

"Who? Who am I?"

"You're the guide this Echtra has been waiting for." She opened the book and skimmed her fingers across the words she had written.

"What's an Echtra, and why do you think I'm the guide for it?"

"An Echtra is an Irish legend which tells of adventurers who travel to Tir Na Nog. Every adventurer needs an Echtra to guide him or her along the journey. An Echtra is a story—but it also becomes the hero in the story."

"But I haven't been there myself, Lottie. I've only been to places *near* Tir Na Nog."

"Nevertheless, you are the one I've been waiting for." She reached for him and threw her arms around his neck. "Tell me what you've already learned, and the rest we'll discover on our great voyage together."

Her confidence brought Reilly new hope. Maybe he had come through the right portal after all.

Releasing him from a long hug, Lottie handed Reilly the book. He flipped through the pages again, just as he had done only a few days before, when he found it in the library near his own home.

The author had only written on a few random pages. Organized in a list with small, daisy-like flowers for bullet points, he read her notations aloud:

- *Forever young*
- *Endless wealth in all forms*
- *Love and joy*
- *Flowers that grow but never die*
- *No death*

Lottie watched him intently as he read. Without looking at the page, she recited the final points in unison with Reilly. "No Deceptors. No war. No sadness."

Reilly's voice trailed off as he finished the words "no sadness." They sat in silence; then Lottie reached for the book and pulled it from his hands.

"What else do you know about me?" she asked.

"Not much," Reilly said absently, trying to makes sense of the warp in time. "My great-great grandmother married a McNamara. When she was pregnant with their first son, who was my Great Grandpa Alistair McNamara, she wrote a letter to him. In the letter, she told him about her own great-grandmother, who had written a book about her adventures in a place called Tir Na Nog. My great-great grandmother hoped to go there herself someday. When I found the book, the letter was in it."

"Well, I guess since I haven't married yet, my great-granddaughter hasn't actually written the letter yet," she laughed.

"Weird."

"Yes, but you also said the letter indicated that your fourth great-grandmother—which is me—wrote about her adventures in Tir Na Nog. That means I go there!"

"You must!"

"It also explains why when I first heard your name, I felt that I knew you, or something about you. And that's why you are my Echtra guide." She giggled, then added, "It makes perfect sense."

"Well, no one wants to find Tir Na Nog more than I." Reilly stood up and took a step toward the water fountain. "It's only been a couple months, but it feels like forever since I've seen my dad."

"I'm sorry, Reilly. I can't imagine losing my father." She stood up and they walked through the garden toward the fountain. "I wonder if your great-great-grandmother went there, too."

"She died in childbirth. But my Great Grandpa Alistair brought his son, my Grandpa Angus, to America, when he was an infant. My dad remembered hearing lots of stories about it. But my Grandpa Angus died before I knew him, too."

Lottie put her hand through his arm, and this time he did not think it was weird. Reilly knew Lottie was his distant, deceased relative, but at that moment he knew she would always be a trusted friend, too.

Chapter Five

The Precipice

When they returned to the top floor of the Embassy, Lottie and Reilly wove their way through the crowd to the front of the platform, where Quin was practising his preliminary speech. At its conclusion, the people cheered wildly, waving red wristbands, flags, and banners.

For the next few weeks, Reilly helped the McKinleys at the Embassy, mostly keeping guard at the Vantage Post. He became an expert at reading auras and successfully prevented several Crumbles. Fortunately, those families did not ignore the warnings from the Embassy to fortify their homes. The Infusionists prepared natural plant elixirs for families at risk—particularly those who suffered from severe depression or despondency. In an attempt to cope with the dire living conditions and lack of food, thievery was common. The elixirs did not take away the people's problems. They simply helped them consider positive solutions. Invariably, families who refused the elixirs suffered a full or partial Crumble, with one or more family members taken by the Deceptors. This served as a warning for neighboring families, but some people naively believed they would never succumb to the Deceptors' traps.

Often when they rode the lift to the McKinleys' tree home, Reilly thought about Sorcha, and wondered what had happened to her. Why had she given in to the Deceptors? The family was not rich, but they did not go without, and they all seemed to work well together. Lottie and Dillon occasionally argued with each other, like normal siblings, but they were respectful to their parents. Quin and Brigid were obviously in love. From everything Reilly could tell, the McKinleys' home should have been safe from Deceptors.

Reilly also thought long and hard about what the Deceptors could do to families in 2015. Poverty was rampant in many countries of the world, and economic downfall had left many Americans without jobs, struggling to pay their bills; the greater threat seemed to be among those who had too *much*. Either they had no appreciation for their abundance, or they used what they had carelessly. Few people Reilly knew seemed truly happy, regardless of their financial status.

Studying auras for hours and days at a time, Reilly had a brutal awakening to his own obliviousness of those who suffered from overindulgence and addictions of every kind. He knew he could no longer ignorantly float in his kayak along ripples of false security. Facing drug lord Travis Jackson and providing evidence for his arrest—he had manufactured fake Stelladaurs laced with drugs—paled in comparison to what Reilly now realized needed to happen. He knew this was only the beginning if he was ever to find his way back through the portal to the library.

It was easy for Reilly to talk with Lottie. She understood him. She reminded him of Norah, which made him miss Norah even more; a heavy longing for her sank ever more deeply into his soul. Reilly and Lottie spent lunch and dinner breaks in the garden. When they were alone, he told her about Eilam, Tuma, Sequoran—the talking tree who had helped him find his Stelladaur—and Nebo, the giant eagle who had carried him to the far Pacific Coast. That was the last time he remembered having his Stelladaur around his neck. He told her about the other portals he had been through, as well. She absorbed all of it wholeheartedly and took notes in her journal, insisting that by doing so she would find clues to help her discover her own Stelladaur.

One evening, only three days before the election, Lottie gasped as they sat by the fountain. "How could I have missed it?" she said, tapping a page of her journal with her pointer finger.

"What do you mean?"

"You told me a person would feel an unexplainable force—a pull to find his or her own Stelladaur. How could I have missed it? My Stelladaur is *here*, in the fountain!" She set her journal down on the stone bench. "Help me look, Reilly!" Lottie leaned over the water, and slowly swirled her hands in the fountain, muddying the water.

They thoroughly felt along the base of the fountain but found nothing. In the center of the fountain stood a jade statue of an angel—a young girl with outstretched arms, her face looking upward. Water cascaded down the back of her long hair and bubbled from her fingertips, falling in thin streams.

"She looks like you," Reilly said, shaking water from his forearms.

"I don't see the resemblance. She looks Asian."

"True. But it's not her features; it's her expression." He stood on the bench to get a better look at the statue's face. Lottie stepped up beside Reilly. "See her smile? And the way her eyes follow us when we move? That's what you do."

"I do?"

"Yeah, it's one of the first things I noticed about you. It's something in your eyes."

Lottie walked all the way around the statue. "But there's nothing here."

"Let's look closer." After taking off his shoes, he stepped into the water and moved his hands over the submerged part of the statue, feeling for anything peculiar; but he felt only smooth jade.

"Maybe near the layers of her skirt," Lottie suggested. She removed her shoes, gathered her own skirt about her legs, and squatted down in the water.

They both crawled around the statue, Lottie moving in one direction and Reilly, the other. Dry only from the shoulders up, they thoroughly explored under the water. Unexpectedly, Reilly felt the same pulsating feeling he had when he searched his dad's sailboat to find his Stelladaur. He looked at Lottie and knew she felt it, too.

"We're close, aren't we?" she said excitedly.

Reilly nodded and reached deeper at the base of the statue.

"What's this?" Lottie fumbled around, both hands stirring the water more.

"Step back. Let the water settle so we can see better."

They watched a thin layer of brownish muck pool on the surface. Lottie gradually separated it with her hands and peered into the water. "It's her foot poking out from her skirt. There's something carved on one of her toes." She continued to encourage the brown silt away from her view. "It's a jewel!"

Leaning in closer, Lottie stretched her hand into the water, looking at Reilly with the same intent focus he had seen in the eyes of the angel statue. "I can feel the top of her foot … and her toes … and the jewe—."

Before she finished the word *jewel,* air swirled around the statue and created a tremendous vacuum, a whirlpool that swallowed the water in a mighty gulp and disappeared under the angel's feet. On the second-right toenail, a star-shaped jewel glittering like a diamond was embedded in the jade.

"Oh my!" Lottie gasped.

Reilly moved closer to Lottie, waiting to see what she would do. She touched the jewel as if it were a delicate flower. "It sends a shiver through my whole body," Lottie said. "But it's pleasant and reminds me of the thrill of plucking a dandelion that has gone to seed, and blowing the wisps away with a single breath."

Reilly smiled. She touched the jewel again, pressing down to feel the contours of the facets. Without warning, the solid mass of jade moved to the edge of the fountain. In the spot where the angel's foot had touched the ground for centuries, a Stelladaur, on a golden cord, glistened in the light of the setting sun.

"Good heavens!" Lottie cried. She covered her mouth with both hands and held her breath.

"It's your Stelladaur, Lottie."

Wide-eyed, she slowly lowered her hands from her mouth and reached for the treasure. The energy that surged through her as she picked it up was so powerful that it flooded through the stone and into Reilly's own body. He remembered the thrill of finding his own Stelladaur, and wished he could feel that invigorating sensation constantly. Lately, it seemed more of a distant memory. When he lost his Stelladaur, Eilam told Reilly that it would, nevertheless, always be with him—and that his dad would be with him, too. In his heart Reilly knew it was true, but after coming through the library portal, doubt crept into his thoughts more than he cared to admit.

Reilly dismissed his conflicting thoughts and gave his full attention to Lottie.

"Put it on, Lottie."

As if knighting herself, she bowed her head and lifted the cord around her neck, letting the jewel fall gracefully between her small, wet breasts. The gem glistened brighter than Reilly remembered his had shone, and he supposed it was because it rested against Lottie's soaking dress. Lottie reached for Reilly's hand—and at that precise moment, they both vanished into a deep tunnel that opened where the angel's foot rested.

The portal was both similar to and different from other portals he had been through. Rather than being immersed in a stream of a particular color, as he had previously experienced, he and Lottie were enveloped by swirling shades of an array of colors. The colors circled and folded gracefully around their bodies in transparent ribbons, like a dance. Reilly and Lottie felt weightless, with no sense of movement, as if they were spinning as fast as the earth itself and an invisible force made them appear still. Their journey seemed to last a long time, and Reilly wondered if they would remain forever in the curious kaleidoscope.

Then, without warning, they landed on the precipice of a narrow ridge on top of a lush, green mountain. The valley floor, if there was one, was farther down than they could see. Barely wide enough for them to stand side by side comfortably, the flat ridge wound in a maze, curving in various directions. The ground was so soft to his bare feet that Reilly hoped the mountain itself was solid.

"Where are we?" Lottie asked, letting go of Reilly's hand.

"Good question."

Lottie touched her Stelladaur around her neck. "I think we should start walking."

"Which way?" Reilly looked out over the massive maze ahead and behind them.

"Let's go this way." Lottie pointed ahead.

They walked carefully along the ridge, glancing down at the seemingly endless ravines on both sides. After walking more than a mile, they came to a crossroad and stopped. Reilly slowly turned clockwise, considering which direction to take. Lottie turned counterclockwise. They met facing each other at their starting point.

They looked to the sky and saw three white birds descending. As each stopped and hovered above one of the paths, a voice echoed softly across the ravines: "The path you choose determines your destiny."

A seagull flapped its wings behind them. "This path will bring you to decisions you've already made, with an opportunity to choose differently," said the voice. A snowy owl hovered to their left. "This path will take you to future choices that will arise from choices you made in the past." A dove fluttered to their right. "This path leads to the secrets of your Stelladaur and to Tir Na Nog."

Reilly and Lottie looked at each bird, hoping the voice would repeat its message, but the birds just circled silently.

It was not an easy decision for Reilly. Even with everything he already knew and believed about his Stelladaur, there were things he would still choose to do differently if he had the chance. He would have shouted "Get down!" when the boom of the sailboat swayed toward his dad. He would have done something to keep his dad from falling overboard and drowning. He would have held his Stelladaur more tightly when he flew on Nebo's back, so it still hung on its golden cord around his neck. And he would have found a way to rescue Norah before it was too late.

Putting logic aside about the possibility of changing the outcome of his previous choices, and not wanting to know about limits on those he would yet make, Reilly knew what path he had to choose. He assumed Lottie was considering her own reasons for which path to choose. But when it came to his dad, his Stelladaur, and Norah, it did not matter what it was called—fate, destiny, or decisions. He desperately wanted to hold each one of them again. Struck with a sudden urge to keep moving along, he pointed to the third path and said, "That one!" He looked at Lottie, astonished! She had simultaneously pointed to the same path that led to the right.

Instantly the ridges behind and to the left of them shifted positions, melding into the path they had chosen, so there was now only a single precipice to walk along. The maze transformed into a straight ledge, extending onward as far as they could see. The seagull and snowy owl disappeared, and the dove flew ahead in the distance.

They walked in silence. Hours seemed to pass as they meandered along the ridge. The other birds did not reappear, nor did Reilly and Lottie see any other animals. The monotony of a cloudless deep-blue sky, set like a never-ending dome above the lush green at their feet, became wearisome.

"I'm getting tired," Lottie said.

"Yeah, me, too," Reilly replied.

"Let's rest a while." She sat down at the edge of the never-ending precipice and dangled her bare feet. "Do you suppose we will truly find Tir Na Nog?"

"I hope we do, Lottie. More than you know." Reilly sat beside her. "But every portal I've been through before only makes it seem further away."

"What do you mean?" she exclaimed. "Do you think just because you haven't found it that it doesn't exist? How do you explain sitting here?"

He had not meant to dissuade her enthusiasm. "I didn't say I could explain any of it. I guess I'm just getting tired of finding answers that only lead to more questions."

Lottie inched closer to Reilly. He appreciated her sensitivity, but secretly felt a little jealous and frustrated. The Stelladaur around her neck was a painful reminder that his was missing.

Dangling her feet and bouncing them off the grassy wall of the mountain ledge, Lottie looked up to the vast open sky. She absently twirled her Stelladaur in her fingers, and as she did, brilliant beams of light shone from the jewel in every direction.

Lottie raised her hands to shield her eyes. "Perhaps you don't know this yet, Reilly, but you *are* an Echtra. My family—*our* family—needs you."

Without replying, Reilly stood up and then reached out his hand to Lottie. With neither sun nor moon or stars—only a steady daylight—they walked along the narrow precipice, following the white dove that flew in the distance ahead. They slept on downy grass when they were tired, and each time they awoke, they found a small pile of white berries beside them. Sweet and juicy, the berries filled their stomachs and quenched their thirst.

After what seemed to be days, the dove stopped and hovered in midair. Lottie and Reilly ran forward, watching the bird land on an ornate, golden perch that towered above them. Standing far enough back so they could see the dove, they waited.

Suddenly, a ray of light struck Lottie's Stelladaur, rebounded off the golden perch with a whoosh, and seared a message in the sky above the dove:

I am eternal, without time or space.

"I've seen that before," Reilly whispered. "But I can't remember where or when."

Then a voice spoke. "You learned the Affirmations of the Stelladaur when you visited Glesig. To you it seems to be in a distant past, but all knowledge and experience happen in the Now. There is no beginning. There is no end."

Reilly felt a surge of hope. "Yes, I remember! Norah was with me there!"

"So she was. So she is."

As if the words were simultaneously rooted in his heart, Reilly gripped his chest and gasped in pain. When he thought of Norah, the physical pain got worse, until he doubled over and fell to his knees. What was happening?

"Why … can't I … see her or … my dad? Why are we … here?"

Lottie reached out to help Reilly, but her Stelladaur emitted a ray that separated her from him.

"Dimension is only limited outside of the Now. All existence occurs simultaneously," the voice reverberated.

Reilly rolled onto his stomach, dug his fingers into the grass, and panted in pain. The dove flew down from its golden perch and circled him. Lottie stood by wide-eyed, unable to help.

The voice spoke again. "Allow the pain of the Now to guide you to joy of the Now. The Affirmations of the Stelladaur will provide complete knowledge when you are ready."

In an instant, the dove and the perch vanished and the beam from Lottie's Stelladaur retracted. She ran to Reilly, then fell to the ground beside him.

"Reilly! Reilly! What can I do?" she cried in desperation, watching him writhe and moan.

Then the earth opened and swallowed Reilly and Lottie down the never-ending Crevice of Now.

Chapter Six

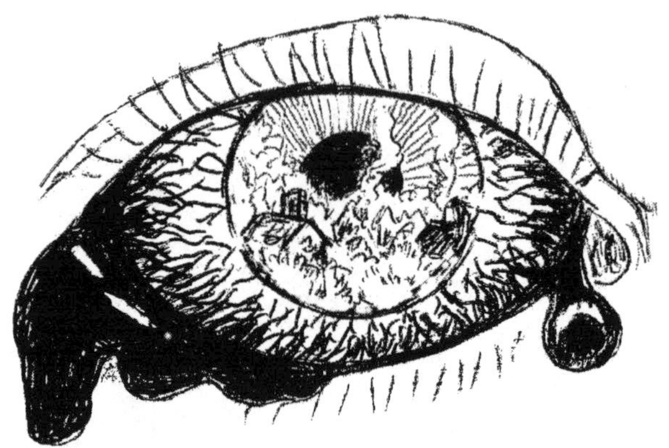

The Crumble

They landed back in the courtyard, where marching-band music resounded deafeningly off the walls.

Lottie turned to Reilly, who was bent over, still catching his breath. "Are you okay?" she said.

"Yeah, I think so." He shook his head and stood up. "I'm fine."

Lottie tucked her Stelladaur into the bodice of her dress. "We missed the election!"

Gathering her skirt above her shins, she ran toward the gate, with Reilly close behind. They turned the corner to the main entrance of the Embassy to find the cobblestone street clogged with people waving red banners and chanting, "Quin wins again! Quin wins again!" Red knitted bands swirled in the air like confetti.

"All the residents of Wicklow must be here! There was talk of supporters coming from counties as far away as Galway, and of course every year many residents from Dublin and Wexford participate," Lottie exclaimed. "After all, the magistrate is responsible for the safety and well-being of families far beyond the borders of our own tree homes."

"Where is your family?" Reilly asked.

"My father likely just delivered his victory speech from the Embassy veranda, so he'd be at the Vantage Post. Mother and Dillon are probably there, too."

She led the way through the crowd to the main doors of the jade building, nodding politely to anyone who congratulated her on her father's behalf. After removing their shoes and not bothering to put them on again once inside the Embassy, they greeted Flynn, grabbed wristbands, and ran down the empty corridor.

"He will be so disappointed we missed the entire election," Lottie muttered, as they ascended the uneven stairwell to the second floor. "And probably angry I wasn't here to help with it." They dodged tables and small crowds of campaign committee members, trying to find the quickest route to the Vantage Post.

The moment they walked into the room, Reilly and Lottie knew something terrible had happened.

"The entire East Forest has been stripped," Quin declared as he looked through a scope. "They've taken every plant in the Forest that our Infusionists use. There won't be enough bark and herbs to make the elixir."

"Father!" Lottie said, stepping behind him.

"Charlotte, my dear, I thought we had lost you in the crowd!"

"Yes, Lottie, it is unfortunate that you could not make your way to the podium when your father was reelected," Brigid added pointedly.

"Not to worry, we have much more to be concerned with just now," Quin said.

Lottie frowned and looked to Reilly. He shrugged his shoulders and smiled, grateful that no one seemed to notice how long they had been missing—or that they were barefoot.

"When did they do this?" Lottie asked. "How?"

"The ground looks charred below the tree homes in that area. The Deceptors must have burned the plants when people came for election events," Quin replied.

"But how did the fire not harm the tree homes?"

"I don't know. The Deceptors' ways are cunning and mysterious." He moved between the scopes, adjusting the focus on each. "Without enough elixir, we're going to lose more people to the Crumbles."

"This is a bittersweet day, indeed," said Brigid. "What shall we do?"

"I'll have the Head Infusionist provide a full inventory and an estimation of when our supply of elixir will expire. The Distribution Committee will need to ration it."

"Can people return to their homes, Father?" Lottie asked.

"I suspect the Deceptors have used this tactic to instill fear. We cannot allow fear to dictate our lives."

"But people *will* be afraid, Father." Lottie said. "How can you assure them they aren't in danger?"

Quin peered over the railing of the Vantage Post and waved to the crowds below, whose cheers led to more victory chants. He turned to face his wife, Dillon, and Reilly. "All I can do is assure people that if their aura is strong enough, they will withstand any Crumble. That is our only defense."

"Sir, may I offer another suggestion?" Reilly asked tentatively, fumbling in a pocket of his baggy pants.

"Of course. What is it?"

"I have a device—similar to your scopes but much smaller—which I think may provide more information." He held the Fireglass in his hand, but kept it hidden in his pocket.

"Certainly. I welcome any solutions from someone who has escaped from The Library!" Quin stepped beside Reilly and placed a hand on his shoulder. "You must surely have seen or heard something that would be of great benefit to us in this precarious situation."

Reilly was finished with erroneous compliments and expectations. "Sir, I've tried to explain before that I did not escape from The Library you speak of. I know nothing of Deceptors, nor do I know their methods of destruction. And I have no idea what one looks like." Reilly paused briefly and noted that everyone in the room listened intently and waited to hear what else he had to say, so he kept going. "I came through a portal door in a library near my home in Seattle. I thought it would lead me to Tir Na Nog. But it brought me here, to Wicklow, back in time, where it is well over a century before my time. I've told Lottie all the details that I can remember, and about other portals I've been through. I … I've learned a lot about how to listen to my own heart, how to act courageously when I'm scared, and how to trust the unknown."

The others moved closer to Reilly and continued to listen. They had never heard anyone speak so boldly about The Library.

"I can't say that I've mastered any of it, and there seem to be more questions than answers," Reilly said. "Lately, I find myself wondering how I'll ever find my way back, or if I will at all. Sometimes I wonder if it's all a strange dream." He paused, took a quick breath, and then finished. "But I'm here to help anyway I can."

He glanced at Lottie, who smiled slightly, acknowledging Reilly's choice not to share his connection to her family.

"I assure you that you are not dreaming, young man!" Quin said firmly. "We are as real as the skin around your bones and the hair on your toes." He *had* noticed Reilly's bare feet. "So where is this device?"

Reilly almost suggested to Lottie that she show them her Stelladaur, but decided that was for her to decide. For now, he wanted to know if the Fireglass could be of help. "It's here," he said, pulling it from his pocket.

He held the device in his palm so they could all see it, and then extended it to its full length, like a small collapsible telescope. They watched intently as the engraving of a Stelladaur spun around the surface, as it had before. Reilly was relieved that it still seemed to be working.

"How is it used?" Quin asked.

"I've only used it once before. I looked through it at a fireworks display, with another device called a Stelladaur, to access a portal to a place called Som. That led me to a place called Bozka."

"Unusual names," Dillon said, joining the conversation.

"I know. Som and Bozka are places in different dimensions, not just different times. In Som, I learned about inevitable and impending change. In Bozka, I learned about the greatest change that must take place inside each of us." He hoped someone might ask for more information about Bozka, but they were more focused on the peculiar device.

"You're right. More questions than answers," Brigid laughed. "And do you have this device called a Stelladaur?"

Reilly glanced quickly at Lottie, who looked at the floor; she wasn't ready to share. "I did have one, but I lost it. When I used the Fireglass to access the fireworks portal with my friend's Stelladaur, we placed her Stelladaur in front of the Fireglass and looked through the devices at the same time. That's how we were transported to Som."

"But apparently *we* do not have a Stelladaur," Quin said. "And we certainly do not want to leave Wicklow at a time like this."

"Of course not," Reilly said, as he collapsed the Fireglass to its original size. "But I wonder if we can use the Fireglass *with* the scopes, and maybe see something that the scopes alone aren't capable of showing." His heart beat faster as he spoke the words, and he hoped his idea was more than a hunch. He did not want his first attempt as an Echtra to be an embarrassment.

"I will allow you to try," Quin said. "Only you may touch the device. If anything should go wrong, I will not have you put my family in danger, nor do I want them disappearing through a portal."

Lottie raised her eyebrows.

"I understand, sir." Reilly nodded.

Reilly stepped to the scope in the center of the room. The music from the band below had stopped, and the crowd had dispersed. All was silent.

He tilted the scope slightly downward and aimed it toward the East Forest. Reilly opened his Fireglass again and waited until the Stelladaur whirred around the surface in a shiny blur. He brought the Fireglass into position, directly in front of the eyeglass of the scope, and peered into the treasure Eilam had given to him.

He drew in a quick, deep breath and adjusted the focus on the scope. "Oh, no!"

"What is it? What do you see?" Quin demanded.

"Sir, the tree homes in the East Forest have been invaded! Every lift has been compromised and there is no support remaining!" He continued to adjust the focus and move the scope and the Fireglass simultaneously to get a closer look. "The auras are blackened—there's hardly any color. A tremendous Crumble is coming!"

"Sound the alarm!" Quin commanded Dillon. The boy ran quickly to the far end of the Vantage Post and struck a brass gong, hung from two ornately carved jade beams, with a hammer that resembled the bone of a large animal. A shrill-pitched tone reverberated off the Embassy walls.

Reilly stepped away from the scope to cover his ears, but then dropped the Fireglass and, crouching, cupped his hands over his right eye.

"Reilly, are you all right?" Lottie ran to him and held him up at his elbow.

"My eye," he groaned. "It feels like it's on fire!"

"Quick! Mother, get cold water! And call an Infusionist!"

The ring from the gong continued to sound. Dillon stood by, not knowing what to do, and Quin looked through the scope Reilly had used, but left the Fireglass on the ground, where their guest had dropped it. Brigid soon returned with a bucket of water.

"Splash water on your eye, Reilly," Lottie said.

Reilly bent over the bucket splashing handfuls of water on his face until the bucket was half emptied. "It still burns," he said, lifting his head.

Lottie gasped. Brigid shrieked. Quin stepped away from the scope.

"My dear young man, whatever happened?" Quin asked.

Reilly's right eye was charred, leaving a black ring around the socket, and his eyeball oozed tarry black pus.

An Infusionist hurried into the Vantage Post carrying a flask, a mortar, and a pestle. "Drink this." He lifted the flask to Reilly's mouth and tilted his head back. "All of it."

Reilly coughed and sputtered from the bitter taste, but drank the entire flask. Quin pulled up a chair and guided him to sit down. "Now hold still," he said.

The Infusionist ground a mixture with the mortar and pestle and used his fingers to smear the ointment over Reilly's right eye. "This should alleviate the pain quickly and heal the wound."

"Thank you," Reilly whimpered, exhausted from the intense pain.

Lottie stroked Reilly's hair while Brigid repeatedly told him to lie still. Within a few minutes he relaxed, and the skin around his eye became normal. He blinked. Everything looked blurry.

"Are you all right now?" Lottie asked.

"Yes, I think so. The burning is gone." He blinked again to focus his vision. "Just a dull ache now."

"That Fireglass is a dangerous device," Brigid said. "We must dispose of it at once!"

"No!" Reilly shouted. He bolted from the chair and picked up the treasure. "A trusted friend gave it to me! He told me that it could be used to 'accelerate passage through any portal.' Maybe there's a portal back to Seattle in the East Forest." He tucked the Fireglass into his pocket. "But my friend also said, 'The same fire that consumes a forest with only one spark also ignites a display of beauty that transcends all doubt.' He said the Fireglass helps to welcome change. The East Forest will soon be consumed by a tremendous Crumble and the Deceptors' bonfire will grow bigger than ever. But somewhere past that forest, beyond the destruction at the Cliffs of Black Castle, there is beauty. Change must occur if we want to discover the beauty."

Brigid dipped a cloth into the bucket of water and placed it on Reilly's forehead. "There, there," she said.

Reilly brushed her hands away. "I'm fine now, thank you. Please listen to me."

"But, Reilly, see for yourself," Quin said as he stepped to the center scope, shaking his head in confusion. "Things looks normal in the East Forest."

The gong had stopped, but a loud hum of alarmed voices below the Vantage Post indicated a growing group of citizens responding to it.

Reilly looked through the scope. "I don't understand. This isn't what I saw before." He adjusted the focus and shifted the scope on its axis, then looked again. "This is different." He moved quickly to another scope at his right, and aimed it directly at the East Forest. "I don't get it!" He jumped to peer through the next scope. "It must be a trick. Maybe the Deceptors have synched the scopes or something, as they do to the lifts."

"But we have someone on guard at the scopes around the clock," said Quin. "Are you suggesting an Embassy member is …?"

"Could be," Reilly interrupted. "I don't know. I only know what I saw through my Fireglass, and we'd better—"

Suddenly the ground shook violently, and a thunderous noise reverberated off the jade walls. Reilly grabbed the base of the nearest scope to steady himself, as the others in the Vantage Post fell to the ground. Lottie tripped in front of Reilly and hit her head on a scope that had become dislodged.

"Lottie! Here!" Reilly reached out his hand.

Clutching him tightly, she screamed for her parents and her brother.

The rumbling continued. Two more scopes collapsed to the floor in a pile of twisted metal and shattered glass. The gong that hung from the beam flew from the open-air window like an oversized discus. The silver bell used to ring for assistance fell, tumbled through the entrance door of the Vantage Post, and rolled down the hallway toward the auditorium. It felt to Reilly as if they would be swallowed into the ground below the Embassy and entombed with the magistrate and his family.

Reilly pulled Lottie closer to him. Blood flowed down her face from a gash on her forehead. He lost his grip on the base of the scope, and they slid to the opposite end of the room, which continued to reel violently back and forth. Slamming into the far wall, Lottie fell unconscious into Reilly's lap.

He jerked off a strip of fabric from the hem of Lottie's dress and pressed the wadded cloth to her wound. Her Stelladaur slid from the bodice, and his palm inched over to reach it. He desperately wished he could claim the jewel as his own, but he knew it was not his for the taking—even if he had good motives for doing so.

Suddenly enlightened, Reilly knew then that he truly was an Echtra. Lottie had summoned him at the moment she believed Tir Na Nog was an actual place. Her belief in Reilly lived in his Stelladaur years before he ever found it, or even knew it existed.

Chapter Seven

Pucatrows

The rumbling and reeling stopped as abruptly as it had begun. Cries faded as the injured people were carried away on stretchers. Those who had assembled in the town square left to find their families and see if anything remained of their tree homes.

"Is everyone all right?" Quin demanded. "Brigid?"

"I'm here, darling. Bruised, but fine. Charlotte? Dillon?" Brigid craned her neck, but rubble from the broken scopes and fallen jade beams made it difficult to see.

"I'm here, Mom," Dillon squeaked from the corner near the entrance to the room. "No broken bones."

"Lottie's unconscious," Reilly said, still holding the blood-soaked piece of cloth to her head.

Brigid climbed over debris and fell to her knees beside her daughter. "Charlotte, my child! Wake up! Wake up!" She felt Lottie's forehead and the girl's lips parted.

"She is alive, Brigid, dear. She'll be all right." Quin briefly rested his hand on his wife's shoulder as he moved toward the one scope still standing. "Hopefully some made it to the Undertunnels," he muttered. He pressed a red button, which Reilly had not noticed before, under the eyepiece of the scope. Maneuvering the scope to various positions, Quin exhaled loudly. "Blessed day! Some made it to the tunnels in time!"

"May I see?" Reilly asked. He carefully lifted Lottie's head, and Brigid took his place to hold her daughter.

Reilly looked through the scope and gasped. "It's like an old-fashioned subway system, without the train."

"A what?" Brigid asked.

"An underground transportation system where people travel from one place to another by train."

"Another time travel mechanism?" Quin asked.

"No, real roads that connect people to various points within their own city, or neighboring cities." Reilly continued to look through the scope. "Like this, but the construction of these tunnels doesn't seem stable."

"During my first term as magistrate, I befriended the Pucatrows, who are experts in tunnel architecture. I exchanged elixir for their skill and workmanship. It took over a decade to build the Undertunnels, and some tree home lifts still don't have access to an escape." Reilly recalled seeing a red button with the letter "U" in the lift with Lottie. "We used the best materials available to us, but Crumbles compromise the stability of the Undertunnels. Sometimes the Pucatrows work day and night to make the necessary repairs. We must prepare for the arrival of the Pucatrows. Reilly, Dillon, come with me. Brigid, I'll send an Infusionist for Lottie as soon as I assess the damage and get things started."

Climbing over fallen debris and rubble, they made their way down the hall to the auditorium. Already people had begun to appear, helping the wounded to the Embassy. Dillon and Reilly began to sweep off tables with their shirtsleeves, kicking broken items out of the way.

"We'll keep only the most critically wounded here," Quin shouted to the group. "Keep them as comfortable as possible until an Infusionist is available. Those who need treatment but are able to walk must go outside to the square. Our space is limited in the auditorium." He scanned the room and then muttered under his breath, "There will not be enough elixir." As he exited the room, he turned and ordered, "Someone find wristbands at once! I'll find the Infusionists!"

Quin left the auditorium, and Reilly turned toward the sound of a shrill alarm that announced the opening of double brass doors along the back wall. He consciously rubbed his wrists. People spilled into the room, mostly women and children. Some carried those who had been injured, and others hobbled or crawled out of the lift as best they could. Reilly ran to hold the doors open for four men who carried two others, one with a severed arm and one with a missing leg. The last person out of the lift, a boy about thirteen years old, collapsed at Reilly's feet with a piece of wood stuck in his side like a dagger.

"Dillon! Get over here!" Reilly screamed.

The two of them lifted the boy and carried him to the nearest table.

"It's Kian!" Dillon said.

"You know him?"

"Yes, he is *mo chara*—my friend."

"You stay with him. I'll find an Infusionist."

Reilly scanned the room, now splattered with blood, whose color only accentuated that of the victory banners and wristbands. Wristbands! Quin had said to find the wristbands. Reilly exited the auditorium and ran quickly down the spiral staircase, grateful it was still intact.

The doors he had previously assumed led to offices remained closed on both sides of the long hallway, and were now guarded by odd, troll-like creatures, each about four feet tall. The unusual-looking sentries stood perfectly still, with slime-green-colored bare feet and matted, orange chest hair. Each held a spear at his right side that towered above a pile of wiry black hair. Their protruding eyes shifted back and forth under bushy eyebrows that curved high on their forehead and across their temples. Reilly observed their wrinkled faces and wide noses, and wondered if they were Irish trolls. Could these be the Pucatrows Quin was talking about? He hadn't said they were guards as well as construction workers. Reilly approached one of them.

"Excuse me, I need to find the magistrate. Is he in this room?"

The guard blinked rapidly, but gave no verbal response. He sniffed loudly, as if he might sneeze.

Reilly approached the sentinel at the next door. "Please, have you seen the magistrate?" The creature gave no reply and he, too, began to sniff loudly. He stepped closer to Reilly and sniffed his torso.

Reilly moved quickly down the hallway, asking each guard if they knew the whereabouts of the magistrate, getting sniffed each time. Finally, at the second to last door, Reilly grew impatient.

"Do you have any idea where the magistrate is?"

The troll moved his spear at an angle, in front of his orange-haired chest, to block the doorframe. "Sciath," he grunted, as if the word was a command. Reilly did not know what it meant, but he could imagine.

"I don't have time for this!" exclaimed Reilly, and he ran toward the main foyer. The guard sneezed loudly.

He spotted Flynn sitting behind the registry desk, knitting as usual.

"Oh, Flynn, you're here!"

"Aye, lad, and why wouldn't I be?" She continued to knit with fury but looked up at him with fire in her eyes.

"But, ma'am … your fingers … they're bleeding!" He reached for the basket of wristbands. "There seems to be plenty of bands here. Why don't you take a break and let your fingers heal?"

Flynn shook her head repeatedly. "No! I must never stop knitting the bands!" She increased her speed and gripped the needles more tightly. "It's my responsibility. And my privilege."

Reilly made a mental note to ask Lottie more about Flynn's obsession and the actual purpose of wearing the bands as he moved the basket closer to the troubled old woman. "Do you want me to get you bandages … or find an Infusionist?"

"Good Heavens, no! The yarn soaks it up just fine."

Reilly glanced at a pile of matted wristbands in her lap. "Is there anything I can do for you, Flynn?"

"Take that basket with you and distribute those bands. I'll keep working so we have enough for everyone."

Frustrated that no one had sufficiently explained what the wristbands were used for, Reilly thanked the woman and carried the basket with him back to the troll he had spoken to last.

"I'm back," he said. "I need to see the magistrate. Now!"

The guard narrowed his eyes and sniffed loudly. "You must be Reilly."

"Yes." Reilly wondered why the guard hadn't figured that out before.

"Then you may go in."

As the guard opened the door, a repulsive smell saturated the air. Reilly held his hand over his mouth to keep from retching. Six men wearing white tunics hovered over six large kettles that ejected green smoke into the air. Floor-to-ceiling shelves, stocked with various plants and herbs, surrounded the perimeter of the room. The magistrate was in the corner of the room, talking with an Infusionist who sat at a desk, busily adding tally marks on a piece of paper with a quill pen.

"Reilly!" Quin called.

"Sir," he said in a muffled tone. He lowered his hand, trying to breathe through his mouth. "Sir, Dillon's friend, Kian, is badly wounded and needs an Infusionist. There are many who are worse off."

The Infusionist continued to add the tally marks and make notations on his paper.

"What can we spare now?" Quin asked the man.

The Infusionist put the quill down on the table and looked up at the magistrate. "With the East Forest under attack, we've lost over half of our supply of Arbutus tree bark and spotted red mushrooms. We can only give elixir to those who we are certain will recover with one or two teaspoons full."

"And the healing ointment?" Quin asked.

"Using what we have now will jeopardize our ability to help those with severe burns in the future, should any be rescued from the bonfire."

Quin paced the floor as he shook his head. Reilly tried to relax his breathing and adjust to the offensive odor still stinging the inside of his nose.

"Sir, may I make another suggestion?"

"What do you recommend?"

"Try to make those who have arrived at the Embassy comfortable. But bring the elixir to those who are still in the East Forest or the Undertunnels. We need to strengthen our front line."

"This young man is right," the Infusionist said. "We can give licorice and horehound to those people upstairs who are in pain but not in critical condition. If they will likely die with anything less than two teaspoons of elixir, then we cannot spare it."

Reilly shuddered at the realization that death was imminent for many people this day, and he closed his eyes in an attempt to remember what the dove had recently told him: *Allow the pain of the Now to guide you to the joy of the Now. The Affirmations of the Stelladaur will provide complete knowledge, as you are ready.* He thought of Norah and hoped she was alive, then wondered why he had the grim thought that she might not be. He felt a deep desire for the missing jewel that had hung around his neck. He took a deep breath to clear his mind and attempt to alleviate his own pain—the anguish that lately accompanied any thoughts of Norah.

"Take those bands to the auditorium, Reilly, and put them on those who aren't wearing one on each wrist." Quin handed Reilly a small bottle. "Then give Kian one sip of this. And give my Charlotte enough until she awakens."

"Yes, sir. Anything else?"

"Meet me at the main lift in eight minutes."

Reilly held the basket under one arm and the small bottle in his other hand as he ran down the long hallway. Pushing his way through the crowd on the spiral staircase, he handed wristbands to anyone who did not wear them. Working his way up the stairs, he finally reached the auditorium, now filled with twice as many injured people as before.

Reilly found Dillon waiting with Kian, who lay motionless on a table.

"He's lost a lot of blood," Dillon said. "Someone came and pulled out the wood, but they couldn't stop the bleeding. Then they left to help the others who arrived from the Undertunnels. I didn't know what to do!"

"You did just fine, Dillon. Your dad said to give him one sip of this." Reilly held the bottle to Kian's lips. The boy did not respond.

"Give him more!" Dillon cried.

"We can't! There's not enough! I've got to bring the rest of this to Lottie." Reilly handed the basket to Dillon. "I'm sorry, Dillon." Reilly wanted to comfort Dillon and tell him his friend would be okay, but he knew it was a lie. "Distribute these and meet me at the lift doors in three minutes."

Without waiting for a reply, Reilly ran to the Vantage Post, jumping over the debris strewn across the floor. Brigid stroked her daughter's forehead as she lay in her mother's lap.

"At last!" Brigid called out as Reilly entered the room. "Hurry now!"

Reilly knelt down and tenderly pried Lottie's mouth open while her mother cradled her daughter's neck. Careful not to waste any drops of elixir, he poured the liquid between her lips.

"A little more," Brigid whispered.

Reilly emptied the bottle and they waited. Then, as if she had been under a spell that had suddenly broken, Lottie sat up, wide-eyed.

"Goodness gracious, that was quite a rumble," Lottie said. "How long was I out?"

"Never mind that, Lottie," said Reilly. "How do you feel?"

"Fit as a fiddle, dear boy!"

"Charlotte? This is no time for shenanigans!" Her mother scolded. "Can you stand?"

"Stand? I want to dance!" She bounded up and twirled around once before stumbling over a broken scope.

"Good Heavens, whatever is in that elixir? The girl is drunk!"

"Here, Lottie, hold on to me," Reilly said. He lifted her up and held her around the waist.

"That's awfully kind of you, to help your Maimeo."

"*Maimeo*?" Reilly asked.

"It means *grandmother*. As I said, she's drunk!" Brigid insisted.

"Well, I may be that, mother dear, but I speak the truth about—"

"Lottie, your father needs us to meet him at the lift and go with him to the Undertunnels," Reilly said loudly. "Are you able to walk on your own now?"

Lottie shook her head vigorously and then held her hand to her forehead.

"I have quite a headache, but I think I'm fine." She held on to Reilly's arm and smiled at her mother. "Yes, I feel better now."

The auditorium was filled with wounded bodies; every table was occupied, and it was difficult to step around those who lay on the floor. But Reilly, Lottie, and Brigid managed to make their way to the lift a minute later.

"Son, I'm so sorry about Kian." Quin had his arm around his son's shoulder. Then he looked out across the auditorium and added, "I need you to stay here and oversee the VP with your mother and sister." Dillon wiped his eyes with his palms and nodded. "Reilly, come with me."

The lift doors opened, and they all stepped back while another few dozen people exited. One man paused in front of Quin. "Sir, the East Forest has been utterly destroyed. There are few people remaining who have not been captured … I cannot say if any more have survived."

"Thank you. Thank you, my friend." Quin held the door. "Let's go, Reilly."

"I'm coming, too, Father." Lottie sprinted on to the lift before her father could object.

"No! Stay here with your mother!"

"Father, there is only one working scope. I'll be more help in the forest." Lottie stepped further into the lift. "I'll have it no other way!"

"She's right, Quin," Brigid said. "Go!"

Quin and Reilly stepped onto the lift and the doors shut.

"The Infusionists could only spare two bottles of elixir and a small portion of ointment." Quin held up a small flask and placed it in his pocket. "Reilly, please keep this with you." Quin handed Reilly a tiny tin canister, which he slipped into his pocket next to his Fireglass.

The lift descended rapidly, creaking alarmingly and landing with a lurch. Reilly wondered if the walls would cave in and crush them, but he dismissed the thought and refocused his attention. A group of the trolls greeted them when the door opened.

"We diverted the remaining Stalwarts to the West Woods." A

Pucatrow with a mound of orange hair covering his broad chest spoke. "We do not detect any others remaining in the East Forest."

"Thank you for the report, Cormack," Quin said. Turning to Reilly, he continued. "Reilly, Cormack is the leader of the Pucatrows. They are a peculiar breed, but loyal to the Embassy."

The Pucatrow's bulging eyes darted back and forth, seemingly uncontrollably. Their noses started to twitch, oozing greenish-blue goop. Reilly crossed his arms when three of the Pucatrows stepped closer to sniff him.

"This is Reilly," Quin said. "He's here to help us."

"He smells different," another Pucatrow snorted. He caught a globule of dripping snot with his hand and licked his palm with a loud slurping sound. Reilly flinched.

"But his hair is beautiful," Cormack added, touching his own wiry, matted mane.

"He's from the far coast," Lottie said.

Reilly's mind wandered to his own home and he thought of Sequoran and Nebo—other unusual creatures—and wished they were with him now to guide him, as they had been before. He closed his eyes briefly and remembered what he had heard as he and Lottie walked along the Crevice of Now: *Dimension is only limited outside of the Now. All existence occurs simultaneously.*

Reilly felt another sudden, searing pain in his chest. He knew then, without a doubt, that Norah was suffering. Trapped in the parallel world of Ireland in 1896, he struggled once again to know what was real and what was not.

Chapter Eight

Bonfire

Six Pucatrows led the way through the maze of Undertunnels, and six followed behind, each carrying their long spears diagonally across their shaggy chests. The damp air smelled of pine and dirt, and reminded Reilly of the Grand Forest near his own home. It seemed to him that the longer he remained in this time warp, the more he felt he had been there before, which puzzled him.

A crackling sound grew louder as they walked quickly through low-ceilinged tunnels. The Pucatrows sniffed frequently, but no one spoke until the Undertunnel opened to a cave-like room made of quartzite.

Noticing Reilly's interest in their surroundings, Lottie explained. "Late at night, the Pucatrows carry sandstone rocks to the

Deceptors' bonfire at the Cliffs of Black Castle of Wicklow, and toss them into the fire. The fire is so intense, the rocks change to quartzite. The Pucatrows use the fired rocks to fortify the Main Stations." Reilly raised his brow. Lottie continued, "There is a Main Station in each corner of the East Forest and the West Woods. During a Deceptor attack, families enter the Undertunnels from their own lift and meet at a Main Station, where the best plan of evacuation or counterattack is determined. Nevertheless, we have yet to execute a truly successful retaliation."

Reilly looked around the room as Lottie explained the details. He sized up each Pucatrow and then looked directly at Cormack. "But how do the Pucatrows retrieve the rocks from the fires without being seen? Or injured?"

"We can morph into fire-resilient black rats," Cormack said. "We creep into the fire and swallow the rocks whole, then carry them to the Main Stations, or wherever we need them, and regurgitate them."

Reilly's eyes widened and he tried to picture rats that could sneak into fire and swallow whole rocks. He thought that if the Pucatrows knew the Deceptor's routine, they might also know more about what happened at the Cliffs of Black Castle, and even The Library, than they may have told Quin.

Intent on his responsibilities at hand, Quin changed the subject. "Let's survey the damage and see if there are more survivors," he ordered.

Cormack pressed a red button on the wall, which opened a lift. Walking toward it, Reilly noticed a snake slither through a crack in the corner of the rock ceiling, and he hoped the ceiling of the lift did not drip with critters, like Lottie's tree home lift. They all squeezed inside. Reilly's stomach turned at the smell of the Pucatrows' warm breath permeating the small space. He could not move his hand to cover his mouth, and thought it might be rude to do so. Establishing a good rapport with the bizarre trolls that transformed into rats seemed to Reilly to be a prudent decision. He was more than relieved when the lift doors opened.

They stepped into the forest air, now pungent with the stench of smoldering plants and other dead life. Reilly's nose twitched uncomfortably from a smell he could not identify. The sizzle of the Deceptors' bonfire sounded in the distance. It was difficult to know which direction to choose; the devastation left no clear path. Trees, limbs, and debris from destroyed tree homes littered the ground, as if a tornado had plundered Wicklow.

"It's worse than I thought," Quin said. "We've never seen such intense devastation in this part of Ireland. It's a miracle anyone survived."

Everyone, including the Pucatrows, stood still and remained silent while the magistrate assessed the damage. "The scopes are no longer adequate. We simply cannot detect changes in some of the auras soon enough. This must be remedied!" He exhaled heavily and looked in the direction of the Cliffs of Black Castle. "Why did we not see the color changes sooner?" He shook his head and added, "This was a well-planned, cunning attack. There was little more we could have done."

Lottie stepped to her father. "We can find those who may still be alive, Father."

The lift doors opened and another two dozen Pucatrows joined the force. Quin took charge and organized three groups. "I'll take the north and west areas. Reilly, you and Lottie go south. Cormack, you go east. The rest of you divide yourselves evenly in each direction. Take those you find alive to the Embassy immediately, but leave a Pucatrow here to tell us where you are. Meet back here in three hours, before dusk."

Reilly and Lottie turned south and stepped over fallen debris. Twelve Pucatrows followed along, using their spears to lift smoldering limbs and branches and push debris aside as they hunted for survivors. For forty minutes they scoured the area, but they found no signs of human life. Reilly silently counted eighteen dead bodies. Everyone listened intently, hoping to hear any sounds of life. Lottie screamed when she nearly tripped on the remains of a woman's severed body.

Another hour passed, and they neared the far edge of the East Forest.

"Stop," Reilly said, as he held up his hand. "Do you hear that?"

The Pucatrows held their spears still and Lottie tilted her head. "What?" she asked.

"Shhh ..."

Reilly moved closer to a massive fallen tree. "Over here," he whispered.

Stepping gently, Lottie strained to hear. "It's a whimper."

Standing on their tiptoes to peer over the fallen trunk, Reilly and Lottie spotted a small child in a filthy linen dress, huddled against the bark.

"Oh, my," Lottie exclaimed. "She can't be more than two years old."

The Pucatrows quickly maneuvered a tree stump for Reilly to use as a ladder. He climbed on top of the fallen trunk and reached a hand back to help Lottie up. Reilly jumped to the ground a few feet away from the child. Lottie walked along the trunk to a thick branch that reached the ground, and scooted down.

Squatting beside the frightened young child, Reilly spoke softly. "It's okay, sweetie. It will be okay."

Lottie scooped the child into her arms and rocked her. "She's shivering."

Reilly took off his shirt and wrapped it around the child. He wandered a little further, looking for signs of her family. The Pucatrows found a way around the massive, fallen tree and scoured the area as well.

"We need to get her to the Embassy, Reilly," Lottie said.

"It'll be dark in a couple of hours," a Pucatrow added. "We'll need to hurry."

Lottie and Reilly took turns carrying the child, and Lottie hummed softly to soothe her cries. When they reached the Main Station, Quin and Cormack had already arrived. They, too, had found only one other person alive. Pucatrows were already transporting the victim back to the Embassy. Quin took the flask from his pocket and gave the child a sip of elixir. She relaxed and fell asleep in Lottie's arms before they reached the Undertunnels.

Moonlight spilled into the auditorium windows when they stepped out of the main lift. Quin left to meet with Infusionists; Reilly and Lottie found Brigid and Dillon in the VP, still keeping watch through the scope. The Pucatrows returned to the Undertunnels.

"Mother, can we name her?" Lottie asked, stroking the child's matted hair.

"She's not a pet, Lottie," Dillon said.

Lottie ignored her brother's remark. "Who will take care of her? Where will the other orphans live?"

"I don't know, Charlotte. Families from the West Woods may open their homes to them," Brigid replied.

"Many have already gone to the West Woods," Reilly began. "Isn't that where your home is? Is your home safe?"

"Yes," said Brigid. "No one can get into our home without giving Katell the command to open the door."

"Stalwart 59, right?" asked Reilly.

"That's right. Each family chooses their own command for their Door Keeper. Stalwarts are those who remain steadfast and strong to the cause of good, regardless of circumstances."

"And the number?"

"There are five in our family," Brigid said. "My husband and I met on the ninth day of May. It's our own secret code." She giggled.

Her smile quickly faded as she looked out to the town square. "We should go home."

"You and Dillon go, Mother. And take the baby with you." Lottie handed the little girl to Brigid. "Reilly and I will stay here. The other VP guards are assisting elsewhere, or have gone home by now to check on their families."

"All right, Charlotte, dear. I'll prepare a tin of food and send it back with Dillon in the morning." She handed Reilly his shirt and wrapped the child in a shawl that she kept at the Embassy for evenings when the breeze blew through the VP open-air windows. "It's nearly midnight. Take turns resting. Let the magistrate know directly if you see anything out of the ordinary."

Reilly chuckled. "You can be sure of that, ma'am."

Lottie moved to the scope, and Reilly stepped over the fallen and mangled scopes to the edge of the window. Order was increasing on the town square; frantic cries had turned to muffled sobs. He watched people doing their best to help one another. Quin was nowhere to be seen, and Reilly assumed he was still with the Infusionists, reassessing the supply of elixir and ointment. There was no sign of any Pucatrows, and Reilly wondered if they had morphed into rats yet.

"Can you see the bonfire?" he asked Lottie.

"No, I'm scoping auras in the West Woods. The Deceptors will likely attack again, and this time we need to be prepared."

"I agree. But we may need to look further. The auras only tell us if a family is at risk, and possibly to what extent. But what good does that do if the people don't know what the Deceptors want from them—what fuels their fire?"

"I told you already, Reilly. The trees." Lottie left the scope and met Reilly by the window. "Like vicious termites, they silently cut away at the tree homes. Once the home is unstable, the Deceptors attack and order the Crumble. They typically attack one or two homes at a time—never the entire forest."

"Yes, I know that much. But why are they cutting the trees? *What* do they *want*?"

"The wood … for their bonfire." Lottie scowled in confusion.

"*Why*?" he nearly shouted.

Lottie sighed, then shrugged. "We don't know much about what happens inside Black Castle, but we do know the Detachment Process begins here."

"In the forest?" Reilly nodded at the West Woods in the distance.

"In our homes. Deceptors separate people from their own families by deceiving them with subtle lies and empty promises. When a person makes decisions based on those lies, he becomes detached from his own self and starts to become detached from his family, too." She turned to look at Reilly and almost glared at him. "That's how they stole Sorcha from us."

Reilly bit his lip and stepped back to the scope.

"The Pucatrows must know more," he said. "And they keep *sniffing* me, as if I have something they want."

He looked through the scope, glancing back and forth from the lens to the scene out the window. "If they capture someone during a Crumble, that person has to carry wood from their own house to the bonfire. Right?" Reilly asked.

"Yes."

"And those people are taken to The Library in Black Castle?"

"Yes. I think that's where they have Sorcha."

"But what keeps the bonfire burning after the trees turn to ashes?"

"We don't know. The legend is that the fire has burned continuously since the beginning of time."

With a sudden insight, Reilly moved quickly back to Lottie. "That's it, Lottie! Remember the first Affirmation of the Stelladaur? *I am eternal, without time or space.* The power of our own Stelladaur—our very essence—is eternal. And time is an illusion! It all happens at once, in the NOW. Nothing happens in a time other than right NOW! Everything that happens also occurs simultaneously in different dimensions, which only appear to be 'past,' 'present,' or 'future.'"

"Like the precipice?"

"And The Library! Do you see, Lottie?" Reilly hugged her. "The flame from the bonfire may burn forever, but so does the light of our Stelladaur! We can use your Stelladaur and the Fireglass to look through the scope lens together—the same way Norah and I did to find the orange butterfly in the fireworks!"

"I'm not sure I understand."

"It doesn't matter." Reilly pulled out the Fireglass as he stepped up to the scope. "Bring your Stelladaur over here."

Lottie held her Stelladaur in her hands and gasped at its brilliance. "But, Reilly, last time you used the Fireglass to look through the scope—remember what happened to your eye? What if that happens again? Or something worse."

"Whatever happens … happens. We've *got* to find out how to get past the bonfire and find The Library inside Black Castle." He twirled the Firelgass in his hands. "And maybe—if *everything* happens simultaneously, then portals are also connected somehow, even ones from Seattle to Wicklow." Reilly was convinced that if he could get into the Deceptors' Library, he could also somehow find a way back to *his* library in Seattle.

Lottie moved closer to Reilly and lifted her Stelladaur so it touched the lens of the scope. "I'm going to look through my Stelladaur first. Then we'll use it with your Fireglass."

"Fair enough."

With the jewel still draped on the golden cord around her neck, Lottie held it in place as she peered through the stone into the scope. "I can see the bonfire," she whispered, "and many people—maybe hundreds—waiting in a long line, about thirty feet back from the flames." She pulled away from the scope and blinked rapidly, then looked again with her other eye. "They're throwing branches and tree limbs into the fire, one person at a time … Then that person walks to the far side of the bonfire and … and disappears. I can't tell where they go. There are people of all ages, but when the younger ones throw their wood into the fire, the flames burst with greater intensity. There are Deceptors, wearing black hooded cloaks, walking back and forth in front of the long line of people."

"Do you see anything else?"

Lottie adjusted the scope slightly. "Only lots of black smoke."

"Let me look now, with the Fireglass."

Reilly extended the device to its fullest length and watched the etched Stelladaur spin around the cylinder. Lottie moved back enough for Reilly to hold the Fireglass up to touch her Stelladaur. Leaning forward, he put his right eye up to the lens of the Fireglass, and looked through all three devices simultaneously.

Suddenly, the room filled with the sound and smell of burning wood, mingled with a rotten Pucatrows-like odor. Lottie coughed. Reilly glowered bitterly.

"The Deceptors seem preoccupied with their new prisoners and not concerned about the rats scurrying at their feet," Reilly said as Lottie held her Stelladaur steady. "But I still think those Pucatrow rats are keeping something from us. They're slithering around in the fire, but they're ignoring the quartzite stones. I can't tell exactly what they're doing, but it looks like they're burrowing … under the soot. The rats disappear for a few minutes and then come back up, swallow a rock … and then slither back out of the flames, and … and cough up the quartzite behind a hedge!"

"I know they're odd creatures … but my father trusts them!"

"There's more, Lottie."

"Yes?"

"I can see through the flames of the bonfire, all the way to Black Castle. The Deceptors in cloaks are standing guard across the entire front of the castle. I can't see weapons … or faces—if they have faces."

Lottie's arm was tired. She switched the hand holding her Stelladaur, and it shifted on the scope lens.

"Hold it there!" Reilly turned the Fireglass and moved his eye closer to the lens. "I can see inside the castle! There's a big room with people waiting … someone is painting on an easel … there are shelves filled with books … and another room with some strange machine … and there's a woman …"

Reilly inhaled sharply and dropped the Fireglass. It fell to the floor and bounced off a piece of twisted metal. With his hand over his heart, he staggered to the open window and steadied himself on the ledge, hunched over as if he had run a race. Lottie let her Stelladaur drop on its cord, and it shone onto Reilly's face. His eye looked normal.

"I … don't … understand," Reilly stammered. "Why is … *she* … in Black Castle?"

"Sorcha? Is Sorcha there?"

"They've captured her." Reilly sank to the ground and whispered faintly, "*Norah!*"

Chapter Nine

Black Castle of Wicklow

"Reilly? Reilly! Are you ok?" Lottie reached out and shook his arm. He didn't look hurt, but he did not respond to her, and his breathing was irregular. Scared, she searched his pockets for the tin canister of ointment. Instead, she pulled out the red flower Reilly had tucked away. She looked at the perfect flower and gently laid it on his chest.

She reached toward the next pocket, but Reilly inhaled abruptly, as if he had not been breathing at all and had just been revived. He saw the flash of red from the flower and picked it up. As he smelled it, his breathing began to return to normal. The wind blew through the Vantage Post, and Reilly's mind flashed to another midnight hour, when he and Norah returned from Bozka through the fireworks display—and he found the same flower that had come with them through the portal and fallen in his lap.

"Everything *does* happen simultaneously in the Now," he whispered. But the flower looked a duller red than Reilly remembered it on the Fourth of July.

"Are you all right?" Lottie sat down on the ground beside him. "Do you need an Infusionist?"

"This flower is my elixir." He smelled it again. "I'm fine," he said with a smile.

"Good heavens! Why do you keep giving me such a fright?" She stood up and brushed off the back of her dress vigorously. "It's quite alarming."

"I don't know, Lottie. It has something to do with Norah." Reilly stood up and held the flower for her to look at again. "Aka-ula gave this to me in Bozka, which means 'Divine Gift.'"

"What is the gift?"

"Love. Aka-ula said 'Love is the most precious of all virtues. Without it, there would be no life.'"

"The flower saved your life?"

"No—Norah's love did."

"But she's not here, and probably has no idea where you are."

"She's in Black Castle! I know it now!" Reilly caressed the petals and then tucked the flower back in his pocket. His fingers brushed the small ruby that Lottie had not noticed.

"Did you see Sorcha?"

"I'm not sure, but she must be there, too! C'mon!" Reilly grabbed Lottie's hand.

"Where are we going?"

"To the castle!"

"What about the scopes? We can't leave them unattended."

"Two are completely broken. Besides, your father concluded the scopes are ineffective. We need to do something more!" They sprinted through the auditorium to the lift, jumping over injured bodies.

Riding down the lift, Lottie pulled out her Stelladaur and studied it. "I wish I knew how to better use my Stelladaur."

"You'll figure it out as you go, Lottie. And there will be others to help you."

"Like Eilam, Nebo, Sequoran, and the others you told me about?"

"Yeah, but maybe different for you. I think we all have our own helpers, who are best suited to us."

"Like an Echtra."

"Sure."

"You must wish you still had your Stelladaur."

"Yeah." Reilly looked at the stone and then touched his chest. "I don't know where I misplaced it, but somehow it's still with me. I can feel it … the same way I can feel Norah is nearby."

The lift stopped, and they stepped into the Undertunnels. It was lit with candlesticks made of bones, posted twenty feet apart on both sides. There was no sign of Pucatrows.

An hour later, they reached the Main Station they had been in earlier.

"There has to be another Undertunnel to Black Castle," Reilly said. "I could see the Pucatrow rats burrowing under the ashes. My guess is that it connects to one of the Main Stations."

The walls of the Station appeared to be solid quartzite, fit tightly together in uneven shapes and sizes. There was nothing on the dirt ground. The rock ceiling was twice as tall as it was in the Undertunnels, creating a cavernous feeling in the room, with only a spray of candles bunched together with twine along one wall. Reilly and Lottie began pushing on the rocks, hoping that one would give way to a secret tunnel.

"We've tried every rock," Lottie said discouraged. "Maybe the entrance is in another Main Station."

Reilly turned around the room to see if he had missed something. He walked the perimeter, looking closely at the ground. Then he thought to look up. His eyes stopped at the spot where he had seen a snake slither into the corner of the ceiling earlier.

"Of course!" he exclaimed.

"It's up there?"

"Yes. We need to go up the lift and bring down a stump tall enough to stand on, so we can reach it."

The East Forest was quiet except for the distant snapping of the fire. They found a stump that had rolled into the pathway just ahead and maneuvered it into the lift and down to the Main Station. Reilly grunted as he heaved the log up and leaned it against the corner wall. He used the nubs of broken branches jutting from the trunk to climb up the log. He could barely reach the rock where he had seen the snake slither out of sight, but when he pushed it, it gave way to a narrow, short passageway.

"We'll have to crawl on our stomachs to get through," Reilly said.

Lottie lifted her skirt, removed her léine, and knotted her skirt between her legs. "I prefer to be as proper as possible," she said as she smoothed her bloomers, "but with all these layers it would be impossible to climb up a tree limb and crawl on my belly."

Reilly laughed at the notion that his fourth-great grandmother wore underwear that ballooned to her shins. "I dare say an Echtra should not find such things humorous!"

"I'm sorry," he frowned, and then quietly watched Lottie tear her petticoat into strips.

After fashioning a makeshift rope from the strips of cloth, she scooted up the log and tossed Reilly the makeshift rope. "Catch this," she said, and she tossed Reilly the rope. After securing it around a large rock wedged along the wall of the narrow tunnel, Reilly hoisted Lottie onto the edge of the opening. Holding tightly to the rope, she teetered on the edge until he positioned himself on his stomach.

"Pull out your Stelladaur so we can see."

The light from the jewel reminded Reilly of his own Stelladaur, lighting the way through the dark caves where he had been taunted and tormented by demon faces of Travis Jackson. *Why does everything seem like déjà vu?* he wondered.

The stench made it obvious that these were, as Reilly had guessed, Pucatrow tunnels, used in their rat form. The domed ceilings were made of quartzite, which explained why the Pucatrows needed more rocks besides those needed for the Main Stations. Reilly presumed that these tunnels went much further than Black Castle. The ground was damp, intensifying the smell and chilling them both.

They crawled along on their stomachs for an hour or more, not once seeing a turn in the tunnel. Soon a gradual incline made it more difficult to scoot along the ground. Lottie stopped. "I can't go any further, Reilly," she cried. "I've worn holes in my sleeves, and my elbows are bleeding."

"Let's rest, Lottie. Can you smell the bonfire? We're not far now." They tried to relax their aching bodies on the damp ground. "Can you tuck your Stelladaur in your dress? Let's see if there is any other light up ahead."

Lottie squirmed and groaned, but she kept her treasure hidden from view. Then they saw a faint red hue seeping through the ceiling.

"I can make it that far," she said with determination.

The red light grew brighter, and the smell of smoke became more intense as they inched their way forward. Reilly wondered why they hadn't seen any morphed rats in the tunnel, but was glad he did not have to deal with *that* just yet. He didn't know exactly what they would see at the opening of the tunnel, but he continued to avoid the fears that crept into his mind with thoughts of Norah.

Just then, the tunnel started to fill with smoke and the ground felt hot. Lottie cried out in pain between gasps for air. They were under the bonfire.

"Hold on to my ankle, Lottie," he said, loud enough to be heard over the intense crackling. "There's a fork in the path just ahead."

As he pulled both of them forward, Reilly was grateful for the muscles built from years of paddling in his kayak. They crept forward until they reached a turn in the tunnel. More heat came from the left; Reilly turned right. Ahead, he could dimly see the edges of the tunnel give way to the regular darkness of night.

Reilly crawled out of the hole and turned to help Lottie. The delicate skin on her arms was raw and bleeding from her elbow to her wrists. His own hands were scratched and had begun to bleed.

He knelt to the ground and held the hem of her skirt. "May I?" Lottie nodded and Reilly ripped a strip of fabric.

"This is no time to be overly concerned about appropriateness in fashion or modesty," she said.

"Modesty? Hah!" Reilly laughed. "You ought to see what the girls wear in my time … or what they *don't* wear." He wadded the fabric into his fist and pressed on one of Lottie's elbows, then the other. Then he reached into his pocket and pulled out the small canister of ointment.

"No," Lottie said. "I'll be fine. We should save that."

"You're probably right. Are you sure you're okay?"

"Yes. Just wrap those other strips around my arms tightly."

Reilly bandaged her arms. Lottie stuffed the soiled fabric in the side pockets of her skirt, not wanting to leave it behind for someone to suspect outsiders.

The tunnel had taken them past the bonfire, to a low hedge about thirty feet long and three feet high, ending just outside the entrance to Black Castle.

"My guess is we've got about an hour before the sun comes up to find out what's going on inside," Reilly said. "We need to get back to this tunnel before then, so we have a better chance of not being seen."

"Yes, I agree." Lottie glanced toward the bonfire. "Look—the line of people from the East Forest is down to only nine."

They watched for another minute while two people threw their branches into the fire. Then they heard a heinous laugh burst from the flame. Both people disappeared behind the fire, just as Reilly had seen through the Fireglass.

"Over there!" Reilly pointed to a second row of low hedges, parallel to them. "It's the same two people. They're heading to Black Castle."

"Should we try to follow them inside?"

"No, let's go in that side door. While the prisoners are entering the castle, we'll cause a distraction and then make a run for it."

"What kind of a distraction?"

"Well … when the Deceptor who leads the group reaches the main door, pull out your Stelladaur and hold it up towards the bonfire, and I'll hold my Fireglass just in front of it."

"All right. Then what?"

"I hope it creates a bit of an explosion in the bonfire."

"And if it doesn't?"

"It will." Reilly felt his chest pulsate for a brief moment, confirming his words as if his Stelladaur still hung around his neck.

A hooded Deceptor approached the main door.

"On the count of three, " Reilly whispered. Lottie began to pull her Stelladaur from its cord. "One … two … three!"

The jewel lit up the night sky around them, and Reilly quickly placed his Fireglass directly in front of it. Brilliant sparks of orange and red erupted in an explosion that ricocheted off the stone walls of Black Castle and back into the billowing flames, like cosmic lasers between the two hedges. The Deceptor at the side door moved quickly to usher the line of people through the main door.

Reilly grabbed Lottie's hand, and they ran for the side door without looking back. Once inside, they followed the sound of footsteps down a narrow, curved hallway. They paused in a small doorway and watched the prisoners file through a room that reminded Reilly of the foyer in the Suzzallo Library, through an adjoining alcove, and then into another larger room.

"Stay close!" Reilly mouthed to Lottie, as they inched their way around the corner to peer into the foyer. Two Deceptors stood inside the main door, their hooded faces covered and their dark robes hiding their true form.

"Stelladaur!" He mouthed as he held up his Fireglass. He pointed to the metal, cobra-shaped door handle. Holding up one, two, and then three fingers, they positioned the Fireglass in front of the Stelladaur and aimed it directly at the cobra. Bright red sparks flew about and rebounded between the cobra handle and the ceiling. Reilly and Lottie dashed into the shadows of the alcove, to the side of a barred, glassless window on the door to the adjoining room.

Lottie peered through the window and gasped.

To their right, the row of prisoners waited in silence on chairs against the wall. In turn, each one stepped in front of a white wall, where an artist with pixie-cut, fiery-red hair studied his or her face and painted a portrait on a small board. When each portrait was completed, the artist clipped the board to a wire that was strung across the entire room, and the prisoner moved to the center of the room.

"That could be Sorcha … she's an artist … but I don't recognzie her from behind." Lottie stood on her tiptoes so she could see further into the room.

"Good heavens!" Lottie whispered. "What are they doing now?"

Reilly shook his head as he and Lottie watched each prisoner place his head in a device that resembled a guillotine.

A Deceptor stepped directly in front of the trapped prisoner, and opened its flowing cape toward the captive.

The eerie silence sent shivers down Reilly's spine.

When the Deceptor stepped aside, Reilly and Lottie stared at a pile of shaven hair that had fallen to the floor. A creature that resembled an ugly troll swept up the hair and put it in a basket nearly the same size as his body. The prisoner was released, and another took his place. Looking further to the left, they saw a large crowd of bald people of all ages waiting to move behind a row of curtains. Each person emerged wearing a red tunic with a single sleeve covering the right shoulder and arm, leaving the left shoulder and arm bare. They wore nothing on their feet, and all body piercings had been removed.

Deceptors lined the perimeter of the room and a few moved about, but the prisoners seemed to know where they were supposed to go without being directed. No one spoke. There was a forced sense of order that made Reilly remember Travis Jackson, and his stomach churned at the thought.

"What are they doing with those metal sticks?" Lottie whispered. Her eyes widened as she pointed to four hooded Deceptors who stood in a circle around a stone cauldron near the back wall, moving the sticks in the huge pot.

Reilly hesitated before he answered, not wanting to say what he imagined they were doing.

"What's that red glow above the pot?" Lottie added. She stood higher on her tiptoes, still trying to get a closer look through the window.

"I don't think they're roasting marshmallows," Reilly whispered, but then wished he hadn't tried to make a joke.

Portraits painted, heads shaved, and clothes changed, the prisoners sat in chairs along the back row. Some of them sat nervously rubbing their heads. A few wrung their hands. Children sat unnaturally still. They all waited, watching the Deceptors turn the metal sticks over and over in the cauldron. A Deceptor wearing a red hooded cloak entered the room through double doors just behind the cauldron. *I wonder if that's Prince Ukobach,* Reilly thought.

All the Deceptors in the room formed a half-circle that closed in on the row of prisoners, their hoods hanging down in front and sleeves tucked together. Reilly and Lottie could only see the backside of the Deceptors' cloaks.

The artist walked back and forth along the rows of hanging portraits, studying each one and blowing on them, her back still towards Reilly and Lottie. The girl wore a white, floor-length, ruffled chiffon dress, with tight-fitting sleeves that came to her wrists. The halter-style neckline bared her shoulders and dipped low in the back. Her bare feet were fettered, connected to a chain hanging down her back from a thick iron collar. Except for the clanking of her shackles, the room was silent.

In unison, the four Deceptors surrounding the cauldron raised their metal sticks in the air and chanted.

Líon isteach dúinn le fuil ar do leanaí go deo.
Líon isteach dúinn le fuil ar do leanaí go deo.
Líon isteach dúinn le fuil ar do leanaí go deo.

"What's it mean?" Reilly hissed.

"It's Gaelic. It means, *Fill us with blood upon your children forever.*" She shivered and reached for Reilly's hand.

The demon with the red hood spoke in a stentorian voice. "With shaven heads your minds are open to accept your fate. Destiny is lost in the blood of vengeance. The curse is now yours to keep and ours to enjoy."

The prisoner in the first chair stood up and stepped in front of the red-hooded Deceptor. The demon bellowed, "Male or female?"

"Male," a quiet voice replied.

The towering Deceptor reached for one of the sticks in the fire, and set it to the bare front left shoulder of the man. The smell of burning flesh permeated the room. The man shrieked in agony. Lottie covered her mouth to keep from screaming. Reilly grabbed the bars across the window. The prisoner's piercing cry stopped after several seconds and diminished to a whimper. He was escorted by one of the Deceptors out the back door.

"Male or female?" the voice boomed again.

"Male." Reilly thought it sounded like someone about his age.

An awful scorching sound accompanied the prisoner's scream before he was escorted from the room.

"Male or female?"

"Female."

The Deceptor chose a different branding iron from the cauldron.

Lottie covered her ears against the piercing scream.

"Male or female? ... Male or female?" he demanded, again and again.

"I'm a girl," a timid voice replied.

"Please!" A woman pleaded. "She's only a child! Spare her!"

One of the demons held the mother back while the horror-struck girl was branded. Then the mother let out a violent shriek and held her breath for the duration of her own branding. Her muffled sobs trailed off as she left the room.

Reilly clutched the window bars of the alcove door until his own shock subsided. He and Lottie watched and listened in horror, stunned by what they had witnessed.

Finally, the four Deceptors escorted the last prisoner out of the room, followed by the demon in the red hooded-cloak. The only person remaining in the room was the artist.

She began to unhook the portraits hanging from the line and placed them in piles on a table near her easel. As the artist turned to straighten a stack of portraits, Lottie suddenly heaved. "*Sorcha!*" she called. "Sorcha!"

Chapter Ten

The Grand Book

Lottie fumbled with the door latch, but it would not move. "Hurry, Reilly!" She moved so he could try to pry it open, but it still would not budge.

"Sorcha! Sorcha!" Lottie shouted.

The artist continued to collect the portraits and stack them in tidy piles.

"She doesn't hear us!" Now frantic, Lottie yanked on the bars of the door window.

"Lottie!" Reilly pulled her back from the door and held his arms around her from behind. "Listen to me!"

Lottie relaxed slightly, but Reilly kept a firm hold of her.

"I don't know why she can't hear you. But we need to come back later."

"No!" She tightened again in his arms. "I won't leave without her!"

Reilly turned her around and held her away from him.

"The sun will be up soon. We can't risk being seen by the Deceptors at the bonfire. We need to get back to the Undertunnels."

Lottie lowered her head and closed her eyes, not wanting to hear.

"We will come back. I promise you."

Lottie opened her silver eyes and saw her Stelladaur, barely visible, tucked in her bodice. It gave her hope and she slowly lifted her head.

"I didn't recognize her," she whispered. "It's been so long. Her hair used to be longer than mine … to her lower back … and not so red."

"She's alive, Lottie. She's alive."

Lottie nodded and sighed deeply. She touched her hand to her breast to feel her Stelladaur through her clothing. "Yes, let's go. We need to tell my family."

They made it safely to the Undertunnels without being seen and crawled the distance to the Main Station of the East Forest in silence. As they climbed down from the tunnel mouth, Cormack greeted them.

"That was an exceedingly stupid thing to do," he snorted. "An Echtra never puts his own interests above the best good of all others."

Reilly looked down at the Puckatrow. "My *own* interests?" He brushed off his clothes, irritated at the accusation. "And why do you think I'm an Echtra?"

"Our tunnels go far past the Cliffs of Black Castle, into the sea, and intersect with all portals that lead to the great Star King and Star Queen." He sniffed again loudly. "The name of every Echtra is written in The Grand Book of Stories."

Reilly remembered Nebo saying that the Star King and Star Queen create a Stelladaur for each human soul … and that every time a child is born, a door opens and a burst of Stelladaur light beams to that child. He started to piece things together.

"Have *you* met the great Star King and Star Queen, through these portals?" Reilly asked with a hint of skepticism.

"I did not say that. But I have seen The Grand Book of Stories."

"And this *book* … each person's story is written in it?"

"As they write it."

"And each story includes an Echtra?"

"An Echtra is assigned to help with each story, or many stories."

Still unsure whether to trust Cormack or not, Reilly nevertheless admitted that he was starting to understand. "Echtras help the writers find their Stelladaur …" he began, as he stared intently at Cormack, "… so they can write their own story."

"Do we write our own story and then live it?" Lottie asked. "Or live it and then write it?"

"It happens simultaneously in the NOW," the Pucatrow responded condescendingly.

Reilly then let go of his doubts and agreed with the strange troll. "Yes! Yes!" He turned to Lottie with renewed hope. "The people who have been caught in the Deceptors' trap of lies are the ones kept in The Library in Black Castle."

"What traps?" Lottie asked. "Are there traps in the lifts?"

"No, it's different than that." Reilly took her hand and they began to walk through the Undertunnels. Lottie pulled out her Stelladaur to light the way. Cormack followed, his spear held across his chest.

"The Deceptors have synched the lifts so they have a place to infiltrate the homes with their lies," Reilly said. "The lies are their traps."

"Similar to those thoughts that persuade us to make choices we later wish we hadn't?" Lottie asked.

"It starts with a thought," Reilly agreed, "but it's more. The Deceptors know exactly what diversions to put in front of us to get us off track. The thoughts turn to negative emotions, and those feelings create more bad thoughts. It's a vicious cycle. Eventually the person caught in the trap feels justified in their bad choices, and they write a story that doesn't honor who they really are, or their Stelladaur light."

Cormack moved closer to Reilly and began to sniff at his back as they walked. Reilly ignored him and continued. "Deceptors torment people with their whispering lies, as well as by silently chopping away at the tree homes. This false information—about themselves, or others, or their circumstances—becomes the story they write. Soon they live the lie they're writing! Each cut in the trunk of a tree home indicates this cycle of lies, skillfully executed by Deceptors."

"Because they live their life and write their story based on deception," Lottie agreed. "That's what Sorcha did."

"Tell me what you mean, Lottie."

"She never felt she was good enough."

"For who?"

"My parents. Mostly my father. He was always so busy at the Embassy, and my mother, too. Sorcha started to think he cared more about the people of Wicklow, and all of Ireland, than he did about her. It wasn't true, but she got it in her mind that it was."

Reilly's mind raced with the multitude of ways in which people believe things that are not true, but he did not interrupt her.

"Sorcha is a painter. My father ocassionally allowed her to paint, but he requires all of us to help in the Vantage Post … which seemed pointless to Sorcha."

Cormack walked closely behind Reilly, his stubby legs tucked behind Reilly's as they walked. The Pucatrow sniffed a snotty, guttural sound, and wiped his nose with his long hair. Reilly turned and glowered at him. Lottie turned back and wrinkled her nose in disgust.

"Anyway," she began again, "you may have noticed her paintings hanging in our house."

"Yes, I did," said Reilly. "They remind me of my home. It's as if the painter had been there."

"When my father remodeled the Embassy, he wouldn't display any of Sorcha's artwork."

"Why? It's so beautiful."

"He didn't say, which only made her feel worse. He said it was for her protection, but that didn't make sense to Sorcha. She was so hurt and angry. She began to spend more time away from home during the day, and sometimes even at night. Worst of all, she stopped painting. My mother cried a lot then, and even now, her eyes water when she looks at Sorcha's paintings. "

Reilly took Lottie's hand. "Then what happened?"

"A Crumble came to our neighborhood. Sorcha wasn't home when it happened … and today was the first time I've seen her since."

Reilly still didn't have all the answers about the Deceptors, but he and Lottie both knew the Demons had enticed Sorcha into their trap with promises that they would allow her to do what she wanted to do most—paint.

Reilly stopped walking so he could give Lottie a hug, and Cormack ran right into him, then fell to the ground.

"What *is* it, Cormack?" Reilly demanded. "Why do you sniff me?"

"You have the smell of a fading heart, which is unusual for an Echtra."

Annoyed, Reilly folded his arms. "And what, exactly, does a fading heart smell like? My heart is more determined than ever. *I'm* not falling for the Deceptor's trap."

"Perhaps not now," Cormack snuffed. "But the scent is here." He pointed to Reilly's pant's pocket.

A sudden realization made Reilly gasp. He quickly retrieved the flower from his pocket and held it in his hands. It still had perfect form, but it was no longer red.

"It's fading! It's barely red anymore." He held it in front of Lottie. "Look!" A wave of pain seared through his chest. He doubled over and dropped the flower to the ground. "Norah is in their trap!" He grabbed Cormack's leg, hoping the pain would subside. He wondered why thinking of someone so important to him consistently brought him to his knees in pain. "How did they … reach *her? Why?*" he said. Then he fell down.

"This happens to him frequently," Lottie said to the Pucatrow. "Is there anything we can do?" She knelt beside Reilly and reached for the flower on the ground.

"It's the pain that comes from true love. He'll experience it until he masters his emotions surrounding it." He spoke as if Reilly was not in front of him, gasping with pain.

"It seems strange that true love would include pain," Lottie said.

"Nevertheless, it does," Cormack added. "And if that desire is true love, it always will."

Lottie picked up the flower. "It smells lovely," she whispered as she placed it on Reilly's chest.

"But not as intoxicating as it once was, correct?" Cormack asked.

"Do they not have the same feelings for one another as they did before?"

"They do. But hearts fade and die without hope."

Cormack picked up the flower and held it to Reilly's nose.

Though the treasured flower from Bozka had previously revived him during an attack, this time he writhed in pain longer. When it finally subsided, Reilly was able to speak.

"Norah's heart … will not … die!" Reilly stammered. He regained enough strength to reach for the flower and take it from Cormack. "I will not … give the Deceptors … the satisfaction!"

A peculiar confidence surged through Reilly with the assurance of what he *did* know. He loved Norah! Reilly had to believe their love would be enough to guide him to Norah—and to keep his own heart from fading.

As they rode the main lift to the auditorium, Lottie tucked her Stelladaur back into the bodice of her dress. When she and Reilly stepped out of the lift, the early morning sun streamed in through the windows, but most people were still asleep on tables or curled up on the floor.

It would be a while before Dillon brought any food. They stepped carefully around the people asleep on the floor, and walked down the spiral stairs to the main hallway of the Embassy. A Pucatrow still stood guard at each Infusionists' door. When they entered the foyer, Reilly and Lottie passed Flynn, asleep in her chair with a skein of yarn in her hands. The main Embassy door opened, and Quin walked in.

"Father," Lottie said softly. She ran to greet him with a hug.

"Lottie, have you been here all night? Who is in the VP?"

"We left the post, Father. We went …"

"But you know how important it is to keep watch, Charlotte!" Flynn stirred at Quin's loud voice. "I know your brother and mother went home many hours ago. Is there another guard at the VP now?"

"I don't know. We went through the Undertunnels to Black Castle," she whispered, as she held her hand on her father's forearm. "Sorcha is there, Father. We saw her! She is alive!"

Stunned with the news of his daughter and exhausted from the recent events, Quin's knees buckled. Reilly stepped forward to steady the magistrate. "It's true, sir. But she didn't see us. We had to leave while it was still dark, so the Deceptors wouldn't catch us."

"Oh, my dear, Sorcha!"

"There's more to tell," Lottie whispered again. She reviewed the details of what they had seen and heard, including their encounter with Cormack.

"Pucatrows are a curious breed with interesting quirks," Quin said. "But they've always helped protect the Embassy."

"Doesn't it concern you that they developed Undertunnels to Black Castle without informing you?" Lottie asked.

Quin began to walk past the main desk where Flynn still slept. He handed two knitted bands to Reilly and Lottie, and slipped one over each of his own wrists. "Pucatrows can be mischievous. But they are also loyal."

Lottie walked quickly to keep up with her father. She pulled his arm firmly to make him stand still, and then stood up straight. "But, Father, Cormack must have known Sorcha was alive. Is that *loyalty*?"

The magistrate stroked his daughter's hair. "Charlotte, my dear child, I will discuss the matter with Cormack forthwith, and then make plans to retrieve our precious Sorcha." He turned to Reilly and added, "You must both be weary after such a long night. Take her home to rest, and tell my wife the good news. I'll send someone to keep watch at the VP."

"I'm fine, Father," Lottie insisted. "Mother said she would send food with Dillon after sun-up. We'll rest in the garden until he arrives." She glanced at Reilly who nodded.

"Very well. Please come and find me after he arrives." He rested his lips on Lottie's forehead. "Today is a day of great hope."

Reilly reached for his chest, as if his Stelladaur still hung there. He wanted to send Norah some of that hope.

Reilly and Lottie sat on the fountain bench and considered their options to access the portal again.

"Cormack said the Pucatrows' tunnels go to the sea, and intersect with *all* the portals that lead to the great Star King and Star Queen," said Reilly.

"Then this portal under the fountain statue must link to those tunnels." Lottie swished her hand in small circles in the water.

"And eventually lead to Tir Na Nog," Reilly concluded.

Although Reilly now had more than one reason to remain in Ireland, he also believed he was closer than ever to finding his dad. He drew in a deep breath to divert the searing pain jolting through his chest.

Lottie pulled her Stelladaur from her bodice and held it in one hand.

"Give me your hand, Reilly. Are you ready?"

He took her hand and nodded. She held her Stelladaur under the water that cascaded from the angel's jade fingertips. Again, a mighty force pushed the statue aside and created a whirlpool.

And once again, Reilly and Lottie vanished into the mysterious vortex beneath the fountain.

Chapter Eleven

Sam

Swirling down a giant, multi-colored helix, Reilly's head began to spin from the centrifugal force. He could see Lottie, rotating in a parallel helix opposite his as they flew down the psychedelic slide. High-pitched squeals reverberated off the walls of the portal; a gurgling noise rumbled in the background.

Dizzy from spinning, his vision blurred. Reilly tried to focus on his surroundings, but everything seemed to melt together with the call of a distant whale increasing in volume as it slowed in tempo. Soon he lost all sense of form to his body, and felt his limbs morph into strange, unidentifiable shapes. The tubular tunnel decreased in size as Reilly accelerated downward. He felt a terrible compression as his body squeezed through the end of the helix just before he shot into the sea. He started to panic and flail until he realized he was breathing underwater. He looked down at his body and saw the body of a seahorse, but he still had his own arms. Lottie, now also transformed into a seahorse with her human arms, admired her new surroundings. Her Stelladaur, hanging on the cord around her neck, shone ahead of them like the beam from a lighthouse.

"Reilly, look at this!" She flipped her curled tail and did a somersault, waving her arms and landing right in front of him. "I always imagined being able to explore the ocean!"

"Not like this!" Reilly protested, his long blonde hair floating around his face. "This is almost too weird for me."

"Oh, stop complaining," Lottie said as she swirled and bobbed around him. "It isn't like you to be so negative."

"Well, I don't exactly *feel* like me." He swished his tail and propelled upward, past a school of fish with multi-colored polka dots. The sudden burst of movement made him change his mind quickly. "Then again … this *is* awesome!"

"Where do you think we are?"

"I hope somewhere near Tir Na Nog."

They shimmied through a giant coral reef and floated past tall grasses that swooshed as they swam by. Reilly's indigo bony-plated body and Lottie's purple, curled body sparkled like iridescent glitter from the light of Lottie's Stelladaur, which caught a stream of light shining in the far distance.

Reilly loved kayaking, but he had never been scuba diving, and had only seen such peculiar fish and creatures on one other occasion—through the first portal he entered. At that time, whatever he saw under the sea was the same color as his seahorse body was now—multiple shades of violet, indigo, and purple. Then, he could see the molecular structure of all the living things: the cells of the fish's scales, the algae's chlorophyll, and the DNA strands in the crabs' vertebrae. Now, he saw the deep-sea wonderland around him as a spray of color and forms that would leave anyone in awe. Bewildered, Reilly wondered why he had been morphed into a sea creature. But he knew enough about portals to expect the unexpected, and to accept that wherever they led him was as real as real could be.

In an attempt to calm his boggled mind, he reached out to touch various fish and creatures as they scurried by. At each touch, he felt a surge of confidence that propelled him forward. He assumed the strange phenomenon of transforming into a seahorse must be connected, in some way, to the place of imagination called Jolka, and to the first Affirmation of the Stelladaur.

Struck with a moment of epiphany, Reilly understood his thoughts more clearly: *NOW is either a mirror of the past at a higher frequency, or a reflection of the future through imagination.* He repeated it to himself again and nodded at the truth of it.

Lottie continued to somersault as they moved ahead.

An eerie melody, like the song of a whale, echoed through the waves with gurgling bass sounds.

A family of giant stingrays moved gracefully through the water, their eyes following Reilly and their fin-like arms waving as they swam by. Reilly waved back and thought he saw one of them smile.

"The life of a seahorse would be blissful," Lottie said. "It's pleasant to be down here, where we could forget about the Deceptors and all that's going on."

"I highly doubt we're here to forget."

Just then, a dark shadow crossed in front of Lottie, almost snuffing out the light from her Stelladaur. She somersaulted back to Reilly and clutched his arm.

"What was that?" she asked, her Stelladaur shining again into the beam of light ahead.

A tremendous clicking sound invaded the water, and Reilly and Lottie covered their ears. More piercing than Katell's staccato pecking, and louder that Sequoran's mighty snores, the noise enfolded them. Visible turbulence accompanied the noise and spun faster and faster, causing a break in the light from Lottie's Stelladaur to the beam still ahead in the distance. Her long white hair twisted around her bony chest and wrapped her Stelladaur to her body.

The undersea went completely dark.

"It's okay, Lottie," Reilly said, gripping her hand. "Close your eyes and just be still."

Soon the clicking stopped and they opened their eyes. Staring back at them, only a few feet away, was the enormous purple eye of a giant blue whale. The whale blinked.

"I am Mor Samhlaiocht," the whale nearly sang.

"More *what*?" Reilly asked.

"It's Irish," Lottie explained. "It means 'great imagination.'"

"Oh. I should have guessed." Reilly swam backwards to get a better look at the creature. "Can I just call you Sam?"

"Indeed," the giant whale said, with a grin that sucked in several passing fish.

"Thank you. Will you show us where we go next?"

"On the contrary. I am here to organize the waves so they can carry messages through the deep seas and then through all portals of creativity and imagination." He blinked, long and slow. "You will need to decide where to go next."

Reilly looked at Lottie, her silver eyes bulging with wonderment. Her hair started to unwind from her body, and the Stelladaur relaxed on its golden cord.

"Like the messages Sequoran heard from the coast near my home," Reilly reminisced, "when he found out Travis had poisoned the waters with drugs."

"Yes. And any messages transmitted from sea-creature to land-creature." The water swirled randomly as Sam spoke. "But the messages are for those who have discovered the gifts of imagination and endless creativity."

"Do all people have those gifts?" Lottie asked.

"Each individual of your species. But few understand that they do, or know how to use the gifts wisely."

"Sam is right, Lottie," Reilly added. "Travis Jackson obviously has imagination, and he created—or invented—amazing things. But his obsession for power overshadowed his ability to use his imagination and creativity wisely. It was his greatest weakness."

"A person's greatest weakness can become an equally great strength," Sam said. "This is another power few of your kind truly understand."

Reilly flipped his tail involuntarily. "But not for someone like Travis!" he insisted. "I can't imagine *he* would ever change!"

"It is not for you to decide if another person will change," said Sam. "Change comes from the most intimate and private part of one's soul—from the heart. Human creatures choose the condition of their own heart."

Reilly knew the whale's words were true. Eilam had told him the same thing. But since Reilly had come to Wicklow—and with his continual thoughts of Norah—he had tried to put Travis's evil heart out of his own mind. Flapping his tail hard, Reilly silently admitted to himself that he blamed Travis for Norah's disappearance and a slew of other unanswered questions.

Frustrated, he changed the subject. "Sam, can you move around behind us? I want to see if that light ahead is any closer now."

"Indeed." A mighty wave swirled around Reilly and Lottie as the giant whale changed his position to clear their view. Lottie's Stelladaur beamed ahead to meet the light in the distance.

"It still seems awfully far away," she said

"Can you take us there, Sam?" Reilly suggested.

"Of course. Hold on to my dorsal fin."

Reilly and Lottie swam hard to reach the whale's fin at the top of his body. It was just big enough for them both to get a secure grip. Sam blinked slowly and gave a mighty swoosh of his tail to move them forward.

Riding on a giant whale reminded Reilly of flying with Norah on Nebo's back. He let his mind relish the memory—the smell of her hair, the warmth of her body pressed against his back, the tickle of her breath on his neck—and waited for the usual sudden pain to hit. He let go with one hand and held it to his chest, waiting for the attack and wondering if a seahorse-man could withstand such pain. But it did not come.

Instead, an angelic, haunting song floated through the waves and resonated in Reilly's ears.

I'll hold my breath within the fire
To keep from utter shame.
I'll bleed inside from every vein
Before I yield my name.
But should my heart fade in the night
Before you come to me,
I'll write my soul's caressing song
And sing my dying melody.
Love is all I ask of you,
Love will make us free.
Imagine love can change it all
And bring you back to me.
Imagine love can change it all
And bring you back to me.

The music filled his soul and suffused the vast ocean. Yet, when Reilly looked at Lottie, he knew she hadn't heard it. Sam blinked and propelled them forward. Reilly's mind raced to remember the words of the song. *Fire ... shame ... love ... free ... imagine.*

Reilly knew he possessed a keen imagination and often saw or heard things differently than others did. In Jolka, he had learned imagination can help a person discover their greatest desire; until then, he hadn't considered the connection between the power of imagination and the power of love. He decided there, in the depths of the ocean, if love was never-ending—which he believed to be true—then imagination and the creative soul also had no limits.

Remembering his experience in Glesig, where the Affirmations of the Stelladaur were seared into his Stelladaur, he turned to Lottie. "The second Affirmation of the Stelladaur is *I am imagination and creativity without end.* If we're going to face the Deceptors and help the prisoners, we're going to need every ounce of imagination and creativity we can muster."

Lottie nodded in agreement, but looked confused. "Is that all?"

"No. We need to find a way to love them."

"The prisoners?"

"The Deceptors."

"That's the most ridiculous thing I've ever heard, Reilly!" Lottie rolled her eyes and glared at him. "How can we have any kind feelings whatsoever for those murderous, lying, evil creatures?"

"I'm not sure. And I don't know if I can do it myself. But if we want to save Sorcha and Norah, and the others, love *must* be our motivation."

"I'm motivated! But I will never love those demons—or like anything about them!"

Reilly knew he needed to be patient with Lottie. She had barely found her Stelladaur and was only beginning to understand how it worked. She would go through her own portals to places like Glesig and Bozka.

"One thing at a time, Lottie," Reilly said as he put an arm around her. "Look! We're getting closer."

She looked ahead and smiled as the brilliant light came into full view. "It's more than one light. It's lots of little lights."

Sam gave a final swish of his tail fin, and they coasted under a sky of lights that dotted the surface of the water for as far as they could see. Glittering like diamonds, the lights reflected some source of illumination further above the water.

"What are they?" Reilly asked Sam.

"Unclaimed and discarded Stelladaurs," Sam replied.

"Oh, no! There must be millions of them!" Lottie said.

"Many more than that," Sam said.

"How does a Stelladaur become unclaimed?" Reilly asked.

"They become unclaimed when a person dies without using their imagination to create the desire to search for their Stelladaur."

Reilly was again reminded of Travis's scheme to deceive others with fake Stelladaurs that stole a person's imagination—or their desire to have an imagination. He clenched his jaw and felt his chest tighten.

"What's the difference if they never had their Stelladaur?" Lottie asked.

"Imagination and desire determine destiny," Sam replied.

"I thought my Stelladaur would determine my destiny." Lottie's seahorse tail curled to her body.

"Your Stelladaur shines a light on possibilities. But destiny begins when imagination brings ideas to your mind. *Then* choices emerge. Your heart determines which you choose."

Reilly had a strange sense that Sam must know Eilam, and this gave him renewed confidence.

"What about the discarded Stelladaurs?" Reilly asked.

"Those are the ones that have been abandoned by souls with fading hearts, and whose bodies have been taken by a Deceptor."

Reilly looked at Lottie and thought of Norah. Lottie looked at Reilly and thought of Sorcha. Both were afraid to ask the question they knew they must know the answer to.

"What do they do ..." Lottie began.

"... with the bodies?" Reilly finished.

The giant blue whale blinked again and shut his eyes for a moment. "The Deceptors take the faded hearts from their prisoners and burn their blood in the bonfire ..."

Reilly's eyes grew wide and Lottie gripped his arm tightly.

"Then," Sam said, "they possess the empty bodies and the Detachment Process is finished."

Chapter Twelve

Ladder of Bones

One thing was clear to Reilly: whenever he got an answer to something important, that answer only created more questions. Not knowing if he would ever come through that same portal again, he was determined to find out as much as he could from Sam.

For the moment, he consciously pushed thoughts of Norah from his mind in an attempt to get more information without jading his perspective. Looking up at the glittering lights, he began again. "What happens to all of these Stelladaurs? Can they be reclaimed?"

"They remain here, in the Sea of Destiny, until the Deceptor who possesses the empty body for whom it was created is destroyed." Sam bobbed in the water as he spoke. "Stelladaurs are rarely reclaimed."

"Is is possible to destroy a Deceptor?" Reilly asked.

"As I said before, Stelladaur light creates possibilities."

"But the Deceptors have been around from the beginning of time," Lottie said. "And apparently, so have Stelladaurs."

"Remember, Lottie, there is no *time*. There is only *Now*," Sam replied. Lottie clutched her Stelladaur. "One of the great lies of the Deceptors is that time will grant what a person wants. Time can help a person better understand *Now*, but what we decide now—what we create now—is all we ever have." The great whale exhaled from his blowhole, and it rippled the unclaimed and discarded Stelladaurs in a shimmering array above their heads. "It is so difficult for your species to let go of time."

Reilly looked directly into Lottie's eyes. "Lottie, Eilam said that only love will conquer the spell of evil." Then he answered her next question before she could ask it. "But it must be the deepest kind of love—compassion and forgiveness."

"I don't understand this riddle, Reilly. I just want to get Sorcha back!" Lottie swam away from Reilly and tried to hide behind a coral cluster.

"I know how you feel," Reilly said, swimming after her. "Finding your own Stelladaur doesn't guarantee there won't be challenges. In some ways, it creates more." She turned her head away from him, but he continued. "We've got to use our most creative imagination to outsmart the Deceptors—create a diversion—so we can begin the conquest and rescue the prisoners."

Lottie held her Stelladaur in an open palm. "I wish I understood how this works." She stared down at the jewel as if mesmerized. "As soon as I think I have it figured out, I realize I don't. It's so frustrating."

"I know."

She looked up at the glistening lights above their heads. "All those people who never found their own Stelladaur, or who gave up …" She turned to look at Reilly. "My own sister."

Reilly put his arms around Lottie and stroked her long hair. "It's not too late. We'll find a way to get her back."

"And your friend, Norah?"

"She's in Black Castle, too. I'm sure of it." He pulled away and held Lottie's Stelladaur. "I need your help, Lottie. Even an Echtra can't do some things alone."

Sam spouted from his blowhole more loudly, and they watched the shimmering Stelladaurs dance on the water.

"You must return now," Sam said. "Swim up to my spiracle and I'll blow you back to the Cliffs of Black Castle. Wrap your tails around each other and hold on tight," Sam said. "This will be quite a ride."

They did as he said, and floated to the center of Sam's blow-hole. The boy and his fourth-great grandmother sailed upward on the tremendous spray of water, piercing through the sky of Stelladaur lights at the surface of the magical sea. As Reilly looked down at the unclaimed and discarded Stelladaurs growing smaller and smaller, he thought he heard Eilam's voice: *It's quite remarkable how far a person can travel by sea.*

Tossing and tumbling in the turbulent water, Reilly and Lottie struggled to hold on to each other. Suddenly unable to breathe underwater, they coughed and spurted, trying to hold their breath, until they landed with a lurch on a rocky beach.

Reilly spit sand from his mouth and turned over on the pebbled beach. Getting used to having legs again, he wiggled his bare toes, poking out of the same pants Lottie gave him to wear when he arrived. He stood up to help Lottie to her feet, and waited for her to squeeze the water from her tattered skirt. They looked out over the water in front of them and saw Sam breach in the far distance.

Then, turning around, Reilly and Lottie dropped their jaws as their eyes followed the perpendicular cliff beside them, up, and up, and up.

"I thought he meant he'd take us to the *top* of the cliffs!" Reilly said.

"I can't even see the top!" Lottie gasped wide-eyed. "Whatever shall we do?"

Reilly smiled, amused by the fact that Lottie was, in the present time, younger than he, but actually so much older. Sometimes she spoke so formally, and reminded him of his mother.

"The only way to go is up."

"But there's nothing to hold on to, Reilly. It's quite impossible!"

He chuckled. "Now who's being negative?"

Lottie frowned. Reilly craned his neck to survey the ominous sheer cliff, glancing to the far right. He sighed and turned to look left. "What's that?" Not waiting for a reply, he added, "It's a ladder, camouflaged against the black rock." He moved slightly so Lottie could look past him.

"Can you reach it?" she asked.

He stretched as far as he could reach, but the ladder was still inches away.

"I'll hold you steady," Lottie said, taking his hand.

Reilly anchored himself against the cliff and reached for the bottom rung again, his fingers barely brushing it. "We need something to grab it." The rocky beach offered nothing. He folded his arms to concentrate, then dropped his hands to his side pockets. "Of course," he whispered as he pulled the Fireglass from his pocket.

"Brilliant!" Lottie said, clapping her hands.

Reilly extended the device to its fullest length, took Lottie's hand again, and reached out against the cliff. He pushed the hanging ladder to make it swing slightly and caught the end with the Fireglass. Pulling the ladder toward him, he handed Lottie the Fireglass and grasped the ladder with both hands.

"Get on my back. Then we'll swing out. Once I've got a good hold, you climb up first and I'll be right behind you."

Lottie ripped her skirt from her dress and stood shivering in her bloomers and chemise. Then she tucked her Stelladaur next to her skin and slipped the Fireglass into Reilly's pocket.

"I'm ready," she said.

She hoisted herself onto Reilly's back as he lunged for a hold on a few rungs from the bottom. Lottie shrieked, but held tightly around his neck until the ladder stabilized against the cliff.

"Now pull yourself up."

Lottie gripped the ladder and screamed again. "It's made of bones … and hair!"

"Just start climbing, Lottie!"

The ladder swayed and the bones rattled as they began their ascent. Reilly looked down, and noticed the beach was now covered by the tide.

They climbed in silence for several minutes, carefully placing their bare feet and grasping each rung. Reilly looked up, but he still could barely see the top of the cliff.

"Take your time," he said. "Rest when you need to."

She groaned softly, already weary from the climb.

Reilly felt the bones—some smooth, some knobby—and shuddered at the possibilities that flooded his mind. He could not tell if the bones—or the hair that was used to bind the ladder—were human or not. He hoped Lottie was thinking of something else but did not want to engage her in unnecessary conversation. She would need her full strength to reach the top.

A wind blew in from the coast, swinging the ladder beneath them. Lottie stopped climbing and looked down at Reilly.

"Are you okay?" he shouted.

"Yes, but I'm getting tired." She titled her head back to look up. "We still have a long way to go."

"A storm is coming in. We need to pick up the pace."

Lottie started to climb again, moving faster. The wind surged, and Reilly heard the waves crashing against the rocks below. They climbed hard as the ladder began to sway in the approaching storm. The blue sky turned grey, and Reilly began to feel the blackness press in around him. Flashbacks of the storm that had taken his father's life flooded his mind. His breathing became shallow as he consciously tried to shake the images away. Lottie continued to climb, but Reilly slowed to a stop. He felt his hands slipping, shook his head to regain his composure, and gripped the rung above him more tightly.

He looked up and saw that Lottie had climbed further ahead. He shouted for her, but his voice was lost in the whistling wind. A gust blew hard against his back and slapped him against the cliff. He wondered how Lottie could hold on. Struggling to catch up to her, his foot slipped on a moist bone.

"Lottie!" he yelled, after regaining his balance. "Lottie, are you all right?"

She looked down at him and nodded but kept climbing.

Struggling to catch up, Reilly was only a few feet away from her when he noticed blood on each of the rungs. Her feet and hands were cut from clinging to the swaying ladder while it collided against the rocky cliff. His own bloodied knuckles stung in the cold air.

When the top of the cliff was in full view but still a significant distance away, Reilly shouted again to Lottie. "Do you want to rest?" She stopped and waited for him to reach her.

"I don't know if … I … if I can make it," she stammered.

"You can do it, Lottie! Hold on!" Looping one arm tightly around the ladder, Reilly ripped his shirttail in two large pieces. "Wrap these around your hands so you can get a better grip."

She nodded and did her best to wind the cloth around her hands. Reilly ripped his shirt again and told her to lift her feet, one at a time, so he could bandage them. She held tightly and lifted one foot as Reilly tied the fabric to cover the cuts and scrapes. Then, as she lifted her other foot, her hand slipped on the bloodied bone and she slid between Reilly and the cliff, grasping at the rungs. The swinging ladder came out from under Reilly, and he held tightly to it with his left hand. At the same moment, the rung beneath Lottie's feet broke, and she grasped for Reilly's hand as she fell. Reaching desperately for her, he grabbed hold of her bandaged forearm and dug his fingers into her skin. Reilly found his footing and turned her body toward the cliff. Lottie grasped the ladder as her legs flailed in the harsh wind. Still holding the ladder with one hand, Reilly reached for her waist and pulled her in.

Seconds later, lightning lit the cliff walls, illuminating them so they gleamed like shiny black obsidian. Reilly and Lottie climbed faster, desperate to reach the top before the rain started. A tremendous crash of thunder rumbled. Then a bolt of lightning struck the side of the cliff directly below them, near the bottom of the ladder. Flames licked the bottom rungs as smoke billowed from the tightly wound hair.

"Faster, Lottie!" Reilly screamed at the top of his voice, but he barely heard himself above the ringing in his ears. "We're almost there!" The fire below spread up the ladder rapidly. Bones bounced off the cliff walls. Reilly pushed her with his shoulder, and Lottie climbed two rungs at a time. Another boom of thunder propelled her forward. Finally, she scaled the top of the cliff and collapsed on a lush bed of grass. Reilly reached the top rung and hoisted his exhausted body up to the ground, dragged himself over Lottie, and fell in a heap beside her. They lay motionless through another crack of lightning, breathing heavily from exhaustion. The wind howled. Moments later, the rain began with a pelting fury. Reilly rolled towards Lottie and covered her head with his torso.

He closed his eyes. He used to love the sound of rain when it fell softly into Eagle Harbor or pattered on the roof of Eilam's kayak hut. But this storm was another deafening reminder of how much he hated the rain after his father died. It seemed never to stop. They had buried his father in muddy earth.

Reilly's temples pounded to the staccato rhythm of the rain. He breathed in deeply, ignoring the pain in his arm muscles, just glad to be breathing.

All at once, the black clouds above them moved away, taking the torrential rain and cataclysmic wind with them. Reilly rolled away from Lottie. Lying on their backs, they watched the clouds part to reveal the light of the early-morning sky.

"Reilly?" whispered Lottie. "We made it."

"Yeah." He chuckled. "Would've been nice if Andre the Giant had been around to help."

"Who?"

"Never mind." Reilly sat up, groaning. "It will be light soon." He stood up, walked to the edge of the cliff, and looked down at the water below. Lottie stood up and joined him.

"I guess no one will use *that* ladder again," she said, looking at the dangling remains of bones. "Another minute and the fire would've reached us."

"I want to know who made it, and why," Reilly said. "Something tells me it was the Pucatrows."

"They discovered a way to Black Castle from the front entrance … they probably wanted another access."

"And maybe they used the prisoners' hair to bind the ladder together. But I want to know what kind of a deal they made with the Deceptors in order to get the hair in the first place."

"Maybe the Pucatrows didn't make the ladder. Maybe the Deceptors did."

"Either way, I expect to find out when we get inside the castle again." Reilly turned away from the cliff and looked across the open grasses. "There it is," he said, pointing to the monstrous silhouette against the sunrise.

"We'll have to hurry if we're going to reach it before it's fully light."

"How are your feet doing?"

Lottie looked down at the bandages. She brushed off her torn clothes, trying to smooth the bloomers. "The grass will be a relief. Let's go."

Reilly smiled at her courage and felt a strange admiration for this girl who would soon become a woman, and live a life that he knew little about. Ironically, he knew he was always meant to be part of her life, and in that moment, he understood the inexplicable truth of timelessness in the endless space beyond three-dimensional existence.

They walked quickly through the tall grass. Smoke from the Deceptors' raging fire rose on the other side of the rock turrets and across the towering edifice. Unlike the front of the castle, there were no hedges for them to hide beneath should anyone approach, and they watched closely for Deceptors. Walking slowly now, Reilly took Lottie's hand.

"I don't see any doors along the back side," he said. "We'll have to find another way."

"Those windows are way too high," Lottie said.

"And it's hard to tell if anyone is looking out of them. But if they are, they could see us." He pulled hard on Lottie's hand. "Get down."

Crawling ahead, Reilly wondered how using his imagination—or any creative ideas that might come to him at a time like this—would bring any solution. The sun had risen higher and started to melt the dew around them. Looking at the droplets nearest him, Reilly thought of the time he and Norah warped through an ice cube to the land of Zora, where they discovered the power of gratitude, which could shine hope in each moment. Reilly tugged at the golden-hair bracelet he had worn ever since Flavio Xanthipee presented it to him. It was given as a reminder to feel gratitude, even in uncertain moments. He wondered if Norah still wore her bracelet.

With that thought, Reilly fell to the ground, groaning in pain. Lottie scrambled to his side. The pain was more intense than ever, and Reilly's eyes rolled back as Norah's song echoed in his mind.

Imagine love can change it all
And bring you back to me.

Chapter Thirteen

The Pawn

"Be still, Reilly," Lottie whispered. She placed a damp cloth on his forehead. "That was the worst one yet."

Reilly tried to sit up, but he could only roll onto his left elbow. He looked around at quartzite walls.

"Here, take a sip." Lottie held a cup of water to his lips as he drank.

"I passed out, huh?" Reilly asked. Lottie nodded.

"I remembered that the red flower revived you earlier in the VP. So I took it from your pocket and laid it on your chest."

Reilly fumbled at his chest. "Where is it now?"

"I gave it to Cormack in exchange for safe passage to the Undertunnels beneath Black Castle."

Reilly's jaw dropped and he started to protest, but Lottie cut him off. "I had no choice! He popped up from the grass like a weasel right after you passed out. He said he'd bring us to safety, but I had to give him something in return. I thought it best that he not see the Fireglass, so I offered him the flower. He liked how it smelled and agreed to the barter."

"What color was the flower when you gave it to Cormack?"

Lottie lowered her eyes. "Barely pink."

Reilly knew he could no longer rely on the perfectly formed flower to alleviate his sudden attacks. He knew his love for Norah must be his strength. He tugged on his golden-hair bracelet and, in his heart, thanked Cormack for providing the safe passage.

Surprised by his own response, he took a deep breath, stood up, and looked around the drafty room. He whirled around at a grating sound and saw a large piece of quartzite fall to the ground. Cormack poked his wiry-haired head through the hole, tossed his spear into the room, and jumped in after it.

"All the Pucatrows will be jealous that my nose has finally stopped dripping. They will wonder how I did it." Cormack smirked and picked up his spear. "Perhaps I will let them sniff my flower, if they can come up with something I want."

Reilly and Lottie looked at each other and frowned.

"Do you think we *like* this annoying curse upon us?" Cormack asked Reilly. "Even the Infusionists have not been able to find an antidote. Yet I could smell the aroma of the flower when I was first near you. I knew you had brought the cure."

"Glad I could help!" Reilly replied. "But it's the only flower like that. I have no idea how long it will last."

"Love's aroma lingers forever," Cormack said.

Reilly considered the Pucatrow's statement. "Then you should know that sharing the flower will only increase its value." Cormack lowered his head in shame, letting his matted hair fall over his face.

Reilly looked at Lottie, then pointed to the hole in the wall. "This must be the way inside Black Castle," he said.

Cormack lifted his head and pulled the hair from his eyes. "It is. But Pucatrows are only allowed to enter from the main doors, and only on shaving days. The Deceptors don't know about this passageway."

Reilly raised his brow.

"Pucatrows may be selfish, but we never lie to people," Cormack said. "The Deceptors know nothing about our Undertunnels, nor do they know we can morph into rats with snake tails. They think we are common rodents, and they prefer to put their efforts into taking possession of human bodies."

"Why do they allow you to enter Black Castle on shaving days?" Lottie asked.

"Without bodies, the Deceptors are hairless. They are more comfortable possessing a body that has as little hair as possible. Once the imprint occurs, they adjust to a body with hair. Our hairiness makes them uncomfortable, but they allow us to sweep up the shaven hair and take it away. We tell them we use the hair to replace our own when it becomes too tangled in our snot."

"Do you?" Reilly asked.

"Yes, but we also use it to make weapons. And now we'll need to collect much more hair to make another ladder," he added pointedly.

Reilly glanced at Lottie. He wanted to ask more about the weapons, but decided to wait.

"But you just said Pucatrows never lie," Lottie interjected. She hugged her bandaged arms. "You lie to the Deceptors."

"I said we never tell a *person* a lie. Deceptors are not people. They pretend to be by imprinting on human bodies, but eventually the person dies, and the Deceptor must find another body to inhabit."

"When does the imprinting happen?" Reilly asked.

"We don't know for sure. As I said, we're only allowed inside the Shaving Room, and only on shaving days. We get little information from the Undertunnels—only what we see or hear through slivered cracks in the ceiling that peek through to their floors. We don't know what happens with the prisoners when they're taken to The Library on the upper floor of the castle." Reilly's eyes widened and Lottie gasped. "As I said," Cormack continued, "Pucatrows are selfish. We don't particularly want to know what happens in The Library—we just want the hair and the rocks."

"It may not matter to you, but it matters to us!" Lottie retorted. "It matters to me what happens to my sister, Sorcha!"

"Sorcha will be at the bonfire tomorrow night. The Deceptors take the prisoners there for a final portrait painting before the bodies are burned. But we are always busy getting the rocks into the fire, or retrieving them—I've never seen the paintings."

Reilly raised his brow and stared at Cormack.

"Our capabilities are limited," snorted Cormack. He pulled the flower from a leather pouch that hung from his waist. "But Pucatrows help the Embassy when we can."

Reilly pulled on his golden bracelet and breathed in the stale damp air. "If you're certain no harm will come to Sorcha, we'll wait to make contact with her until tomorrow night."

"No! We've come this far!" Lottie cried. "I won't leave again without her!"

"Our best defense is more information, Lottie," Reilly insisted. "Sorcha will have the information we need."

"How can you make her the pawn?" Lottie cried more loudly. Reilly put his arm around her shoulder, but she jerked away from him.

"She's the only prisoner who hasn't been taken to The Library. She's the only one who can help us."

Lottie felt for her Stelladaur.

"We'll need the Pucatrows' help," Reilly said, turning to Cormack. "You'll need to distract the Deceptors so we can get close enough to communicate with Sorcha."

Cormack tucked the flower into his pouch and twitched his nose. "It won't be easy. When the Deceptors prepare to inhabit bodies, they become insanely obsessed. Not much that can be done to distract them."

"Then the distraction must happen before the next imprinting. Think, Cormack! There must be *something* that will sidetrack them."

Cormack waddled back and forth on his stubby legs, his overly long arms swaying awkwardly at his side. "We could fake an attack on the rats. Instead of shape-shifting, a group of us could stay in Pucatrow form and attack the rest of us, in our rat form, in the bonfire." Cormack stopped pacing and giggled. "It's risky but doable. We stay hidden from the far side when we've tossed our rocks into the fire. But the Deceptors will surely see us in the commotion—it could jeopardize our arrangement to collect the hair." Cormack twisted his wiry hair around his finger and glared at Reilly. "There would be great repercussions for all of us."

"Make the arrangements, Cormack!" Reilly said firmly. "Lottie and I will meet you here just before dusk."

"Very well." Cormack sniffed. "But if it does not have an acceptable outcome, there will be a price to pay." He stepped close to Reilly and pulled on a strand of his blonde hair.

Reilly took Lottie's hand to leave the Main Station, but turned and walked back to the Head Pucatrow. Looking down into his bulging eyes, he added, "And I want my flower back."

Cormack grinned, showing his crooked and rotted teeth. "Then you will need to make another exchange." He twirled his hair again and sniffed loudly. "We can discuss this arrangement after the attack … if you still want the flower."

The creature smiled eerily, making Reilly's chest burn. He ignored the sensation and affirmed his desire. "I will always want whatever leads me to Norah. The flower is mine, Cormack. But I'll give what you want—you have my word."

The Pucatrow narrowed his eyes and glowered at Reilly. "A person's word is only as valid as his actions. I'll give you back your flower if you promise, in blood, that you will give me whatever I ask."

"What do you want?"

"A blood promise does not require that the exchange is known to both parties in advance." Cormack sniffed the flower before he handed it to Reilly. "I'll make my demand tomorrow night."

Reilly and Lottie returned to the Embassy through the Undertunnels and the main lift. They found Dillon waiting for them at the VP with a basket of food.

"Thank you, Dillon," Lottie said as she swallowed a bite of rye bread. "I didn't realize that I was so hungry. Have you seen Father yet?"

"I saw him talking with Cormack in the auditorium when I first arrived," said Dillon. "I could tell he didn't want me to interrupt them, so I came in here. I haven't seen him since then."

"Huh!" Reilly said. "We've been with Cormack for the past few hours."

"True," Lottie agreed, "but remember, time is elusive. And a rat-Pucatrow can scamper back and forth through the Undertunnels much more quickly than their knobby troll-legs can run."

Reilly wasn't convinced, but he let it pass.

"Dillon, I have something wonderful to tell you," Lottie began again. "Sorcha is alive! We saw her inside Black Castle!"

His eyes widened. "Are you sure?"

"Yes! Father knows, too, and he's working on a plan to get her out. Cormack will help him." Lottie decided not to tell her brother about any other details, or the plan she and Reilly had devised with Cormack.

Reilly nodded. "Go tell your mother. We'll take care of things here."

"All right," the boy replied. "Do you think Sorcha is all right?"

"Of course," Lottie said, half lying. She hugged her brother. "Now off you go!"

Dillon left the basket of food for his sister and Reilly and stepped over the rubble into the doorway. Turning, he said, "Mother said she will keep the baby if no one claims her. I'd rather have a brother."

Reilly waited until Dillon was out of sight before he pulled out his Fireglass and stepped to the only remaining scope. Lottie reached for her Stelladaur and met him at the end of the dented device.

"It's remarkable this still works," she said as she adjusted the lens.

"Without your Stelladaur and my Fireglass, it's just a chunk of metal now."

Reilly reached into his pocket for his Fireglass, but first he handed the container of ointment to Lottie. "Just in case."

Lottie nodded her head but said nothing. She lifted her Stelladaur to the scope as Reilly raised his Fireglass to meet the jewel. He leaned forward and peered through the eyepiece.

"The West Woods seem calm enough." Reilly adjusted the level of the scope and did a wide sweep. "I don't see any auras that we should be concerned about now."

"People tend to be vigilant right after a Crumble. I've seen it before. People are on guard for a little while, and then they seem to forget."

"Human nature is to forget the stuff we should remember, and remember the stuff we'd be better off forgetting. Either way is a vulnerable position."

"Can you see my house?"

Reilly adjusted the scope. "Yeah, there it is. Ummm … there appears to be a darker yellow in the aura that I didn't notice before. Maybe even tinges of faint orange."

"I wonder if the people from the East Forest who are staying with my family have infected our home."

"That could be." Reilly turned and looked at Lottie with a sudden realization. "Could it be coming from the baby? Can Deceptors influence someone so young?"

Lottie nodded as she considered his questions. "Infants' auras are extraordinarily bright and strong, so Deceptors infiltrate the weaker members of families instead. Young children can usually feel any disturbance in a home's aura, but they don't have the language to communicate what they know. Unfortunately, by the time children *are* able to communicate, they've been infected, too."

"And life gets sucked out of them before they have a chance," finished Reilly.

"'Sucked out?' You mean they die?"

"It's a phrase people use when they don't like what's going on in their life—it's too hard, it's not what they thought it would be, or they just feel like giving up. But it's quite literal! When a person says 'life sucks,' they affirm what they don't want, so that's what they get. Life is hard for everyone in different ways—harder for some than others—but one of the Deceptors' lies is that it doesn't matter what a person chooses, because life will just *suck* no matter what. When a person believes that lie, little by little he loses his dreams and the ability to imagine, and to feel joy. So, yeah, they die."

Reilly saw a look in Lottie's eyes that told him she understood. She held her Stelladaur up to the morning light now shining through the open window. "And that's what you meant when you told me that you need to help others find their own Stelladaur."

"Sort of."

Lottie looked out the window at the people who had spent the night on the town square.

"They must be hungry," she said. "If we can't return to the bonfire until tomorrow night, let's see what we can do to help around here."

Most of the critically injured people in the auditorium were still asleep or unconscious, and those who were awake seemed delirious with pain. Even the Infusionists could not provide adequate remedies for severed limbs.

Reilly and Lottie headed down the spiral jade staircase. They moved aside as three people carried another casualty out of the building. The bodies were taken to a burial site between the West Woods and East Forest. Survivors of the Crumble knew to look there for their missing family members.

Pucatrows still guarded the Infusionists' doors down the long hallway to the main entrance, and they sniffed loudly as Reilly passed by. Lottie asked several of the trolls if they had seen her father, but they had not. Reilly and Lottie passed Flynn at the registration desk, and offered her something from the basket of food.

"Such a lovely color," Flynn said. She held a single strawberry in her hand as if she had never seen one before. "It will make a beautiful dye."

Lottie glanced at Reilly. "You have plenty of red yarn here," Lottie said. "These berries are for you to eat."

"How kind of you, my dear. I will save them for a special occasion."

Reilly stepped closer to the registration counter. "Today is already a special occasion, Flynn. Everyone in the Embassy is wearing the wristbands that you made … and …" He looked to Lottie.

"… and without you, Flynn, none of us would be protected while we are here at the Embassy."

Flynn held the berries in her hand, squeezed them, and watched the juice run through her fingers. "The wristbands will soak up the blood." She licked her fingers and smiled as Reilly and Lottie walked outside to the Square.

"What are the wristbands *really* for?" Reilly asked Lottie.

"We've only known of a few survivors who escaped from The Library. One man named Deaglan lived there centuries ago for almost his entire life. But somehow he escaped and was found, near death, hiding in a hollowed-out tree in the East Forest. It's said that his dying words were these: 'Cover your wrists in red, as if to wear their band. If you don't, the blood of the storytellers will stain your hands, and your heart will slowly fade.'"

Reilly's eyes widened. "What does that mean?"

"Some people believe Deaglan was delirious with fever and that his dying words were nothing more than a superstitious riddle. But if Deceptors find a person who is not wearing the red bands, he or she is at greater risk of being captured because wearing the bands indicates loyalty to the Embassy. Deceptors take weaker ones first."

"I thought people only wore the bands when they were at the Embassy."

"My father is not a superstitious man, but he requires people to wear the bands when they are at the Embassy. He cannot force people outside those walls to follow rules or the laws which are meant to keep them safe."

Reilly turned to look back at the main door. "Did Flynn escape from The Library?"

"We aren't sure. They terrorized her, no doubt," Lottie said as she lowered her head. "I've only ever known her as she is now. Father thinks it's her belief in Deaglan's riddle that fuels her obsession to knit the bands. But he said everyone needs purpose, even if they are clearly mad."

"What do you believe, Lottie?"

She held the basket in one hand and touched her Stelladaur with the other.

"I believe if more people found their own Stelladaur, there wouldn't be as many Crumbles."

Reilly wished again that his own Stelladaur still hung on its golden cord around his neck. Eilam had said Reilly's Stelladaur lived inside his own heart, and Reilly believed it—but that was before he came through the portal to Wicklow all by himself. It frustrated him that seven Affirmations of the Stelladaur had been magically seared into his stone—and allegedly into his heart—but now he could only remember the two he had recently rediscovered with Lottie.

He felt certain they would need to know and use each Affirmation if they were to rescue Sorcha … and if Norah's haunting song was to lead him to her.

Chapter Fourteen

The Great Basin

After distributing the remainder of the food to people at the Embassy Square, Reilly and Lottie retreated again to the courtyard. Even with all the commotion, the garden seemed undisturbed. The sweet-smelling air helped revive Reilly's fatigue and waning strength.

He walked toward the fountain with his hands in his pockets, rolling the ruby between his thumb and fingers. He brushed the flower with his fingers. As much as he wanted to lie down on the ledge of the fountain, fall asleep, and just dream of the days he spent with Norah back home, he knew he could not afford the luxury of doing so. Besides, Lottie had already opened the portal.

"Come on, Reilly!" she hollered. "We have no time to waste. And resting will have to wait. Let's go!"

This time, Reilly and Lottie simply stepped into the swirling water at the base of the angel statue, and instantaneously transported to yet another dimension.

In that moment, Reilly realized that dimensions are limitless. Knowing also that time, space, and imagination are endless, Reilly felt no sense of movement as he and Lottie shifted from one place to another through the portal. They simply arrived, wherever it was they had arrived.

Glimmering brightness—so bright that Reilly and Lottie lifted their hands in an attempt to shade their view—filled a vast space around them. Blinking repeatedly, they looked across an immense panorama that resembled a diamond mine. Fluffy clouds hovered above them against a piercing, azure sky. Like grains of fine sugar, the ground beneath them shimmered brilliantly.

"You must use the Stellagoggles within two minutes of arrival, or you will be blinded," said a fairy creature fluttering about. "The light is too powerful for human eyes."

The creature handed Reilly and Lottie each a pair of white-rimmed glasses. The lenses were shaped like a Stelladaur but otherwise resembled ordinary sunglasses. They put the glasses on and looked again across the cavernous pit in front of them. Narrow roads wound in a great circle around the perimeter, and others disappeared into the walls of the excavation site. Reilly saw three spectacular waterfalls. One began near the top and the others cascaded further down, all spilling into the mine.

"This must be where Stelladaurs are mined," he blurted, but instantly he knew that what he had said did not make sense.

"Star Doors are not mined. They are imagined and then created," said the fairy-creature. "One for every child born to your sphere."

Embarrassed, Reilly nodded.

"I am called Sitara," said the fairy. Her translucent wings whirred like a hummingbird's in front of Reilly. "You are in Jolkavatar."

Reilly pushed his Stellagoggles further up on his nose and tucked the bendable stems tightly around his ears. "Then we are near Jolka?" he asked.

"Jolkavatar is found deep within Jolka," Sitara replied.

"Then we are also near Tir Na Nog!"

"Tir Na Nog is always near. It, too, is within."

Reilly sighed, frustrated because the portals always provided *few* answers and always *more* questions.

"Follow me," Sitara said. Her black pixie hair shimmered against her iridescent wings, and her flowing dress trailed behind her in a blur of white light. "The Fairies of the great Star King and Star Queen await your arrival."

Again Reilly thought about the portals he had been through. They all started to blend together. Although he knew each one was as real as the next, sometimes he could not distinguish one from the other. It was as if all of his barely sixteen years of existence melded together in a recurring, familiar dream—that recently felt more like a nightmare.

Reilly looked at Lottie to determine if she had experienced the same realization. *Probably not,* he decided. *She hasn't yet gone through the same portals as I have.* Sitara turned back from her flight just ahead of them and winked at Reilly.

Something that resembled an oversized white lily pad with two white toadstools perched on top hovered barely above the ground, and Sitara invited them to step in. Reilly and Lottie boarded the transportation device and sat down on the huge white mushrooms. Sitara led the way along the road, which spiraled downward so far that Reilly could not see the bottom, even with Stellagoggles. When they finished circling the perimeter once, Sitara stopped in front of a glass doorway, and the floating lily pad came to a slow halt.

"First we will explore that which is understood through the human eye," said Sitara.

Reilly and Lottie stepped to the sugary ground and followed Sitara through the doorway into a room that appeared as endless as the circular pit outside. Tens of thousands of delicate fairies, each resembling Sitara, flittered about like honeybees gathering nectar, storing something tiny in apron pockets at their waist. When their pockets bulged to nearly overflowing, the fairies flew to a pool of crystal clear water and emptied them.

Thinking that he ought to know more about what the fairies were doing than he did, Reilly hesitated to ask any questions. He was relieved when Lottie spoke.

"What are they doing?" she asked Sitara.

"The Star Fairies are gathering every nugget of truth that is possible for humans to understand with their eyes. The nuggets are liquefied in the Pool of Manifestation and then poured into the Great Basin." Sitara pointed to a river, which led out from the pool and disappeared beyond it.

"The waterfall," Reilly mumbled.

Sitara smiled.

"*Every* truth?" Lottie questioned.

"The human eye is limited by the brain's ability to process what is seen. So truth seen in any form can only be partially understood, not fully comprehended. Vision is a great gift for those who use their Stelladaur to truly see."

Lottie touched her own Stelladaur and turned to look at Reilly. He nodded in agreement.

"How many truths are there?" Lottie asked Sitara.

"Truth is endless," the head fairy replied.

"So the fairies will do this forever?"

"Until a Stelladaur is created for every human soul."

Lottie scowled. "It's still a bit confusing."

Sitara swooped around Lottie and hovered just in front of her. "Truth is the first ingredient of a Stelladaur. It is what makes the jewel shine so brightly. Every truth is manifested as its own grain of light." The humming of her tiny wings harmonized with her melodic voice. "Whenever a truth is presented merely through the eyes to a human soul, he or she has the option to affirm it. If the truth is affirmed, it will manifest itself in various forms of light, over and over, until it embodies the entire soul."

"The second Affirmation of the Stelladaur," Reilly whispered. "I remember it now: *I am realization and manifestation as One.*"

"Yes," said Sitara. "But when a truth is disregarded, ignored, or in any way shunned, the grain of light will fade."

Reilly watched the fairies empty their pockets full of brilliant specks into the Pool of Manifestation, spilling them like a stream of precious jewels. He tugged at the golden thread Flavio Xanthipe had tied around his wrist, and remembered looking into the Well of Infused Light, where he had seen a vision of his father drowning. Even then, fear had gripped him as he relived the horror of what had happened. For a few moments, his mind wandered. *When did that actually happen? Has it only been a few months since Dad drowned? And since I went through the portal in the Suzzallo Library to look for him?* Soon the clear river, flowing from the Pool of Manifestation and weaving around the room with gentle bubbling sounds, assured Reilly that he was closer to his dad than ever before. He understood more completely the significance of gratitude in relation to the second Affirmation of the Stelladaur.

"We disregard the things we see every day and take them for granted … like water … and family," Reilly said.

"Gratitude nuggets are also infused into each Stelladaur," Sitara replied. "The warmth of gratitude soothes the sting of evil and the chill of deceit."

"Are you saying we should be grateful for *everything*? Even Deceptors?" Lottie interjected.

Reilly knew how she felt. He knew her own Stelladaur would help her understand, so he didn't say anything. He breathed in deeply and twirled the thread at his wrist.

"Deceptors are masters of deception because they speak only part of a truth," said Sitara, now flitting in front of Lottie. "A partial truth can also be a partial lie."

"I thought Deceptors *only* told lies," said Lottie.

"Not so. Deceptors hide at least one truth in every lie they tell."

"How do they do this?"

"First, they disguise each lie in the human brain as distorted thoughts—thoughts about entitlement, justification, selfishness, revenge, abandonment, inadequacy, and despair." The fairy's wings slowed, and she landed on the sandy ground. She picked up a sparkling grain and flew again to look directly at Lottie. "Without the light of a Stelladaur, it is impossible to know where truths stop and lies begin." She held the shimmering grain of light in her tiny hand and held it up for Lottie to see.

"You may have eyes to see, but you must watch most carefully that which you cannot see," said Sitara.

Reilly watched Lottie touch her Stelladaur at her chest, and he knew she was beginning to understand. "Our thoughts?" Lottie asked.

"Indeed. When thoughts linger, they quickly turn to human emotion." Sitara's wings continued to flap as fast as a hummingbird's. "These emotions can be so intense that they can overpower reason and hide truth. I will show you."

Reilly and Lottie followed the fairy back to the open mine and stepped onto the lily pad. They circled around the tremendous cavity three times, passing under the first waterfall, which drained from the Pool of Manifestation into a river and cascaded far below them.

Then, just ahead, Sitara stopped in front of the second giant waterfall. The lily pad slowed, and Reilly and Lottie stepped to the sandy ground.

"Here, a drop of every emotion is added to each nugget of truth. Humans have the capacity to feel the deepest of all emotions," Sitara said.

Thousands of fairies darted in and out of the waterfall, trailing miniature rainbows behind them, while their light reflected off the water like multicolored fireflies.

Reilly's mind wandered to the portals he had gone through from his home, and he struggled with a flood of his own emotions that made him wonder if what he was experiencing was real at all. His mind raced, and he thought his brain might explode in a burst of multicolored blood. He questioned why he would have such a thought to begin with! Battling to shake off the oppression, he put his hands to his temples and pressed hard. He began to sweat profusely. Or was it spray from the waterfall? He couldn't tell. Where was Lottie? All the fairies were a blur of conglomerate colors. Thoughts of home—of his mom, the bakery, Chantal, Eilam, and Tuma ricocheted through his mind, as if in a movie playing in fast reverse. Reilly remembered hooded creatures in a dark cave—each one being Travis Jackson—and then fireworks … portals … Norah … the library!

"No!" Reilly screamed as he threw off his Stellagoggles. "Make it stop!"

Intense light enveloped his entire body and he fell to the ground to cover his head. Reilly felt something brush the back of his hair and he swatted it away.

"Living in thoughts of what you call the 'past' can be the worst torture," Sitara said soothingly. "The past is only a reflection of what was the NOW, and it will only serve you well when you use it to feel gratitude for what is."

Reilly squirmed on the ground with his head still covered. A gust of wind blew a spray of water over him.

"Put the Stellagoggles back on, Reilly," Lottie said. "If we're going to find Tir Na Nog, we need to move on." As he heard her voice, he saw in his mind the same words written on the pages of the book she was writing, which he had found in the Suzzallo Library. "Here." Lottie knelt beside him and nudged his shoulder.

Reilly uncovered his head and reached for the goggles. When he put them on, he turned over completely and sat up. "I don't understand. What just happened?"

"You saw the rainbows in the waterfall and it reminded you of your experiences through the other portals. But sight can only give glimpses of truth. Once the glimpse is processed, which happens in the human brain instantly, millions of thoughts collide," Sitara replied. "But you have the power to slow thoughts down. There are many ways humans attempt to do this, some of which do not come from a place of stillness at all and ultimately cause the person's own destruction."

Reilly pushed his Stellagoggles up further on his nose and latched them again tightly behind his ears. "Go on," he said.

"You look at an object and think you know what it is, but it is only an outer reflection of what it truly is. You call a reflection of light off the water a *rainbow*. But you have learned it is much more than colors in the sky—it is a doorway to other realms."

"I think I understand," Reilly said. "A Stelladaur isn't a jewel at all. It's all truth inside of me. That's what Eilam meant when he said I didn't need it around my neck anymore, and that it would always be with me."

"That's part of it, Reilly. Stelladaurs are made of truth, but also of all thoughts and all emotions. Each thought is given an accompanying emotion. Thoughts often come without intent or invitation, but you choose the thoughts that serve you best by deciding which emotion you want to affirm. It's a powerful gift."

"The Stelladaur?"

"No. Choice."

"But not all people have the same choices," Lottie said.

"True. Many of your species attempt to steal this power from others."

"Like Travis Jackson tried to steal people's imagination by coating fake Stelladaurs with drugs," Reilly said. "And like Deceptors, who I believe are also trying to steal choice."

"That is a thought, Reilly," said Sitara. "Now determine if that particular thought is true by considering your emotions around it. If the thought is only a thought and you can't affirm its assigned emotion, then you may be dwelling on a thought of deceit rather than truth."

"Don't we choose our emotions?" Lottie asked.

"Yes, but only as it relates to what comes into your mind and the thoughts you continue to hold on to. You can be sure a thought is a thought of truth when the emotion aligns with it. That is why emotions are added to the creation of each Stelladaur. In other words, don't believe everything you think. Make sure the accompanying emotion is in response to truth, not deception."

Lottie nodded and touched the jewel around her neck. Reilly looked at the fairies darting in and out of the great waterfall.

"I know the Deceptors try to steal choices," Reilly said. "But I'm almost certain they do this in a calculated way, so the prisoners believe they have no choice at all."

"So the emotion you feel is *certainty*?" Sitara asked.

Reilly nodded, then added, "And *urgency*!"

"Then let's move on," Lottie declared.

The lily pad floated under the second waterfall, lit in multicolor reflections. After spiralling through the cavernous hole in the earth several times, they reached the top of the third waterfall, from where they saw the other two cascading across the divide, one at their right and one at their left. The road ended in a tremendous spray of rushing water that spilled into whiteness far below.

"If feelings and emotions are stripped from thoughts, humans have no way to experience the greatest truth," said Sitara.

Reilly stood up from the toadstool and peered over the edge of the cliff.

"We have to go down there, don't we?" he said.

"The Great Basin arranges all truth, thoughts, and emotions in every Stelladaur. There they are polished so they can resonate within the heart."

Reilly took Lottie's hand and they stepped to the edge of the cliff. He listened to the cascading grains of light chime a melody he had heard before—when his Stelladaur had hung around his neck, and when he had stepped to the portal door of the Suzzallo Library. The song of his own soul sang across the Stelladaur mine above the sound of rushing water.

"This is where the greatest truth lies," said Sitara.

Still holding Lottie's hand, Reilly tilted his head to listen to a haunting descant lingering in the air.

Hearts must be polished—or they fade in empty bodies, he thought. Then he and Lottie leapt into the Great Basin.

Chapter Fifteen

The Rowan Tree

The portals in Wicklow seemed to operate differently. Back home, they took Reilly on journeys he experienced with heightened sense-awareness, but jumping into the Great Basin was different. He and Lottie simply jumped off the cliff's edge, and landed sitting on the ledge of the fountain in the Embassy garden, with the evening sun poking through the flowering trees. He stretched as he stood up.

It was clear in Reilly's mind and heart that he could not save everyone from the Deceptors. Just as Jaida, the Guardian of Nature, had told him, it would take more courage and strength than he had ever known to rescue Norah—a greater sacrifice. Reilly knew that if his courage failed, Norah would be the sacrifice.

Without warning, he fell to the ground, gripping his chest.

"Not again!" Lottie wailed. She wet the hem of her tattered skirt in the fountain and pressed it to Reilly's forehead. She fumbled in his pocket to find the flower and placed it on his chest.

He writhed in pain longer than he had before. Lottie waited for the spell to pass.

"It's even paler now," Reilly whispered, as he opened his eyes and looked at the flower. "Hold on, Norah."

Lottie put her hand on Reilly's shoulder and smiled at him.

"We need to rest." He yawned. "This time tomorrow, we'll talk with Sorcha."

"And bring her home!" Lottie said firmly.

"I hope so. But we need more information first. "

"What about Cormack? He still knows more than he's saying. Can't *he* be the bait?"

"Let's find the magistrate and find out what he and Cormack have discussed." Reilly yawned again and put the flower back in his pocket.

They searched the Embassy courtyard and the main foyer. They asked the Pucatrows guarding the hallway doors if they had seen Quin or Cormack, but the trolls only sniffed Reilly and grunted that they did not know their whereabouts. The auditorium was still filled with wounded people. A chill ran down Reilly's back as he noticed more empty tables than there were before.

As they approached the Vantage Post, it was obvious that neither Lottie's father nor the Head Pucatrow was there.

"Your father told me to tell you to meet him at the edge of the East Forest," said the volunteer at the scope. "He looked for you all morning. Cormack is with him."

"Thank you," said Lottie.

"The magistrate said not to take the Undertunnels," the volunteer added.

Lottie glanced at Reilly. "Very well," she said. "We'll take the trails in the woods, as I usually do."

"Have you seen any other disturbances?" Reilly asked the man, whose hand rested on the top of the scope as he spoke.

"Nothing."

Reilly wanted the man to step aside so he could look through the scope with his Fireglass, but he hesitated and then decided against it.

As Reilly and Lottie walked through the forest, they passed the Wicklow Cemetery, where a mother and five children huddled together near a newly dug gravesite. Mounds of fresh dirt dotted the grassy hillside.

A large rowan tree creaked nearby, and Reilly stopped to listen.

"Me ruby berries restore the blood," a voice called from somewhere.

"Did you hear that?" Reilly asked Lottie.

"Hear what?"

"Listen."

They stood still and waited.

"Me ruby berries restore the blood."

Startled, Lottie spun around. "Who said that?"

Reilly pointed to the large tree on the far side of the cemetery.

"I've never heard a tree speak before," said Lottie. "I had no idea!"

Reilly smiled. "Magical things don't just happen in unlikely places. They happen all around us, wherever we are."

Lottie walked quickly toward the tree, and Reilly followed. He wanted to see the expression on her face when she talked with a tree for the first time. Approaching cautiously, Lottie stepped under the canopy of red berry clusters.

"Hello," she whispered. She looked up the trunk and pointed to something near the top. "Did this tree *speak*?"

"Me ruby berries restore the blood," said the feminine voice again.

"I believe she did just speak, Lottie." Reilly laughed.

Lottie raised her brow as she looked at Reilly, and then walked around the tree.

"I'm Lottie—Charlotte Louise McKinley. This is Reilly McNamara."

"Of course," the tree replied. "I am called Grania O'Keegan. Me name means Heart O'Fire. Me fruit is bitter. Therein lies its power."

Lottie stepped back to stand beside Reilly and get a better look at Grania.

Reilly thought about bitterness and power, and felt his heart skip a beat. "Will your berries ease the pain I feel when I think of Norah?"

"If ye are willin' to taste o' the bitter juice, ye will know the answer to that question." The tree lowered a branch filled with red berries. Reilly picked seven plump ones and held them in his hand.

"We should have an Infusionist analyze the fruit before we eat it," Lottie warned. "We believe rowanberries are poisonous."

Reilly studied the berries as if mesmerized by their beauty.

"The taste o' bitter is poisonous only when the heart resists what is. It then changes to bitterness within," Grania said softly. "But at least one drop o' sweetness is in every swallow o' bitterness. Such a drop is precious and more powerful than the most vile bitterness."

There were already so many uncertainties in Reilly's life that eating the mysterious berries seemed to be the only solution left. Without second-guesssing his decision, he popped the handful of berries into his mouth and chewed them all at once.

Puckering as if sucking on unripe gooseberries, Reilly's mouth contorted and he swallowed hard. "That wasn't so bad." He coughed.

"Do you feel any different?" Lottie asked anxiously.

"A bit of a pit in my stomach, but nothing more. Do you want to try some?"

Lottie shook her head and grimaced.

Reilly clicked his tongue a couple times in an attempt to diffuse the taste of blood now lingering in his mouth. He purposely thought of Norah and rehearsed the first few lines of her song in his mind.

I'll hold my breath within the fire
To keep from utter shame.
I'll bleed inside from every vein
Before I yield my name.

Reilly stroked his chest, aware that he felt no pain. He reached for Grania's branch, scored a clump of berries in his hand, and stuffed them into his left pocket.

"What are you doing, Reilly?" Lottie asked.

"The berries may taste horrible, but they completely take away the pain in my chest."

He stuffed another handful of berries into his pocket. "How long will it last?" he asked Grania.

"Until the blood o' the storytellers is restored by a jewel placed in the wound," Grania replied.

"Why do you speak in riddles?" Lottie demanded. "Tell us what this means!" But the tree lifted her limbs high above their reach, and her mouth closed tightly.

Reilly understood Lottie's frustration but remained confident. "She's told us all she can, Lottie. Now we must rest."

"How do you keep such calmness about you? This is madness! I want to know how to get Sorcha back!"

"Lottie, tomorrow will be here soon enough, and sooner if we sleep for a while. C'mon, let's go." He took her hand and pulled her away from the tree. "I'm doing my best to be this Echtra you've waited for, but you're going to have to trust me."

Lottie nodded and smiled half-heartedly.

Reilly knew how frustrating it was to get tidbits of information … to see only scattered puzzle pieces … to wonder where someone he loved had gone, and if he would ever see that person again. He also knew that life's uncertainties often came in large doses—and that the only antidote seemed to be love.

The trouble was, the more Reilly thought about how much he loved Norah, the more he thought he might never be able to tell her. Determining whether that thought came from his head or his heart, or somewhere in between, seemed more perplexing to him than the fact that he was trapped back in time, walking further into the East Forest of Wicklow, Ireland, hand in hand with his fourth great-grandmother. For now, he was simply grateful that the berries allowed him to dwell on thoughts of Norah without any pain.

When they arrived at the lift to the McKinleys' tree home, Reilly noticed something was different.

"There are more nicks in these walls than there were before," he said as they ascended. "A Deceptor has been here."

"You're right, Reilly! Look at this." Lottie knelt down and picked up a small chunk of fallen wood. "I've never seen one this big before. Not even when Sorcha was in trouble … before she was taken."

They reached the top and greeted Katell.

"Stalwart 59," Lottie said.

The bird struck his beak on the door in the usual staccato pattern, and it swung open. Reilly stopped and looked back at the bird. "Did you detect any danger near this tree home since the last Crumble?" The bird blinked only once and twisted his head sideways, and then toward the ground.

"Katell?" Lottie asked. The bird flinched and ruffled his feathers. "Did you see anything?"

Katell blinked twice and shook his head.

"Thank you," Lottie said, as she stepped inside her home.

Reilly and Lottie followed the smell of bacon, fried zucchini, and fresh bread, and they found the McKinleys seated at the kitchen table. Cormack sat across from Dillon and snorted loudly but did not look up.

"Charlotte, my dear!" cried Brigid as she jumped up from her chair. "You look such a fright!" She hugged her daughter tightly and cradled Lottie's head. "I have been worried to my bones."

"You look as if you've not slept in days," Quin added. "You must be hungry. Come and sit down." He pulled a chair out for her and grabbed a stool from the corner for Reilly.

Brigid released Lottie and quickly grabbed Reilly in an embrace. "And you, young man! I understand you have been quite a help to my husband." She patted him hard on the back. "I thank you, indeed."

"Yes, ma'am, thank you," Reilly said. He sat down on the stool and looked at Cormack, who still had not lifted his eyes to greet Reilly or Lottie.

Brigid ladled a few spoons of zucchini onto Reilly's plate and slapped four pieces of bacon on the side. Reilly reached for the bread, torn into big chunks and piled into a serving basket.

"Now tell us more about Sorcha!" Brigid exclaimed. "You saw her, yes?"

"Yes, Mother, we did," Lottie said. "But she didn't see us. Her back was to us and I hardly recognized her."

"But you are sure it was my Sorcha?"

"I'm certain, Mother. But she looks quite different." Lottie twisted a strand of her hair around her finger.

Quin nodded. "As I told you, my love, our daughter has been spared the torture that the others have been subjected to, but she is a chained prisoner, nevertheless. Cormack and I have been discussing the best way to get into Black Castle for her rescue," he said.

At the mention of his name, the Pucatrow finally looked up and wiped the bacon grease that drooled from his mouth with the back of his hairy hand. "I smelled you comin' up the lift," said the troll.

Reilly was determined to stay focused on what really needed to be discussed. "Sir, I noticed a slight discoloration in your home's aura. And your lift has fresh nicks."

"I noticed the nicks but was not aware of the change in the aura," Quin replied.

"After the last Crumble in the East Forest, did you take in any house guests who managed to escape? Lottie and I wondered if they could be the cause of the discoloration."

"Yes," said Brigid. "A childless couple and the man's sister stayed with us only one night. Perhaps the crying child we have taken in was a painful reminder of their added misfortune. They were anxious to leave the next morning." Brigid wiped the corners of her mouth with a napkin and replaced it on her lap. "The poor thing doesn't sleep well and keeps us all awake at night."

"It wails all night long!" Dillon added, chewing a piece of bacon. "I want to sleep in the Undertunnels, but Father won't allow it."

"As I've told you before, Dillon, your little sister's name is Roisin."

Lottie raised her eyebrows and looked at her father.

"Your mother has become quite attached to the baby and feels she must be given a suitable name, in order that she might thrive and grow in this treacherous time. Her name means 'little rose.'"

"Maybe the couple's inner pain brought a shadow on your home's aura," Reilly offered. "But there could be other causes." Reilly looked directly at Cormack, who held his glance briefly and then stuffed his mouth with bread.

"The nicks generally occur at night, or when we are off guard." Quin pulled away from the table and began to pace the floor. "Even Katell was probably distracted with the crying child. And our attention has been elsewhere, for obvious reasons."

"Sir, in addition to being concerned about disintegrating auras, don't you think our main focus should be on how we'll get into Black Castle tomorrow night?" Reilly said.

"Yes, definitely! Cormack and I have discussed this at length. There are only two options we can conceive of."

"What are the options, Father?" Lottie asked.

"The first plan of attack is simple but not likely to be effective: The Pucatrows would cause a distraction. They would each change to their rat-snake bodies, and instead of puttering about in the fire waiting for their rocks to turn into quartzite, they would scurry out of the flames and scuttle about under the cloaks of the Deceptors. Cormack believes the Deceptors will simply pick up the creatures by their tails and toss them into the fire, and assume it would be the last of them. Meanwhile, Reilly and I would move up behind Sorcha and take her."

"I'm going, too, Father!" Lottie demanded.

Quin ignored Lottie and continued. "The problem with this idea is that once the Deceptors know Sorcha is gone—which wouldn't take long—they will attack in Crumbles greater than any that Ireland has witnessed before. We hardly have the support to recover from our own recent disasters. Anything worse may result in annihilation."

"With all due respect, sir, that doesn't seem to be a real option, then," said Reilly. "What's the second option?"

Quin stopped pacing, cleared his throat, and looked at Cormack. Lottie squirmed in her chair at the awkward silence, now hanging thick in the air. Brigid folded her napkin and placed it on her half-emptied plate. Reilly looked at the Pucatrow and narrowed his eyes.

"Cormack knows more than he is saying," Reilly blurted loudly but steadily, and then looked directly at Cormack. "Why didn't you tell Mr. McKinley and his family about their daughter?"

Lottie sat up straighter and glared at their dinner guest.

The troll sniffed loudly and let a long thread of snot drip onto his plate. He lowered his head until his wiry black hair fell over his face. "We needed the hair."

"Yes … for the ladder … I know," said Reilly. "But that isn't all of the truth. If, as you say, a Pucatrow *never tells a person a lie*, then he must also tell the *whole* truth!" Reilly slammed his fist on the table, and saw Brigid and Lottie flinch. Cormack looked up. Reilly stared directly into the troll's eyes. "Otherwise, a Pucatrow is also a Deceptor!"

Lottie and her mother gasped, and Dillon dropped his fork. The magistrate waited for the troll's reply.

"The whole truth is this: As rats, we hide in the fire under the cover of the night sky, but as bald trolls, we bring shame to all of Ireland. Centuries ago, we were beautiful creatures, with hair as fine and shimmering as spun gold. With our hair, we could live as Pucatrows, and we didn't have to scuttle about as rats. But when Ukobach, one of the most powerful and jealous of all Deceptors, struck us with a curse, he stole our hair."

"Why?" Reilly demanded. "Why did he want your hair? I thought Deceptors were uncomfortable around people—and trolls—with hair. You said that was why the Deceptors shave their prisoners' heads."

"Hair is a threat to Ukobach because he believes it is a source of great strength and power, yet all Deceptors are bodiless and therefore hairless."

"He allows the Pucatrows to sweep up the hair from the shaven prisoners and take it away so the Deceptors don't feel threatened?" Reilly asked.

Cormack pushed his chair away from the table and stood up. "Yes, but the prisoners don't know this. They are told their heads are shaven as a reminder that unprotected minds create thoughts that are not their own; and, as prisoners, the only place their minds are protected is in The Library."

Reilly persisted. "It still doesn't make sense to me."

"In time, insanity feeds on the vulnerable mind," Cormack continued. "First, the Deceptors steal the mind." He took a step closer toward Reilly. "Then, they drain the heart." He sniffed loudly near Reilly's pants pocket. "Finally, they take possession of a mortal body."

Lottie gasped and held her hand to her Stelladaur under her bodice. Brigid told Dillon to go to his room. The boy's father insisted he should stay. Reilly stood up and towered over Cormack, studying the hair on his head.

"Do the Deceptors know you use the discarded hair to transplant into your own heads?"

"Yes, but they believe once the hair is cut from the body it loses its power. They think we are stupid trolls with no more sense than a rat."

Reilly fumbled in his right pocket. He looked around the room at each of the McKinleys, but they remained silent, as if they expected Reilly to say something more. Reilly rubbed his hand over his head, pulling his own blonde hair over his shoulder. Then he stopped directly in front of Cormack.

"Do you know how they steal the prisoners' minds?"

"No," Cormack answered. "No Pucatrow has been allowed in The Library."

"Then there is only one solution," Reilly said firmly. "I will shave my head and disguise myself as a prisoner. I must get into The Library."

For a moment, everyone was too stunned to move or speak. Then Quin stepped up to Reilly and gripped his forearm tightly. "That is precisely the second option Cormack and I discussed. But I could not ask you to do such a thing, Reilly."

Reilly touched the flower in his pocket and smiled. "You didn't ask, sir."

Chapter Sixteen

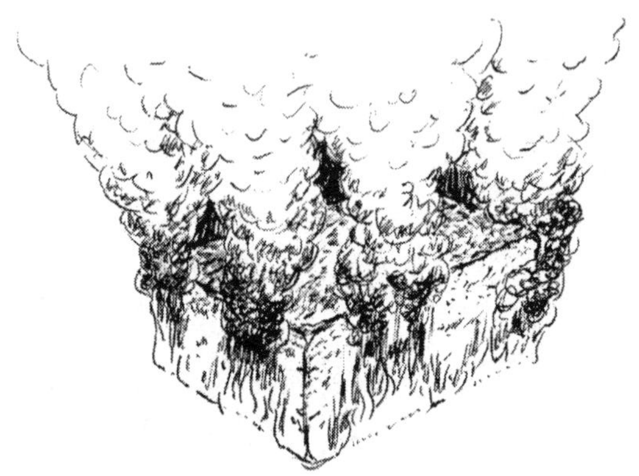

The Exchange

Reilly had been asleep for just an hour when Roisin started to wail. Not having younger siblings of his own, he could not remember ever hearing a baby cry so loudly. He tried covering his head with a pillow and plugging his ears. He even ate two rowanberries, hoping they would help, but nothing lessened the noise of the bawling baby. Reilly gave up and got out of his hammock.

He emptied his pockets and counted the remaining berries. Small, perfectly round, and shiny, there were one hundred and thirteen left. As an experiment to determine if the magical effect of the berries he had eaten earlier was still potent, he focused on thoughts of Norah. He was relieved to discover that the only pain he felt was in his ears, which was more an annoyance than discomfort. A sense of urgency about Norah's fate weighed on his soul.

Reilly pulled the flower from his pocket and set it on the table beside the pile of berries. When the flower was red, it gave him strength. Now, although it was still as perfectly formed and soft as it was when he tucked it behind Norah's ear, its waning hue was a harrowing reminder that Norah was in danger. She, too, was fading fast.

Roisin's shrill cries added to Reilly's sense of unrest. Tomorrow night was too far away—he could not sit around and do nothing!

For a brief moment, the baby stopped screaming. The unexpected silence felt strangely charged, as if the hush itself seized people's attention. Then Reilly heard Brigid hum softly, and the baby began to wail again. Reilly made a mental note to let Mrs. McKinley know she couldn't carry a tune, and not to try to do so. In an effort to distract his own thoughts from the racket, Reilly set the small ruby and the Fireglass on the table. The ruby glowed in the moonlight against the darkened room.

He placed it on the pile of berries and reviewed in his mind what the rowan tree had said: *Me ruby berries restore the blood. Me ruby berries restore the blood.*

Reilly didn't know how many of his one hundred and thirteen berries he would need for Norah, but he assumed it would take more than seven. *Restoring blood would definitely be a bigger undertaking,* he thought as he continued to contemplate the tree's words: *Until the blood o' the storytellers is restored by a jewel placed in the wound.*

He shuddered to think how many people the Deceptors confined in their library prison. Reilly decided it would be a good idea to pick as many ruby-red berries from the tree as possible. Maybe Dillon could take on that task. That idea triggered thoughts of yet another responsibility: Who was at the Vantage Post tonight? He wished he had looked through the scope with his Fireglass another time before they left the Embassy.

A gust of cold air whooshed through the open window and scattered the berries across the table. The ruby and many of the berries fell to the floor. The ruby rolled along a crack to the corner of the room. Reilly crawled on his hands and knees, picking up the spilled berries, until he reached the ruby. Barely visible, the jewel was wedged tightly in the crack. He tried to pry it loose, but the stone only became further imbedded in the wooden plank. Reilly looked around the room, but he could not find anything with a sharp enough point to dislodge the gem. He missed the knife that Eilam had given to him for his sixteenth birthday, just a few months ago. Reilly knew it had been on his belt loop when he went through the portal in the Suzzallo Library. Why some treasures came with him to Ireland and some did not, he couldn't say. He let out a melancholy sigh and found comfort in the fact that no one in all of Wicklow would find the ruby, or even knew it existed—not even Lottie.

Reilly picked the remaining berries up off the floor and reshaped the pile on the table. The Fireglass lay on the table, too, and he noticed the Stelladaur etched on its side glowing steadily in the dark. He picked up the device and opened it fully. The Stelladaur began to spin around the cylinder faster and faster in a blur of white. He walked to the window and lifted the Firelgass to his eye.

Scanning the surroundings, he saw Katell perched on his post at the main door. The bird twisted his head and looked up at Reilly. With the Fireglass, Reilly could see deeply into the bird's eyes, and into its brain, which looked like a stream of computer data. Surprised that it was mechanical, Reilly also felt perplexed by the advanced technology that had been used to make the creature; it was uncharacteristic of Wicklow at this point in time. He thought the data probably kept an account of who had entered and exited the McKinleys' tree home, and when, but he could not decipher it. Like the Fireglass, Katell was a device—one that could do more than Reilly understood at first.

He raised the Fireglass higher to look around the neighborhood. A candle flickered in a nearby home, but most of the people in the East Forest seemed to be asleep. Reilly wasn't high enough to see many homes' auras. He could make out smoke from the bonfire filtering through the neighborhood. The Vantage Post was definitely a better location for scanning distances.

Reilly adjusted the Fireglass slightly and searched the inside of the McKinleys' lift. The critters dripping from the lift ceiling wriggled in and out of the hanging vines, and a few more fresh nicks scarred the walls. Reilly shuddered at the thought that Deceptors had invaded the McKinley property again, without anyone knowing. He wondered if Katell had seen any signs of intruders, and if so, why the bird-guard hadn't sounded an alarm. If an alarm had been given, what could have been done to prevent the subtle attack? He thought about informing the magistrate of the intrusion, but decided it would be best to get more information first.

Reilly scanned the entire lift, searching for more clues, and felt the device pull him to examine the ground. Instantly, the ground peeled back, leaving a gaping hole that opened directly to an intricate web of Undertunnels. Reilly was stunned by the sheer number of pathways that wove in and out and intersected at various Main Stations in a sophisticated maze. Looking back through the strange diorama and up to the ground level, where forests and grasslands dotted the landscape, it was obvious that the tunnels led to towns far past the East Forest and the West Woods—even throughout all of Ireland. Reilly peered into the device to search the tunnels more thoroughly.

Dark shadows from inside the tunnels clouded his view. Barely enough light came through the Fireglass to bounce off the quartzite ceilings of the Main Stations and partially illuminate the long corridors. But Reilly could clearly see that above ground there was only one Embassy, because no other building exuded such obvious respect. There was also only one Black Castle—no other building oozed such evil. Yet, from what he could see through the Fireglass, many of the Undertunnels eventually led to the infernal prison.

At that moment, Reilly believed that Cormack had told the truth about the trolls being Pucatrows that change into rat-snakes. It now made sense to him that only rats that could survive fire could also survive living in such a tainted environment. The thought lingered in his mind long enough to resonate in his heart. Reilly smiled to himself and decided to find Cormack.

He carefully filled one pocket with berries and was surprised by how well they kept their form without getting squished. He picked up the flower and held it in his palm. *Hold on, Norah,* he prayed, and he tucked the flower into the other pocket.

Still holding the Fireglass, Reilly quietly opened the door to his room, looked to see that no one was down the hallway, and darted through the tree home and out the front door. He motioned for Katell to remain silent, and the bird obeyed, blinking once in acknowledgment. While Reilly waited for the lift, he extended his Fireglass, thinking that if he pressed the lift button, he would not have access to all the tunnels. It arrived, and as soon as he stepped inside, he looked at the ground through the device, and watched as the earth rolled back to reveal the gaping hole.

Reilly jumped through the hole and landed with a thud on the ground. Cormack, who had been sleeping, jumped up with a start and grabbed his spear.

"Halt!" shouted the Pucatrow, and he pointed the spear under Reilly's chin.

Reilly quickly retracted the Fireglass and tucked it inside his pocket so the troll wouldn't see it. "It's me, Cormack. Reilly!"

"Blimey!" The troll sniffed loudly. "Where did your smell go? I didn't know you were comin'!" He sniffed again more deeply and lowered his spear. "Well. It's you all right."

Reilly looked around. This was different than the other Main Stations. The walls, instead of quartzite, were a putrid green. "What part of the Undertunnels is this?"

"The Main Gate. It's much further away, beyond the bonfire, past the Undertunnels near the edge of Black Castle. This is where we bring all the hair to make the ladder and our weapons."

Reilly looked more closely around the room. "I don't see any weapons. And you're here by yourself."

"As Head Pucatrow, I keep guard at the Main Gate the night before a shaving takes place. The others guard the doors for the Infusionists or prepare rocks in the fire."

Reilly's jaw dropped. "Then you know when a Crumble will occur and when prisoners will be taken! Yet you don't warn them?"

"Even the magistrate can detect a Crumble through the VP scopes. He does all he can to fortify the families, yet many people ignore his direction and refuse the help of his Infusionists." Cormack held his spear at his side, like a staff. "Pucatrows are valued for their physical strength but considered by most people to be no smarter than rats that have a keen ability to design tunnels. I discuss strategies with the magistrate privately, so the people have confidence in their leader. After all, how much can a rat know?"

Reilly considered Cormack's words carefully. "The Deceptors are planning another attack on the McKinleys' home. Lottie and I both saw the marks in their lift."

"Yes, but Deceptors go swiftly to the weak and stealthily to the strong. The McKinleys are strong enough … for now." Cormack circled around Reilly. "You are strong, too. But once your hair is gone, you may feel weakened."

Reilly grimaced. "My hair doesn't have anything to do with my strength. That's a ridiculous superstition." He reached up and pulled his wavy hair into a ponytail. "I'm not saying I'm looking forward to being bald, but hair grows back. By the way, are the prisoners re-shaved when their hair grows back?"

"It doesn't grow back."

Reilly's eyes widened. "What do you mean?"

"The branding stops hair growth."

Reilly felt rooted to the ground, and his heart started pounding. "Will I need to be branded?"

"Yes."

"And what weapon will you make with *my* hair?"

Cormack pulled his own hair away from his face and stood on a large rock in the center of the room so he could look directly into Reilly's eyes. "We have never used the hair of an Echtra. We believe it will provide more power in the bricks than all the other hair combined."

"What bricks?" Reilly insisted. "And how did you know I was an Echtra?"

"Pucatrows make it a point to be well-informed rats." Cormack chortled. "As for bricks, we chop the hair small and add the juice of Sam's seaweed to make a thick paste."

"You mean Sam, the whale?" Reilly interrupted.

Cormack nodded. "The seaweed is only found in the depths of the sea off the cliffs of Black Castle, where Sam regurgitates it after chewing it like cud. The seaweed can extinguish fire."

Reilly glanced down at Cormack's green feet and then around the room at the putrid green walls. He scowled, demanding a further explanation.

"Bricks put out fire," Reilly stated as if it were a fact, and then he questioned it. "Right?"

"That, they do," Cormack replied. "The seaweed juice bonds with the hair fibers to make bricks more solid than rock."

"Please tell me you've attacked before, with some rate of success." Reilly was losing faith in Cormack again.

"It's only been in the last century or so that we discovered the power in the prisoners' hair. Over time, we discovered that we could use hair to make bricks, thinking we could build our own fortress. Then, by chance, we realized that the bricks could extinguish small fires in the forest. If we can extinguish the bonfire, the souls of the prisoners that the Deceptors have stolen will be freed. But we can only make one or two bricks from the hair of each prisoner, and we'd need five times that, or more, to attempt to put out the bonfire. We've never had enough bricks for a full attack. If we fail the first time, there will not be another chance. The Deceptors will know *we* have deceived *them.*"

Reilly raised his brow. "Go on."

"If we don't stop the Deceptors, the Gods of Ifreann—the rulers of Prince Ukobach and all the Deceptors—will destroy our kind and, in time, all of humankind."

More questions without answers collided inside Reilly's brain. He closed his eyes and rubbed his temples. "What can *I* do?"

"It's not only Charlotte and the people of Wicklow who have waited for you. All of Ireland has waited for an Echtra. Even the rats have waited, because if we can extinguish the bonfire, the spell will be broken and we can permanently return to our Pucatrow bodies, with hair of fine gold."

Reilly wrinkled his forehead and began to pace again, twisting the golden bracelet at his wrist as he realized the weight of his responsibilities. Shaving his hair seemed to be the least of his concerns.

"You want my hair in exchange for the flower."

"The hair of an Echtra is more precious than our hair of gold. We must have it to put out the bonfire."

"And what's the strategy?"

"Once every year, at the eleventh hour of Hallow's Eve, the Deceptors shed their cloaks in the bonfire and perform a ritual dance for the Gods of Ifreann. The souls of the bodies that the Deceptors possess at that time are trapped in the flames forever. However, for only this brief hour, the Deceptors are totally spellbound as they dance. At midnight, the rats will scurry into the fire with the bricks."

Reilly tried to picture it in his mind, but the plan seemed too elementary. "You believe if you simply carry the bricks into the bonfire, at that precise time on Hallow's Eve, the flames will be magically extinguished?"

"We've experimented with our regular bricks on ordinary fires, and the flames sputtered and diminished, sometimes leaving smoldering smoke. Perhaps if we use bricks from an Echtra's hair, the great flames of the bonfire will disappear. Then the Pucatrows' curse will be lifted." Cormack grinned and pulled on his wiry hair. "And the Deceptors will cower in fear and jealousy of our hair of gold."

"And the prisoners?"

"The soul of each prisoner will be restored to his or her own body."

"What happens to the Deceptors?"

"Without the infernal fire, they would have no power, and they would leave Black Castle."

Reilly hoped the plan would work, but there was one fatal flaw in it. "No one knows what happens in The Library itself, or how a Deceptor chooses which body to possess. I can't wait until Hallow's Eve to find out—that's still a few weeks away, and it may be too late for Norah." Reilly turned toward Cormack, who was still perched on the large rock in the center of the room.

He stepped closer to the troll so they stood eye-to-eye. "If saving Norah means shaving my head, risking my soul, and living in Black Castle, then tomorrow night can't come soon enough. Let's do it now."

"Tonight," Cormack said flatly. "You must wait to enter Black Castle with the prisoners who are taken during today's Crumble."

Chapter Seventeen

Possibilities

Cormack lifted his spear and used the pointed end to brush the ends of Reilly's hair. "Your hair is a great temptation to me. I could cut it now. Only my loyalty to the Embassy—and to my fellow Pucatrows—holds me back."

Reilly held Cormack's stare and grabbed the handle of the spear, holding his own hand over the troll's. "If you've lied to me in the slightest, I'll kill you with this spear." His voice trembled with intensity. It came out of his mouth before he put any thought behind the words. The vow startled Reilly, but he did not flinch. He kept his gaze and held his grip tightly. Cormack lowered his eyes to watch his snot drip to the ground.

"You're not yourself, Reilly. You need rest." The Pucatrow looked up at Reilly and snorted, wet and loud. "This night is almost gone, and you have a lot to do before tomorrow night."

Reilly dropped his hand and stepped back. He shook his head and rubbed his temples with one hand. "Yeah. Yeah, you're right." He put his hand in his pocket to run his fingers across the flower. "I've got to sleep."

It was well past midnight when Reilly returned to the McKinleys' tree home. Roisin had stopped crying; finally it was quiet. Reilly collapsed into his hammock with Norah's song playing over and over in his mind: *I'll write my soul's caressing song, and sing my dying melody.* He slept fitfully with a recurring nightmare of dark caves and hooded creatures, until he heard a loud knock at the door.

"Reilly? Reilly … are you awake yet?" Lottie called.

He pulled the blanket over his ears, hoping for a brief moment that he was back home in his own bed. "Uhhh …"

"May I come in?"

"Uh-huh," he muttered.

Lottie entered the room, carrying a tray of food. "I brought you lunch." She set the tray on the side table and pulled up a chair. Swinging her satchel from her hip to her lap, she sat down. "I thought my ears would ring for hours after that child finally stopped wailing."

"She does have a set of lungs." He sat up and wiped drool off of his mouth with the back of his hand. "Did you sleep past breakfast, too?"

"No. I spent most of the morning writing in my journal. I had a lot to catch up on. But you slept over twelve hours."

"Not exactly," Reilly nodded. "I went to the Undertunnels and met with Cormack. Apparently, I need to wait to get into Black Castle with the prisoners who are taken during the Crumble today."

"Today! How do you know? We must tell Father! And what do you mean *apparently*?" Lottie's voice got louder and faster with each exclamation.

"I just hope Cormack is telling us the whole truth. I can't quite figure out the Pucatrows."

Lottie handed Reilly a plate of food. "But Father trusts them completely. I suppose there should be no cause for alarm."

Reilly picked up a sharp knife to cut a slice of ham and then speared a few potato chunks. "Maybe." Annoyed by his continued hesitations about Cormack, he told Lottie about their most recent conversation. Looking at the blade of the knife, he added, "I wonder if I'll look funny without hair. What if … after all this … Norah doesn't recognize me?"

Lottie swept her long blonde hair over her shoulders. "Hair may help with recognition," she said, as she twisted her hair down her front torso. "But real identity is reflected in the eyes." The corners of her mouth turned up in a Mona-Lisa smile, and Reilly felt her silver eyes look right through him.

"It's so weird … you look like … as if I've always known you," he said.

"I know what you mean. I've felt the same way since we first met." She let go of her hair and smoothed it out with her fingers. "Even your name sounded familiar to me. I think that's how I knew you were the Echtra."

Reilly chewed his last bite of ham as he looked at her. "You have such beautiful hair, Lottie. It's almost white."

"Thank you. My mother said a woman's hair is her crowning feature. I wear it down because when I'm sixteen I'll have to wear it in a braid on my head."

"Why?"

"When a girl becomes a young lady, she must maintain a more mature appearance."

Reilly looked into the blade of the knife again. "I'll probably look like an old man when my hair is shaved off."

Lottie threw her head back and laughed. "Nevertheless, you won't be as old your fourth great-grandmother!"

Reilly chuckled and set his empty plate back on the tray. "I hope Norah recognizes me."

"She will," Lottie said.

Reilly changed the subject. "Lottie, I had a ruby that came with me through the portal from Bozka to Seattle, and then here to Wicklow." He maneuvered out of the hammock and walked to the corner of the room. "It's over here. I dropped it yesterday, and it got stuck in the floor planks." He squatted to the floor and picked at the jewel to try to dislodge it. "Bring me that knife?"

Lottie flipped her hair behind her back and reached for the knife. She handed it to Reilly, who wiped the blade on his pants. He poked into the wooden plank, and the gem popped out and bounced along the floor.

"Grab it, Lottie, before it gets stuck in another groove."

Lottie knelt on the ground and cupped her hands over the ruby. Reilly set the knife on the table and knelt beside her. When she opened her hands the ruby glistened off the reflection of her Stelladaur hanging at her neck. Reilly picked up the ruby and reached for his Fireglass in his pocket.

"It's time to go through another portal." Reilly was developing a sense about when and where he needed to go through portals. He knew there was more to learn about the other Stelladaur Affirmations, and he figured he ought to do it *before* he was stuck in Black Castle for a time. He imagined that portals accessed from a place as horrific as the castle might lead to other places of hellish darkness.

"Then we should get to the courtyard fountain right away," Lottie said. "We never know exactly how long we'll be gone, and we must be back before tonight."

"I think we can access the portal from here. Remember, I told you that Eilam said it could be used to accelerate passage through any portal?"

"I'm not sure," Lottie muttered.

Reilly held the Fireglass ready in one hand and the ruby in the other. "On the count of three, hold your Stelladaur just above the ruby, and I'll look through my Fireglass into both jewels. One … two … three!"

Brilliant flames of orange and red danced out of the Fireglass and bounced off the jewels.

"Our tree home will burn to the ground!" Lottie cried.

"These are only flames of beauty, not of fire." Reilly's eyes widened. "Touch my hand, Lottie! Now!"

The instant she placed her hand on top of Reilly's, the flames wrapped around both of them and swept them through the jewels.

Reilly and Lottie warped through the portal and landed in a two-person vessel, floating on a sea of flaming fire. Reilly registered it as a coracle—Eilam had told him about this kind of boat. As far as they could see in any direction, the ocean of fire rolled in great swells. Tremendous waves lifted the vessel high into the sky; then it fell deep into a trough, like a colossal roller coaster. Finally looking up, they saw that the unusual boat could not only float on the waves but also hang in the air, much like a blimp.

Barely able to catch their breath from their first descent on the waves, Reilly and Lottie held tightly to the side of the little craft. Fire crackled and whooshed all around them, although the heat from the flames was no more intense than that felt while standing in front of a campfire. Reilly looked for signs of life—a creature, a fairy, or an Irish gnome—some magical being to explain what they should do. But here, no such creature made an appearance or gave any instructions.

"I'm getting seasick, Reilly," said Lottie.

"Are you going to throw up?"

"No, I just feel dizzy. Queasy." Lottie gripped the rope rail more tightly, and closed her eyes. "Tell me when it's over."

Looking out across the never-ending conflagration, Reilly thought hard about what it might have to do with the fourth

Stelladaur Affirmation: *I am all possibilities.* He knew now that more possibilities existed than he could even imagine.

Until recently, he had never imagined that anything he did—or did not do—would make any real difference to anyone. He was content to glide in his kayak across Eagle Harbor, visit Eilam, and go to school—like any other kid. But now Reilly understood that extraordinary things happen all the time, even to those who don't know that they themselves are extraordinary.

Riding the waves of the flames, Reilly held tightly to the ledge of the coracle. Lottie put her head between her legs. Reilly fumbled for the rowanberries in his pocket, knowing that if Lottie ate one, her nausea would subside, but he decided he needed to save the berries for real emergencies.

The flames licked the side of the coracle, and wrapped around it like octopus legs flailing gracefully in a deep sea. Riding up and down on the crest of each swell, he started to make out something far away. He grabbed his Fireglass with one hand and wrapped his arms around a side rope to steady himself as he looked through the device.

Through the Fireglass, the tremendous waves of flames looked like waves in the ocean. Then water splashed over the blimp with a mighty force, knocking him over. He was barely able to hold on to the Fireglass.

"What's happening now?" Lottie cried, as she coughed water.

"When I looked through the Fireglass, the flames transformed to water!" Reilly shouted so she could hear him above the roar of the waves.

"Well, don't do that!" Lottie screamed. "We'll drown!"

They rode out the swell. When they pulled themselves up, they could only see flames again, soaring above them like a tidal wave.

"Burned alive or buried alive!" Reilly shouted. "Take your pick!"

"I don't care for either option!"

"Then we need other possibilities—fast!"

Lottie gripped the side rope as she reached for her Stelladaur. "This works every time. Why do I wait until circumstances are bleak before I remember how powerful it is?"

"Don't be so hard on yourself. Sometimes I feel so consumed with what's going on around me that it's hard to remember there are any solutions at all." Reilly smiled.

"Why are you smiling?" Lottie scowled. "It's hardly the time to relax and grin."

"But that's just it, Lottie. It's impossible to see through the flames if we don't relax and look past them."

"Whatever do you mean, Reilly?" She flipped her soaking hair over her shoulders. "Will you stop speaking in riddles?"

Reilly ignored her comment and held up his Fireglass again. "All things are possible, Lottie, if we look further …"

"Further than where?" she demanded.

"… than whatever is blocking our view." They ascended on another great wave of fire and Reilly looked into his Fireglass. "There's something ahead … I can barely see it … but it looks like … a boat!" With that, another great wave of seawater showered them.

Lottie's feet shot out from under her and she slammed into the side of the coracle-blimp. She grabbed her Stelladaur to keep its cord from rising over her head, ensuring that the jewel wouldn't disappear into the depths of the strange waves. She held it tightly in one hand as she struggled to keep a hold on the side rope.

Alternating with each ascent between water and fire, Reilly and Lottie rode the peculiar tidal waves. Finally, Reilly was able to get a closer look at the boat through his Fireglass.

"It looks sort of like *The Ark*," he said.

"The what?"

"My dad's sailboat. It's difficult to tell from here … we're still so far away, and it's hard to hold this thing still enough."

"Let's try it now with my Stelladaur."

Reilly gripped the edge of the coracle-blimp to move closer to Lottie. "On the next ascent."

Lottie held up her Stelladaur as the giant wave lifted them high into the air. At the pinnacle, Reilly set his Fireglass in front of the Stelladaur and looked through the lens. Although the boat was still far away, Reilly could now see it more clearly.

"It's *The Ark!* It looks just like it!" He shouted above the roar of the fire. "But I don't see anyone on board!"

"Are we getting any closer to it?" Lottie lowered her jewel to rest her arm as they descended the fire wave and crested the next swell.

"Yes … I want to see what's inside and figure out why it's *here*!"

With several more attempts, as they rode atop the waves, he failed to see more details. Then the wind shifted dramatically, swirling and tumbling them about. There was a sudden, horrific bolt of lightning. In that instant, the fire receded and the noise stopped, and the boat floated inches above a serene sea of glass. Light danced off of Lottie's Stelladaur, reflecting a spray of multi-colored bursts. The etched Stelladaur on Reilly's Fireglass whirred around the treasure in a blur. About one hundred feet away, *The Ark* hovered.

Everything was mysteriously still and quiet. Lottie turned completely around. Reilly kept his eyes on the sailboat. The coracle glided steadily closer, but Reilly still could see no one on board.

His heart beat rapidly as he anticipated what he hoped to find. If he was there to better understand all possibilities, perhaps this strange place was Tir Na Nog after all.

Their small boat came to a gentle stop at the edge of *The Ark*. Reilly closed his Fireglass and slipped it into his pocket.

As Reilly stepped onto *The Ark*, a strange calmness settled on him. He waited while Lottie pulled herself up; then he reached for her hand to help her jump onto the deck of the sailboat. As Lottie bounded across the threshold, she instantly morphed into a beautiful, longhaired albino dog and landed on the deck on all fours.

Stunned, Reilly jumped back. "Tuma? *Tuma!*"

The dog barked. Once.

"Tuma … is that you? But where is Lottie? How did …?"

Tuma barked once again. Reilly felt tears. He bent down and hugged his dog tightly around the neck. "I thought I'd lost you! When you didn't come with me through the portal in the Suzzallo Library, I didn't know if I'd ever see you again." He stroked the dog's long hair over and over across her back. He scratched under her chin and behind her ears. "It's really you! But where's Lottie?"

Reilly held his dog's face in his hands, hoping for her to lick his face. Then he looked deeply into Tuma's silver eyes and paused.

"Lottie? Is that you in there?" As surely as he knew he was alive, Reilly knew it was so. "It was you all along! Eilam said my dad sent you to me, through the portal, and that your name means 'everlasting.' It makes sense now … your eyes … I saw it in your eyes. But I couldn't have imagined it would be possible!"

Tuma barked again, her usual single bark to affirm Reilly's words. She nuzzled her nose under his hand, begging for more scratches. Reilly scratched his dog vigorously and then patted her head. "By now I ought to know that *anything* I can imagine *is* possible! Right?"

Again, the dog barked once.

"All right then. Let's take a look on deck."

Reilly walked around the sailboat, breathing in the salty smell that reminded him of Eagle Harbor. The boat bobbed almost imperceptibly as it floated above the glassy sea. He walked to the port side of the vessel, where he had stood the afternoon his dad fell into the water. He looked across to the exact spot on the boat where his dad had plummeted to his death. He looked down at Tuma and then walked tentatively to the starboard side. He peered cautiously over the edge … but only his own reflection stared back at him.

Reilly gazed deeply into his own green eyes. In an instant, everything he had seen and heard and learned in all the portals he had ever been through flashed across his mind. When the vision he witnessed caught up to his present moment, he finally understood.

"Possibilities are endless. *I am endless possibilities!*" He blinked and continued to stare into his own eyes. "I create! I decide! All possibilities exist inside of me!" Reilly repeated the affirmation again to make sure he not only *believed* it was true, but that he *knew* it was true. He stood up and looked down at Tuma. "I get it now." Tuma wagged her tail and gave her usual woof. "Let's go inside."

Reilly led the way into the galley. It seemed to him as if this moment was months ago, and he was on the boat for the first time since his dad died. But now there was no eerie feeling—only a sense of excitement. He flung open the door of the stateroom, not expecting to relive anything from the past, but with great anticipation for something new to reveal itself.

The room was neat and tidy. The bed was made and throw pillows were perched around it. He didn't remember the room ever looking so well kept.

Reilly emptied his pocket and set his items on the bed: the Fireglass, the tiny canister of ointment, and the perfectly formed flower that was no longer red. Tuma jumped up on the bed and lay down, watching intently. Reilly sat next to his dog and picked up each treasure, one at a time, and studied it to assess its usefulness.

It was obvious to Reilly that the Fireglass had been, and would continue to be, an essential tool. The ointment from the Infusionists healed, and may even have kept him from going blind after the strange reaction he had had while looking through the scope and the Fireglass at the same time. The faded flower gave him hope that transcended time; without the flower, he doubted he would have heard Norah's song or known that she was nearby.

Finally, Reilly transferred the rowan tree berries from his other pocket and spilled them onto the bed, too. Like the flower, the berries were still perfectly formed, but they had kept their deep red color. The ruby rolled out into the middle of the pile of berries. Though Reilly had carried it since Bozka, he still did not know its practical use.

He held the gem up to the porthole window and twirled it between his thumb and finger.

"Something about the ruby … and the berries," he whispered. "What did Grania say?" He looked more closely at the gem and studied the tiny facets that looked similar to those of his Stelladaur, though the jewel was round and much smaller. The ruby was, in fact, the same size and color as each perfect berry lying on the bed. He picked up a berry with his other hand, and twirled it in the light.

Reilly brought his fingers together to compare the jewel and the berry to each other. Touching them together, as if in a trance, he squished the bitter berry onto the ruby and let the red juice drip around the precious jewel and onto his fingers.

"Until the blood of the storytellers is restored by a jewel placed in his or her wound." Grania's voice resonated around the stateroom.

Reilly licked the skin of the berry and the lingering juice from his fingers. Rather than having the bitter taste he expected, the berry was sweeter than a fully ripe raspberry.

"One drop of sweetness is more precious and powerful than the vilest bitterness," Grania whispered again.

Although he did not yet understand the riddle, Reilly knew the number of berries scattered on the bed would not be enough. He hoped Dillon had picked many more from the tree, as Reilly had asked him to do.

"I could be wrong, Tuma, but I think we'll need one berry—one ruby—for each prisoner at Black Castle," Reilly said, as he stroked his dog's head. "Somehow, we need to change the berries to rubies. The Deceptors won't think a berry is valuable. But given the opportunity, their greed may override their intent to take possession of a body."

Tuma barked loudly and jumped off the bed. She wagged her tail rapidly while Reilly collected the rowanberries and stuffed them back into his pocket with the ruby and the other items. They walked out of the stateroom and into the lower deck room.

"Once I'm inside Black Castle, we need to be able to communicate with each other … Lottie." Reilly looked down at his dog as they walked past the galley. "We need to figure this out before we get off *The Ark*, 'cuz I expect you won't look like a dog anymore." The dog whined. "Of course you don't look like a dog … Lottie … I mean, Tuma … except when you *are* a dog. You know what I mean!"

The dog stuck out her tongue and drooled.

"Look, I'm sorry! The thing is, it's going to be a lot easier to get information back and forth to each other in the castle if you're Tuma, not Lottie." They climbed up the steps and out of the galley onto the main deck.

"I know the Pucatrows and the magistrate have a plan, but things could come up that they haven't considered. Who knows what it's like inside The Library? Besides, your father isn't going to allow you anywhere near Black Castle or the bonfire again. C'mon, help me out, Tuma."

Tuma circled around the wheel, wagging her tail, and bounded onto the outside deck. Reilly followed her. The dog stopped on the starboard side and started to bark.

"What?" Reilly asked. "The reflection? What about it?"

"All right! Let's take a look."

Reilly moved to the rail and rested his hands on the edge. He looked down at his dog, who continued to bark. "You want to see, too? Is that it? All right." He lifted Tuma in his arms, barely able to hold her.

Together they peered over the edge of *The Ark*. Though Reilly held Tuma in his arms, the sea of glass below them reflected Lottie looking back at them, her silver eyes shimmering in the light.

"I get it," Reilly said. "Somehow, I need to explain to you—when you're Lottie again—that you're not only my fourth great-grandmother, but that you also appeared in my life, out of nowhere, as a magical albino dog. And I should expect that you'll believe me … and that you'll willingly change into Tuma in your own present time … and that I can help you figure out how to do that!" Reilly shook his head. "I'm losing my marbles."

He hugged Tuma, then set her down. "Anything is possible with a little imagination."

Reilly went to the bow of the sailboat, where he found a large empty cooler. He pushed it up against the starboard side. He stepped onto the cooler and climbed onto the edge of the boat, holding onto a side rope. "Up! Up!" he called. Tuma jumped onto the cooler. "Okay … let's go."

With that, Reilly and his dog jumped off *The Ark*. As they landed on the sea of glass, the portal opened. Tuma transformed back into Lottie, and she and Reilly landed, sitting cross-legged on the wooden floor of her tree home.

Chapter Eighteen

Everlasting

"That was most unusual!" Lottie said as she picked up the ruby from off the floor and held it in her hand. "When we jumped onto *The Ark* there was a flash of light and I couldn't see a thing. What happened?"

Reilly stood up and reached for Lottie's hand to pull her up.

"You transformed into my dog." He tried to sound nonchalant.

"Your *what*? How?"

"I have no idea *how*! It just happened!"

"Why don't I know it happened?"

"Again, Lottie, I don't know! But anything is possible with a little imagination. You've got to figure how to change back into Tuma at will, because it may be the only way for us to communicate with each other once I'm in Black Castle."

Lottie shrugged and continued to listen.

"As soon as there's another Crumble, I'll go with the other prisoners to Black Castle. I'll pretend to be one of them, until we know how to rescue Sorcha and Norah, and the others, of course. I have no idea how long that will take, or if we can do it. But Tuma has powers—*you* have powers that are essential, like going invisible. Without you, we can't do it."

Lottie smiled, despite her apprehension. Being able to go about invisibly at will appealed to her. She picked up the ruby and held it to the light of the window. "There's something about this ruby ..."

Reilly watched her twirl the gem between her fingers as she looked intently at it.

"It's different than my Stelladaur, but somehow the two are related," she said.

Reilly stepped closer to Lottie, watching flickers of red light shine in her eyes as she studied the ruby. Her Stelladaur caught similar red reflections that ricocheted between the two jewels. He watched the light dance like fire in Lottie's eyes and knew this was, as Kokumo had said in Som, a moment of impending and inevitable change. *Impending* because it would be continuous—all change is—and because it would occur in the very next moment. *Inevitable* because it was going to happen, regardless of what he or anyone else did or did not do in that particular moment.

Sure enough, as quickly as it had come, that moment passed. In the next few moments, Lottie instinctively and with a hint of reverence touched the small ruby to her Stelladaur. Instantly she changed again.

"Tuma!" Reilly exclaimed. "Lottie! You did it!"

Tuma barked and Reilly hugged his dog tightly. "I can't decide if I like you better as a dog or a girl or my grandmother." He laughed as he stroked her thick fur. Reilly set the ruby on Lottie's dresser table. "It was so simple." He wondered where Lottie's Stelladaur had gone.

"Okay, girl, let's make plans for tonight."

Reilly left Lottie's room carrying the tray and empty dishes, Tuma following behind. He approached Brigid in the hall just outside the kitchen. Roisin gurgled and wiggled in Brigid's arms.

"Thank you for lunch, Mrs. McKinley. The sausage was delicious."

"You are welcome, my dear. Will you please just set them in the sink for me?" Reilly smiled and nodded. Then, looking down at Tuma, Brigid continued. "Well, what in heaven's name do we have here?"

"Uh … Lottie found her. She must have been caught in the recent Crumble. She … just showed up here."

"My, my but she is lovely. And such beautiful eyes!"

"Yes, ma'am."

"And where is Lottie?"

"She … said she was awake early this morning, so she decided to take a nap. I'm just going for a walk."

"Indeed, this poor child is happy enough now, but she is overtired from so little sleep. I must get her to take a rest, as well." Brigid shifted Roisin in her arms. "I'm sorry if the child kept you awake last night. She's been through such an ordeal and cannot be expected to be content with people she doesn't know."

"It's no problem, ma'am. Is there something I can do for you?"

"Yes. If you see the magistrate at the Embassy, please ask him to bring a vile of elixir if it can be spared. I think this child has a colic that will not be quieted without a drop of the tincture. And we could all surely use more sleep tonight." She patted Roisin's back briskly and headed down the hallway. Reilly knew he would not be sleeping much that night, regardless of Roisin's incessant crying.

Reilly and Tuma left the tree home. He chose to walk to the Embassy aboveground, through the forest trails, rather than using the Undertunnels. The warm afternoon air smelled of early fall, and he wondered what season it was back home. Knowing that time wasn't equally measured between parallel worlds, he wondered if it was later in the season in Seattle in 2015. Or maybe it was an entirely different year altogether, and he was much older now. He admitted to himself that he did not know if time existed at all, anywhere beyond where he currently was. He briefly wished for his smart phone so he could call home … but assumed it would probably be useless anyway.

As they approached the cemetery on the edge of the West Woods, Reilly spotted Dillon picking berries at the rowan tree. Dillon waved and nodded for Reilly to join him.

"Wow! She's a beauty!" Dillon said as he looked at Tuma. "Where did she come from?"

Reilly hesitated as he remembered asking Eilam the same question. "She just showed up. She's sort of attached herself to the family … your family, I mean. Lottie's taking a nap, so I thought I'd take the dog for a walk and see if I can find your dad at the Embassy."

Dillon set the small bucket of berries on the ground and petted the dog.

"What's her name?"

"Tuma. It means *everlasting*."

Dillon smiled and continued to give the dog attention.

Reilly peered into the bucket. "You sure got a lot of berries. The tree is almost picked over."

"I didn't have much else to do. Mother is constantly busy with Roisin. Besides, you said it was important to get as many berries as I could."

"It's very important, Dillon."

"What are we going to do with them? I tried a few, and they taste nasty."

Reilly noticed Grania was quiet; the tree had not revealed her identity to Dillon. "We're going to use the berries to help us rescue Sorcha."

"Are you giving them to the Infusionists … to make some sort of evil potion for the Deceptors?" Dillon's eyes grew wide with the suggestion.

"Not exactly. But you're doing a great job and as I said, it's very important that we get as many berries as possible."

"It's tricky climbing high enough to get the ones at the top. I just came down to have a bite to eat. But I'll get all of them!" Dillon said with enthusiasm.

"I know you will, Dillon. Thanks. Just leave the bucket outside Lottie's bedroom door."

Reilly looked up at Grania and figured it was good that Dillon did not know more about the tree.

The town square was empty. Flynn was knitting, as usual, and Reilly noticed a new basket overflowing with wristbands. He wondered how she could make so many of them in just one day. Flynn hadn't looked up when Reilly and Tuma entered the building, and she only stopped briefly to smile at Reilly as he helped himself to two wristbands. She did not notice Tuma.

Pucatrows guarded the Infusionists' doors and sniffed loudly as Reilly walked by, but, like Flynn, showed no interest in the albino dog. Surmising that the magistrate was in the Vantage Post, Reilly moved quickly past the snotty-nosed trolls and up to the main auditorium. There, only half a dozen people still lay on tables; several moaned softly, others looked lifeless. Three people walked between the tables, offering comfort to those who were conscious. Reilly shuddered, knowing more patients would not make it through the coming night. Tuma walked at Reilly's heals with her ears drooped and her tail barely swaying.

Reilly noticed the debris in the Vantage Post had finally been cleaned. The Magistrate was looking through the one remaining scope. Cormack stood on a chair, peering out the window.

"Excuse me, sir," Reilly began. "Do you see anything new?"

Quin turned around. "Ah, Reilly! Very good. And who is this?"

"Lottie found her. Your wife may want to adopt a child, but your daughter seems to prefer dogs."

"I hope she's quieter than the child!" Quin said.

Reilly laughed and stepped toward the window. "How are you, Cormack? I didn't expect to see you here."

"The magistrate and I are discussing the plan of attack." Cormack snorted loudly. "I could hardly smell you coming with that creature overpowering your scent."

Reilly sniffed. "I can't smell her."

"Of course not. You're a far cry from a Pucatrow," Cormack said. "Her hair is strangely bright … for a dog."

"She's albino."

"She's beautiful," Quin said. "And where is Lottie?"

"Resting."

"Just as well. I don't want her to be a part of this attack anyway. She will not be happy with me when I tell her that she must stay home tonight." Tuma barked a few times. "She has quite a booming bark. If she barks at night, she will be staying outside with Katell." Tuma whined and lowered her head. "Cormack told me about the plan the three of you came up with. There is certainly *no possibility* that Charlotte will be joining you at the bonfire tonight, or going anywhere near Black Castle of Wicklow."

Tuma barked again, only once, and Reilly patted her head. "Sir, will you be coming with us?"

"I can't. If Sorcha sees me, she will run to me, and our hope for a full attack and rescue of the other prisoners will be for naught." Quin looked through the scope again. "This is not an easy decision, but it's the only logical one. Reilly, are you sure you want to risk your own safety and be taken to The Library during the next Crumble?"

Reilly stroked Tuma. "Yes, sir." He surmised that Cormack hadn't told the magistrate about Norah, and he was glad about that. "Getting into The Library may be the only way for me to figure out how I can get back home. However, as an Echtra, I, too, must put the good of all above my own desires."

Quin stepped next to Reilly and slapped him on the back. "You are quite the young man."

Reilly glanced at Cormack, who grinned and nodded slightly. Reilly returned the nod. "Are there any changes in the auras, sir?"

"Not that I can see. But the focus mechanism seems to have been damaged. It's more difficult to read the auras than before."

"May I take a look?"

Quin nodded, and Reilly stepped up to the device. He twisted the focus knob back and forth, trying to get an accurate reading. "I see what you mean. Can it be repaired?"

"Three of our most skilled technicians were killed. Both of our apprentices were captured. I have tried to fix it myself, but I'm afraid my expertise is in conceptualization, not with the intricacies of mechanical functions. For now, this will have to suffice."

Reilly thought of suggesting that he try looking through the scope with his Fireglass again, but still felt it was best that Cormack not see his treasure.

"Sir, I noticed some fresh nicks in your lift. I should have told you sooner."

"I saw them, as well. We must be more vigilant."

Reilly nodded and changed the subject.

"Mrs. McKinley asked if you could spare a drop of elixir for Roisin. She says the baby has colic."

"I'll need to survey the inventory at the lab and see what the Infusionists can spare. Will you stay here while Cormack and I go downstairs?"

"Of course, sir. Tuma will keep me company."

"Hmm … Have I heard that name before?" He offered Tuma the back of his hand and she licked it. "And those eyes … they remind me of Charlotte's eyes … so enchanting."

Tuma barked once and Reilly told her to shush. Quin and Cormack left the Vantage Post, and Tuma jumped onto the chair to look out the window. Reilly pulled his Fireglass from his pocket.

"Let's see what's really going on out there, Tuma."

Reilly carefully positioned the Fireglass in front of the scope lens and looked through both devices. Scanning the West Woods, he zoomed in on the McKinleys' home. Dillon was placing the bucket of rowanberries outside Lottie's bedroom door. Brigid was in the kitchen, chopping vegetables and tossing them in a pot on the stove. Roisin played on the floor with a wooden spoon, hammering it on the leg of a chair like a drumstick. Zooming out, Reilly noticed a dark orange color around the edges of the aura above the McKinleys' tree home. He felt a slight pain singeing the area around his eye. He quickly pulled away and dropped the Fireglass to his side.

"It's Roisin," he whispered. "Roisin is in danger." Then, as if he knew that what he had said wasn't quite accurate, he rephrased his statement. "The family is in danger because Roisin is there."

Tuma barked and jumped off the chair.

"But how can a child bring danger? There is no way Brigid is going to believe me on this." Looking directly at his dog, he added, "Lottie, we can't say anything about it until we know more. Promise me you won't say anything." Tuma barked.

"Of course," Reilly laughed. "Since neither of us knows how long you will remain as Tuma, or how you change back when you want to, I shouldn't worry about you running off to tell your mother anything. I'm sorry."

Reilly pulled out the tiny canister of ointment, smeared a small dab around his eye, and rubbed it in. "Does it look better now?" Tuma barked.

"Thanks, Tuma. Hey, we need to figure out a different system of communication to use while I'm inside Black Castle. I don't imagine the Deceptors will take well to a barking dog. Of course, you can play the invisible trick so they don't see you, as you did when we were at the Suzzallo Library. That worked well. But I still may need feedback from you."

Tuma barked once and wagged her tail swiftly.

"Yes, I know. But tell me you agree without barking."

Tuma whimpered.

"And no pouting. This is serious business."

Reilly looked at Tuma's silver eyes and had an idea. "That's it! Give me *that* look when you disagree." He waited to see if Tuma would hold the look. "Good. Now, if you agree, perk up your ears. Can you do that?" Tuma responded perfectly. "Okay. Now … if you know there is danger … can you do something different?"

Tuma gave the "yes" look. Then she silently bared her teeth. Reilly laughed. "That's good, Lottie! You make a great watchdog!" He stroked her long fur and rubbed behind her ears. "Good girl. Since your father won't allow you to come to the bonfire tonight, or go anywhere near Black Castle, you'll need to come as Tuma—visible to Sorcha, but *in*visible to the Deceptors and their prisoners. What do you think?"

Tuma perked up her ears.

"Great. We'll need to figure out what to tell your parents—you can only take so many naps." Reilly paced the floor, trying to come up with a solution. "You're the key, Tuma."

Without warning, and as if awaking from a dream, Reilly thought he heard the *clink* of James's key, which had dropped to the floor of the Suzzallo Library when he came through the portal door. Then he heard Eilam whisper, "Tuma will help you perceive the door and see the everlasting."

Another haunting déjà vu crept over Reilly. He shivered, knowing without a doubt that what happened *then* was simultaneously happening *now*.

Chapter Nineteen

Portraits

Quin returned to the Vantage Post without Cormack, who had gone to rally the other Pucatrows for the attack that evening. Reilly and Tuma found Brigid at home, pacing the floor and frantically trying to calm Roisin.

"They could only spare half a vile," Reilly nearly shouted. He handed the vile to Mrs. McKinley and watched as she tilted the baby back in her arms and cautiously poured drops of the liquid into the child's wide-open mouth. Seconds later, Roisin stopped screaming and relaxed into a solid sleep. "Thank heaven! I thought my eardrums would burst. The poor child!"

"The magistrate said he'll be home for dinner," Reilly said. "He's not going with the Pucatrows to the bonfire tonight. He said if

Sorcha sees him, she'll run to him, and that will mess up our plan for the full attack on Black Castle."

"I don't understand."

"Well, ma'am, Sorcha will have to stay there until after the next Crumble. I'll need her help at the castle. We'll know more tonight at the bonfire."

"Lottie must not go!"

Tuma barked loudly and Reilly glared at her.

"Of course not, Mrs. McKinley. I'm going to explain it all to her right now. Is she still asleep?"

"I haven't seen her all afternoon—I've been tending to Roisin constantly." She shifted Roisin onto her shoulder and turned to leave the room. "Hopefully this child will sleep through the night and we can all get rest. Please tell Lottie I need her help with dinner."

"Yes, ma'am."

Reilly and Tuma passed Dillon in the hallway.

"I picked almost all the berries, Reilly," Dillon said proudly. "There were only a dozen or so just out of my reach. I tried shaking the branches, but it didn't work well."

"I'm sure what you got will be enough. Thanks."

Dillon bent down to pet Tuma. "Are you going to the bonfire tonight?" He looked up at Reilly as he stroked the dog. "Can I come, too?"

"No, Dillon. Your family must stay here."

Dillon frowned. "Even Lottie? You know she'll insist on going. Sometimes she's extremely stubborn."

"I know!" Reilly agreed wholeheartedly. "But tonight, unless you're a Pucatrow or an Echtra, you've got to stay home."

Tuma barked again.

"You should take Tuma," Dillon suggested. "Maybe she can help."

Pretending he hadn't already thought of the idea, Reilly agreed. "Good thinking, Dillon. I think you're right."

"Let me know if there's something else I can do," Dillon said as he stood up and started down the hallway. "Twelve-year-olds are smarter than you might think."

"Definitely."

Reilly picked up the bucket of rowanberries outside Lottie's bedroom door, and he and Tuma walked in.

"Okay, Lottie, Tuma—you stay here. I'll go help your mom with dinner. Did I mention that my mother owns a bakery and that I can bake a few things?"

Tuma perked up her ears in agreement, which made Reilly laugh. "I think you've got it down. I'll tell your mom you're not feeling well and Tuma is keeping you company."

Reilly spent the next hour in the kitchen with Brigid, who wanted to hear all about Bainbridge Island and Blackberry Bakers. She even inquired about the boating accident. He answered her questions openly but kept the details to a minimum. Nevertheless, the conversation left him feeling homesick, and he wished he had never gone through the portal. Whatever waited for him at the bonfire, especially as a prisoner of Black Castle, now seemed more ominous than anything he had yet experienced.

"The scones should be about ready," Reilly said, changing the subject. He opened the cast iron oven and pulled out the pan. "They don't look the same as the ones I've made before."

"They smell delicious," Brigid said. "The lemon flavor will be a tasty complement to our pumpkin soup."

"I think I'll take a bowl to Lottie."

Reilly left the room with a bowl of soup and two scones. Tuma swallowed the scones whole and lapped up the soup enthusiastically. He and Tuma returned to the kitchen just as Quin walked into the room. Reilly explained that Lottie was still not feeling well, and she thought she would try a bowl of soup before settling in for the night. Quin and Brigid both seemed to have too much on their minds to question the matter.

After dinner, Quin announced that it was time for Reilly to depart for the bonfire with Cormack. "I'm sorry I can't go with you, Reilly. But you do understand why I must stay here, don't you?" Quinn asked.

"Of course, sir." Reilly said.

"Be safe, my dearie," Brigid said as she pulled Reilly into her arms and hugged him tightly. "You are like family, and I simply could not bear it if anything happened to you. Please give my sweet Sorcha this hug." Reilly's eyes bulged as she squeezed him harder.

"Yes … ma'am … I will," he choked. When she released him he added, "And don't worry. Tuma will protect me."

Brigid bent down to look into Tuma's eyes. "I expect you're right."

Cormack and a dozen other Pucatrows were waiting in the Main Station when Reilly and Tuma arrived. Reilly covered his nose to keep from losing his dinner at the smell of so many trolls in such a confined space.

"That mongrel is not coming with us," declared a stubby-toed Pucatrow.

"Tuma is a purebred albino!" Reilly retorted, surprised at his own defensiveness. "She goes where I go." Tuma looked up at Reilly for added reassurance.

"I object!" the Pucatrow replied.

Tuma perked up her ears.

"Shut up, Dubhghall," Cormack said. "You don't get a say in the matter."

Dubhghall stamped his foot and lifted his spear across his chest. "Keep her at a distance from me or I'll not hesitate to use this."

Cormack stepped to Dubhghall's side. "Tuma is here to help us. She will not harm you." Turning to Reilly, he added, "Dubhghall witnessed a pack of white wolves kill his parents when he was young. It has haunted him for centuries."

"Tuma is not a wolf," Reilly said.

"Call her what you will," Dubhghall blustered. "Just keep her at a distance from me."

"Enough!" Cormack shouted. "The night is upon us. Let's go!" He motioned to a Pucatrow near the back of the group. "Basil, you stay close to the boy and his dog."

"My pleasure," Basil said as a string of snot from his bulbous nose dripped to the ground.

Cormack led the way through the Undertunnels with Dubhghall beside him. None of the trolls seemed to notice Tuma silently bare her teeth at Dubhghall before the others fell in line. Tuma walked beside Reilly, just in front of Basil, who was the last one out of the Main Station.

The steady *thwunk* of the Pucatrows' long spears tapping the ground as they took each step forward made Reilly feel uneasy—as though he was already a prisoner, sentenced to solitary confinement. The stench of the trolls attacked more than his nostrils; he didn't know how much longer the pumpkin soup would keep sloshing around in his stomach. He and Tuma both watched the ground carefully to avoid puddles of snot. Just when Reilly was sure the lemon zest in the scones would curdle the soup, he saw the opening of the Undertunnel ahead, and the air, reeking with trolls, became smoky.

Most of the Pucatrows had already changed to rats when Reilly, Tuma, and Basil emerged from the Undertunnel.

"We'll wait behind the laurel hedge until the Deceptors arrive," Cormack instructed. "From there, we'll have a complete view."

Reilly noticed that the four-foot hedge grew in a giant half circle at the far end of the bonfire, just beyond the edge of the forest. "And Sorcha?" Reilly asked.

"Yes. She stands at her post there." Cormack pointed to two stone archways that stood about six feet apart, with the flames of the bonfire providing a harrowing backdrop. "After she starts to paint, we'll crawl under the hedges and pretend to attack the rats."

Reilly wanted to ask about the paintings, but Dubhghall, who hovered next to Cormack, interrupted his thoughts. "Make sure you keep the mutt away from me, or she may get singed, too."

"Here, girl," Reilly said as he clapped his hand to his thigh. Tuma snuggled against Reilly, and again silently bared her teeth. But this time, Dubhghall saw the warning.

"I'll take her now!" Dubhghall snarled, as he jabbed his spear toward Reilly and his dog.

"Silence!" Cormack commanded in a loud whisper. "Dubhghall, you will keep your distance from Tuma. Remember, she's part of our strategy. We need Tuma to distract Sorcha while we distract the Deceptors. Now let's get behind the hedge and wait."

The heat from the fire grew hotter with each step. When they crouched in position, Reilly began to sweat, and Tuma panted heavily. The three trolls lowered their spears so they wouldn't poke up above the laurel hedge. Reilly squatted uncomfortably, glancing up and down to be sure he wasn't visible. In front of the hedge, the rats scurried about, waiting for the signal from Cormack.

Reilly held Tuma close and stroked her head and soft ears. It was as if the dog had been a part of his life for as long as he could remember. Now, knowing that Tuma was his deceased ancestor, sent by his dad to comfort him, Reilly felt unusually anxious. He glanced over at Dubhghall and clung more tightly to Tuma.

Peering through the laurel, Reilly saw the Deceptors approach in a line, each with a person walking feebly at its side. Reilly counted: there were seventeen Deceptors and seventeen prisoners, who each wore a red tunic with the left shoulder bare. With their shaven heads and bodies obviously gaunt with hunger and fatigue, Reilly could not tell if the prisoners were men or women, but the last one was noticeably shorter than the others. Reilly shuddered as he considered what was about to happen to the prisoner who seemed much younger than himself.

The first Deceptor approached one of the stone arches with a prisoner at its side. Both stood still and waited. Reilly heard a loud clanking noise and watched as Sorcha appeared from out of the shadows. She carried her easel under one arm and a small basket in the other hand. Positioning herself directly under the other stone archway, she set the basket on the ground and unfolded her easel. Then she placed a small canvas on the easel and took a brush from the basket. She swirled the brush in the wells of a small palette and stared into the bonfire for a long minute. Then she turned and faced the first prisoner and Deceptor, who stared at her from a few feet away.

The prisoner stood like a wax statue, as if oblivious to the dangerous heat. In just a few minutes, Sorcha completed the portrait, and placed it on a stone ledge.

Without warning, the Deceptor wrapped its flowing cape around the prisoner, lifted up the victim, and walked directly toward the bonfire. Reilly gasped and covered his mouth. Tuma bared her teeth and furrowed her brow. The rats scuttled about, still unnoticed by the line of Deceptors, who began to chant.

Líon isteach dúinn le fuil ar do leanaí go deo.
Líon isteach dúinn le fuil ar do leanaí go deo.

Reilly buried Tuma's head in his chest as he watched the Deceptor and its prisoner walk into the fire. The flames rose higher, and a burst of deep purple swirled into the sky.

Confused, Reilly looked at Cormack. "I don't understand what's happening here, but we've got to stop this now!"

"When the chanting begins again, I'll give the signal. Dubhghall, Basil, and I will crawl under the hedge and start spearing at the rats," Cormack said. "We'll make a lot of noise and hope the distraction will cause enough of a disruption for you to get to Sorcha."

Reilly nodded and waited while the next Deceptor and prisoner stepped into place. As before, Sorcha looked into the fire, then faced the statuesque figures in front of her, and began to paint. When she finished, she methodically placed the painting on another ledge of the arch, and the chanting began.

Cormack and the two other Pucatrows bounded under the hedge and raised their spears high in the air.

"Weee-aaakkah! Kooo-shatah-mu'apa!" Cormack hollered, and Basil and Dubhghall echoed the sounds.

Suddenly the ground seemed to heave with rats. The rodents scampered along the edges of the bonfire as the three Pucatrows pretend-speared at the rats and flung them by their tails into the fire.

As the Deceptors waiting in line left their prisoners and converged on the yelping Pucatrows, Reilly and Tuma made their way to an opening in the hedge. The prisoners remained as still as statues. Reilly and Tuma jumped through the hedge and landed a few feet from Sorcha.

Startled, Sorcha jumped and dropped her paintbrush to the ground.

"We're here to help!" Reilly declared. "The Pucatrows, too."

Tuma picked up the brush in her teeth and presented it to Sorcha.

"Who are you?" she asked.

"My name is Reilly. This is Tuma. Please, you must trust me."

Sorcha's face was pale, but not gaunt. Her sapphire eyes glistened in the firelight as she took the paintbrush from Tuma.

"We only have a few minutes, Sorcha. There's no time for me to explain. But I will tell you this: your family is safe. Your father is working with the Pucatrows to make a full attack on Black Castle … but we need your help."

"Of course." She whispered the words, her eyes wide with amazement. "What do you want me to do?"

"I need to know what's going on here. During the next Crumble, I'll join the other prisoners as they're taken to the castle. I'll pretend to be one of them so I can get into the Library."

Sorcha was too stunned to speak. Reilly stepped directly in front of her and held her shoulders. "Sorcha, we're going to get you out of here, but I need more information so I know what I'm walking into. Have you been in the Library?"

"No."

"Do you know who is there?"

"I know the names of all the prisoners. I paint each of their portraits when they arrive. It becomes the front cover of their book. When they leave, I paint another portrait for the back cover of their book."

"What book? What do they do with the books?"

"I don't know. I only know that if I paint the portraits, the Deceptors will not send me to The Library. If I refuse, I will become one of them."

"You'll become a Deceptor?"

"No, one of their prisoners."

"But you *are* a prisoner." Reilly pointed to the shackles at her bare feet.

"No, I'm here by choice. I choose to paint. I choose to keep my own name and my own identity."

Confused, Reilly glanced at the Pucatrows, who were still making enough of a ruckus to divert the attention of the Deceptors. But he knew time was short.

"Do you know a prisoner named Norah?" he asked Sorcha.

"I remember painting Norah. She was so beautiful."

Reilly's chest seared in pain and he inhaled sharply. Disappointed that the effects of the rowanberries were wearing off, he breathed shallowly through the throbbing.

"When did you see her?"

"After the last Inner Crumble," Sorcha said.

Reilly frowned.

"Inner Crumbles bring people from other times and places, but The Library can accommodate every book."

Reilly's head began to hurt, though he didn't know whether it was from trying to piece the information together, the inescapable smoke, or the exhaustion that came after an attack of chest pain. "How long ago was it when you last saw her?"

"I lose track of time here, but I would imagine she is about ready for imprinting."

"Imprinting?"

"After the prisoners arrive, the Deceptors look through my paintings and choose a body they want to possess. Deceptors don't have mortal bodies of their own, so they have to borrow bodies. They are specific about whether they want to imprint a male or a female. Once the prisoners are shaved, it's harder to tell which sex they are, so they're branded. The Deceptors are obsessed by hair, but they also fear it because they are bodiless and of course hairless. Oddly, they especially prefer bodies with a lot of hair. Norah had beautiful hair."

Reilly grimaced and closed his eyes briefly. "Then what happens?"

"The imprinting occurs when the prisoners are brought here to the bonfire. I paint their portrait just before their demise. It's a reminder to the Deceptor that although they are inhabiting the body of a mortal—for a time, at least—even a hairless mortal is more powerful than a hairy Deceptor."

The commotion subsided, and the Deceptors began to disperse. Abruptly, Reilly shifted gears with an idea that had popped into his mind.

"I'm going to leave Tuma here with you. She'll wait at the edge of the laurel bushes until you give her a red tunic to bring to me. I'll ask Brigid to sew an inside pocket for me where I can hide a few things that I'll need when I'm in the Library."

"My mother," Sorcha whispered. "Oh, how I miss my mama."

Reilly stepped closer to Sorcha.

"I can't take you back with me yet, Sorcha. But I promise—you *will* see your mother again." Reilly wiped a tear from Sorcha's cheek. "Here," he added as he embraced her, "this is from her."

Reilly gave Tuma a quick hug and crept back behind the laurel hedge to wait for the Pucatrows. He thought it peculiar that the prisoners remained in their positions and didn't take the opportunity to escape, even when the Deceptors' attention shifted to the rats and the bonfire. He saw Cormack conversing with one of the hooded demons as he waved his spear high in the air. The rats were no longer visible in the fire, but they continued to make grotesque screeching and squealing noises. Gradually, the Deceptors returned to their former posts with the prisoners.

Cormack, Basil, and Dubhghall walked back to the hedge and slipped through the hidden opening.

"That went well," Cormack said.

"It did?" Reilly asked.

"Much better than I expected. At first, the Deceptors were annoyed we had interfered with their ritual. But when I told them we were there to celebrate with them, they thought our chants were troll cheers, not sounds of attack, so they joined the screeching."

"I would've thought they were smarter than that."

"Deceptors have a strange affinity for Pucatrows. Often, we can be convincing with them."

Reilly was anxious to collapse in the hammock at the McKinleys' house and bask in the success of the evening, but Cormack reminded him about their unfinished business.

"Now we will complete the exchange," Cormack began. "You agreed to give me what I want."

Reilly touched the flower in his pocket. "Yes."

"As I warned you, the transfer must be done with a blood promise." Cormack lowered his spear and held it just above the sharp point. "Extend your right forearm."

Reilly pulled his hand from his pocket and offered his arm. He flinched as the sharp spear pierced his skin and left blood oozing from a letter "T" halfway between his elbow and wrist. Cormack quickly did the same to his own arm.

"Now make a fist and crisscross your arm to mine," the troll said.

Reilly thought Cormack would ask for Reilly's hair. He never dreamed the Pucatrow would demand what he did next.

"I will have Tuma! Or you return the flower to me."

Chapter Twenty

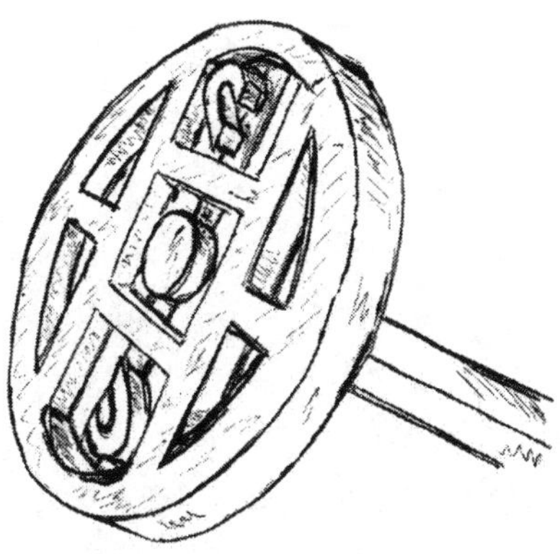

Familiar

Reilly lay awake most of the night, trying to understand why he had not seen it coming, and why he had not ascertained the seriousness of a blood promise with a Pucatrow *before* making the promise. Cormack had assured Reilly that if anyone did not honor his blood promise, a Pucatrow could imprint the body of the one who had failed to keep that promise. It wasn't until then that Reilly recognized why the Pucatrows got along so well with the Deceptors: they had more in common than most were aware of.

Reilly had been so consumed with holding onto anything that he thought would bring him to Norah that he had inadvertently sacrificed something else he loved deeply and thus jeopardized

Norah's rescue. But it was done. There was no going back on an exchange with a Pucatrow.

Reilly drifted in and out of sleep during the early morning hours, waking each time in a heavy sweat, crying out for Tuma. Just before he woke, a harrowing image of Norah flashed in his mind. Tears streamed down one side of her face, while the other half was the silhouette of a demon. Norah's song seemed to echo throughout the night between the cracks of the treehouse.

Reconciling in his heart his past behavior and current responsibilities frightened Reilly more than facing Travis Jackson.

For two days, he managed to convince the McKinleys that Lottie was ill and simply wanted to be left alone, and that he had come down with the same flu. Brigid seemed so preoccupied with Roisin—and did not want the baby coming down with anything worse than colic—that she believed the white lie. Meanwhile, Quin was consumed with his increased pressures and demands. Reilly spent most of the time in the bedroom, pacing the floor until he was so exhausted and anguished that he made himself ill. Another day later, in the late afternoon, there was a loud knock at the guestroom door, and Quin burst in.

"Reilly! Reilly! They have taken Charlotte! The Crumble has begun and she is nowhere to be found!"

Reilly jumped out of the hammock and shook his head vigorously to clear his mind from the recurring scene of Norah, masked with the face of a demon.

"Are you well enough?" Quin demanded. "You must join the others now, before they reach Black Castle."

"Yes, I'm fine." He brushed his tangled hair from his eyes and held it briefly in a ponytail. "Give me a minute and I'll meet you outside."

Tuma hadn't shown up with a red tunic, and there was barely time for Reilly to make sure his treasures were still in his pockets. He dug into his left pocket and pulled out the Fireglass and the small canister of ointment. From his right pocket, he pulled out the red ruby and the perfectly shaped flower, now an ashen color.

Reilly gripped his chest at the penetrating pain and stumbled to the bucket of rowanberries in Lottie's room. He grabbed a small handful and popped them into his mouth at once, then stuffed a satchel with as many berries as it would hold.

"Bail o Dhia ort!" Brigid shouted above Roisin's shrill screams. Reilly bolted past them to the front door. He knew what it meant: "The blessings of God on you." Reilly did not know much about God, but he presumed there was one—at that moment, he decided he could use any blessings offered. If nothing else, knowing Brigid McKinley was praying for him gave Reilly more courage.

"That was a long minute!" Quin bellowed. "We'll have to run to catch them before they leave the far edge of the woods!"

Much of the West Woods now reminded Reilly of his tumultuous arrival through the portal to Wicklow. Fallen trees and limbs lay in huge piles; tree homes had collapsed on the ground; numerous small fires had erupted; and a hundred or more people scrambled toward the Main Station, some screaming like banshees. No one seemed to take notice of the magistrate and Reilly, who headed in the opposite direction, toward Black Castle.

The ground beneath them rumbled, and deep cracks revealed tree roots, some of which were thicker than trunks. When crevices were too wide to jump across, Reilly and Quin found alternate routes.

In the distance, Reilly could see the light from the bonfire. As the forest trees thinned, dozens of prisoners marched in a line, each dragging a tree limb behind them or carrying a branch in his or her arms.

Quin and Reilly stopped briefly to catch their breath and strategize Reilly's entrance into the line.

"If you veer to the left and cut across that embankment, you should be able to step into line without being noticed," Quin said.

"It looks as if there are two Deceptors in the lead, one in the middle, and two taking up the rear. Your best chance is to sneak in somewhere near the middle, when the Deceptor is not facing your direction."

"Yes, sir."

Quin patted Reilly hard on the back. "You are doing more than is required of an Echtra. Should you return with my sweet Sorcha and dear Charlotte, I will leave the Embassy in your hands."

Reilly wasn't sure what Quin meant. *What good is an embassy that's under attack anyway?* he thought. *Even if it's made of solid jade.*

Reilly sprinted toward the embankment and scaled the ditch with a high leap. He picked up a fallen limb, thick with leaves, and used it to camouflage himself as he crept toward the line of prisoners. Crouched behind the leaves, he waited for the front half of the line to pass by him, then dropped the branch and grabbed another, smoother limb as he stepped into line, clutching the satchel of berries in his other hand. Undetected by the Deceptors, Reilly wondered what the few people directly behind him thought, but he marched forward without looking back.

Figuring it would be a full half-hour before they reached the bonfire, Reilly used the time to study the movements of the Deceptors in front of him. Their cloaks flowed in wide ripples, as if there was a breeze, though there was not. The arms of fabric hung long, and the hoods drooped steadily in front of their bodiless forms, concealing their identity in the folds of the black fabric.

With each step he took closer toward the bonfire, he considered his situation. He had successfully become a prisoner in order to rescue Norah, but how would he proceed now? The treasures in his pocket were an advantage, but he would have to assess his surroundings quickly when they reached the Portrait Room, to determine how to conceal them in the tunic he would be given to wear. Sorcha was aware of his plan, and would be on the lookout to provide assistance.

Hopefully Tuma was with Sorcha. Reilly was determined to figure out yet another exchange that would satisfy Cormack. Finally, he rehearsed in his mind the Affirmations of the Stelladaur.

> *I am eternal, without time or space.*
> *I am imagination and creativity without end.*
> *I am realization and manifestation as One.*
> *I am all possibilities.*

There were seven affirmations in all, but he could not remember the other three. He trusted that the information already revealed would aid him in rescuing the victims held at The Library.

As for liabilities, Reilly could think of three that were most pressing: the unknown, the unexplained, and the unanswered. He was confident that if he could somehow overcome those obstacles, he would prevail.

On the other hand, Eilam had told him that it was not necessary to know the end from the beginning. He only needed to take the next step. But it was at times like this—when he had given himself up as a prisoner to infernal demons without knowing for how long or to what end—that it took all he could muster to put one foot in front of the other.

Nevertheless, he marched on across the open meadow with the others. On toward the bonfire and Black Castle. On toward a plethora of liabilities and possibilities …

His arms started to tire from carrying the tree limb, but he noticed a few victims ahead of him dragging much larger ones. He wondered if the others had been allowed to choose the wood they carried. He was glad his piece was small. The bonfire crackled like gunfire in the distance, and the heat grew more severe.

The Deceptors at the front of the line stopped, and the line came to a slow halt.

Relieved, Reilly lowered one end of the tree limb to the ground. Others dropped their limbs to the parched grass beneath them. Leaning on his tree limb, Reilly strained to hear anything a Deceptor might say. He assumed the prisoners' rest would be brief when he saw the first person in line step closer to the fire and hurl his branch into the flames. He counted fifty-seven prisoners as they fueled the fire with branches and limbs. Nine more prisoners waited ahead of Reilly.

The flames were so tremendous that Reilly wondered if the fresh pieces of wood made any difference—it seemed the fire would burn forever, regardless. The whole procedure seemed more ritualistic than anything else, symbolizing the disappearance of their homes, and their old lives with them.

As he stepped to the edge of the bonfire, Reilly glanced quickly around for Sorcha or Tuma, but could see no sign of either of them. He hurled his tree limb into the flames with a vow to rescue them both—and to return to his home on Eagle Harbor Drive, with Norah.

The heat from the fire consumed the branches almost instantly. Reilly shuddered as he thought about the imprinting he had watched a few days before. Why didn't the prisoners protest? Why didn't the victims scream as they met their horrific deaths in the fire?

Reilly felt his skin burn from the heat as he marched around the edge of the bonfire and toward Black Castle. His eyes felt bruised far back in their sockets. He blinked rapidly to soften the sting and clear the smoke. The entrance to Black Castle was now in clear view, and the people at the front of the line were entering the towering front door.

Reilly knew he needed to find somewhere outside the castle to hide the satchel of berries. Figuring Tuma was around somewhere, and counting on her to find the satchel, he quickly crouched down and stashed it under the low hedge.

As he entered Black Castle, the searing pain in his chest reappeared and he wished he had eaten another handful of berries before ditching the satchel. Instead, he stuck his hands in his pockets and breathed in deeply. He needed to figure out what to do with his treasures before he, too, wore only a tunic, which might not have pockets. Sorcha was his only hope that he wouldn't lose his treasures.

The prisoners stood in line and watched Sorcha paint. When it was his turn, he took his place in front of the easel and relaxed his arms at his sides. Glancing in each direction, and seeing that the hanging portraits blocked his view of the Deceptors who stood guard at random points around the perimeter of the room, Reilly mouthed the word *Tuma*. Sorcha kept painting but nodded ever so slightly. She took her time with the portrait, waiting for any other communication from Reilly. He glanced down at his pockets, moving his eyes quickly back and forth from left to right. Sorcha furrowed her brow, not understanding what he meant. Then, looking straight ahead so he appeared to be standing at attention, he put his hands in his pockets. This time Sorcha understood.

Sorcha removed the canvas from the easel and blew on it. Then she stepped just beside Reilly and held it up, as if examining her work.

"As you walk past me, quickly drop the items into my basket," she whispered. "The Deceptors are more concerned with what's going on in the Shaving Room. I have never given them reason to doubt me."

Sorcha found a spot to hang Reilly's portrait while he pulled the Fireglass and small canister from his left pocket, and the ruby and flower from his right, and dropped them as discretely as possible into her basket. Then, as he walked ahead in line to wait with the others on the row of benches outside the Shaving Room, he noticed Sorcha cover the items with a paint cloth as she nodded for the next prisoner to step into place.

So far, so good, Reilly thought.

He sat on the bench, moving up in line each time a prisoner advanced to the next room. He made eye contact with Sorcha a few times, and felt comforted having an ally. Two Deceptors stood guard at the Shaving Room door. One moved his armless sleeve in a sweeping motion for the next victim in line to enter the room, as the other guard said "Next" in a deep, hollow tone. Each time the door opened, Reilly shuddered at the sound of screams coming from further on. First the shaving, then the branding—that much he knew would happen.

Next, he walked into the Shaving Room and watched others wring their hands; some whimpered in distress. Cormack, Basil, and Duhghall busily swept up the hair and tossed it into barrels behind them. Reilly stroked his wavy blonde hair. He hadn't noticed before how soft it was, or how long it had grown in the past few months. It hadn't been trimmed since before his dad's funeral, at his mother's insistence. For a moment, Reilly closed his eyes and imagined the wind blowing through his hair, as if he were slicing through the waves in his kayak. It seemed so long ago.

Someone pushed him from behind—another Pucatrow—and Reilly stepped up to the shaving device. Resting his head in position on the contraption that resembled an ancient guillotine, Reilly looked at Cormack's stubby-toed, filthy, bare feet. The lead troll bunched Reilly's hair into his hands and cut it off, close to Reilly's scalp. Reilly flinched as the blade touched the back of his neck and scraped toward his forehead. He shivered slightly as he felt the warm breath of the Pucatrow across his half-naked head. After half a dozen more scrapings, the lock released, and Reilly stood up. He shivered as a deep chill flooded his skull, and his entire body trembled.

Reilly took a deep breath and glared at Cormack, then put his hands into his empty pockets and walked to wait in the next line.

When it was his turn, he stepped behind one of the curtains, took off all his clothes, and dropped them into a large barrel with the other prisoners' items. He took one of the red tunics from a brass hook behind him and slipped it over his head. His right arm slid into the single long sleeve, and he pulled the frock down over his body. It hung to mid-calf. Reluctantly, he removed the golden Thread of Gratitude from his wrist and dropped it on the pile.

He stepped from behind the curtain, and caught a glimpse of Sorcha as she exited through a side door, along with Tuma.

She's done with the portraits, he thought. *That must be where she goes when she's not painting. She said she hasn't been allowed inside The Library.* He counted it another asset that he had noticed where she went, and that he knew Tuma was with her.

The shaved and changed prisoners sat on benches along the back wall. Soon, four Deceptors raised branding sticks in the air and began to chant:

Líon isteach dúinn le fuil ar do leanaí go deo.
Líon isteach dúinn le fuil ar do leanaí go deo.
Líon isteach dúinn le fuil ar do leanaí go deo.

Once again, the demon with the red hood bellowed, "With shaven heads your minds are open to accept your fate. Destiny is lost in the blood of vengeance. The curse is now yours to keep and ours to enjoy."

The Deceptors lowered their sticks, and another series of brandings began.

"Male or female?"

"Female."

An agonizing screech filled the room.

"Male or female?"

"Female."

Another bloodcurdling cry, and the stench of burned flesh.

"Male or female?

"Male."

A gasp of air—and a scream.

And so it went. Reilly counted the screams of fifty-seven prisoners ahead of him being branded. Moving into place, he clenched his fists and jaw, his heart pounding wildly. When the hot metal touched his bare left shoulder, his fingers spread open wide and he let out a long, shrill cry. Unexpectedly, as he stepped aside and was ushered through the main exit door, the pain subsided to a dull throb.

Looking down at the wound, Reilly was perplexed. He couldn't remember where he had seen the design before. But as he stepped into The Library, he knew: it was the same symbol as one of the petroglyph drawings chiseled into the rock off Bainbridge Island, near home.

Reilly now better understood how the first four Affirmations of the Stelladaur were interconnected. He finally got it: *Time is only measured where limited dimensions exist.*

He was where he was. He was *there* in that particular *now. Now* was all he had. If he wanted to go somewhere else—anywhere else—he could utilize other dimensions, and he would be *there* in *that* now. It made sense to him in his brain … but his heart kept telling him there was little time remaining before Norah would cease to exist in the now he understood right then.

Chapter Twenty-One

The Library

The new prisoners walked through a long, dark corridor, lined on both sides with Deceptors who whispered torments as they groped at the red tunics. He kept his arms at his side and did his best not to look directly at the demons. Parents shuffled their children along in a feeble attempt to guard them from the taunting grasps. At the end of the hallway, a tremendously tall iron door swung open with a *clang* so loud that the prisoners covered their bare ears in a half-crouched position.

Reilly uncovered his ears as he entered The Library. It was so similar to the Suzzallo Library! Stained-glass windows lined the perimeter of cathedral-high ceilings, supported by massive, arched wooden beams covered with strange carvings. But unlike the Suzzallo, which was beautiful, bright, and inspiring, this cavernous room reeked with debauchery. Reilly closed his eyes for a moment and decided it would do him no good to focus his thoughts on the vile window designs. He vowed to look only straight ahead, and no higher than the tops of the full bookshelves that surrounded the room.

The Library covered a great distance. Reilly could barely make out the far wall in the dim light. He estimated the shelves reached about twenty-five feet high; the number of books seemed incalculable. Extending the length of the room were rows of small tables, with one person seated at each table. Reilly quickly counted thirty rows—he figured there could be a thousand prisoners or more seated in The Library. The back four rows of tables were empty.

Each new prisoner took his or her place at an empty table and waited anxiously. Looking at the rows further ahead, Reilly could see that the other prisoners appeared to be working at their desks—a faint red light glowed in front of them and gave the entire room an eerie aura.

Glancing around, Reilly noted a young woman seated to his right. To his left was a man who, by the looks of his wrinkled hands and face, Reilly guessed was quite old. Directly in front of Reilly was someone shorter than he was, though looking at the baldness from behind, he could not determine if that prisoner was a girl or a boy. To the right of that prisoner was a large person who appeared to be a woman; and to her left was someone about Reilly's size, whose toes and hands looked male. Reilly did not turn around to see who was seated behind him.

An opaque screen opened out of Reilly's desk and displayed an image of the portrait Sorcha had painted of him. Under the portrait, in a font resembling dripping blood, words appeared: **MY STORY, by Reilly McNamara.** A keyboard flush with the desk emerged. **Press Any Key to Begin** flashed on and off the screen in a deep red hue.

Reilly glanced around The Library again. Many of the new prisoners were typing, but he could not see what was displayed on their screens. He looked further ahead, searching for Deceptors. He couldn't see any but assumed they lurked in the shadows.

With one finger, he pressed the "R" key.

The white screen was blank except for the heading, which read, **Chapter One.**

An eerie silence hummed below the sound of fingers tapping on keyboards. Reilly could hear his own steady breathing. He shifted slightly in his wooden chair, raised his hands to the keyboard, and began to type.

Hello.

He waited. There was no response. It wasn't an instant messaging system. He tried again.

Hello. Is anyone there?

He waited longer this time. The screen still offered no response.

My name is Reilly.

Suddenly, his own mirror image appeared on the screen. Reilly stared at his baldness. *It's not so bad,* he thought. *I do look older, though.* He continued to write.

I am sixteen years old.

Like a hologram, images of his sixteenth birthday celebration faded in and out of the screen. He saw Eilam, his mom, and his dad, all enjoying time together at the birthday picnic on Blake Island. He watched himself blow out all the candles on the cake, except for one. It burned on the screen in a single red flame that overtook the entire display until the rest of the birthday images disintegrated.

Reilly was no stranger to images related to past events magically appearing through strange devices. But he knew this was different. Horrifically different.

I live on Bainbridge Island in the State of Washington in 2015.

Images of his home and various island locations emerged.

But right now I am in Black Castle of Wicklow, typing on a strange computer, in the year 1896.

His own image, sitting in Black Castle, faded on and off the screen. The hologram would show him whatever he typed, as he typed it.

He started to write whatever came to his mind: random thoughts, details about his surroundings, what it felt like to be shaved and branded, the fact that he was hungry, and a list of his favorite foods. He figured he didn't know enough about what the device could or could not do, so he didn't write anything too personal.

He stopped to observe the victims around him, who each typed feverishly. The old man to his left wept as he typed. The young woman stared at her screen and gasped, as if in pain. Reilly wanted to lean over and ask them if he could help, but he resisted. He turned around and made eye contact with the person directly behind him, another boy about his age. The boy held Reilly's gaze with a look of sheer determination.

"I'm not staying in this place!" the boy whispered.

Reilly raised his brow and slowly turned around.

Just then, someone a few rows over screamed. Prisoners in the nearby rows stopped typing, but quickly returned to their screens as if they wanted to ignore what was happening around them. Soon others let out cries of pain, holding a hand over their branding wound. The large woman nearby doubled over in pain, clutching her bare upper chest. Reilly noticed that the outbursts came mostly from the new prisoners, with only occasional moans from those in the rows further ahead.

Not knowing if the peculiar devices were preprogrammed like a computer, or synched like the tree home lifts—either of which could be to his disadvantage—Reilly decided not to type anything else until he had more information.

He touched his branding wound and studied it carefully. It was circular, about two or three inches in diameter, with a solid dot in the center, about the size of a dime. Two vertical lines divided the circle into thirds, with two short horizontal lines dividing only the center section also into thirds. In the top third of the center section was a symbol that looked like an upside-down J. In the bottom third of the center section was a right-side-up J. The circle was divided in half by two short horizontal lines that came from the outer edges to meet the two vertical lines.

The healed skin over his wound left a well-defined branding that gouged into his chest slightly. The wound no longer hurt, but a dull ache lingered on the surface.

Reilly leaned over the side of his desk and looked up the long row toward the front of The Library. With the sea of red tunics and shades of crimson emanating from the desks, he recalled that the color red symbolizes blood, hatred, war, and evil, but it also represents love, selflessness, and forgiveness.

Everything has its opposite, he thought. *So no matter what appears to be here in Black Castle, there also exists something different than what I see, or know, or understand, in this moment. Something good.* He traced the branding mark with his finger. *I've got to remember this.*

As he pondered that thought, he pressed on the solid dot in the center of his marking. In an instant, his soul warped into the screen in front of him, leaving his body at the desk, watching the screen.

For a moment, Reilly wondered if he had died. He wore typical clothes for an October day: his Mariner's sweatshirt and jeans. A celestial-looking creature dressed in flowing white gossamer floated around him. Her blonde hair trailed behind her like folds of liquid gold.

"When the body aligns with the spirit within it, the power exists for the soul to overcome all darkness," said the creature.

"Are you an angel?" Reilly asked.

"I am a messenger for the Great Star King and Star Queen," she said. "My name is Parisa."

Reilly looked at her and waited. He had been through enough portals and met enough rare characters to know she would only be there until he understood her message well enough to warp back through the portal.

"The fifth Affirmation of the Stelladaur is this: *I am the open mind and the gentle heart.*"

"Yes," Reilly agreed. "I remember that now."

"And what does it mean to you now?"

Reilly blinked and thought hard. "A courageous person can overcome the fear of doing what must be done if he or she has a clear mind. But it must be done with a gentle heart, and without any ill will."

"If a person is clear in mind, does that mean they know what the outcome will be?" Parisa swooped around Reilly and hovered beside him.

"No. They have to be open to the possibility that it may have a different result than they expect." Reilly reached into his pockets to feel the flower or one of his other treasures, but his pockets were empty. "Open to all possibilities."

"And how does one get rid of ill will if it fills their heart, or even lingers there?"

Reilly looked directly at Parisa and said, "The mind will not be settled if the heart is filled with anger, hatred, revenge, or envy. Those emotions must be replaced with their opposites."

"You've learned much, Reilly. It's obvious you have mastered this knowledge intellectually."

Parisa took Reilly's hands in her own. He thought it was peculiar that he could feel a spirit. But as she touched him, he felt a power more intense than that which he felt the first time he touched his Stelladaur, and it settled in the deepest part of his soul.

"If you are to be the master of a truly gentle heart, it will come from the source of your greatest strength," Parisa whispered. "Find your greatest strength, so your heart will not fade like the others."

She lifted her arms high. As she embraced him in folds of flowing whiteness, he found himself sitting again at his desk in Black Castle. He started to write.

My story begins right now. Right here in Black Castle of Wicklow. I'm here to rescue Norah and the others. I'm not sure how I will do it, but I will. I gave myself up as a prisoner of the Deceptors so I could get inside their castle. My head has been shaved because the Deceptors believe mortals' power comes from the hair on their heads. They fear this power. They tell the prisoners that our heads must be shaved to open our minds and accept our fate. But it is a lie. Our fate is determined by the story we write.

Every prisoner of Black Castle must write his or her own story, but I don't think many prisoners understand this. What we write will not only be what we see on the screen—it will be our life's story.

No one else can write my story. I am the author.

If I don't like the plot or the setting, or if unwanted characters invade my story, I can change it. I can delete what I don't want.

As he typed, only his portrait painting appeared on the screen in front of him. No other scenes appeared. Reilly looked at his long blonde hair in the painting, knowing the Deceptors likely considered him a greater threat than others because of his abundant hair. He chuckled at their stupidity. Although he didn't know yet what his greatest strength was, he knew it did not come from his hair. He continued to write.

In order to write my truest story, I must be true to myself. And if I want to know my greatest strength, then I must know my greatest weakness. Eilam would agree.

I admit three things: #1. I detest the Deceptors. #2. I don't trust Cormack. #3. I will sacrifice anything for Norah—even my own heart.

Reilly gasped suddenly from the intense pain that gripped at his chest, deep under his branding. The screen revealed Norah, who lay on a stone floor in a small empty room. Her body was frail and grey. Her long auburn hair was gone. Reilly's hands fell to his side, and he felt as if the blood ran directly from his heart, through his veins, out his fingertips, and onto the floor.

Shaking his head to clear his mind, he reread his words. Relaxing his hands, he raised his fingers to the keyboard, highlighted the last sentence, and pressed 'delete'. Then he rewrote part of his story.

#3. Only my heart knows my greatest desire and my greatest strength.

Reilly looked around and studied each of the prisoners in his view. It occurred to him exactly what The Library of the Deceptors was: a prison for humans who are deceived by the Deceptors' lies. The Deceptors prey on their victims—using those very lies. Once they are captured, the victims are taken to The Library, where they are forced to write their own story. Each time a prisoner writes something that is contrary to the essence of his or her own soul, his heart burns with pain; soon his heart fills with fear, which then becomes disgust, revenge, contempt, and eventually, hatred for the Deceptors. Deceptors feed on negative emotions, which is their most powerful tactic to begin the Detachment Process. In time, numbness takes over each prisoner's body, until the writer's heart is empty of all emotion. Then the Deceptors drain the blood from the heart, and it fuels the endless flames of the bonfire.

Then the imprinting occurs.

Chapter Twenty-Two

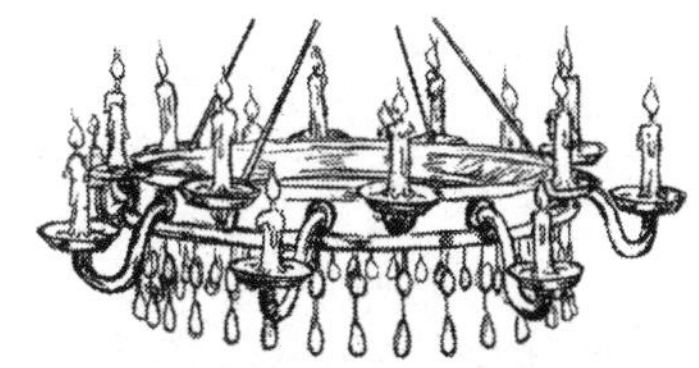

The Feast

Reilly quickly deleted his typed words, hoping the Deceptors had not yet read it. For the next three hours, he wrote about his earliest memories as a child: the bakery, his family, his kayak, and Eilam. He wrote mostly facts, leaving out his life during the past six months.

He figured the story he had now rewritten was mundane enough.

When making decisions, Reilly tried to consider his options, weigh pros and cons, and then do what he felt was best. There had been plenty of occasions when his thoughts did not jive with his gut or his heart, and he did something he later wished he had not done. Reilly purposely left those details out of the story.

Regardless of everything, discovering his Stelladaur had improved his ability to listen to his own heart. He had learned enough to know that right now, sitting in The Library, he could not write anything related to his Stelladaur, or he would risk handing his heart over to the Deceptors.

Just as he began to wonder if, in addition to stealing hearts, the Deceptors also starved their victims, an announcement sounded throughout the room.

"Nourishment and rest yield healthy hearts." It was a low, feminine voice with a taunting lilt.

"It's about time," said the boy behind Reilly.

Like an army stepping in line, chairs scraped against the wooden floor as the prisoners stood up at their desks.

Reilly turned around and smiled at the boy behind him. "I'm Reilly."

"Eoghan." The teenager shrugged to relax his broad shoulders and simultaneously twisted his head and jaw with his palms. When his neck popped, he added, "Now what?"

"We go that way." Reilly nodded to the front of the room where everyone was exiting, one row at a time.

"I hope the rest of the accommodations are more comfortable," Eoghan whined.

Reilly raised his brow. He wasn't sure if Eoghan meant to be funny or was naïve.

The prisoners filed quickly toward the far end of The Library. *There must be a million books in here,* Reilly thought. As they approached the front of the room, the line veered off toward an exit door to the left. Reilly slowed his pace as he came to an alcove with paneled doors, which reminded him a great deal of the alcove in the Suzzallo Library, and the door he had opened to go through the portal from Seattle to Wicklow.

"Get going!" Eoghan said. "I'm starved."

"Look at that inscription," Reilly whispered, as he pointed to the wall of stone surrounding the alcove.

"I can't make it out. Probably one of their stupid chants or something."

Reilly halted. Eoghan bumped into him and motioned for the other prisoners behind them to move on. Then Reilly read the inscription. "It says, *Good books are a priceless possession. They reveal the minds of creative man and enrich life with fine experience.*"

"Huh. Sort of long for a chant." Eoghan scratched his stomach. "It's nonsense to me. But books don't exactly strike my fancy."

"I've read this before," Reilly said as he stepped closer to the alcove. "On another library wall."

"The Deceptors have more than one dungeon?"

"I don't know. The place where I first read this is far away from here, near my home."

"I noticed you're not from around here. Your accent is weird."

"I live on a small island near Seattle, Washington."

"Never heard of it."

"It's on the West Coast of the United States."

"Blimey! What are you doing in Wicklow?"

"Uh … visiting family."

Part of Reilly wanted to jump over the railing into the alcove and find the portal back home. His mind raced with various scenarios, and he imagined life the same as it was before—before he stepped through the portal … before he met his fourth great-grandmother … before Norah and Eilam left without saying goodbye … before his dad drowned … before he ever knew anything about his Stelladaur or Tir Na Nog or Black Castle.

But in that moment, he realized that his heart was stronger than his thoughts, and more powerful even than his imagination. He simply wouldn't leave Black Castle without Norah, Tuma, and Sorcha.

Eoghan nudged Reilly to steer him back into the line. "What does it mean? The inscription."

Reilly turned slowly and stepped behind one of the other prisoners. Eoghan followed closely at his heels. "It means the Deceptors get around," Reilly whispered.

Eoghan shrugged as they left The Library. They walked down a long hallway lined with brass plaques with dates engraved sequentially by century, both B.C. and A.D. Reilly noted where the plaque marked "2010-2020" was located.

They entered a grand dining room, where rows and rows of banquet tables draped in purple silk filled the length of the room.

"Unbelievable!" Eoghan exclaimed.

"I bet the forks and knives are solid gold," Reilly said. "And the plates are probably sterling silver." He shuddered as he noted the multi-jeweled chandeliers that dotted the ceiling, like mesmerizing gems across a black sky.

When all the prisoners settled into seats at the decorated tables, the same woman's taunting voice made an announcement.

Refreshments will please throughout night,
No treats will be withheld,
For stories are more truly writ
When hunger and thirst are quelled.

With that, bursts of color exploded from the hanging jewels and transformed into platters filled with gourmet foods of seemingly endless varieties, floating just above the tablecloth. The aroma of seasoned meats mingled with the smell of tangy sauces, stewed vegetables, and sweet breads.

Oohs and aahs wafted through the room as the prisoners watched and waited.

"Let the feasting begin!" The invisible woman cheered.

The clattering of utensils erupted as people lifted serving spoons and forks to fill their sterling plates. Reilly noticed that each dish was arranged like a chef's work of art, and his favorite foods were displayed directly in front of him: pesto pizza in a plain take-out box; smoked salmon with mango salsa; steamed green beans; pecan pull-a-parts and pumpkin chocolate chip muffins—just like the ones his mom made at the bakery; and a bowl of red grapes.

"Don't just look at it!" Eoghan squealed. "Dig in! It's the best food I've ever tasted!" Eoghan ladled every food within reach onto his plate, and began to shovel it in.

Reilly wasn't sure if it was the blend of so many flavors permeating the room, or the stench of self-indulgent decadence, but his stomach churned—and it wasn't from hunger.

"I guess I don't have much of an appetite tonight," Reilly said.

"Suit yourself," Eoghan said, "but the restaurant may be closed tomorrow."

Reilly sat back in his chair and held his stomach. He closed his eyes and breathed deeply in an attempt to ward off nausea. The noise of so many people eating and chatting was almost deafening. He considered the possibility that the Deceptors used food to divert the prisoners' attention away from the conditions of their captivity.

He opened his eyes, and suddenly he wanted to tell all the prisoners they were being fattened up to the liking of the Deceptors, who would imprint their bodies sooner rather than later. Then he wondered why the victims at the bonfire were so gaunt; and why, when he saw the image of Norah, she looked as if she was near death from starvation. Did the Deceptors starve them, or had those prisoners chosen not to eat? Or was something strange about the food in Black Castle of Wicklow?

Eoghan refilled his plate three times. Two women seated across the table gasped at the boy's belches but continued to gorge themselves. Just when Reilly thought he might lose any food still lurking in his stomach from his previous meal, a high-pitched chime rang above the chatter and the hostess spoke again.

Salt and spices warm the body,
Aiming for a short night's slumber.
Savoring sweetness on the tongue
Ensures the soul will never hunger.

The almost-empty serving platters and bowls suddenly transformed into elegant gold trays and crystal dishes, each filled with delectable desserts by the dozens. Reilly's stomach switched from churning to growling, and he admitted to himself that he really was hungry. Beautifully displayed, the sweets were tempting. He thought he would have just one cookie or a small piece of pie. Then his eye settled on a dessert that made him reconsider.

In the center of the table, partially hidden by tall cakes, caramel fountains, and meringue pies, was a birthday cake—a German chocolate cake, just like the one his mother had made for his last birthday—with sixteen lit candles.

Reilly felt a tickling sensation, as if he was being watched. He couldn't see any Deceptors in the room, though, and the prisoners were preoccupied with the banquet.

He leaned over the table to get a closer look at the cake. The candles were black, and they were made not of wax, but a thin metal. In the flames, he saw an image of Norah. She sat on the stone floor with her arms around her knees, gently rocking back and forth.

Reilly stood up and scooted the other desserts out of his way, piling them in front of Eoghan. Then he reached for the cake platter and lifted it closer to him. He set the flaming cake on the table where his plate had been and inhaled deeply. Blowing hard and long, he extinguished all sixteen candles. Seconds later, the flames returned on the tips of the candles with a loud *whoosh*. Reilly attempted to blow them out again.

"Save your breath and eat a piece of the cake," Eoghan laughed. "They're obviously trick candles."

Reilly considered Eoghan's suggestion. "You're right," he nodded. "It's all a trick."

He watched Norah rock back and forth in the flames. From somewhere inside Black Castle, he heard her singing softly.

I'll hold my breath within the fire
To keep from utter shame.
I'll bleed inside from every vein
Before I yield my name.
But should my heart fade in the night
Before you come to me,
I'll write my soul's caressing song
And sing my dying melody.
    Love is all I ask of you,
    Love will make us free.
    Imagine love can change it all
    And bring you back to me.

Why do they have Norah? Why is she here? Fierce pain attacked Reilly—the same debilitating pain he invariably got when he thought of Norah, or could feel that she was near. He fell back into his chair, covering his branding mark and gripping his chest.

The elixir from the rowanberries has worn off, he thought. *I've got to find Sorcha and Tuma—tonight—and get those berries!*

"What's wrong?" Eoghan demanded. "Are you all right?"

"It … will … pass …" Reilly stammered. "I'm … fine."

Eoghan and the other prisoners nearby stopped eating and watched Reilly writhe in pain. None of the others offered assistance. Eoghan poked his fork into his palm and watched helplessly.

"Get rid … of that … cake," Reilly stammered.

Eoghan stood up and grabbed a large crystal bowl filled with lemon sorbet and dumped it upside down on the cake and burning candles. The bowl filled with yellow smoke and then exploded, shattering glass, and spewing coconut frosting and chocolate. Nearby prisoners jumped up. The two women who sat across from Reilly and Eoghan held their hands over their eyes and ran down the aisle screaming. Seconds later, the sixteen burning candles hovered above Reilly's head, rearranged to spell his name. The other prisoners jumped away to avoid the glass, some gasping and pointing at the sight above Reilly.

Shards of crystal pierced Reilly's face and head. A thick piece stabbed Eoghan in the shoulder, just above his branding mark. He reached for a silk napkin and quickly pulled it out. Just then, the candles dropped with a thunderous crash onto the table in front of Reilly, and the flames were finally extinguished.

Blood streamed down Reilly's face from a deep wound in his head. Eoghan pulled a large piece of glass from his friend's face, but before he could remove the smaller pieces, a frightened hush engulfed the dining room. Deceptors infiltrated the room and loomed around the perimeter.

The red-caped Deceptor swooped past Reilly and bellowed a command.

Be careful who you speak to
Within the dining hall.
Those like Reilly McNamara
Jeopardize you all.

Reilly felt all eyes in the room on him. Then, as if on cue, the prisoners heaved in unison as the pain from their own brandings returned briefly, but more intensely.

Eoghan squared his shoulders and whispered to Reilly, "Some trick!"

The red-hooded Deceptor swooped past Reilly again and bellowed, "Come!"

Reilly followed the demon down the length of the room, through the countless prisoners, each of whom stepped back as he walked past—as if *he* were a demon! Blood dripped to the floor, and his face contorted in pain.

Reilly didn't know whether he was being taken to a dungeon worse than The Library or to his death, but he felt strangely calm. In that moment, he recognized something remarkable: he felt no ill will.

Chapter Twenty-Three

Sorcha's Parlor

The Deceptor led Reilly through a narrow corridor that wound behind the main rooms and ended abruptly at an ornately carved door. The demon walked right through the door as it simultaneously opened for Reilly. Reilly stepped into the room and saw Sorcha seated, facing him.

"This one is bold," the Deceptor said. "Be sure to use your brightest reds. When you finish, mend his wounds and return him to the sleep chamber. He will need to be fresh for tomorrow's work in The Library."

The Deceptor passed through the wall and left Reilly in Sorcha's studio.

"Reilly!" Sorcha cried. "Oh, dear, you do look a fright!"

Reilly looked around the room for other Deceptors.

"Don't worry, they can't hear us, and they won't be back."

"Are you positive?"

"Yes. They only come here to bring me prisoners who are going up for auction."

"They're going to sell me? To whom?"

"Whichever Deceptor gives Prince Ukobach the highest price. Let's do this quickly, so I can take care of those wounds." Sorcha tugged at his elbow and positioned him in front of a black silk curtain hanging from a rod suspended in air. Then she stepped up to an easel with a fresh canvas.

"I know you're in pain, but please be as still as you can."

"Okay."

"Once I get the outline of your face and the shape of your head, I'll clean away the blood from your eyes. They like to see the eyes in my paintings, especially of prisoners who are auctioned."

Reilly squirmed as blood coursed along his jawline and down his neck.

"The Deceptors discovered I could paint and used it as a decoy to capture me. My father didn't think I should spend my time painting. I am his eldest child, and he wanted me to contribute more at the Embassy. We argued a lot about it. Anyway, the Deceptors told me all sorts of lies, and one day during a Crumble, I was captured. I had no choice. Of course, like any prisoner, I had no idea what was inside the castle. When I arrived, they immediately separated me from the other prisoners and brought me here, to this studio. They told me their previous painter had been imprinted the night before, and I would be their new resident artist."

Sorcha dabbed her brush in the paints and worked on the canvas.

"But—"

"Shh! This will go much more quickly if you don't talk just yet." Sorcha started to paint long strokes, forming an outline of Reilly's face. "Besides, I'm quite sure I know what questions are running through your mind, so I'll do my best to answer them. First, resident artists are only imprinted if they show signs of rebellion. As long as I willingly paint the portraits, stay in my quarters, and don't attempt to take off these chains, I live in one of the most hospitable places in the castle and get plenty of good food. They even grant an occasional request. It's not so bad."

Reilly squinted and caught a glimpse of Sorcha's expression. He was relieved to see that it was not one of complete resolve.

"I think I've been here over three years, and I've only painted four auction portraits—after all, not many people come to The Library with the intent to rescue other prisoners, and those who tried didn't succeed. I've heard that only a few people have escaped in the past century. Don't write anything in your story that will tip them off any more than you already have. Keep it basic and boring. You've probably already figured out that you have to tell the truth, and it has to be your own story. When you write something that indicates you made a choice to please someone else—because you felt compelled, rather than free—your branding symbol will surge with pain. It's a paradox, because the only thing the Deceptors can't take from you is your own will—your power to choose—which comes from your heart. They can only take your heart when you give it up, a little at a time, when you are not true to yourself."

Sorcha walked to Reilly, turned his shoulders slightly, and returned to her easel.

"I'm lucky. When I'm not painting portraits, I am free to paint whatever I choose. My story is told in my art. I can show you when we have time."

"Okay," Reilly muttered.

"Hold on a few more minutes. I'm almost done." She continued to guide the brush onto the canvas, now using shorter strokes. "I told you before, Deceptors are quite particular about whether they want to imprint a male or female body. I don't know if you've noticed or not, but the female branding mark is exactly the same as yours, except for the half-circled dot in the center. The males have a half-circle to the left, and the females, a half-circle to the right. The Deceptors typically remain in an imprinted body until that body dies a human death. Then they choose another body, and often a different gender, but I don't know why. On rare occasions, a Deceptor decides to vacate a human body before it expires, but only when the human is able to resist the evil spirit repeatedly. I think the Deceptors get bored when there isn't enough wickedness in the imprinted bodies."

Sorcha stepped back from her easel. "There. Now I can remove the shards and clean you up before I paint your eyes." She walked to a nearby table, immersed a cloth in a basin of water, and squeezed out the excess. She carefully wiped the blood from Reilly's eyelids before she began to pull pieces of glass from his face. "I'll get them all from your face first. Those two pieces in your head will bleed more when I remove them." She worked quickly and rinsed out the cloth three times. Then she daubed strips of cotton fabric to his facial wounds. "Okay, let's take out the real culprits." She snatched the two shards from his head and quickly pressed a clean cloth to the wounds. "Hold this firmly while I finish the portrait. Look straight ahead, please."

Reilly's head throbbed, and he thought about using the last of the ointment from the canister in Sorcha's basket with his other treasures. But he decided against it, knowing that if the Deceptors saw that his wounds had healed, they would realize something was up.

"Do you still have the things I dropped in your basket?" he asked.

"Of course. I've been intrigued by them, but Tuma has not told me what they are for."

"Tuma? Is she here? Is she all right?"

"She's in the next room. I didn't want you to get too excited before I completed the portrait."

"But how did you get her in here without the Deceptors knowing?"

"They know. As I said earlier, occasionally they allow me a special request. Whenever Deceptors feel inclined, they acquiesce to a resident artist in an attempt to keep them satisfied, so the artist doesn't rebel. Apparently, portrait artists are not easy prisoners to find. When they first captured me and told me I would be the resident artist, they said I could have one request. I asked that they not shave my head. When I was younger, my mother stroked my head and ran her fingers through my hair as I fell asleep. Sometimes my father would, too. The Deceptors do not allow me to grow my hair long, but at least I wasn't shaved. When a prisoner is shaved in Black Castle, the hair on his head never grows back."

"Never?"

"Not unless they escape."

Reilly pressed the cloth more firmly to his head, trying to soothe the throbbing.

"Are you almost finished with the portrait?"

Sorcha bit her lip as she looked across the room into Reilly's eyes, and then back at her canvas. "I'm done." She stepped back to critique her work. "It should go for a high price. The paintings are sold along with the prisoner himself."

"No!" Reilly exclaimed. "They can have the painting, but they don't get me!" Still holding the soiled cloth to his head, he walked across the studio to the easel. He gasped at the painting. "I look terrible! I mean, you've done a great job … you are truly gifted, Sorcha … but I look like a monster!"

Sorcha stepped closer to Reilly as she looked at the portrait with him. "A monster would never have eyes like yours." She smiled at Reilly. "Now let's see how your head is mending. Bend over a bit."

Reilly released his hands from the cloth as Sorcha took over. She peeled the stained fabric from his head. "It looks worse than it is. If we rinse it well, it won't become infected."

She pulled him toward the table and told him to lower his head over the basin. She lifted a pitcher to cleanse his head. He flinched … she poured … and he sighed with relief. The liquid was warm.

"That should do it," she said. "I'll layer more cotton over the wound, and it ought to close up in a couple days."

"Thank you, Sorcha," he said, and thought about how much she looked like her sister. "Can I see Tuma now?"

"Of course. She's in my parlor."

They exited the portrait studio through a side door and entered a well-appointed bedroom. Tuma leapt off the bed when she saw Reilly, wagging her tail.

"She never barks," Sorcha said. "But she looks at me as if she knows me."

Reilly hugged his dog. "I know what you mean." He stroked her ears and kissed her head. "I'm surprised the Deceptors didn't have *her* shaved!" Tuma whimpered and lowered her ears. "Sorry, Tuma."

"They aren't interested in animal hair. It's human hair that they feel threatened by. If the Pucatrows didn't haul away the shaved hair, they would probably be shaved, too. I don't quite understand the relationship between the Pucatrows and the Deceptors."

"I don't trust Cormack. Or Dubhghall. Or Basil."

"Hmm …"

"Your father insists they are quirky but loyal. Did you know that the Pucatrows have built tunnels from Black Castle to the Main Stations?"

"I've wondered why I see them so often at the imprintings. The Deceptors are preoccupied with the prisoner they have chosen to imprint and don't seem to notice the Pucatrows poking their heads through the hedge. But I can see them when I'm painting under the archway. This last time, the Deceptors were quite annoyed by the intrusion of the rats."

Reilly and Sorcha sat on the bed, and Tuma jumped up between them. Reilly told Sorcha what he knew about the Pucatrows, the rats, and the most recent Crumbles.

"And my family? Are they all safe?" Sorcha asked.

"Yes. Your mother has taken in a baby who was abandoned during a recent Crumble. She named the girl Roisin."

"I imagine Dillon isn't happy about that."

"Roisin screams a lot. She has colic."

"And my sister? How is Lottie?"

Tuma nosed Sorcha and licked her face. "Stop, Tuma! Settle down," Sorcha said.

"Lottie misses you terribly. She wanted to come with me, but your father would not allow it. Now he fears she was taken in the last Crumble."

"But she didn't come through with the others."

"No, she … uh …"

"She what?"

Reilly was silent.

"What is it?" Sorcha demanded.

"Sorcha, this may seem unbelievable, but … Lottie is …"

"For goodness sake, tell me! Where is Lottie?"

Reilly faced Tuma, who barked once.

Sorcha caught the dog's face in her hands to quiet her and then looked deeply into her silver eyes. "Lottie? It's *you*?" Sorcha threw her arms around Tuma's neck and hugged her. "It's those eyes! You kept looking at me as if you knew me … really knew me! But how did this happen?"

"It's a long story, Sorcha," Reilly said.

Reilly lay back on the pillow and told Sorcha the story: how he got to Wicklow, where Tuma came from, portals, and such—but he didn't tell her anything he hadn't already told Lottie. He was relieved that Sorcha listened and believed his story as easily as Lottie had.

"So I'm your fourth-great auntie!" Sorcha laughed. "I suppose anything is possible after knowing that! "

"My point exactly!" Reilly added as he sat up. "Which leads me to the next challenge. I left Lottie's satchel filled with rowanberries under the hedge just outside the main entrance doors to the castle. The berries have healing powers. Norah must have some … as well as the other prisoners who are in the most danger."

"I can get the satchel in the morning. The Deceptors allow me to walk around the front courtyard for exercise three times a day. Tuma—I mean, Lottie—can join me."

"Great. How will you get the berries to me?"

Sorcha scanned the room. "There is an extra tunic in that closet. It's been there since I arrived here, and the Deceptors seem to have forgotten to remove it, because they don't have me wear tunics. I'll sew a few inside pockets into the tunic, and you can trade it out tomorrow. I'll tell the Deceptors I didn't have time to complete the eyes of the portrait because you simply couldn't stay awake. They will likely agree because they insist auction pieces be perfect."

"If you think that will work …"

"It's the best and quickest solution."

"The pockets won't hold all the berries, but we'll just take one thing at a time. Can you please also sew a pocket where I can keep my other treasures?"

"Yes, of course. The canister, the ruby, and the flower should be small enough not to be noticed." Sorcha reached for the basket under her bed and pulled it out. "But this other instrument is rather bulky. What is this?"

"That's the Fireglass I told you about."

"It's lovely," she said, admiring it. "I haven't found my Stelladaur yet, though you say Lottie has, and it doesn't appear that her

Stelladaur came with Tuma. But I wonder if we could still access another portal with just the Fireglass."

"Hmm … maybe." Reilly jumped off the bed and knelt beside his dog. "What do you think, girl?" Tuma perked up her ears and licked Reilly's face. "I believe you're right, Sorcha. Lottie is giving me the look that says she agrees, too."

"What are we waiting for?"

Sorcha handed the Fireglass to Reilly. He rolled it over in his hands a few times. "I never know quite what's going to happen when I use this." He lifted the device to his eye and pointed it directly into Tuma's eyes. Twinkling white lights began to swirl inside her eyes, like stars from a distant galaxy.

Then Reilly and Tuma were gone.

Chapter Twenty-Four

Return of Jaida

Once again, Reilly and Tuma stood within a circle of fire with flames that rose high into the air. Turning around repeatedly, Reilly looked for an escape.

He noticed the only sound was Tuma's incessant barking.

"Shh!" he whispered. "Tuma, be quiet." Still barefoot and wearing the red tunic, Reilly held the Fireglass in his hand.

"There's no heat," he said. "These flames are like a mirage. C'mon."

He stepped toward the edge of the fire with Tuma at his side and walked boldly with her into the smokeless, silent flames. Then, encompassed by a blossoming orange and red glow, they stopped and waited.

Moments later, a single flame leapt at Reilly's feet and transformed into a small evergreen tree. Almost simultaneously another flame transformed into a similar tree. Soon Reilly and Tuma stood in the middle of dozens of three-foot-high pine, cedar, and spruce trees, while the flames in the distance unfolded even more trees. Standing at the top of a mountain and looking across a vista of what looked like baby Christmas trees dotting the landscape, Reilly breathed in deeply.

"Remember, Reilly, it is my purpose to protect the spirits of all living things," he heard a woman's soft voice say behind him.

Reilly spun around. "Jaida?"

"Yes, of course." The Guardian of Nature appeared before Reilly as she had in Gwidon, with her flowing green cloak teeming with critters and creatures. She lifted her moss-covered arms and pointed a finger on her maple-leaf hand. "Each flame cleanses the forest so new life can grow."

Reilly looked at Tuma, who sat at attention, looking back at him.

"This is the process of Nature," Jaida continued. "Life emerges and begins to grow. In time, the elements of Mother Earth converge, and transform all life into the greatest potential within it."

Reilly tried to relax and just listen. He stroked Tuma and looked intently at the strange creature, her upper torso covered in iridescent scales and the rest of her body covered in feathers.

"Humans must learn to welcome and appreciate not only the lushness of life, but the uncertainties. Stepping into the flames of uncertainty is the only way to allow real change. Nature teaches the greatest lessons of life and the deepest understandings of death."

Reilly stepped back when he caught a glimpse of a hissing scorpion crawling across Jaida's foot. He shifted slightly on his own two feet as the Guardian of Nature looked down at the scorpion.

"There is competition for survival only on earth. When Nature is truly understood and respected, the sting of the scorpion is also honored."

Jaida lifted her arms up high and spread them wide to reveal the myriad of critters beneath her, all mingled together harmoniously. "Fire purifies living souls."

Reilly couldn't resist speaking any longer. "But fire also destroys."

"There is purpose in what appears to be tragedy."

"What about all the prisoners who will be killed by imprinting at the bonfire? What purpose is there in that?"

"There is no death, only refinement."

Reilly stepped closer to Jaida. "Are you saying that being imprinted by a Deceptor is *necessary*? That it's a *good* thing?" He watched the scorpion scuttle around her feet.

"Goodness comes from within all living creatures, as does the power to resist Deceptors."

"Are Deceptors considered living creatures?"

"They become alive when they inhabit a human body."

"We're going in circles!" Reilly protested.

"The Circle of Fire is the Circle of Life."

"No!" Reilly shouted. "They cannot have Norah! They'll have to take me instead!"

Jaida lowered her arms and wrapped her cloak loosely around her shoulders. "Sometimes Deceptors consider a trade," she said. "But only if they believe the replacement is more passionate, more valuable, and more powerful."

"How do they determine that?"

"By reading the stories. Your story must be convincing. You must write your deepest emotions and strongest passions. These qualities are innate in the human soul—body and spirit combined—but eternally devoid in Deceptors, so it is what they crave more than anything." Squaring her bare shoulders, she added, "But most importantly, you must reveal your greatest desire, as well as your greatest weakness."

"Why would I give the Deceptors that advantage?"

"Vulnerability is essential if you are to discover your greatest strength." She opened her arms as if to embrace Reilly. "This they do not know … and therein lies your greatest strength."

Reilly knelt down to hug Tuma. Looking into her eyes, he knew she agreed. Then, as if spooked by something unseen, the dog tucked her tail between her legs and cowered behind Reilly.

"What is it, Tuma?" He stroked her long white fur over and over. "What's wrong, girl?" As he spoke the words, Reilly realized one of his greatest obstacles to convincing the Deceptors to spare Norah and take him instead.

"She's a girl. I'm a boy. The Deceptor who intends to imprint Norah most likely wants her not only because of the story she's already written, but because she is female. Sorcha said they are particular about which sex they choose each time they imprint. But I will be up for auction for Deceptors who want to imprint a male." Reilly stood up and looked to Jaida. "Is this situation my greatest weakness?"

"It is only a complication."

For a moment Reilly wished he hadn't looked through his Fireglass. But he knew it was not a wish of substance, and it did not come remotely close to being his greatest desire. Nevertheless, it was a good reminder of what he knew about such desires. He repeated in his mind what his Great Grandpa had said: *A wish becomes a greatest desire at the very moment when a person's belief in the seemingly impossible is stronger than any doubt.*

It wasn't that he doubted any specific seemingly impossible thing—there simply seemed to be so many things that appeared impossible.

Reilly inhaled deeply and exhaled as he looked down at Tuma. "We better get going, Lottie."

Without asking Jaida anything else, Reilly lifted the Fireglass to his eye. "C'mon, girl."

When Reilly awoke the next morning, he couldn't recall how he had reached his sleeping quarters. He hoped Tuma was still safely with Sorcha. There was no sign of his Fireglass, either. He rubbed his temples and massaged his forehead. His hand brushed against a piece of cotton stained with dried blood. He stretched and looked around the room.

Simple cots, about two feet apart, lined both sides of the room, with another row down the center. Reilly quickly estimated about sixty boys and men—probably newcomers—had spent the night in the damp room. Swinging his legs over the side of his cot, he noticed Eoghan beside him, squirming restlessly. Without warning, the metal door clanged open.

There is little time to rest
With stories still untold.
Words not truly written
Make destiny unfold!

As if those in the room did not understand the rhyme, further instructions were given, this time in a more commanding voice.

Today you write the words
Which give luster to your name.
Soon secretly you'll wish
To match it with a frame.
But as the fire flickers
And burns within your breast,
Until you write the truth for us
Your soul will never rest.

As they lined up and filed out, Reilly noticed many prisoners avoided walking near or making eye contact with him.

"Their rhyming antics are so annoying," Eoghan whispered behind Reilly.

Reilly glanced around quickly. "You think it's funny?"

"Not really. I just don't believe what they say, that's all." He leaned closer and added, "It's a bunch of malarkey."

Reilly knew the Deceptors were masters of deceit. He knew they laced partial truths with subtle lies. But he wondered what Eoghan's story was, and why he seemed so aloof to the obvious doom that awaited the prisoners of Black Castle. As they walked down a long corridor, Reilly felt Eoghan nearly bouncing along a few steps behind him.

Soon they met a line of women and girls, who filed along beside the men and boys. Mothers pulled small children closer to avoid walking near Reilly.

"I've got your back, Reilly," Eoghan whispered, patting him on the back.

"Thanks."

Walking into The Library, Reilly mentally added Eoghan to his list of assets. He hoped Sorcha would arrange for him to return to her parlor soon. He wrote more than he thought he could truthfully write about his life without adding details that would alert the Deceptors, but hours later, there was still no indication that he would be allowed to leave. Eoghan kept trying to talk, but Reilly did not want to draw attention to himself so he finally told Eoghan they would have to wait until they were in the dining hall, where everyone was permitted to talk.

Reilly's stomach growled, and he guessed it was near dinnertime, though the computer screen did not have a clock. Nor did it provide the Internet, or any capability to connect with the outside world. It was simply blank pages on a screen, waiting to be filled.

Hoping to distract his hunger, he decided to write a chapter about his favorite foods and the smells and sounds of the bakery. Three pages later, he only felt worse.

"What was that?" Eoghan whispered.

"My stomach!"

"Yeah, the service here is wretched," Eoghan replied with a grin.

Just then the metal doors that reached half way to the ceiling swung open with their usual clang.

Nourishment and rest provide healthy hearts.

It was the same eerie voice that had chanted the first haunting rhyme he had heard in The Library. But before chairs scraped in unison against the floor, she continued.

Tonight the feast must wait
And bodies wither on,
While portraits for the auction
Are perfected without song;
For one among you swears
That he will rescue all,
But no price is sufficient
To exchange hearts filled with gall.

Reilly's chair slid with a long screech as he pushed away from his desk and stood up.

"Blimey!" Eoghan cried. "This can't be good!"

Reilly shook his head slightly. "I won't be long," he muttered.

A Deceptor met Reilly at the front of the room. Reilly said nothing, but followed the hooded creature out of the room and through the back hallways to Sorcha's studio.

"Prince Ukobach has declared the auction will be held on Hallow's Eve," the demon intoned, "at the hour before the Festival of Fire begins." The Deceptor vanished through the wall as silently as before.

Reilly glanced quickly around the room before speaking to Sorcha. "When is Hallow's Eve?"

"In two weeks, on the last day of October."

Reilly did several quick calculations. In real time, it had only been a couple of months since he left the beautiful Suzzallo Library. But going back in time to 1896 made him feel as if a hundred years had passed since he was home—or had last seen Norah.

Tuma walked up to Reilly and nuzzled at his legs.

"And what is the Festival of Fire all about?" He scratched Tuma's neck and stroked her soft ears.

"Once a year, Deceptors who are dissatisfied with the bodies they have imprinted can choose another instead, rather than waiting for the body to die a natural death," Sorcha said.

"What happens to the body that was first imprinted?"

"It is deemed useless and destroyed in the fire."

Reilly tried to sort through what Jaida had taught him, and how it might apply to Sorcha's comment. "But if a soul is released from imprisonment by a Deceptor, wouldn't it then be free?"

"There are many situations worse than death." Sorcha led the way through the door to her parlor. She handed Reilly a tunic. "I hope you'e right about the rowanberries."

Reilly took the tunic and searched for the pockets Sorcha had sewn. "Nice job. The stitches are practically invisible." He inspected it more closely and found three pockets sewn inside the front hem, each covered by a flap.

"I tried to position the pocket for the berries somewhat between your knees, so it would be less noticeable when you walk."

Reilly stepped behind a screen, changed into the modified tunic, and returned to model it.

"Good heavens! Don't waddle like a duck!" Sorcha laughed. "Just walk normally."

Reilly paraded back and forth in the small room.

"That's better," Sorcha said. "I counted out thirty-seven berries. I didn't put in any more than I thought would fit easily. You probably noticed the small pocket to the left has the flower and the ruby. The one on the right has the ointment."

"Thank you, Sorcha. What about the Fireglass?"

"It just didn't work to make a pocket that would hide it effectively, Reilly. You'll have to work with what you've got."

"Then we have to come up with another excuse for me to come back here," Reilly insisted.

"I can't ask for another favor right away, or they'll be on to us. Asking to keep Tuma was a big risk."

Reilly stopped pacing and petted his dog again. As he had often done when searching for answers, he looked deeply into her silver eyes. "Then we need to offer something to the Deceptors. Make them think we can give them what they want more quickly."

"What do you have in mind?" Sorcha stepped closer to Tuma. "My sister stays with me!"

Reilly chuckled. "Of course. At least I know the two of you are not in immediate danger. By the way, where is my Fireglass?"

Sorcha reached into the folds of her chiffon dress. "I have a couple of pockets, too." She smiled as she held up the treasure, and reached out her fettered arms. "These chains are a fine distraction. The magical device will not be noticed."

"Awesome!" Reilly squealed. "This should work perfectly with my plan."

"Which is …?"

"We need to outsmart the Deceptors—let them think we have something they want."

"They want our bodies! Isn't that enough?"

"But first they try to take our stories." Reilly stroked Tuma's head. "Let's give them a reading!"

"I don't understand, Reilly." Sorcha looked at Tuma to see if she understood what Reilly meant. Tuma wagged her tail harder and let her tongue hang down with a dog smile. "A lot of help you are, Lottie!"

"You said the Deceptors will grant you requests as long as you show no signs of rebellion, right?"

Sorcha nodded.

"Tell them you want to thank them for allowing you to keep Tuma."

"*Thank* them?"

Reilly ignored her skepticism. "Yes. Propose a reading of the stories. Tell them … when I came here for the auction portrait, you were impressed with the sound of my voice. Suggest that a reading of the stories—narrated by the one who is up for auction—will create a greater sense of competition. They'll think I am even more valuable, and offer a higher price to Prince Ukobach."

"How ever did you come up with such a preposterous idea?"

Reilly laughed. "It's called *calculated imagination*."

"I call it *confounded desperation*!"

"Either way, do you have any better suggestions?"

Sorcha admitted she did not.

"It's settled, then," Reilly declared. "If they accept your offer, suggest that I be allowed to come here to practice the readings, so they are perfect—like the portrait. There must be a book where all the stories are kept together."

"We can only hope." Sorcha rolled her eyes, still not convinced. "I'm agreeing with the idea simply because I can tell that Lottie also agrees with you."

"That's good enough for me." Reilly rechecked the positioning of his tunic to make sure his pockets didn't pucker when he walked. "I'd better get back now. I don't want to keep the others from dinner any longer. My number of friends in The Library is limited."

"Be careful, Reilly."

Reilly gave Tuma another big hug and then hugged Sorcha, too. "Don't try to use the Fireglass without me. We'll utilize it to find the last portal and the last Affirmation of the Stelladaur, and then we can all go home."

Chapter Twenty-Five

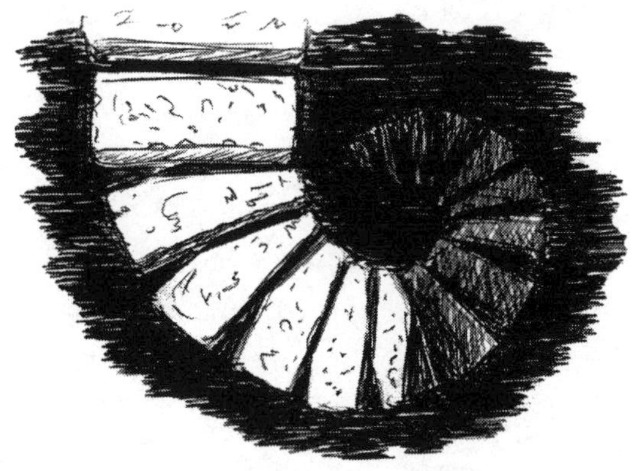

Priceless

A week passed without Reilly hearing anything from Sorcha, and he often wondered if Quin's plan to attack Black Castle with the Pucatrows was still on track. Nevertheless, he spent his days writing in The Library with the other prisoners, trying his best to keep the content of his story basic, boring, and before the time of his dad's accident or the discovery of his Stelladaur. Since dinner was still the only meal of the day, he knew he needed to keep his strength up, so he ate something each night, and hoped the food wouldn't cause any lasting adverse affects. He noticed that many prisoners were beginning to look pale, and there was less conversation among them in the dining hall.

Whenever he heard the haunting echo of Norah's song in his mind, he was tempted to eat one of the berries, but he dealt with the pain as well as he could, knowing there were others who needed the berries more than he did. Yet to his utter frustration, he still did not know how to get the berries to the prisoners who needed it most—those who, like Norah, were kept in seclusion somewhere beyond The Library. The berries, safely hidden in his pocket, kept their form as perfectly as the flower, and they were still bright red.

Late one night, after hearing Norah's cries again, Reilly awoke with a stabbing pain that pierced his chest and infused his entire body. He gasped loudly, gripping the sides of his cot with both hands. Not wanting to awaken the other prisoners, he muffled his cries by biting his bare arm. But Eoghan, on the cot next to him, heard Reilly grunt and sat up.

"Blimey!" Eoghan whispered. "Can I do something?"

Reilly opened his eyes wide. "Help … me … sit … up!"

Eoghan bounded to his feet and lifted Reilly to a sitting position.

"I … need … to … stand!"

Eoghan lifted Reilly's legs over the side of his cot and hoisted him up. Reilly bent over, flipped his tunic back at the hem, and unfolded the flap to the pocket. He retrieved two berries, painstakingly put them both in his mouth, and sat on his cot, waiting over a minute for the berries to take effect.

"Thank you," he whispered.

"Yeah, sure," Eoghan replied. "Are those magic berries or something?"

"Not really. But they have healing powers."

"What causes these attacks?"

Reilly knew Eoghan kept his ears and eyes open for any information that might be helpful, and he trusted the boy. Reilly leaned forward to whisper more softly.

"I came here to Black Castle on purpose—to rescue a friend named Norah and another friend's sister, Sorcha, who has been here for years."

"Years? Reilly, we've got to get out!"

"I know. Sorcha is the portrait artist. Sometimes she can ask the Deceptors for a special request. I've been waiting for her to make arrangements for me to go back to her studio again, so we can move ahead with our plan."

"What's your plan?"

"It's complicated. But we need to find out where the Deceptors put the prisoners who are kept in confinement. I think that's where they've taken Norah. I don't know how much longer she can hold on."

"Let's find her right now!"

"Shh!" Reilly admired Eoghan's zeal but knew he did not understand what they faced. "I'm not sure we can just go wandering the halls of Black Castle."

"Why not? It's been weeks since the explosion of glass in the dining hall, and nothing else seems to be happening. You said yourself that Norah may not be able to wait."

Reilly looked around the darkened room. With only the moonlight peering in through a few high stained glass windows, he reconsidered. "No one else seems to be awake." He shrugged. "All right, then. Let's go."

They walked quietly out of the sleeping chamber and down the hall past other dormitory rooms. Since they knew their way to and from the dining hall and The Library, Reilly decided it would be best to begin at The Library and work their way backwards, exploring corridors they were familiar with.

As they passed through the hall with the brass plaques, Reilly stopped when he noticed something out of the ordinary.

"The one dated 2010 to 2020 is missing."

"It's a weird calendar system." Eoghan shrugged. "Why do they post dates so far in the future?"

"They aren't future dates. They represent the time periods of different prisoners at Black Castle. I came from 2015."

"Blimey! This just gets weirder and weirder. I live in Dublin in 1981. I was visiting my cousin in Wicklow when the Crumble hit. Somehow he managed to escape." Eoghan scanned the wall filled with plaques. "What about Sorcha and Norah?"

"Norah is from my time. Sorcha lived over a hundred years ago."

"Blimey!"

"Black Castle of Wicklow has been here for centuries. The Deceptors? Probably since before time began."

Eoghan was too stunned to respond.

"The castle is the holding place for people who are captured by the Deceptors' lies, regardless of when or where they came from," Reilly said. "My guess is they're preparing for the next imprinting, and that it will be with prisoners who came here from the same decade as I did. That means Norah, too."

Reilly led the way to The Library and stopped outside the metal door. He pressed his ear against it. Eoghan followed.

"I can't make out what they're saying," whispered Reilly. "But it sounds like one of their chants. We've got to look inside."

The boys stepped back and Reilly pulled the handle to open the door a crack. Eoghan bent further down to peek through. Their eyes widened as they watched a single hooded figure wearing a red cape dance around the room, flailing wildly. The figure had no distinguishable body features except for a ghostly face with a grotesquely contorted mouth and eyes like balls of fire protruding hauntingly through a red cloak.

A muffled wailing sound rebounded throughout the cavernous room. The cloaked creature seemed so caught up in the dance that it didn't notice Reilly and Eoghan at the door. They cracked it open wider and peered further into the room. The demon swooped along the towering walls, swirled around the desks, and whooshed under the chairs. It darted up to the ceiling and shot back down like a flaming bullet, then ricocheted off a chandelier.

Eoghan nudged Reilly. "No one else is in there," he said. "Let's get going before that devil sees us."

"Wait," Reilly whispered. "Look!"

Just then the satanic creature let out an eerie laugh that made Reilly's knees wobble. The demon swooped into the alcove and hovered near the inscription on the wall, which lit up from the reflection of its fiery eyes. Reilly's mind filled with confusing flashbacks to the Suzzallo Library. The alcoves were similar, but the inscription, which he first noticed the night he came to Black Castle, was exactly the same. *Good books are a priceless possession. They reveal the minds of creative man and enrich life with fine experience.*

But the monster, which Reilly now suspected was Prince Ukobach himself, emitted a chant that left Reilly with a distorted interpretation of the inscription.

The stories soon will all be mine!
There's no price for exchange.
Hidden in their silent words
Even a child will be deranged.
I need not wait now to possess
My desire within the flames.
The fine experience of a body
Keeps emptied souls in shame.

Prince Ukobach screeched horrifically and swooshed around the alcove again. Then he disappeared through the wall, just above the inscription.

Reilly slowly pushed the door open, just wide enough for him and Eoghan to squeeze through. He rubbed his arms, trying to warm himself. Eoghan's teeth started to chatter, and he clenched his jaw to keep it still.

"I thought Hell was supposed to be hot," Eoghan whispered.

Reilly glanced around the entire room, and then focused on the alcove. "Maybe Hell isn't a place," he said as he walked toward the alcove. "Maybe it exists inside souls who have no heart." Reilly stepped closer to the inscription and reached his finger up to the word *life*. As it touched the wall, he continued, "Hearts fade in the fire, but they die when they become as cold as stone."

"Now what?" Eoghan asked.

"We go through the wall."

"Riiight!" Eoghan drawled.

Reilly ignored his response and ran his hands along the wall.

"What are you doing?"

"There's got to be an opening somewhere." Reilly moved his hands deliberately around the contours of each large stone, pushing slightly and feeling for anything unusual. Eoghan started to prod the stones at the other end of the alcove.

For a moment, Reilly hoped that if they found an opening, it would be another portal that would lead them somewhere far away from Black Castle. But the frigid air did not evoke the warmth or stillness he had felt when he entered the other portals.

Walking toward the center of the alcove, where the inscription on the wall began, the word *priceless* caught his eye. The *i* was not dotted. Instinctively, he bent over and retrieved the ruby from his hidden pocket. Holding it firmly between two fingers, he lifted the gem to the wall and placed it into a round indentation that was barely visible, where the dot on the letter was missing. The jewel sparkled in the dark room. Suddenly a section of the floor beside Reilly swooshed open to reveal a wide spiral staircase that descended into a dark abyss. He heard a strangled heave from Eoghan.

"You go first, Eoghan. I'll grab the ruby and follow right behind you."

"Maybe you should leave it there," Eoghan suggested as he peered below. "What if the floor closes up when we're down there?"

"We'll find another way out. Go!"

As Eoghan stepped into the darkness, Reilly snatched the ruby and leapt into the floor. Just as his head cleared the surface, the floor slid shut. Reilly lifted up the ruby to cast its reddish glow ahead. He descended a few more stairs until he stood beside Eoghan.

The steps declined gradually, leading the boys into damp air. Without a railing to hold on to, the boys walked close to each other and avoided looking over the edge.

"It's a good thing you grabbed that rock," Eoghan whispered. "We wouldn't be able to see a thing without it."

Reilly nodded.

Something swished below them with an eerie moan. Reilly cupped both hands over the ruby, and for a moment, he and Eoghan stood in utter darkness.

Whoosh! Reilly shuddered. Something swept against his bare shoulder … a moan blew past his ears … Holding the ruby tightly in his left fist, Reilly spontaneously brushed off his shoulder with his empty hand … and he heard the demon plummet down the stairwell! Losing his balance, he knocked into Eoghan, and the two boys tumbled down into the black hole.

They screamed, somersaulting through the darkness. Reilly dug his fingers deeply into his palm, squeezing the ruby more tightly. The stench was nauseating—thick and pungent—and reminded him of the forest smells when he first arrived in Wicklow, in the middle of a Crumble. Seconds later, Reilly and Eoghan plunged into warm liquid, thick and vile. He resurfaced, gasping for air and holding the ruby above his head. He coughed and sputtered from the bitter and foul taste of the liquid.

"Eoghan? Are you there?"

"Right behind you. Is this what I think it is?"

"It tastes like blood."

"Blimey! I'm gonna puke!" He retched but nothing came up.

"Look!" Reilly shone the gem ahead of them. "The stairs end there, at that ledge."

Clutching the ruby, he swam hard in the putrid blood towards the edge of the pool. He hoisted himself onto the narrow ledge that curved into the darkness and reached out his other hand for Eoghan. Together, they scrambled to their feet. Facing each other, they watched the slimy blood slide down their arms, over their tunics, and off their bodies, as if it was alive. They shook their legs as the remainder drained from their feet onto the ledge, and then slid into the pool.

Reilly lifted the hem of his tunic, which now hung almost to his ankles. He fumbled for the pockets and lifted the flap where he kept the berries. He found only a small clump of mashed red guck, but the canister of ointment was safe inside the left pocket.

Lifting the flap on the right pocket, he gingerly pulled out the flower. It had changed from ashen to dark grey and, for the first time since the night of the Eagle Harbor fireworks when he placed it behind Norah's ear, it had wilted.

"We're too late," he whispered.

He lifted his right arm across his chest and held it at his heart, covering his branding symbol with his clenched fist, which held both the ruby and the clump of petals. For a moment, he hung his head and just tried to breathe. He had come so far to find Norah, and now he feared he would never see her alive again.

The thick darkness closed in on Reilly, and he started to hyperventilate.

"Bend over," Eoghan said, as he pushed Reilly's head down.

The sudden movement caused Reilly to open his fist, and the ruby lodged in the center dot of his branding mark. The petals fell to the rock ledge. At that moment, a faint melody rang up from the pool beneath them.

Imagine love can change it all
And bring you back to me.

Reilly stood up tall and listened harder.

"Did you hear that?" he asked.

"I did," Eoghan replied. "What does it mean?"

"Maybe she's still alive!" Reilly was infused with hope that welled up from his soul and seemed to shine from his heart through the ruby imbedded in his skin. He picked up the wilted petals and began to walk along the ledge.

Illuminated by the ruby, he and Eoghan moved along the ledge, circling the pool. Spotty red footprints trailed behind them. A slow dripping sound began to reverberate off the walls. Inching their way further along, they noticed a narrow pipe that jutted from the wall and steadily drained more blood into the pool, one drop at a time. On the other side of the pipe, there was an opening into another dark corridor.

Reilly watched the blood drip for a moment. Then he walked with Eoghan into the dark tunnel.

Chapter Twenty-Six

Hell

The tunnel reminded Reilly of his nightmares about hooded monsters chasing him in a dark cave. But he knew he wasn't sleeping. This was real. He pulled his shoulders back and lifted his chin higher. The ruby glowed, lighting the way a few feet in front ahead of them.

Reilly feared that at any moment he and Eoghan would be surrounded by Deceptors, groping and grappling for their bodies. Nevertheless, he moved ahead steadfastly. He had faced demons before and was prepared to face Prince Ukobach himself, if he had to.

Just then, it occurred to Reilly why they had not seen the Deceptors in the tunnel.

"They must be planning another Crumble," he whispered.

"Finding more victims," Eoghan agreed.

"What's your story, Eoghan? How did you fall into their trap?"

"I just got lazy and didn't see them coming. I thought it was some kind of elaborate joke."

"And now?"

"There's nothing funny about Hell."

Some time later, a dim light appeared in the distance. Relieved, Reilly sprinted forward and soon saw a light trickle through bars at the top of a closed metal door. He stopped in front of it and looked for a handle, but there was none. He returned the flower petals to his pocket.

"Give me a hand," he said.

Eoghan clasped his fingers, and Reilly raised a foot to Eoghan's hands for a boost. Reilly reached for the bars and grasped them firmly to hoist himself up.

Too stunned to speak, he stared into a barren room, lit only by a small torch jutting out from the back wall. A person with a shaved head and both shoulders bare lay on the ground, facing the barred door. It looked lifeless. Reilly knew it was Norah.

He tried to rattle the bars, but they would not budge. Eoghan lost his grip, and Reilly fell to the ground.

"It's her," Reilly said softly. "She looks near death."

Eoghan's eyes widened. He didn't know what to say, so he simply clasped his hands again and boosted Reilly back up the door.

"Norah ..." Reilly whispered. Then again louder, "Norah! Can you hear me?" She wore a red sleeveless tunic, but her branding mark was visible on the front right shoulder. He watched the mark to determine if it moved with the rhythm of her breath, or if she breathed at all.

Reilly pulled himself up higher, so the glow of the ruby implanted in his shoulder would project into the room. Glancing around, he saw nothing in the room except Norah and the torch.

He wondered what happened and how she had come to Black Castle. Why did Ukobach want *her*? The door he was clinging to appeared to be the only way in or out, but he could neither feel nor see a handle on the inside.

"Norah! Norah!" He spoke a little more loudly. "It's Reilly! Can you hear me?" She still did not respond. "Let me down," he whispered, and Eoghan moved out of the way.

Out of habit, Reilly placed his hand to his chest, but he felt no piercing pain. What he felt now was something deeper than he could describe. He knew the ruby was protecting his heart from dying the moment he saw Norah. The imbedded gem magically filled his entire soul with a love for her so deep that he could not fully comprehend it. He began to wonder if, by some peculiar decree of fate, his love for Norah had put her life in peril, rather than being the power that could reach her. Could Prince Ukobach know that Norah and Reilly felt for each other something that a demon was not capable of feeling? Was that why the Prince of Hell was so obsessed with Norah?

Reilly considered his assets: a small canister of ointment, a crumpled grey flower, remains of mashed berries, and his new friend. He knew the ruby must remain imbedded in his chest, at least until he returned to The Library. If it did not, even the thought of Norah would attack his body, leaving no strength for him to save her.

Trying to think of any possible solution, he consciously summoned his ability for imagination, and an idea surged into his thoughts and resonated in his soul. He remembered Grania telling him, *"One drop of sweetness is infused into every swallow of bitterness."* He retrieved the canister from his pocket.

"Hold this," he said, handing it to Eoghan.

Then he fetched all but one of the petals, and placed them in Eoghan's other hand. He scraped the remaining ointment from the canister and smeared it onto the cluster of petals, then rolled it all into a small ball. He took a handful of the mashed berries from his other pocket and rolled the ball into the red mush. The remains of the bitter berries clung to the ball, and Reilly held it up to inspect it. A sweet odor permeated the air around them.

"It's the only thing I can think of," he said.

Eoghan raised his brow, but nodded in agreement. Cupping his hands tightly again, he hoisted Reilly up to the barred window of the door.

"I've got one shot to make it land close enough that she can smell it. Hopefully, it'll be strong enough to wake her."

Reilly focused on Norah's face and drew in a deep breath. He held the ball of balm and aimed it directly toward her nose. He fired it like a spitball. As it flew through the air, he held his breath and gripped the bars more tightly, watching the ball fly as if in slow motion—and land a foot from Norah's mouth.

"Good enough," he said. "Norah! Norah!" He continued to call her name.

Eoghan lost his grip again, and Reilly landed on the ground.

"Sorry." Eoghan shook out his fingers and stretched his shoulders.

Just then they heard a noise come from inside the dungeon room. Eoghan quickly hoisted Reilly up again, and Reilly peered into the room. Norah's chest rose slightly and Reilly saw her move a finger.

"Norah!" he whispered. He did not want to frighten her. "Norah, it's me, Reilly."

Norah breathed in more deeply, and whimpered softly.

"Norah, wake up. I brought you something to eat."

She let out a longer moan, and Reilly saw her struggle to open her eyes. She lay still as she focused on the sticky ball in front of her. With a labored effort, she slid her hand along the ground to reach the ball, placed her fingers over the gift, and rested a moment.

"You've got to eat it, Norah," Reilly urged. "It will taste bitter, but it will give you strength."

Closing her eyes again, Norah carefully held the ball and moved it closer to her mouth. She inhaled deeply, fluttered her eyes open, and stared at the delicacy.

"Reilly," she muttered.

More than anything, Reilly wished he could break through the door, hold Norah gently in his arms, and feed her the healing balm. Instead, in an effort to infuse energy into her, he focused on breathing calmly and steadily, blowing his intentions toward her.

"You can do it, Norah," he whispered.

She picked up the ball and slowly brought it to her mouth. She parted her parched lips wide enough to take only a nibble. Norah sucked softly until the delicacy melted enough to swallow.

"That's great, Norah," Reilly encouraged. "Now finish the rest of it."

Norah opened her mouth wide enough to eat the remainder of it. Still lying on her side, she lifted her cheek and faced the ceiling as she chewed. Reilly was quiet; he wanted her to finish eating before he spoke to her again.

Eoghan groaned and dropped Reilly to the ground again. He shook out his fingers and rubbed them together rapidly. A cold breeze blew through the barred window and chilled Reilly to the bone. He quickly covered the jewel in his chest with his hand. Then he and Eoghan both froze and stared at each other. Reilly motioned for Eoghan to boost him up the door again. Still keeping a hand over his chest, he stretched up to grab the bar and pulled himself high enough to peek into the room.

Reilly peered past the window and saw Prince Ukobach in his red hooded cape, hovering above Norah. She had regained enough strength to sit up but kept her eyes closed, refusing to look at the demon.

Ukobach began to chant.

I've chosen you above the rest
To be my endless heart,
For when we two become as one
Our bodies never part.
Your compassion ever drains
Into the pool of sin;
There's no escape for emptied souls—
The story starts again.

The light cast a dark shadow across Norah's face, and Reilly saw a single tear fall down her cheek. She opened her eyes and looked toward the door into the darkened room. Prince Ukobach swooped against her body, lifting her to her feet. She closed her eyes, waiting for the assault to end.

Opening her eyes once more, Norah held her gaze on Reilly until the monster covered his prize with his cape. Then the Prince of Hell disappeared, clutching Norah in his despicable cloak.

Chapter Twenty-Seven

Shooting Stars

Reilly could only hope that the prince from Hell was so distracted by his own insatiable desire for a body that he hadn't noticed his presence.

The climb up the winding staircase took much longer than Reilly expected. He and Eoghan were exhausted by the time they reached The Library. As they approached the final few steps, the ruby fell from his chest; he just managed to catch it as the stairwell opened into the alcove. The floor closed behind them, and Reilly and Eoghan returned to their sleeping quarters unnoticed. The blood on their bodies disappeared; traces of it had dried and now blended in with their red tunics.

Within minutes, Eoghan started to snore. Reilly lay on his cot and stared into the darkness. He reviewed in his mind the Affirmations of the Stelladaur.

I am eternal, without time or space.
I am creativity without end.
I am realization and manifestation as One.
I am all possibilities.
I am the open mind and the gentle heart.
I am nature.

He had done his best to understand each one and embody its meaning since he had arrived in Wicklow. But he knew one more affirmation remained, and he would need his Fireglass to find the portal where he would learn about it in more detail.

Morning arrived before Reilly thoroughly determined his next plan. When they arrived at The Library for another day of work, his hope for a new chance to help Norah dramatically increased: dozens of freshly-shaven newcomers filed into the room. Another Crumble meant the Deceptors would have more stories to choose from and more bodies to imprint. With luck, they would be more inclined to agree with Sorcha's idea to allow Reilly to narrate at the reading—not that he wanted to read all the stories, but he needed to get back to the parlor to retrieve his Fireglass.

Finally, after the usual chant to announce dinner, Reilly was summoned to the parlor. When his escort disappeared through the parlor wall, he turned to Sorcha.

"I guess you didn't get much sleep last night either," he said. "You look exhausted."

"More prisoners than usual were captured this time," Sorcha replied. "They were taken from a town further north. But there's talk of an even bigger Crumble coming to the West Woods. I'm worried about my family."

Tuma stood beside Sorcha and leaned against her leg. Reilly greeted his dog and hugged her tightly. "What are we going to do, girl?"

"There's something else, Reilly."

Reilly stroked his dog and looked up at Sorcha.

"I used the Fireglass last night. I know you said not to, but after I was done with the portraits in the Shaving Room, I heard this awful wailing I hadn't heard before. I couldn't tell where it was coming from, and Tuma was upset." Reilly stood up to listen to Sorcha. "Anyway, I asked Tuma if the noise was coming from somewhere outside Black Castle. She perked up her ears—the way she does when she agrees—and I knew the Fireglass would help. I looked through it, right into Tuma's eyes, as you did before."

"What did you see?"

"My mother. She was trying to calm a baby. It must have been Roisin."

Reilly nodded.

"Roisin screamed uncontrollably and arched her back, as if she was having a seizure. Reilly, she looked as if she was possessed by something—or someone."

"She was imprinted?"

"I don't know. I think imprintings only occur at the bonfire, and I've never painted a portrait of someone as young as Roisin before."

"Lottie told me Deceptors prey on weak members of a family. A baby's aura is usually strong." Reilly paced the floor. "Babies and young children are sensitive to any disturbance in a home's aura, so Roisin may carry negative energy."

"Someone else in my family may be in danger!"

"Or maybe Roisin was possessed."

"What do you mean?"

"Last night I saw Prince Ukobach in The Library, doing a bizarre dance. He was wailing a chant about possessing the body of a child, and then he disappeared through the wall with a horrific laugh."

"Oh, that dear baby!" Sorcha lamented. "We've got to do something!"

"We will, Sorcha, but we've got to be careful how we do it. Did the Deceptors agree to your suggestion of a reading?"

"Yes. The reading will be the morning of the auction."

"What? A reading, an auction, and a festival—all in one day? That will be a busy Hallow's Eve."

"It's only a week away, Reilly. Prince Ukobach has agreed to order you to come here each day to practice. He believes if you do this, the stakes at the auction will be higher. Auctions are rare, and the Deceptors thrive on competition."

"What do they offer Ukobach in exchange for the person being sold?"

"The prince prefers to imprint the strongest ones. Prisoners who dare to challenge his power by saying they will escape Black Castle—or worse, declare that they will rescue someone else—are the ones he wants most. For them, the price is high. Often, a Deceptor will bid on several imprintings."

"But what do the Deceptors who win the bid give to Ukobach?" Sorcha pressed.

"Their claim on a body—a claim that is irreversible even at a Festival of Fire."

"I don't understand. I thought they could only imprint one body at a time."

"I'm not sure. But currently there aren't enough captured prisoners to keep every Deceptor in a body at all times. Black Castle is like a holding place for them. But they're impatient—they would give up multiple imprintings for the opportunity to possess a stronger soul."

Reilly sat on a chair and stroked Tuma's back. He knew Lottie was a strong soul and was glad she was safely disguised.

"You're a strong soul, too, Sorcha."

She looked down. "I used to be," she said. "Now I'm not sure strength is an advantage."

"Your privileges here remain because of your strength, not in spite of it."

Sorcha nodded and sighed deeply, then walked to a table in the corner of the room.

"They brought me the master Story Screen," she said. She tapped a point on the desk and a holographic screen appeared. "We can access all the stories the prisoners are writing. They are sorted, with the author's portrait, by his or her date of arrival."

"How many will be imprinted this time?"

"I'm not sure. The Deceptors wait until a prisoner's heart has been weakened at Black Castle. Apparently, human blood fuels their fire."

Reilly grimaced and walked to the desk.

"It's important to write your own story," Sorcha continued. "Whenever you try to write someone else's story or write just to please others, a bit of your heart fades."

Reilly scanned the portraits that appeared randomly on the hologram. He recognized a few of them from the Embassy courtyard. There seemed to be about the same number of men and women, as well as a cast of young people of various ages, but no babies. He wondered if that was not just because an infant's aura is strong, but also because someone else tells his story until he is old enough to write it himself.

"Of course she would scream," he whispered.

"Who?"

"Roisin. She must be so frightened every time Ukobach, or any Deceptor, casts a spell on her."

"Then you mean she *was* imprinted?"

"Not exactly. But she senses evil is near. My guess is Deceptors sometimes prey on babies—haunt them, so to speak—until they're old enough to be taken." Reilly stared at the portraits on the master Story Screen and then added, "Ukobach will use any tactic to disrupt a family."

"And yet she can't explain to anyone what happened to her," Sorcha added with a sigh. "She can only cry."

"But is it the child or the demon who is crying?" he said. Sorcha frowned and Reilly paced. "No one can completely understand another person's story."

Sorcha walked over to Reilly and knelt beside him. "Are you okay?"

Reilly stared into Tuma's silver eyes. "Maybe people are in so much pain that it's impossible for them to find words to write their story."

Sorcha put her hand on Reilly's shoulder. He blinked back his tears.

"Love is the only language that truly understands every story." As he spoke, he had the extraordinary feeling that he had in his soul the ability to love all people. Not just his family and friends, like his mom and Eilam … and not just Norah, the girl he ached to be with … but also those who were difficult to love because they seemed strange to him, like Pucatrows … or even those who were despicable, like Travis Jackson. Perhaps people like Travis had been taken so skillfully by Deceptors, their hearts evaporated. "Can I have the Fireglass, please?" he asked Sorcha.

"Of course." She reached into her pocket for the treasure and handed it to Reilly.

"We won't be long, Sorcha." With that, Reilly held the device infront of Tuma's eyes and adjusted the focus as he looked through it, directly into Tuma's eyes.

"Wait! Can I—?"

But Reilly and Tuma had already zipped through a sliver of space to another dimension. This time when they arrived, Lottie did not take the form of the albino dog.

"Cover your eyes!" Reilly shouted before he registered the silence surrounding them. He wished he had spoken more softly.

A terrific sandstorm whirled about and obscured their view. They shielded their eyes with both arms and squinted at the endlessly swirling, silently colliding white particles. The sand did not feel harsh against their skin—to their surprise, it was as soft as silk. Reilly breathed in deeply and noticed that it was easy to do so. This was no ordinary sand.

"It's beautiful!" Lottie whispered. "It sparkles like millions of delicate diamonds."

Reilly smiled and relaxed as the magical particles danced around them. He reassured himself that travelling through portals invariably brought him experiences that expanded his imagination. Portal travel provided new awareness about things that were in front of him but which he had not noticed before. Just as he thought something similar was occurring again, the sand dissipated and settled on the ground.

Blinking hard, Reilly focused on what was, indeed, right in front of him. "Wow!" He gasped and pointed to a huge structure. "That's more spectacular than the solid jade Embassy!"

"It's made entirely of glass!" Lottie whispered.

Reilly took Lottie's hand, and they walked toward the main entrance, gazing up at the brilliant colors and light that emanated from inside the building. As they stepped up to the front door, he reached for the knob, which looked like an oversized Stelladaur. When he touched it, he felt as if his entire body was infused with an exhilarating light. The cosmic energy coursed through him with a force more powerful than it was when he first touched his own Stelladaur. Allowing the feeling to permeate his soul, he turned the knob and the door swung open.

They stared up at a vast ceiling of multicolored nebulae, each one moving into and out of globular forms as it transformed into intersecting shapes. A melody that reminded Reilly of his own Stelladaur song resonated throughout the cavernous glass rotunda. With the strange music enveloping his soul, Reilly thought if Tuma had been with him, he might have found the portal to return home.

Nevertheless, consistent with each time he had accessed portals before, an unusual creature greeted him.

"The view is much clearer after the dust settles," the sand creature said. "Don't you agree?"

"Uh … yes. Yes, I do." Reilly focused his eyes to make sure he was seeing the creature accurately. He could not tell if it looked more like a small, oddly shaped Christmas tree, with glittering white lights and a strange star for a head, or if it was a giant twinkling Stelladaur with eyes and a mouth. "Are you made of sand?"

"Stardust, actually." Gracefully, the creature moved closer to Reilly and Lottie. "I am Anusha, the Morning Star Princess."

"What is this place?" Lottie asked.

"You have come to the Star Palace. This is where we create a Stelladaur for each child born on your planet. Stardusters also make the doors."

Reilly looked at Lottie and knew she did not understand.

"Star Palace? What doors?" she asked.

"A Stelladaur is created for each human soul," Reilly explained with a smile. "When the soul is ready, he or she will find his own Stelladaur, to hold and to keep."

"That's right," Anusha said. "When a person searches for light—or greater understanding of themselves—his search causes stardust light to emerge behind his own Star Door, and then to transform into a Stelladaur jewel. The Stelladaur travels through the Star Door to Earth."

"Like a shooting star?" Lottie asked.

"Precisely," Anusha said. "It lands in the spot where the one who summoned it can find it."

Lottie nodded her head. "Maybe so, but it didn't seem easy to find *my* Stelladaur."

Reilly stepped closer to Anusha. "I know what's inside the stardust," Reilly said.

"Of course you do," Anusha agreed softly.

"Love. The seventh Affirmation of the Stelladaur is *I am Love.*"

Reilly closed his eyes to allow the extraordinary feeling to fill his soul again. *Was it possible to love the unlovable? Could he love someone he did not trust? Could compassion reach even the truly wicked?*

At that moment, he realized that if he accessed the power of light that emanated from his Stelladaur—the essence of his own soul—he could truly know love.

"But from where does the light in the stardust come?" Reilly asked Anusha.

"Follow me," Anusha said. "I will show you."

The Star Princess led the way out of the rotunda and through a solid, translucent door decorated with a circle of etched Stelladaurs. They stepped into a vast open space—a room that appeared to extend forever. Hundreds of Stardusters worked busily at long tables, scooping and pouring the glittering particles that spilled from a conglomerate of glass pipes intertwined above their star-shaped heads and sparkling hands. As the workers allowed the light-filled stardust to trickle from their hands, Stelladaurs took form and the jewels were carefully handed to another worker. The priceless gems were then placed on an invisible conveyer that moved around the perimeter of the tables and disappeared behind a wall of multicolored glass.

"The Stelladaurs stay in the Waiting Sky until it's their time to emerge through their Star Door," Anusha said softly. "Follow me."

She led Reilly and Lottie past dozens of rows of colorful glass worktables, smiling at other Stardusters as they went. The newly formed Stelladaurs glistened in an endless array of colors.

Soon Anusha stopped in front of a glass escalator. She stepped onto the transporter and motioned for Reilly and Lottie to join her. They ascended effortlessly and silently into a glittery night sky.

"Once the Stelladaurs are placed in the Waiting Sky, they twinkle continuously until they are claimed," Anusha explained. "They do this to try to get the attention of the children they were created for. But often children are reprimanded for wishing upon stars, and soon they grow old and fear the power of their imagination. In time, they forget to look up."

Reilly nodded, making sense of what the princess said. "We saw the unclaimed Stelladaurs from under the sea, with Sam."

"And the discarded ones, too," Lottie said. "There are so many of them! Isn't there something more we can do?"

They approached a landing and stepped off the escalator. "Everyone must find his or her own Stelladaur, Lottie, and then decide what to do with it. Stardusters open the doors and send each jewel on its way. Occasionally we provide assistance from here, but usually we rely on those who have found their Stelladaur to help those who haven't."

Anusha moved to a silver railing with a gossamer curtain suspended behind it. She spread her arms wide, and the curtain opened. "The Waiting Sky!"

Reilly and Lottie grasped the railing and stood spellbound at the vast expanse glittering before them.

The Stelladaurs twirled in place, each one suspended in front of a shiny silver rectangle with a unique star shape cut in the center. Brilliant light emanated from the Stelladaurs, and Reilly wondered how his eyes could withstand such intense brightness. "Those are the doors … hanging in front of each Stelladaur," he whispered, not wanting to intrude on the majestic space around him.

"Yes. Each door is designed to fit each unique Stelladaur precisely," Anusha said softly. "Look, over there." The princess pointed to a nearby Star Door. As it opened, a celestial echoing melody sprang from it. The Stelladaur zipped through the door and launched downward in a streak of light, then disappeared from view.

"It's so beautiful," Lottie whispered, as she wrapped her arms around herself.

"It's sad that so many are unclaimed or discarded," Reilly said. "I wish we could bundle up all the Stelladaurs and deliver them ourselves."

The princess replied, "You cannot rob another of the opportunity to search for his or her own light." She gathered a bit of stardust from the air into her hands and continued. "Yet, you can help restore hope with the treasures you already have."

With that, Anusha blew the dust from her hands onto Reilly and Lottie … and in an instant, they transported back to Sorcha's parlor.

"Where did you go?" Sorcha demanded. "I wanted to go with you!"

Tuma wagged her tail and nuzzled Sorcha's leg.

"I'm sorry, Sorcha. I don't know exactly what will happen when I go through a portal."

Sorcha frowned. "Well … now what?"

Reilly paced the floor, thinking hard about Anusha's message. He caught sight of something glittery out of the corner of his eye, walked to the table, and reached for Sorcha's basket of rowanberries.

Sorcha looked into the basket. "What is that on the berries?"

Reilly smiled. "It's stardust."

Chapter Twenty-Eight

Sea of Stelladaurs

Reilly lay awake most of the night, searching the corners of his imagination to come up with an explanation for the stardust on the berries. What was Anusha trying to tell him? The healing power of the berries sometimes only lasted for a little while, and he wasn't sure they were potent enough for the prisoners of Black Castle. He wondered if the stardust increased the berries' effectiveness.

As the autumn morning light peeked through the high windows, it occurred to Reilly that Grania had said the *ruby* berries would *restore the blood.* He thought the value was in the berry itself, but now he wondered if the berries could change into real rubies. Could he use precious gems to barter with the Deceptors?

Overriding these questions and speculations was his most desperate concern: determining where Ukobach had taken Norah and whether she was still alive. He listened for her melody and the lyrics to her song—even a single note would have been encouraging. But there was nothing. The best he could do was play it over and over in his mind and listen for his heart to tell him what to do.

When the other prisoners started to move about their sleeping quarters, Reilly decided to face the inevitable. But he was not ready to deal with Eoghan.

"Blimey! Were you gone all night?"

"It feels like it." Reilly stretched and sat up on his cot.

"What happened?"

"It's complicated." He leaned forward on his knees and lowered his head. "It's about love."

"Obviously! I know you love the girl." Eoghan sat down next to Reilly. "Tell me something I *don't* know."

Reilly turned to face Eoghan. "I've got to find a way to approach the Deceptors … with love," he whispered.

"What the hell are you talking about?"

Reilly spoke firmly but softly. "*Hell* is exactly what I'm talking about. It's not a place. It's what we feel when our heart is tormented, either by our own choices or because of someone else. And sometimes when bad stuff happens, because of either or both."

"Call it what you want, but that bloody dungeon—no pun intended—felt like Hell to me." Eoghan shook his head. "I'm sorry, chum, but I'm getting out of this place tomorrow—with or without you."

"You can't just walk out. They'll bring you back, or worse."

"I heard a group of the newcomers talking about another Crumble—an even bigger one—in the works for tomorrow. I'm going to make a run for it when the Deceptors take the new prisoners to the Shaving Room. Those monsters seem to be preoccupied at that time, and it's my best chance to make it to the tunnel you told me about."

"Eoghan, please! Don't try it!" Reilly took Eoghan by the arm, but he jerked it away.

"I'm going, Reilly, and you should, too. I'm sorry." Eoghan stood up and joined the other prisoners lining up for The Library.

Twice more during the day, Reilly tried to convince Eoghan to wait, but he refused to respond. Reilly battled with his own inability to do something that might make a difference, let alone save lives. He managed to write more of his story, though there were long periods when he stared at the hologram and waited for words to come. He was more than relieved when the usual voice announced dinnertime.

He had just taken the first morsel of bread when a Deceptor summoned him. The prisoners watched as the monster escorted him out. On his way, he saw Eoghan glance his way and then quickly lower his eyes. The Deceptor led him to Sorcha's studio.

Although Reilly didn't have a friend in the cavernous dining hall, he understood why Eoghan felt the way he did. Reilly had considered Eoghan both an asset and a liability, but unless something changed, he could not rely on anyone in Black Castle except Sorcha and Tuma.

Once inside the studio, Reilly went directly to the basket of rowanberries. He sifted them through his fingers and watched as they fell back into the basket.

"What are you doing?" Sorcha asked.

"Thinking," he said. "Imagining."

Sorcha and Tuma watched as Reilly reached for the ruby in his tunic pocket. He held the gem closely to his eye and inspected it. "The ruby berries restore the blood," he whispered. "But they must be real rubies."

"What are you mumbling?" Sorcha asked.

Ignoring her question, Reilly asked for his Fireglass and she handed it to him. He opened it to its full length and waited for the etched Stelladaur to spin, as it did each time he prepared to go through a portal.

"I suppose I must stay here again." Sorcha pouted.

"Yep," Reilly said. "Once you find your own Stelladaur, you can access the portals, too."

Reilly grabbed the basket and pulled it up his arm so it hung below his elbow. He wrapped the same arm around Tuma and held the ruby with his fingers in front of her eyes. In his other hand, he grasped the Fireglass and looked through it at the jewel.

In an instant, Reilly and Tuma were transported to the bottom of the cliffs of Black Castle. As they landed Tuma transformed back into Lottie.

"Thank goodness," Lottie said. "It's difficult to remain quiet for so long. And Tuma doesn't enjoy being cooped up in such a small space. She needs some exercise."

Reilly laughed. "Good to see you, too, Grandma."

Looking across the sea, Reilly drew in a deep breath and closed his eyes. "Someday maybe I'll open my eyes and be back at home," he said.

There was a mighty whoosh, and Mor Samhlaiocht surfaced in front of them.

"Climb aboard," Sam said. "The Sea of Stelladaur awaits."

Reilly held the basket above his head as he and Lottie slid into the water. They swam far enough out for the giant whale to take them on his back. With a mighty thrust from his flippers and the thwack of his fluke, Sam propelled them forward across the sea until the cliffs disappeared behind them.

Reilly and Lottie gripped the edge of Sam's front blowhole. Soon they spotted lights on the horizon. As they approached the shore, Sam slowed down and gave a tremendous burst of water from both blowholes. Reilly lost his grip on the basket and watched it soar to the top of Sam's blow. He and Lottie somersaulted along the whale's back and caught Sam's dorsal fin, sixty feet back.

When the blow subsided, the berries miraculously landed undisturbed in the basket, which sat calmly on the membrane covering of Sam's nostril. Reilly and Lottie managed to stand up and run toward the basket, watching as an array of jewels danced like diamonds on the surface of the water.

Reaching Sam's blowhole, Reilly picked up the basket of berries and stared ahead at the brilliant reflections on the water. "The Sea of Stelladaurs!" he said.

"Unclaimed jewels!" Lottie added.

"Indeed," replied Sam. "They are launched from the Waiting Sky when it is determined that they must be reassigned."

"Is there ever a time when a Stelladaur can be claimed by someone other than the person it was created for?" Reilly asked.

"Stardust light is never wasted. When a Stelladaur is underutilized, it can be redesigned and used to help someone else," Sam said.

"Redesigned? Will it still look like a Stelladaur?" Lottie asked.

"The light will take a different form so that others can more easily recognize its value," the whale said.

Reilly looked down at the basket of berries. "I imagine it could change color, too. And even become a different jewel?" he asked.

Sam bobbed slightly in the water. "Now you are beginning to understand."

"Like a ruby." Reilly raked his fingers through the berries. "How can they be transformed?"

"By casting them into the Sea of Stelladaurs. As each rowanberry strikes a Stelladaur, its juice explodes and covers the gem so it appears to be a ruby. The Stelladaur shrinks and changes to the shape and size of a small pea, so that the jewel will be a recognizable treasure."

Reilly walked toward the point of the whale's head. Drawing his hand back, as if he were going to pitch a ball, he threw a handful of berries as far as he could. On impact, the berries exploded and coated some of the Stelladaurs in red. The jewels shrunk and glittered on the water amidst countless glistening Stelladaurs.

"I want to try!" Lottie exclaimed. She reached into the basket, scooped a small handful of berries, flung them outward, and watched more Stelladaurs magically transform. Together, Reilly and Lottie threw the remaining berries into the sea.

Sam released a blow that pulled the gems like magnets to the top of the spray above his blowhole. Reilly and Lottie watched the jewels glitter above them like tiny sparks of fire. It was a fire that Reilly knew would warm the prisoners' hearts and somehow win them victory over the Deceptors … but he did not expect what Sam was about to reveal.

"The rubies will only restore the blood if they are placed directly in the heart," Sam cautioned. "You may offer the prisoners the gift, but each one must accept the ruby without coercion, or it will not save him from the flames of the bonfire."

With that, the blow dispelled and the rubies tumbled into the basket at Reilly's feet. He reached for the basket and gazed at the sparkling jewels.

"There are not enough for all the prisoners," Reilly said.

"Even though the gift is priceless, some will refuse it," Sam replied.

With his own energy waning, Reilly felt the weight of his enormous responsibilities as an Echtra.

"Are you ready?" Reilly asked Lottie.

"She cannot go with you, Reilly," Sam said. "Lottie will return to her home. Remember, you are the Echtra."

Suddenly Reilly felt alone. "What about Tuma?"

"Tuma will be nearby when you need her most. She will remain part of your story, as she always has been."

"I don't understand," Reilly said.

Sam released another mighty blow through his blowhole. The stream of sea spray enveloped Reilly and instantly transported him to the parlor, where he found himself seated in a chair with the basket on his lap.

"Where's Tuma?" Sorcha demanded. "Where's my sister?"

Reilly scowled and shook his head. "She wasn't allowed to return. Apparently she had to go home."

"Will she be safe there?" Sorcha's eyes widened. "There's talk of another Crumble—the worst yet. They are planning to attack the Embassy, Reilly!"

"I know."

Reilly didn't say anything to Sorcha about his deal with Cormack. He shook his head, trying to make sense of what he had done. Would Cormack somehow know that Lottie was also Tuma? And would the troll then demand *Lottie*?

"What are we going to do?" Sorcha demanded.

Reilly lifted the basket so Sorcha could see the berries.

"Mercy! Are those rubies?" she asked.

"Yes." Reilly scooped up the gems and dropped them back into the basket.

"They must be worth a lot of money! That much wealth could change the lives of the poor people of Wicklow!" She stared at the jewels as Reilly stirred them inside the basket. "We must get these to my father!"

"No, Sorcha. These are for the prisoners."

"But the treasure will do them no good here!"

Looking at the brilliant gems, Reilly tried again to make sense of his assignment.

"At first I thought the Deceptors might want them in exchange for bodies. But then I realized their insatiable desire for a body is much greater than their greed." He set the basket on the table.

"Besides, Deceptors can't do anything with money unless they have bodies. Then they can wreak all kinds of havoc. It's so twisted."

Sorcha pulled up her chair to sit across from Reilly and waited for him to continue. Reilly thought about Sam's words. It bothered him that there were not enough rubies for all the prisoners. He was more troubled by the fact that he had to make such a difficult choice: either determine which prisoners to offer a ruby to or offer one to each person and hope there were enough for all who wanted to accept the gift. It wasn't fair that anyone should be given this responsibility, not even an Echtra.

Reilly stood up and paced back and forth, trying so hard to think about the answer that he actually overlooked it. His eyes shifted to the main Story Screen.

"I should take a look at some of those stories," he said.

"Of course. Do you want to practice reading aloud to me?"

"No thanks, not now." He walked across the room to the screen and pulled up a chair. "We have no way of knowing what stories the Deceptors will choose to have me read." He tapped the keyboard and continued. "Look … the list is practically endless. It could be any of these! And with more prisoners arriving tomorrow, I'm not sure reciting any of them right now would help much."

"You'd better sound well-rehearsed during the reading," she said anxiously. "If any portion of this plan goes awry, it could be my demise."

Reilly scowled at Sorcha.

Sorcha's eyes softened. "I'm sorry, Reilly. I know you're doing all you can."

"I just hope it's enough."

"I'm sure you will be convincing." Sorcha stood behind him and put her hands on his shoulders. "Is there something more I can do to help?"

Reilly reached for the basket of rubies on the table beside the Story Screen, and handed it to Sorcha. "Yes. Guard the rubies until

Hallow's Eve. I can only take enough with me to fill my pockets. I need to distribute the rubies to the prisoners who will most likely see their value and hope they will use the jewels correctly to free themselves." Reilly reached into the basket and took a small handful of the jewels. He handed her the empty ointment canister to make more space to carry berries. "I don't need this anymore. Find somewhere to hide it. If the Deceptors see that you possess anything out of the ordinary, the entire plan could turn against us in an instant." Sorcha nodded and took the canister from Reilly. He tucked the rubies into his pockets. "And keep the Fireglass safe."

"I will, Reilly."

"You need to take care of your responsibilities here, just as you regularly do, no matter who shows up at Black Castle tomorrow night after the Crumble. Do you understand what I mean, Sorcha?"

She reached into the basket, gathered a handful of berries, then let them trail back in from her fingers. "Yes," she said as the jewels bounced off the chains around her wrists.

"We don't have the luxury of knowing what's going on in the West Woods right now, or what strategy your father and the Pucatrows have for an attack. But Lottie is home now. When she tells your family what she knows, we can hope they will all be safe."

Sorcha shook her head. "She may not tell them everything."

"She'll tell them what they need to know."

Sorcha walked back toward the far wall, dragging the chains around her ankles. She stopped a foot from the wall and stood still. Then she faced Reilly and softly declared, "My sister came here to rescue me. Now, I may need to help my family—even before I am freed."

"Freedom is found in one's heart, Sorcha. As the Echtra for your family, I will protect it with my life."

Chapter Twenty-Nine

Storybooks

Everyone was asleep when Reilly returned to the dormitory, but for him, it was another restless night. Eoghan's snoring didn't help.

Although Sorcha had given Reilly a little food each time he came to the parlor, it was only a portion of her daily allotment. He felt weak with hunger when he lined up with the others to leave for The Library. The day was wearisome as he tried to think of something mundane to write about. Food was a safe topic, and he spent hours inventing and writing new recipes. Then, by accident, he discovered something about his Story Screen.

Up to this point, to avoid disclosing anything to the Deceptors about his Stelladaur or the portals, Reilly had been careful not to write about his father's death. Today, however, as he wrote about a time when his mother had taught him to make raspberry cheesecake, *the screen* took over and began to reveal random scenes to him. Rather than typing what came to his mind about an event that had already occurred, he began to write about the random scenes appearing on the screen as if they were happening in the present moment, revealing things to him that he did not yet know.

My mom keeps things going at the bakery. She told everyone I've been in Ireland for the school year, staying with relatives. Business has picked up more than ever since Travis was convicted and sentenced to prison.

Travis appeared on the screen, sitting by himself in a cell. This information comforted Reilly somewhat, but he shuddered as he tried to make sense of time. It was July 2015 when Reilly was last at home, and when Travis was arrested. But Reilly knew sentencing usually took many months, and if there was a trial, it could be a year or more. Why did the screen reveal that his mom had been telling people he was staying with relatives for the school year, as if the school year was nearly over? Even though it was, at that moment, October 1896 in Ireland—and it seemed logical that it had only been three months since he had come through the portal in July—he suddenly considered the possibility that he had been in Wicklow much longer than that. He hit the delete button to erase what he had written—still not wanting to divulge any information to the Deceptors that might put him in peril—but the device wouldn't allow it. He kept writing.

James and Chantal are still dating, and they divide their time between running Eilam's Kayak Hut and working at the bakery. They've been back to the Suzzallo Library numerous times to see if they could follow me through the portal.

Reilly pressed the delete button repeatedly, but still, nothing happened. It had worked before, so why, he wondered, wasn't it working now? The pictures continued to appear, and he was compelled to know more, so he continued to write.

They found the key I dropped when I went through the portal door, but it was actually James's key. James is the only one who can use it to go to Tir Na Nog. Unfortunately, James hasn't figured out how to get there.

Everyone has to find his own key to open the portal to his own dreams. Each door can be unlocked only with the right key.

Reilly stopped. He did not know why he was giving this information to the Deceptors, but he wondered if they already knew since he had no control over the scenes that were appearing on the screen. His hands were sweating and his head was swimming. Did this new information mean that in addition to all that he had to face in The Library, he also had to find a key to return home?

It would be Hallow's Eve in two more nights! He would be auctioned and sold to the highest bidding Deceptor. He had tried to fulfill his responsibilities as an Echtra, but the thought of a demon imprinting his body suddenly made Reilly panic.

I can't do it all! I need to look out for myself! Where is my key to the portal? I've got to get out of here! Maybe I should talk to Eoghan and try to escape with him tonight.

He turned around to look at Eoghan.

"Are you still planning to escape tonight?" Reilly whispered.

Eoghan nodded.

"I might come with you. Let's talk about it at dinner."

Eoghan shrugged and Reilly continued to type.

Norah will not survive ...

He dropped his hands from the keyboard.

On the screen, Norah appeared to be looking directly into Reilly's eyes. Tears streamed down her right cheek. On the left side of her face was the dark image of a demon. As if she knew Reilly was watching her, Norah began to sing through her tears. He typed the words as she sang.

I'll hold my breath within the fire
To keep from utter shame.
I'll bleed inside from every vein
Before I yield my name.
But should my heart fade in the night
Before you come to me,
I'll write my soul's caressing song
And sing my dying melody
Love is all I ask of you,
Love will make us free.
Imagine love can change it all,
And bring you back to me.
Imagine love can change it all,
And you'll come back to me.

"How could I forget so quickly?" Reilly whispered.

He shook his head vigorously and took a deep breath before he continued to write.

Love is the only key! I do love you, Norah! But is love enough? What is love?

Dinner was announced, and Reilly's screen shut off automatically. He did not understand why his Story Screen had functioned differently today, but as he walked into the dining hall, three Deceptors surrounded him, and he knew he was about to find out. He hoped the other prisoners would be allowed to eat, rather than being bound to wait for him again.

Winding through countless empty corridors of the castle, Reilly followed one Deceptor, with two more behind him, until they came to a closed door that Reilly had never seen before. The leading Deceptor walked right through it. It swung open, and Reilly entered a circular room that he quickly decided could be Hell itself if he hadn't already determined Hell might not be an actual place. The walls were stamped in blood with branding symbols—a gruesome display of the evil that occurred in Black Castle. Reilly looked up at the high-domed ceiling, where books were suspended and twirled. The front covers showed portraits of prisoners with hair, and the back covers showed them with shaven heads.

Prince Ukobach stood in the shadows at the far end of the room. Reilly walked toward the demon and saw Norah lying on a table behind him. She looked dead.

"What do you think of my gallery, Reilly?" Prince Ukobach jeered.

Reilly watched the other Deceptors leave the room.

"It's just you and me, now," the demon declared. "And of course, your true love." The prince's evil laugh violated Reilly's soul, as well as his ears. "Unfortunately, she is useless to you now. By Hallow's Eve, most of her blood will be drained, and she'll be taken to the bonfire for her imprinting."

Reilly breathed heavily. He stepped closer to Ukobach and saw a tube dangling from underneath the table to the floor.

"Do come. Take a look at her!"

Reilly stopped, but the devil continued.

"Her story was the perfect addition to my private collection—after you deserted her. I especially enjoy those who first seem to have a power greater than my own, but then give it up. Not even I know why they do this. When it's a younger one, I usually possess the body for a much longer time."

Reilly closed his eyes and tried to summon any hint of imagination or affirmation that would help him. Nothing came. He opened his eyes and glared at Prince Ukobach. Intense hatred welled up inside of him, and he was unable to resist the emotion.

"Your contempt is delicious!" The prince cackled loudly. "Now come closer!"

Reilly stepped forward, feeling the rubies in his pockets bump against his knees. He looked away from the demon, focused on

Norah, and approached the table from her right side. Her delicate cheeks were chaffed and ashen, as if charred.

Now only inches away from the table, he wished he could lift her into his arms and warp through a portal home. But doubt surged through his veins like a mad fire, and he knew his wish was not yet a greatest desire. If he were to save her, it would have to become one.

"You are powerful, too, Reilly. I've waited long to imprint an Echtra." Reilly looked up at the demon. "Did you think I didn't know this about you?" Again the prince laughed and then swept his arms around the room. "As you can see, I find enjoyment in possessing both genders. However, I recently left a female body, and I would prefer a male this time." The prince swooped close to Norah and waved the sleeve of his red cloak over her face, brushing her right eyelashes. Her pallid eyelids remained closed. "I will release her body to the Deceptor who bids the highest price—for you!"

Reilly glared, bewildered.

"It's simple, Reilly-boy. The bodies I imprint have no hope of an exchange during a Festival of Fire—or ever! However, bodies taken by other Deceptors can *sometimes* be saved by an Echtra—though this happens rarely. The game will be much more intriguing if we play it with a double exchange. You see, first I will display you to the Deceptors. Then each of them will bid to trade the body they previously chose to imprint in exchange for you. But at the end, I will give Norah to the winner instead—in your place!" Prince Ukobach sneered, pleased with the deception he had planned. Then he glowered at Reilly and said, "She will have a chance to return to Black Castle during a future Festival—but you will not!"

Reilly clenched his jaw and held his hands firmly behind his back to resist the temptation to punch the prince—if only he had a body to punch. He wanted to release Norah immediately, but he knew any attempt now would be futile.

He knew the infernal prince did not have the power to read Reilly's mind, and that engaging in conversation would not be to Reilly's benefit. The voice in Reilly's head was an asset only if it did not drown out the song in his heart.

He reached for Norah's open hand, which hung lifelessly off the narrow table, and cradled her fingers. He gently lifted her hand and tucked it carefully at her side. Trying to look past the demon that hovered above and the grotesque masked image on Norah's face, Reilly wiped the tears from her right cheek with the back of his fingers.

"Your feelings for her are strong," Prince Ukobach said. "But unless she reciprocates on her own, those feelings are useless."

Reilly knew that was a lie. If his love for Norah was to save her, it would be despite her inability to respond to his feelings for her at that moment.

He had loved her from the moment he first saw her in Jolka, and even then he did not know if he would ever see her again. As he held his hand over hers, he continued to feel that Norah was just out of his reach. He stood there, wishing he could take her from the hell she was in. At that moment, his wish came from a place deep inside his soul that he had never felt before. At last! It was a greatest desire!

If he could only have one greatest desire, it would be to be with Norah forever. Reilly wanted this more than he had ever wanted anything before—now, even more than he wanted to go to Tir Na Nog to be with his dad.

Now he understood what Jaida meant when she said if he truly listened, the Spirits of Nature would be felt in his heart and teach him about sacrifice. Even though he was standing in Hell, he listened to his heart and finally understood love.

"I will give you my body for imprinting," Reilly said to Prince Ukobach.

The demon laughed heinously. "I will have it, no doubt, but your magnanimous declaration will not deprive me of amusement at the auction on Hallow's Eve. The dance for the Gods of Ifreann will follow, and at the final hour, during the Festival of Fire, the exchange will occur—all as I have planned."

The door behind Reilly opened. Two Deceptors escorted him back to the dining hall, where the other prisoners waited hungrily. Reilly felt their glares as he walked down the long rows of tables to his chair beside Eoghan.

"What took you so long?" Eoghan whispered. "You should hear what the prisoners are saying about you."

"It doesn't matter," Reilly said.

The jewels above their heads burst into vibrant colors and transformed into platters of food that lowered to the tables as usual. Prisoners dug in with as much enthusiasm as ever.

"You're still not eating much?" Eoghan asked.

"Sorcha gives me food to eat at the studio."

Reilly looked around the room, hoping to see a Deceptor who would take him to the studio, but there was none.

"I'm loading up good," Eoghan said with his mouth full. "From what I hear, the Crumble is underway, and new prisoners will arrive soon. I'm going to need my full strength for the escape." He chewed noisily and looked at his food as he spoke, rather than directly at Reilly. "You coming with me?"

"No."

"Suit yourself." Eoghan washed down his food with a tall glass of strawberry milkshake. Then he shifted in his chair to look at Reilly. "Blimey, mate! You're a damn fool to stay here. You know more about how to escape than anybody else."

"If you believed that, you'd take my advice, Eoghan. You don't know what you're up against."

"I've seen enough to know that I have no chance of survival if I stay here. Getting out tonight, while the biggest Crumble ever occupies the Deceptors, *is* my chance. Any last words of advice?"

Reilly leaned toward Eoghan, pretending that he was going to tell him something important. Instead, he reached for the hem of his tunic and pulled out a small ruby from the hidden pocket. "Take this with you. If you're captured, put it in the center dot of your branding mark."

Eoghan took the jewel and held it in his lap so no one else would see it. "Blimey! It must be worth a ton of money! Not sure why I'd implant it into my chest in a bad sci-fi ritual when I could take it home with me and make some good hard cash. Besides, I've already been captured!" He pointed to Reilly's chest. "The gem you put in your own mark the other night didn't seem to help much. When exactly do you want me to do this bizarre thing?"

Reilly rolled his eyes. "Not here. You'll know when. Just do what I've told you, Eoghan, or you won't make it to the Undertunnels alive."

After dessert, the prisoners filed into place to return to their sleeping quarters. From the corner of his eye, Reilly watched Eoghan sneak out of line into a dark corridor.

Chapter Thirty

Stoney Arch

It was the first night in a long time that Deceptors hadn't escorted Reilly to Sorcha's studio during dinner. He came up with numerous reasons why this might be, but the only logical explanation was that the Deceptors were preoccupied with incoming prisoners from a Crumble, and Sorcha was busy painting their portraits.

Reilly wasn't about to sit on his cot and wait to be summoned.

The hallways between his sleeping quarters and the Portrait Room were unusually quiet. He didn't hear any screaming from the direction of the Shaving Room. When he approached the door to the Portrait Room, he headed left, toward Sorcha's parlor. Reilly had the eerie feeling that he was being followed, though he turned back a number of times and saw no one.

Arriving at Sorcha's parlor, he quietly turned the knob and peeked his head inside.

"Sorcha," he whispered. "Sorcha, are you here?"

He stepped in and the door shut behind him. Reilly heard a sniffing sound coming through the door that connected Sorcha's parlor to her studio. He tiptoed across the small room and pressed his ear against the door. The sniffling sounded like snorting now, and Reilly opened the door a crack. After peering into the room, he swung the door open wide.

"Cormack!" Reilly exclaimed.

The Pucatrow spun around on his dirty heels. "Reilly!" he sniffed. "I'm glad to see you are alive!"

Reilly was glad to see the troll. "How did you get into Black Castle?" he asked.

"Over the years I've made somewhat of a friendship—an association rather—with one of the guards. He admires my spear and has asked for it numerous times. But I could never part with it—until tonight."

"Why tonight?"

"The Crumble in the West Woods has hit so hard that I decided to warn you of the destruction and the possible repercussions." The troll sniffed again. "You smell different, Reilly. That disappoints me."

Reilly crossed his arms. "So you traded your spear in exchange for entrance to Black Castle?"

"The guard would only allow me to enter through the side door into this studio."

"Where is Sorcha?"

"I would imagine she is preparing the Portrait Room. She will have to paint more than usual tonight."

"Then you'll need to be in the Shaving Room."

"Yes, soon. But the guard heard that you were brought here each night to prepare for a reading at the auction, which will be held in forty-eight hours."

"I'm the one being auctioned!"

"Of course."

"Why do you say that?" Reilly remembered he could only be around Cormack a few minutes before the creature fiercely annoyed him.

"Imprinting the body of an Echtra is a rare honor."

Reilly, frustrated that Cormack still seemed to know more about the Deceptors than he would let on, tried to shift his attention. "Tell me about the West Woods. Have the McKinleys been taken?"

"Almost all homes have been destroyed. The Undertunnels were overloaded and several collapsed, trapping hundreds who had hoped to reach the Embassy. The McKinleys arrived safely, though—even Lottie."

"Lottie?" Reilly pretended to be surprised.

"After you left, she went to the Embassy for respite in the courtyard garden. Quin and Brigid thought the Deceptors had taken her, but she told her father she had discovered another tunnel—she called it a portal—that led her to a place of beauty, peace, and even wealth. Apparently that's where she was the whole time she was gone."

This was more information than Reilly expected to hear from anyone other than Lottie. He hoped she hadn't divulged too much information to the Pucatrows just yet. "Did she say what the place was called?"

"Indeed she did!" The troll grinned, displaying his rotten, crooked teeth. "Lottie found Tir Na Nog itself!"

Reilly realized that Lottie had gone directly through the portal to the place he still only dreamed of. "Did she say if anyone else went with her?"

Cormack's smile changed to a pout. "Unfortunately for me, Tuma went with her and remains there."

Reilly glanced at the floor to hide his relief. "I see."

"Hmphf!" the troll snorted. "I find that I am now without my spear and without the promise of Tuma's white hair to bring me solace from the curse of all Pucatrows. I feel naked indeed!"

"I'm sorry," Reilly said. "But if I understand the blood promise we made, our exchange is now voided."

The troll looked genuinely sad. In that moment, Reilly recognized Cormack for who he truly was—a Pucatrow who wished to be free from the curses brought upon his own kind centuries before. Reilly bent down and took the last wilted, ashen flower petal from the pocket in his tunic hem. "I only have one petal left, but I'll give it to you, if you still want it, in exchange for the information you've given me."

Cormack reached for Reilly's hand. He barely touched the petal with snot-covered fingers. "Love dies." He looked up at Reilly through the wiry hair that covered his eyes. "And so I must remain a fire rat forever."

Reilly pulled the troll's hair away from his face and tucked it into a knotted mound on top of his head. Cormack snuffled, this time with tears streaming down his wrinkled face. "No, Cormack," Reilly said. "Love never dies."

The troll blinked as he held the petal tightly in his fist and dropped it in his own pocket. Reilly put his hand on the troll's shoulder and said, "Tell me more about the Crumble in the West Woods."

"Small fires burn throughout the woods, and all the plants for the Infusionists have been destroyed. The attack came more swiftly and with more force than the magistrate had anticipated. He did not have time to prepare the people. There are more deaths than ever before, and resources are extremely limited. Even the rowan tree was burned to the ground."

"You know about the rowan tree?"

"It was a relief to talk with Grania when I felt weighed down from the responsibilities as Head Pucatrow." Reilly's eyes met Cormack's, and he smiled. Even someone like Cormack might need a true friend!

"And you are sure all the McKinleys are safe?"

"Yes. But the child screamed so loudly and for such a long time that Brigid herself wondered if they should find Roisin another home. The magistrate surmised the child may have aided the Deceptors in locating prisoners."

Still not knowing if Cormack knew all that the Deceptors were capable of, Reilly continued to probe. "Did the magistrate say how a baby could do that?"

"No. He just said he had a feeling about it."

"Anything else?"

Cormack wiped his nose on his sleeve and nodded. "After you left, an older gentleman arrived uninvited at the McKinley tree home. Katell didn't sound the house alarm and the gentleman already knew the family code, so the bird let him pass. The man was able to calm the child instantly—Brigid said it was almost like magic. He said he came from a town far away, west of Wicklow, to help the magistrate at the Embassy."

Reilly's eyes widened and his heart beat rapidly. He took a step closer to Cormack, waiting to hear more.

"Apparently the man is skilled in understanding the Deceptors' tactics. He and the magistrate were impressed by my plan for the Pucatrows to put out the fires with our bricks. But now that many of the Undertunnels have collapsed, it's doubtful that we can transport enough of them to the bonfire." Cormack lowered his head. "We don't seem to be of much use to the magistrate right now."

Reilly patted Cormack's back. "Of course you are. Things change all the time, but the Pucatrows are needed now more than ever." Reilly kneeled so he would be at eye level with the troll. Even though he knew the answer to his next question, he had to ask it. "What is the old gentleman's name?"

"The people of Wicklow call him Malie the Magician."

Reilly closed his eyes and whispered, "Eilam!"

Cormack wrinkled his nose. "No, it's Malie, and he can do all kinds of tricks."

Filled with renewed courage, Reilly stood tall. "Cormack, you must get to the Shaving Room and take care of your responsibilities there. We don't want to create any suspicion. I'll stay here and practice the readings."

Cormack nodded and grinned. "I hope we can finish repairing the ladder with this next batch of hair." The troll exited the studio through the outside door so he could re-enter Black Castle the way he usually did on shaving days.

Reilly tapped on the Story Screen keyboard and flipped through the portraits. He randomly chose stories and read them aloud. He tried to read with enthusiasm and expression in his voice, but the truth was that many of the stories were so depressing that it was difficult to make the person sound enticing. Reilly considered changing his voice inflection based on the content of each story. Maybe the chances of the prisoners remaining at The Library and of delaying the imprintings would increase if he read the stories in a monotone.

But that wouldn't work. For Prince Ukobach's double exchange to work—which meant Reilly would be auctioned at a high price and then exchanged for Norah—Reilly would need to sound enthusiastic and convincing while reading the stories. The greater the number of bodies chosen for imprinting on Hallow's Eve, the greater the likelihood that Prince Ukobach would take his body, and Norah would be given to another Deceptor—and then she might escape at a future Festival of Fire.

Reilly tapped through the portraits to find another story to practice, but he was interrupted when the outside door blew open. A Deceptor stepped into the room and commanded him to follow.

The night air was filled with smoke and the smell of burning wood. Reilly followed the Deceptor to the front corner of Black Castle and watched as hundreds of new prisoners waited in line to enter the main doors. He wasn't close enough to identify the incoming prisoners, but he was sure they included people the McKinleys knew well. He rubbed his bald head as he followed the Deceptor past the far hedge toward the bonfire. The rubies in his pockets bumped at his shins, and he panicked because he still did not know how he would distribute them. How would he convince each prisoner that the gem could save his or her life?

Rounding the corner beyond the hedge, he watched as more prisoners threw their tree limbs into the fire and returned to their place in the line. Further ahead, he saw someone standing under the stone arch across from Sorcha's station. He squinted to see through the smoke. It was Eoghan, chained to the stone arch.

No! He got caught! Reilly didn't think Eoghan was there for an imprinting. He wondered what was about to happen?

When they passed the archway, Eoghan's eyes met Reilly's with a look of hopelessness and resignation. The Deceptor instructed Reilly to stand under the other arch. Then a booming voice sang out into the night above the crackling of the bonfire, and all the prisoners stopped, as if frozen in fear.

> ***Hail, all young and old!***
> ***Hail, all rich and poor!***
> ***Welcome to your new abode,***
> ***Your home forever more.***
> ***Should you think for but a moment***
> ***That escape is your desire,***
> ***In your useless quest for freedom***
> ***Be devoured in the fire!***

Sparks erupted at Eoghan's feet and created a small ring of fire around him. Another ring of fire burst around the arch where Reilly stood. Great flames leapt from the bonfire and set Eoghan's tunic ablaze. He screamed as Reilly and the other prisoners watched in horror. Many closed their eyes and covered their ears. Parents did their best to hide their children's faces from the sight.

Reilly tried to see if Eoghan's branding mark glowed with a ruby. The wind blew the smoke away from him and Reilly had a clear view of his burning friend. He could no longer scream. There was no ruby in his chest.

A chorus of Deceptors burst into discordant laughter.

Reilly closed his eyes. It was too late for Eoghan. Now, Reilly could only wait.

When it was over, the flames imprisoning Reilly disappeared into the ground, and a guard escorted him back toward Black Castle. Following the Deceptor, Reilly walked past the laurel hedge and caught a glimpse of something red sparkling under the bush. Pretending to trip, he grabbed the ruby and held it tightly in his fist.

Restless again before falling asleep that night, Reilly wondered if any of the prisoners who had witnessed the murder might think Eoghan had been spared something worse than death.

Chapter Thirty-One

Reilly's Meditation

The next morning, the Deceptors had rearranged The Library to accommodate the many new prisoners. Desks were closer together and there were fewer aisles. Most of the veteran prisoners were moved to an overflow room. The new prisoners from the West Woods were assigned seats and Story Screens at the back of The Library. Reilly was moved up to the row nearest the alcove. Deceptors swooped in and out throughout the day, preparing for the reading and the auction.

Reilly decided to pick up his story where he had left off. Rather than write about his love for Norah, he decided to write about his understanding of other aspects of love. He hoped the device would cooperate.

The first thing that came to his mind was the love he had felt from his family—he wished he had not taken that for granted. But as he wrote his story, he realized there were many things he hadn't been able to appreciate until they were gone. It was something he was just beginning to understand.

Next, he wrote about various kindnesses others had shown him. He was surprised by how many instances he remembered. Though there were punks at school who had bullied him, there were many people who had been kind to him in simple ways, even strangers. Though by nature Reilly was kind-hearted, he wondered how often he had gone out of his way to reciprocate kindnesses. Had he sequestered himself in his kayak, or in the comfort of Eilam's friendship, at the expense of maturing his ability to show kindness? Reilly knew he had more to learn.

It was strange that he felt both compelled and free again to write anything he wanted at The Library. Though it was the darkest place he could imagine, he was still free to choose love.

He continued to record other memories of love: when he experienced nature or enjoyed music, when he was with his sister, when he whittled a feather on the dock with Eilam, and when he could sense his dad nearby. Then his words expanded to include the times he had done something kind for other people, just because he knew it would brighten their day.

Reilly wanted to write about Tuma and Eilam, but he hesitated to expose his closest friends. Then, before he typed their names, Tuma and Eilam appeared on his screen. As he wrote, he discovered he could describe how he felt about his friends and how they felt about him without disclosing details of where they were. He wrote about long chats with Eilam on the dock, and eating cheese and rye bread with him in his hut. He wrote about Tuma's soft fur, how she had been welcomed at the bakery, and how he felt when he hugged her.

Reilly relived his experiences as he wrote, but the emotions that the words evoked were much more important than the words. He understood that love was only a word people used to try to describe something beyond definition, but he still wanted to try.

Love encompasses all good things.

Love is inclusive.

Love is universal.

Love is given freely, without demanding anything in return.

Otherwise, it is not love.

As he wrote, euphoria filled his heart, and he began to understand things in a new way.

Love is the key.

That's it! he thought. *The key is only a symbol for love. Love can unlock any closed heart. Nothing else has enough power to override all the duplicity and destruction caused by the Deceptors, whose greatest weakness is my greatest strength.*

Admitting this seemed easy—after all, he already knew it. But now, he also knew he must become vulnerable enough to admit his own weakness—and even reveal it to others—before he could identify his greatest desire. Otherwise, he would never have the power to claim it. Intuitively, he knew utilizing this power would be a process, not an event.

He began to write again.

My greatest weakness ...

Before he could finish the sentence, an image appeared on the screen. It was his own face, obscured behind the hooded cloak of a Deceptor. He gasped and glanced around to be sure no one was looking in his direction. Then he continued.

... is giving power to the Deceptors whenever I refuse or forget to show love to others.

The words came from his fingers before he could question them. Reilly stared at the admission. Instantly, scenes from his life flashed on the screen at random. Each one was a brutal reminder that his ignorance and fear had increased the Deceptors' evil power.

Reilly had been so unaware—but ignorance was not bliss! His own ignorance had, in fact, contributed to other peoples' living hell!

Stunned that he had caused pain to others, even if it was unintentional, Reilly stared at the screen. The decisions he had made that were based on negative emotions had a collective negative impact on all of humanity! The truth of this gripped his soul more deeply than he thought anything could.

Yet, he alone was not accountable. This was true for every decision made by every person. The evolution of humanity could only occur through pure love—otherwise, humanity would eventually destroy itself.

To be with Norah forever was his greatest desire, but he now realized that what he had thought he wanted was a step toward knowing what he *truly* wanted. Figuring out what would be his *true* greatest desire involved a making choice. Now he understood what that choice must be.

My greatest weakness will become my greatest strength because my greatest desire is simply to love.

I am love.

The words on the screen vanished. Without warning, his keyboard burst into flames. Reilly pushed back from the desk and jumped to his feet as his screen disintegrated in front of him.

The prisoners around him gasped and lifted their hands from their own keyboards. The flames continued to burn in front of Reilly until all that remained was a charred outline of a hooded creature emblazoned on his desk.

Deceptors emerged from The Library walls and ceiling, swooping through the room. Up and down the aisles, they whooshed in black blurs while the prisoners clutched their chairs and desks. Reilly's desk ascended to the ceiling in a whirling cloud and exploded into pieces, which dropped to the floor like bullets. Prisoners took cover under the furniture; a few ran to the doors, only to find they were locked.

Reilly instinctively reached for one of the rubies in his pockets and placed it in the center of his branding wound. The jewel disappeared under his skin and changed the dot in the center to bright red.

Seconds later, Prince Ukobach appeared in front of Reilly and lifted him off his feet. Reilly and the demon levitated above the prisoners, circling The Library until they hovered above the alcove at the front of the room. The prince cackled as he pulled his hood away from his head, revealing the face of an evil Reilly. Horrified, Reilly stared blankly and the prisoners screamed in a burst of hysteria. Ukobach wrapped his cape around Reilly, and the two vanished in a burst of red smoke.

Reilly was suspended briefly near the ceiling. Then he fell and crashed on the stone floor below. He landed on his side and lost consciousness.

Some time later, he awoke groggy, groaned, and rolled onto his back. With his eyes still closed, he thought for a moment that he had transported through the portal in Seattle into the forest of the West Woods again, because a pungent smell invaded his nostrils, and it hurt to inhale. He wondered if he had cracked a rib and dislocated his shoulder. He moaned as he pushed himself up to a sitting position. Rubbing his shoulder, he was relieved that it was all right. Although his ribs ached fiercely, he struggled to stand, and it felt good to stretch his body slightly.

Reilly lifted a hand to cover his mouth and nose. The air reeked of blood. He blinked to focus on the door across the room. There was no door handle, only a barred window at the top. Reilly realized he was in the same room where he and Eoghan had seen Norah imprisoned.

He walked around the perimeter of the room, looking for any signs of possible escape. The door was solidly embedded in the wall. The barred window was too high for him to reach, and making a running jump for it was not possible in his current state. The walls were made of something resembling cement, without cracks or crevices. Getting on his hands and knees, he crawled on the stone floor, inspecting it carefully, but determined it was a single mass of stone. He saw no way to escape.

Figuring it must be the morning of Hallow's Eve, Reilly expected it would not be long before he was summoned for the reading. He sat down in the center of the room, tucked his knees to his chest, and pulled his tunic over his ankles to stay warm. He traced his finger around his branding mark and looked down at the red dot in the center. Doing so gave him strength and eased the pain in his ribs. He removed the jewels from his tunic pocket to count them. Reilly had brought one hundred thirteen with him from the Sea of Stelladaurs; now there were one hundred twelve. He stared at the gems cupped in his hands and tried to clear his mind.

He wanted to have a plan in place to distribute the rubies, but nothing came to him. So many unexpected things were happening that he was not sure a plan at this point would do any good, anyway. He closed his eyes and reviewed the Affirmations of the Stelladaur.

I am eternal, without time or space.
I am imagination and creativity without end.
I am realization and manifestation as One.
I am all possibilities.
I am the open mind and the gentle heart.
I am nature.
I am love.

He breathed deeply through the pain in his ribs and focused on each affirmation. Then he examined the ways he had done his best to utilize what he had learned. It had not been easy—even for an Echtra.

With his cupped hands resting in his lap, Reilly gazed at the rubies and started to hum the melody that was his own Stelladaur song. As before, the notes came from deep inside, and he rocked back and forth to the tune. The meditation relaxed his body, cleared his mind, and soothed his soul.

It occurred to Reilly that his song lacked lyrics. Norah's song had lyrics—she had written them herself. Reilly knew each person's song appeared the day his own Star Door opened. But now he also understood that each melody came without lyrics, and in addition to writing his or her own story, each author must also compose the lyrics to his song.

He did not question why this message came to him while he meditated. He simply closed his eyes again and continued to breathe deeply. The acoustic melody echoed in his ears with an ethereal descant, just as it had played before. At that moment, Reilly had an epiphany—his song was not a solo! Norah had sung *her* song to bring him to her. Now he needed to write lyrics to *his* song so their duet would harmonize—so he would have a chance to be with her again.

When the melody ended, Reilly opened his eyes and replaced the rubies in his pockets. He trusted he would know what to do with the jewels the moment he needed to do something. He also knew his heart had already written the lyrics to his song. Soon, he hoped to sing them for Norah.

Reilly's meditation ended abruptly. A Deceptor appeared in the room, lifted him to his feet, and covered his body with thick, wet breath, methodically moving from his head to his toes. It drooled down his body like the blood that had drained off him in the pool not far from this cell. But Reilly touched his finger to the red dot on his shoulder and remained steadfast in his mind and heart.

When the attempted torment ended, the demon howled, "Now to The Library, where the preliminary rituals continue!" The monster captured Reilly in its cape before they disappeared from the room.

Reilly stood in the center of The Library alcove on a platform that towered over the massive room where the prisoners waited. The desks were gone and the prisoners sat anxiously on long benches arranged in neat rows facing the alcove. Some Deceptors swooped in the air above while others placed themselves around the perimeter of the room.

Reilly tried to make eye contact with a few people near the alcove in order to give them hope. Some refused to look up and kept their eyes on the floor; others quickly looked away when he caught their eye.

None of the prisoners spoke to each other. The only sounds were the Deceptors' screeches as they flew about the room. *This must be another ritual,* Reilly thought. He held the platform handrail and ran his fingers back and forth in its deep groove. Prince Ukobach was nowhere to be seen. With the Deceptors occupied in their frenzy, Reilly had the idea to drop the rubies into the concave groove of the handrail in front of him. Trusting his instincts, he bent over and removed all but one ruby from the safety of his tunic pocket and let them spill into the groove. He noticed some of the prisoners watching him, but he wasn't sure how he could communicate to them with the Deceptors still whooshing about the room in a dither of excitement.

Moments later, Prince Ukobach entered the room and levitated to the alcove, opposite Reilly. The Prince raised the arms of his cloak and spoke in his grating, hollow voice.

Hallow's Eve begins anew
With stories to please each devil.
Readings reveal each author's fate
And seal the end with evil.

The Prince cackled and focused his gaze on Reilly. "Let the Story Screen display the names for today's reading!"

With that, a jumbotron screen descended from the ceiling in the center of the room and hung midair. Another screen the size of a laptop hovered in front of Reilly. The first name flashed in bright red letters on both screens.

"Julie Bennett!" boomed a demonic voice. "Take your place on the author's platform!"

A young woman seated twelve rows back from the platform stood and walked hesitantly toward the alcove. She glanced up at Reilly and mounted the steep stairs to the top of the platform. She took her place beside Reilly, gripped the handrail, and looked out to the prisoners below. The jumbotron displayed Sorcha's portrait of the girl, and simultaneously, her story appeared on Reilly's screen. Before the shaving, her shoulder-length hair had been black with wide streaks of pink and purple, and she had piercings above her eyebrows, numerous ones on both ears, and two in her left nostril. The facial piercings had disappeared. Reilly took a deep breath and began to read.

"I am twenty-six years old. For as long as I can remember, my life has been a living hell. I'm not sure what this Black Castle is, but I feel as if I've been here before." Reilly stopped and looked at the girl, but she lifted her head high and did not look at him. He breathed in deeply and continued to read. "I know all about demons and devils. An ugly one began to invade my body when I was barely old enough to speak. I suffered for twelve years. My mother did nothing and I hate her because of that. My sister did nothing.

How could she? We both lived in Hell. I was only fourteen when my child was born. I named her Sadie. I gave Sadie to a family who I trusted to take care of her. They took my child but wouldn't include me in their lives. Soon after my baby was gone, another demon engulfed me. The depression was so heavy … so dark … always so much pain! Drugs became my only satisfaction. At least with the drugs, I didn't have to think … or remember … or feel. I wished I didn't have to breathe."

Reilly choked. He reminded himself to sound convincing. Yet, how could he give Julie over to the Deceptors to be imprinted? Wouldn't she be better off writing her story in Black Castle forever than going back to the life she knew before? He had to do well enough in the readings to merit his exchange for Norah. She was the one for whom he would sacrifice his own life!

"During my last visit to the ER, something happened that I hoped would change my life. When I was in the recovery room, a nurse who was at least twice my age stayed with me around the clock. She sat by my bed and held my hand for hours and hours. I could hear her voice even while I was in the coma. She told me I was courageous. And beautiful. And loving. No one had ever said those things to me before, and I didn't believe her. At first, I thought she was lying to me. Maybe she was a demon, too … but her hand was warm and her voice was kind. I was afraid to wake up because I thought she would go away if I did. Her name was Grace. No matter what happens now in Black Castle, I know Grace loved me."

Julie blinked rapidly and took a deep breath.

"When I think of Sadie, in my heart, I remember Grace. I love my daughter. This memory comes from a love somewhere deeper and more powerful than all the demons inside of me. As I write this, I hope Sadie will know I love her."

Reilly glanced up to see Julie smiling through her tears.

A Deceptor scoffed loudly and declared, "This one is not ready for imprinting!"

Julie gripped the handrail and looked to Reilly to see what she should do next. He diverted his eyes to her hands, which covered the groove where the rubies waited. Julie moved her hands slightly along the rail as the Deceptor continued.

"Summon another author!"

Julie's portrait disappeared from the big screen. Simultaneously, Reilly nodded to Julie. She wedged a ruby between her fingers as she removed her hands from the handrail. When she stood up to leave, Reilly lifted his hand to his shoulder as if to adjust his tunic. Julie noticed the red mark in his branding. She smiled faintly as she walked down the steep steps while the next name was announced.

"Patrick Fairbank! Take your place on the author's platform!"

Reilly watched a young man limp from the back bench in The Library up the center aisle. As he moved toward the alcove, Reilly thought Patrick couldn't be much older than he was. The young man's portrait appeared on the large screen: his nose and mouth looked chiseled against a square jaw, dark eyes, and short blonde hair. Patrick ascended the stairs and took his place on the platform. When he noticed the rubies, he raised his eyebrows and looked at Reilly. Reilly nodded almost imperceptibly and started to read.

"Isn't it enough that I've been deployed three times for my country and killed more people than I can count? What the hell do these demons want from me?"

Reilly had never met anyone who had killed someone, even in defense of his country. He felt his knees weaken and he clasped one hand on the rail to regain his composure.

"They called me a hero and gave me a purple star when I returned home. I didn't accept it. It meant nothing to me. A moment of honor and glory was useless. No medal could ever stop my nightmares!"

Patrick crossed his arms.

"This place I am in … Is it a secret foreign government facility? A place where the enemy tortures those who killed their own?" Patrick raised his arms aimlessly as Reilly read. "Just kill me now! Get it over with! This place looks so much like my nightmares, I expect I'll wake up and be stuck again with my agonizing memories."

Reilly did his best to read with expression, but it was so much more difficult than he thought it would be. Why did he have to be the one to assist with Patrick's sentencing? He vacillated, questioning his intent for his task. Did he have to choose between his love for Norah and his compassion for Patrick and all the other prisoners?

He read a few more sentences, and then a screech pierced his ears. Next, the horrific laughter of the Deceptors filled the room. Startled, Reilly jumped back and nearly lost his balance. Patrick gripped the handrail in front of him. Reilly caught himself and nodded at the rubies. Patrick let go of the rail.

"This one is ready! Who will claim him?" the announcer declared.

Instantly, a swarm of Deceptors engulfed the platform and swooped between Reilly and Patrick. Reilly fell to his hands and knees, trying to grip the floor. When he looked up, Patrick was gone.

Another name appeared on the jumbotron.

"Sarah Callaghan! Take your place on the author's platform!"

Reilly read stories for over five hours. His voice became tired, and he worried constantly that he wasn't speaking with enough enthusiasm to interest the Deceptors. His body was fatigued, but more than anything, his chest hurt with a deep, hollow throb that even the ruby in his branding mark only dulled. He almost forgot about his cracked rib.

He noticed that all the stories, regardless of the age or gender of the author, had similarities: each person was confused about why he was in Black Castle, and each person wrote about wanting to make the torture of their lives end, though he did not know how to do so. So far, there were no signs that the Deceptors had noticed the rubies, and Reilly hoped they were just too enthralled by their zealous mood. It also occurred to him that by some uncanny twist of magic, the rubies might only be visible to the prisoners, not to the Deceptors.

Perhaps there were things that could only be seen by those who understood something about love.

Reilly lost count of how many prisoners the Deceptors had taken, but near the end of the reading, he realized that the groove of the handrail was empty. Only a single jewel remained. That ruby was still safe in his pocket—for Norah.

Chapter Thirty-Two

Death's Duet

After Reilly completed the reading, he and the other prisoners filed into the dining hall for the Feast of Hallow's Eve. He was not summoned to Sorcha's studio. To his surprise, a few prisoners showed him signs of good will. They smiled at him, and several offered him a place to sit. Reilly thought word of the jewels must have spread among the captives.

Judging by the number of prisoners, at least ten times fewer had a ruby than those who did not. No one's branding mark glowed red, so he knew those who had a jewel did not know what to do with it. He felt people watching him closely now, some with a guarded sense of respect for him. Others continued to snub him; he could feel their eyes on his back.

The prisoners were served an early banquet, even more epicurean than usual. Reilly was starved. During his stay at Black Castle, he had only eaten enough to sustain himself. Although the food was delicious, he still wasn't convinced it was good to eat. Nevertheless, he ate more that night than he had in days, hoping it wouldn't harm him.

Three prisoners who Reilly had seen remove a ruby from the groove in the handrail sat near him, one on each side and the third across the table. When he felt the others were absorbed in eating the delectable food on their plates, he whispered to the woman at his left.

"The ruby will restore what the Deceptors have taken. It will keep you from believing their lies."

The woman leaned in toward Reilly. "How?"

"It carries a power strong enough to dispel the forces of the demons."

The middle-aged man across the table looked up to hear what Reilly was saying. The young boy to his right stopped chewing and raised his ears.

"But the power can only be accessed through your heart," Reilly continued.

The woman glanced at Reilly's marking. He nodded.

"Yes, you need to put the ruby in your branding mark, like mine. I know it sounds strange," he added, "but trust me. The ruby will save you from imprinting."

"What about you?" the boy whispered. "I heard you are going to be auctioned. Will it save you, too?"

Reilly bit into a piece of fish covered in Alfredo sauce. "I don't know for sure. But it's given me strength when I otherwise wouldn't have survived."

"That's good enough for me," the woman said. She took the ruby from her fist and pushed it into the center of her branding mark. Those around her watched as the gem melded into her body and made her skin glow in a small dot, like Reilly's.

"Well?" the boy asked. "How do you feel? Does it hurt?"

"Not at all," she said. "It's comfortable, as though it's always been part of me."

"We've got nothing to lose," the boy said. "Here goes." He placed his ruby to his chest and it disappeared under his skin, leaving the same ethereal glow.

The man opened his fist and then quickly closed it again. He stared at it closely.

"This reminds me of another gem I found many years ago, only this one is much smaller. That one was clear and brilliant. I thought it was a valuable diamond, so I took it to a jeweler for an appraisal. He said it was worthless—only glass. So I tossed it." The man lifted the ruby to his chest. "I believe the appraiser was wrong. That jewel was more valuable than this ruby, and I think my life would have been very different if I hadn't discarded it."

Reilly's eyes widened and he smiled. "Yes! But it's not too late!"

"It seemed hopeless in this place," the woman said, "until now."

Others nearby leaned in to hear what those with the rubies were talking about. The ensuing conversation ended abruptly, when their voices were drowned out by heinous laughter echoing throughout the room. It was followed by a demonic chant summoning Reilly to the auction. Before the Deceptors led him away he had just enough time to whisper to his three neighbors, "Tell the others! There are more rubies!" He hoped his instruction wouldn't cause more chaos among the prisoners, and that those with a ruby had somehow tucked it in the hem of their tunic or concealed it somewhere between the fabric and their body.

The benches in The Library were gone, and Deceptors filled the room. In front of each demon, cloaked in the folds of its cape, stood a prisoner. Reilly knew these were the ones whose stories the Deceptors had liked and therefore chose for imprinting. Having given up the hope for freedom, none of them had taken a ruby.

The platform was gone. An assortment of black candles hung around the perimeter of the room, lighting it with eerie shadows. Suspended in the center of the alcove were Sorcha's portraits of Reilly: one painted before he was shaved, and the other done in her studio specifically for the auction. Reilly's eyes were compelling in both renditions.

Prince Ukobach swooped into the room from behind the walls of the alcove and trapped Reilly in the folds of his red cape. He carried him to the center of the stage and deposited him on the floor with a jolt. Reilly gained his footing and stood still between the portraits, waiting.

The prince swept his cape around the room, extinguishing all the candles in succession. The prisoners in the room gasped with fear. Without thinking, Reilly lifted his hand to his chest to cover his branding mark. He braced himself firmly, knowing what would come next. The thick darkness in the room crawled over him, attempting to assault him.

Reilly spread his fingers across his chest, and a subtle red light gleamed in front of him. He lowered his hand to his side and the light spread toward the Deceptors, enabling him to make out their shadowy forms holding their prisoners captive.

Reilly had read the story of each prisoner in front of him. He breathed deeply and felt the power of his ruby fill his mind and heart with insight. As its glow intensified, its light revealed to him the fear in the prisoners' eyes, but also, something deeper—tremendous sadness. Then he saw past all the anguish, disappointment, and injustice in their lives. Deep inside each one, he saw a glimmer of hope. In a flash, the light swirled. It simultaneously transported each one's ray of hope to the hope in his own heart, and then boomeranged it back to the prisoners in the form of a warm flame.

A fire in Reilly's soul burned as brightly as the jewels that had danced on the waves of the Sea of Stelladaurs. At that moment, he understood that everyone—even the prisoners that were soon to be imprinted by demons—would still have some Stelladaur light within them. The demons that took over the bodies and minds had no light, but the human soul always would. That light came with them the day they were born and could never be completely extinguished, regardless of the circumstances life might bring them, and regardless of whether they found their Stelladaur. It was Reilly's responsibility—and anyone else's who found his or her Stelladaur—simply to love.

Love without judgment. Love without expectations. Love simply because it is the light within all people.

Without warning, Prince Ukobach's voice punctured the darkness. "Let the auction begin! Bids will only be considered for young bodies as fresh and strong as that of this Echtra. I want a challenge! I've been so bored with the recent imprintings—a boredom that appears to be madness to the humans. Give me something subtle I can sink my teeth into." Ukobach cackled and floated above Reilly's head. "Convince me that the body you've chosen to imprint is more exciting than Reilly's, or I shall devour him myself."

Over half of the demons wrapped their victims in their capes and disappeared from the room, heading to the bonfire to imprint them.

A demon from the back spoke. "This one is slightly older than the Echtra. He recently questioned all he has believed to be true and is undecided in his resolve."

"A good start to the bidding," the Prince said. "But not enough!"

"This body is beautiful and perfect," said another Deceptor. "He's also older than the Echtra, but he understands the power a body can have over those who are weak. He uses his body for his own pleasures."

"This is to my liking," Ukobach laughed. "Give me more!"

"I have one who is much younger," chimed a Deceptor near the front. "She has something similar to the Echtra—innocence. She was born to poverty but is still fresh."

"You tempt me!" Ukobach crooned.

"I have a body even more tempting!" A Deceptor from the side moved with his victim to the front of the stage. "She, too, is younger than the Echtra, and she embodies something more powerful than innocence." The devil pushed the girl forward so Ukobach could see her more clearly. "She is beautiful but does not know it. She sees only her flaws and obsesses over them. Already she has made severe changes to her body and is destined to continue with this for many years. She would be an invigorating body to imprint."

Prince Ukobach fumed in frustration. "Give me more! This Echtra is worth more to me than any of these! He has power! It is a power I have yet to possess. No body I have ever imprinted has given me this power. I must have it!"

Reilly closed his eyes and meditated on the fact that no Deceptor, demon, or devil would ever have the power Prince Ukobach desperately wanted to claim. As each Deceptor in the room placed a bid to purchase Reilly, he stood resolute and calm.

The final Deceptor brought his victim forward from the back corner of The Library and stood at the front of the stage. Prince Ukobach floated next to Reilly and waited anxiously for the Deceptor to place his bid.

"I will buy your Echtra in exchange for this body. He is young and more intelligent than most. Since his birth, he has fought to stay alive. He was abandoned by his mother and many times beaten and almost killed by his father. His father took the life of his younger son, this young man's brother, and then his own life—all in front of this one's eyes. He has learned to use his knowledge to encompass what the other prisoners have to offer, and more. The power in this one is strong—and he uses our greatest tactic to keep increasing it. Deception!" The Deceptor shifted the victim to face the prince. "With training, he will become one of us, Prince Ukobach."

Ukobach darted around the prisoner and then around Reilly. Shrieking wildly, he swooped back around the prisoner, carried him up to the ceiling, and then whooshed him down again. The prisoner now stood directly in front of Reilly.

Reilly looked more closely at the young man. Something in the prisoner's eyes made him shudder. He breathed in deeply to regain the calmness and love he had sustained in his heart and mind throughout the auction. As he shifted, the light from his chest shone on the prisoner's face. The man smirked, and Reilly recognized him. Standing before him was the person he feared and hated most—Travis Jackson! It was a younger Travis, about Reilly's own age, but he knew it was Travis.

Before Reilly could process what was happening, Prince Ukobach declared his decision. "Sold!" A rush of putrid air laden with the smell of blood wafted through the alcove as Ukobach wrapped his cloak around Travis and disappeared. Simultaneously, the Deceptor who had purchased Reilly snatched him up and escorted him out of The Library.

The bonfire raged. Flames billowed higher than any Reilly had seen before. He stood under a stone archway, with the Deceptor that had purchased him hovering inches behind. Travis stood under the other archway in front of Prince Ukobach. The Deceptors circled the entire bonfire with their victims clasped tightly inside their capes. Sorcha stood between the two archways and the fire, at the side of a stone altar upon which Norah's lifeless body lay.

The roaring sound of the flames ended abruptly in a haunting silence. Reilly could hear his own heartbeat. He was almost close enough to touch Norah, but he knew he must wait. He needed perfect timing, or the Festival of Fire would be the last time he ever saw Norah or Sorcha.

Prince Ukobach announced the beginning of the dance for the Gods of Ifreann. At his command, the Deceptors began to sway back and forth to the accompaniment of their own garbled chants and satanic rhythms. Soon a discordant tune pierced the air as the Deceptors and Prince Ukobach joined in with their screeching laughter. Disrobing with a single swoop, the Deceptors quickly changed their movements to grotesque distortions resembling ghastly bodies.

Reilly could not see the Gods of Ifreann, but he knew they were there, either invisible in the flames or watching from a distance.

He closed his eyes long enough to consider the gruesome circumstances he faced. As soon as the dance was over, he and all the prisoners encircling the bonfire would be imprinted. The only chance at freedom from the curse of the demons would be on another Hallow's Eve—but only if a Deceptor became bored and wanted to imprint a different body. Otherwise, the person would remain imprisoned by his Deceptor until death—or until, by some improbable and rare fate, an Echtra could save them. However, whomever Ukobach imprinted would have no chance for freedom. Not for all of eternity.

Reilly also knew Ukobach had not yet completed the double exchange he had intended to be the finale for the evening's festivities. Ukobach wanted Reilly as much as he wanted Travis and Norah! And although Reilly did not comprehend how it was possible, he knew without a doubt that the Prince of Hell could possess more than one body at a time.

Opening his eyes, Reilly moved his head slightly to look at Travis. Now knowing the boy's past—as well as what his life was to be in the future—Reilly's heart ached for him. But Travis's destiny had already been determined.

With only one ruby remaining in his pocket, how could he save Norah and change destiny at the same time?

The chanting intensified, and the dance increased its frenzied tempo. Reilly knew he needed to act quickly. He felt the Deceptor behind him relax his hold as he swaggered to the music. Prince Ukobach twisted around Travis and the stone archway.

Just then, Sorcha glanced back at Reilly and pointed discretely to the hedge just beyond the arches. Cormack, Dubhghall, and

Basil poked their heads through the bushes with large bricks raised in their hands. All the Deceptors were too engrossed in their ritual to notice.

The Pucatrows began to pull bricks from under the hedge and stack them in piles, while the volume and pitch in the air increased to a deafening level. Reilly looked quickly to Sorcha and nodded toward the Pucatrows. He knew only seconds remained before either the Deceptor behind him would come out of its self-induced trance, grasp him, and have him imprinted in the fire or Ukobach would claim him forever.

In that instant, Reilly looked at Norah and knew what to do.

He bent over and grabbed the ruby from his pocket, then bolted towards the altar. At the same moment, Cormack hurled the first brick into the fire. First a sizzling noise, and then an explosion of flames. Ukobach instantly retrieved his red cape, swept over Travis, and jetted toward Reilly and Norah.

"Run, Sorcha!" Reilly screamed as he scooped Norah in his arms and thrust the ruby into her branding mark.

Norah opened her eyes and clung to Reilly while he ducked under the altar, out of Ukobach's reach.

Sorcha tripped over the chains that bound her. She fell in front of the Deceptor that had won the bid for Reilly. Dubhghall hurled another brick into the flames and temporarily distracted the Deceptor.

The other demons, garbed in their capes, jumped into the flames with their victims to complete the imprintings, then disappeared in the smoke that swelled in the night sky.

Ukobach swooshed over the altar. It vaporized, and the Prince of Hell descended on Reilly and Norah.

"You are mine!" Ukobach shrieked as he plunged forward.

The Pucatrows threw more bricks into the fire. Sorcha crawled toward the hedge to help. The Deceptor who had intended to imprint Reilly was enraged, having been tricked by his own master. In his shame, he disappeared into the flames.

Reilly knew he would rather die, with Norah in his arms than see her held captive by the Prince of Hell forever.

Clutching her more tightly to his chest, Reilly prepared to run into the flames to save them both.

As the glow from their rubies intertwined, Reilly's song sounded above the sputtering flames.

When dark shadows steal my breath
And take you from my arms,
Love will be the only key
To block the flame that harms.
But fire can't consume a love
As still and pure as ours,
For ashes turn to whispered dreams
Like ruby-colored flowers.
Love is all I have for you—
A light to set us free.
If we know love changes all
Our love will ever be.
In this spell I give my heart—
Now love will make us free.

Norah's descant lilted above Reilly's melody and harmonized in a perfect duet that washed over their bodies like a gentle summer rain.

As the last note sounded at midnight on Hallow's Eve, an ominous thunderbolt boomed through the clouds above. The Prince of Hell swooped above the fire to finalize the imprinting of his prisoner, held securely in the folds of his red cape. With frenzied wrath, he opened his cloak and laughed heinously as Travis

Jackson plummeted into the flames. In a streak of red, Ukobach plunged, caught his victim before he landed, and simultaneously melded into the helpless body. Travis's soul was demonized forever.

Chapter Thirty-Three

Invitation

"Sorcha!" Brigid screamed as Sorcha and Reilly, with Norah still in his arms, burst through the auditorium door at the Embassy.

Brigid ran through the room filled with injured people and debris from the Crumble that had destroyed the West Woods. When she reached her daughter, she embraced her tightly, sobbing uncontrollably.

"Reilly!" Lottie swept a pile of debris and paper from a table. "Lay Norah down here!"

Reilly gently laid Norah on the cold table. "She's in shock," he said. "Is there any elixir left?"

"I'm afraid not," Lottie said. "But I managed to grab the leftover rowanberries before we evacuated our tree home." She reached into the satchel around her shoulder. “These are all of them.” She held out a handful of berries for Reilly.

“Thank you, Lottie,” he said. He bent over the table and stroked Norah’s cheek and forehead. “Norah,” he whispered. “It’s Reilly. Can you hear me?” Norah returned only a blank gaze.

Dillon burst into the room and ran up to the table. “I thought I’d never see you again!” he cried, hugging his sister. “Is it really you? Why are you in these chains?” The boy stepped away and lifted part of the chain that hung from Sorcha’s wrist.

“Never you mind, son,” Brigid said, her hand waving a light scolding. She looked again at her daughter and continued. “As soon as your father arrives, he’ll release you from this horrible contraption!”

“Will Norah be okay?” Lottie asked Reilly.

Reilly did not answer. He slowly forced a few berries between Norah’s lips. “You’ve got to swallow them, Norah. Please!” he whispered. He leaned in closely and began to hum his song in her ear. He stroked her brow and cheek over and over.

“Try a few more berries,” Lottie suggested.

Reilly looked up at her and nodded. He put three more berries in Norah’s mouth and waited. “C’mon, Norah,” he said as he took her hand. “Stay with me.”

Norah’s eyes fluttered and she took a deep breath.

“Reilly?” she whispered.

“Yeah,” he said. “I’m right here.” He lifted her hand and kissed it.

“I … I … was so dizzy … after the …”

“Don’t talk yet. You’re going to be just fine. Here, try to eat these.” Reilly lifted her head slightly and fed her the remaining berries, blinking away tears.

Norah sucked the berries for a few moments and swallowed them. She wrinkled her nose the way she had done when she first caught Reilly’s attention long ago. “They’re nasty,” she whispered.

"I know." Reilly chuckled.

A few minutes later, Norah looked around. "Where are we?"

"We're at the Embassy … in Ireland."

"Ireland? I saw a post on Instagram … someone from your school said you'd gone to Ireland … to stay with relatives for the school year."

"Instagram?" Lottie interrupted. "What does she mean, Reilly?"

Reilly ignored Lottie. "Yeah, sort of. But how did you get here, Norah?"

Norah pushed herself up and leaned on her elbows. Reilly helped her sit up, and she sat cross-legged on the table. "It's all a bit vague. After I was taken from Travis's guesthouse, they put me with Child Protective Services. I stayed with a foster family for ten months, but life fell apart again. It was too much, Reilly! I couldn't think straight anymore … and I couldn't find my Stelladaur. I was so confused about everything!" She raised her hands to her eyes and started to cry.

"We can talk about this later, Norah," Reilly said as he sat down beside her and wrapped her in his arms.

She shook her head. "No. No, I'm fine. Anyway, when I found out you were in Ireland, I contacted your mother and she said it was true. But she sounded confused and worried, as if she wasn't sure where you were. I knew then that you must've gone through a portal—not flown to Ireland on a plane."

"A plane?" Lottie asked.

Norah peered around the room and then focused on Reilly's clothes. "Are we both in Ireland … in the past?" she asked Reilly.

"The berries are working," he said. "Yep. It's 1896."

"Well, that explains it," Norah said.

"Please explain all these details!" Lottie persisted.

Reilly smiled at Lottie. "Norah, meet my fourth-great grandmother, Charlotte Louise McKinley."

"She's *who*?" Brigid piped up.

"It's true, Mother," Lottie admitted. "Reilly *did* come back in time as the Echtra for our family—because he *is* part of our family!"

"This is nonsense!" Brigid replied.

"I can't say how or why, Mother. Some things just are." Lottie stepped in front of Norah. "Pleased to meet you, Norah. Reilly has come a long way to help our people. And to find you."

Norah nodded. "Thank you." She swung her legs over the side of the table and looked at Brigid and Dillon. "And you two are ...?"

"This is my mother, Brigid McKinley, and my brother, Dillon."

"Well, it is indeed a pleasure to meet you, dearie," Brigid said. "How, may I ask, did you come to Ireland?"

"Through the portal at the library."

"In Black Castle?"

"No, in Seattle," Norah replied.

"What exactly happened?" Reilly interjected.

"Well, as I said, when I was finally able to speak with your mother and she sounded so strange—as if she didn't want me to know where you were—I called James to ask him what he knew. He didn't hesitate to tell me."

Everyone around the table looked intently at Norah.

"James and your sister, Chantal, saw you go through the portal in the library. You dropped James's key as you went through it. He and Chantal tried to use it several times, but nothing happened. They said they'd been learning to use their Stelladaurs but couldn't figure out why the key didn't work. Your mom couldn't make sense of it—she'd been through so much—so she told people you'd gone to Ireland to stay with distant relatives." Norah smiled at Lottie and then at Brigid and Dillon. "Apparently, she was right."

Reilly nodded. "Go on. You said something about staying for the school year. When did you come through the portal?"

"When I left, it was May."

Reilly paused to calculate the time warp. "I've been gone my entire junior year?"

"It feels like forever," Norah said, resting her head on Reilly's shoulder.

Reilly pulled her closer to him. "It's only the end of October here. That means going this far back in time actually accelerates the speed of time as it occurs in the present."

"Something like that," said Norah. "That's probably also true for the prisoners who were captured from different times and places and taken to Black Castle." She wrapped her arms around Reilly's waist. "They took me before I knew what was happening. I should have seen them coming."

"They work overtime on the strong ones, Norah. Don't be hard on yourself."

Brigid and Dillon fidgeted, frustrated because they did not understand everything Reilly and Norah were talking about. Lottie listened eagerly.

Reilly continued. "There were no other Deceptors near the bonfire after Prince Ukobach disappeared with Travis. I saw some go back to Black Castle, but others had already imprinted a body and disappeared."

"I couldn't watch!" Sorcha said. "I stayed behind the hedge with Cormack and did my best to hand him bricks." She shuddered, then added, "What about the rubies? Were any of the prisoners spared?"

"Yes! I saw a dozen or so running towards the woods. They could only have been the prisoners who actually placed a ruby in their mark, freeing themselves from an imprinting. The others, with and without a ruby, must still be in Black Castle with the Deceptors who remained there. We can only hope the message about the power of the rubies eventually reaches all of them."

Brigid stepped forward. "Some of them are our neighbors!"

"I know," Reilly said. "The Deceptors imprinted many of them. It will be next Hallow's Eve, or later, before they have a chance to escape, assuming their captors want to trade them for another body at the Festival of Fire. Or maybe those who are still in the castle and *do* use the ruby will find another way to escape. Who knows?"

"Mercy!" Brigid said as she wrung her hands. "We are all tired. It's time to settle down for the night."

"Yes, Mrs. McKinley," said Norah. "That's a good idea."

"Very well, then. We cleared out the VP as well as we could. It's our home away from home," Brigid chimed. "Come along, everyone."

Reilly supported Norah as she stood up. She wrapped her arms around his waist as they carefully stepped over the people already asleep on the floor. When they reached the Vantage Post, Norah saw the brilliant harvest moon shining through the open windows and caught her breath. A dusty-red cloud blew across it in the night sky.

It occurred to Reilly that some of the McKinleys were missing. "Brigid, where is your husband? And Roisin?"

Lottie stepped forward and put an arm around her mother, who looked down at the ground, trembling. "The baby died," Lottie said, "just before the Crumble."

Reilly did not know what to say. He was convinced Prince Ukobach himself had possessed Roisin's body in one of his fiendish fits, impatient for the imprinting that would occur on Hallow's Eve.

"My father left hours ago to lead the Pucatrows in the attack," Dillon said. "I wanted to go with him, but he wouldn't allow me."

Reilly nodded and found a place in the far corner for him and Norah to rest. She snuggled in his arms, and silently they watched the moon rise.

It was early morning when Reilly awakened with the sense that something was happening at the Town Square.

"Norah," he whispered in her ear. "Lottie isn't here. C'mon."

They stepped out of the Vantage Post and through the auditorium. No Pucatrows were guarding the doorways in the long hallway to the main foyer. Flynn's basket was empty, and she was nowhere in the reception area. Reilly instinctively knew Flynn was gone, freed from her torment forever.

Reilly led Norah by the hand through the main doors of the Embassy into the chilly morning air. The fog from their breath blew in front of them and mingled with thicker fog, obscuring their view as they walked down the jade steps to the Town Square. There they met Lottie, who stood next to a massive statue.

"You just missed him," Lottie said.

"Who?" Norah asked.

Reilly looked at the massive gargoyle statue gaping in front of them, and knew. "Malie," he said.

"Yes," Lottie said. "I couldn't sleep, so I went to the fountain in the garden." Reilly noticed a tone of serenity in Lottie's voice. "I found it, Reilly. I found Tir Na Nog."

Norah gasped and squeezed Reilly's hand. "Are you sure?" she asked.

"Oh, yes. I'm sure. I brought home more than enough wealth for my father to rebuild Wicklow!" Lottie stepped closer to Reilly. "I was just coming to wake Mother and tell her the good news, but when I walked around the corner at the edge of the garden, I saw someone through the fog. It was Malie."

Reilly gripped Norah's hand and waited for Lottie to continue. "He's like a magician, Reilly! He met me in Tir Na Nog and helped me bring the jewels back for the people. When we returned, he made this gargoyle appear before my eyes. He said it represented the evil that would linger in our town until we each discover the key to unlock the spell. When the spell is broken, there will never be any more Crumbles, and the Deceptors will disappear forever."

Reilly and Norah looked at each other.

"Love is the only key that will unlock the spell," Reilly said. "Malie told me the same story when he first told me about the magistrate … and the gargoyle … and Tir Na Nog." His voice trailed off. "Did you write it all down, Lottie, in your journal?"

"Yes, I did."

Reilly smiled. He let go of Norah's hand and stepped close to Lottie. "Don't ever let anyone else write your story." He hugged her and held her tightly. "Did Malie say anything else?" he asked.

Lottie pulled away and reached into her satchel. "I gave him this treasure from Tir Na Nog to thank him for all he had done to help us. He told me to give it to you." Lottie handed Reilly an ornate knife with a handle made of intricately carved ivory and a Stelladaur carved on the silver tip.

Norah grasped Reilly's arm.

Reilly reached for the knife with the same awe he had felt when he first held it over a year ago, on his sixteenth birthday, when Eilam had given it to him. At that moment, he knew the portal wasn't a location at all. It wasn't a destination, or even a warp in time.

It was just there, wherever he was.

Reilly and Norah wrapped their arms around each other, and together they held the knife, with their hands entwined. They pointed the blade directly into the gaping mouth of the gargoyle and walked toward the statue.

As the rays of the early morning sun bounced off the Stelladaur at the knife's tip, Reilly and Norah disappeared.

Reilly inhaled the smell of leather, floor planks, and oiled hardwood furniture. Still holding Norah's hand, he looked up at the globe that dangled from the cathedral-high ceiling of the Suzzallo Library and watched it sway gently.

They glanced around the room. Had any of the students studying at the long desks noticed that they had just arrived—as if out of nowhere? Reilly looked at Norah and decided that it didn't matter either way. He ran his fingers through her long auburn hair, looking deep into her green eyes. Pulling her closer, he cradled her face in his hands and bent to kiss her. She reached her hands around his neck and grasped the soft, wavy hair at the back of his head. Their lips met, tenderly at first, and then in a passionate first kiss that transcended time and filled their souls.

They clung to each other until they heard the rustling of papers and someone coughing awkwardly, attempting to get their attention. Norah wiped her mouth and giggled. Reilly pulled her by the hand, and they walked quickly toward the center of the Reading Room.

As they walked past the desks, Reilly noticed the screen on a student's laptop displaying a news headline: Travis Jackson Acquitted. He stopped and peered over the student's shoulder

"Excuse me," he whispered. "That headline caught my attention. Do you mind if I read the article? It's important."

The student moved aside and motioned for Reilly to read the article.

> After only one year of imprisonment, world-renowned scientist and philanthropist Travis Jackson was released with all charges dropped and a full pardon granted by the courts. New evidence substantiates all claims against Jackson were false. Respected Seattle criminal attorney Lee Oliver contends that Jackson was released on a technicality, not on any new facts brought to the court's attention that might exonerate him. Jackson and his attorneys refused to give any comment.

"Lee is James's step-dad!" Norah whispered.

"I know," Reilly said. "C'mon."

As they prepared to exit the room, something else caught Reilly's eye. He walked to the familiar leather-wrapped door in the middle of the glass-cased bookshelves, with wooden drawers at the bottom. The entire section of the wall resembled a walk-in closet with picture windowpanes. Reilly dropped Norah's hand and pressed his nose against the dark glass. The last time he looked, nothing was on the shelf and the door was locked. Now he saw a single book.

He turned the brass doorknob and reached in for the book. He knew what it was before he brought it into the light of the Reading Room. He ran his fingers across the small leather cover and turned it over in his hands. Then carefully, he opened to the first page: *Finding Tir Na Nog*, by Charlotte Louise McKinley.

He held his breath as he flipped through the pages and stopped at the end.

> I found it at last! Please come and see it with me, Reilly! Tir Na Nog is beautiful indeed! Come and find me ... through the paneled door of the library. Our family will always need our Echtra.

Reilly closed the book and held it to his chest. Lowering the heirloom to his side, he reached for Norah's hand. Fragments of eternity had been scattered throughout history, and then gathered into one piece with the sands of endless time and glistening stardust. He knew he would have to find more lost pieces and fit them together.

As they walked out the main doors of the Suzzallo Library, Reilly paused on the front steps and looked up at the magnificent edifice. This time, without a doubt, the three stone statues above the arched entrance moved—first the Greek god, then the winged angel, and finally the bearded sage. Each shifted slightly at its post and smiled down at him.

Facing Red Square, Reilly squeezed Norah's hand. The crisp Northwest air breezed against their faces. As the library faded behind them in the dense fog, Reilly heard Lottie's voice echo in his soul: *I'll show you the way through the door. Just look for me, and I'll be there.*

Reilly turned and thought he saw Charlotte, her long blonde hair streaming in the wind. He saw her silver eyes looking into his as she came closer … and closer. The fog was dispersing …

"Tuma!" he called, as he ran to greet his dog.

Book Three

Fraction in Time

Something bizarre happens to Reilly when he returns from Ireland through the portal to the library. He feels different. Almost as if he's not the same person he was before he left … or worse! Maybe that's how everyone feels after a first kiss. Maybe. But what if that first kiss was also his last?

Unexplained flashbacks haunt him until one day he finds himself trapped and alone in a cavernous room under the ruins of Stonehenge. When three familiar statues deliver the Stelladaur Scrolls to him, Reilly must learn the secret of keeping history from repeating itself, or all he knows and loves will vanish forever—even before it exists.

About the Author

Author, educator, and Founder and President of The Stelladaur Academy, S. L. WHYTE was born in Minnesota and raised in Victoria, British Columbia. "I inherited my love of stories from my aunt, who was a professional storyteller on Mississippi steamboats. As a teenager, I wrote short stories, poetry, and song lyrics. Diagraming sentences became a strange obsession in tenth-grade English class. When I write, I see more clearly, feel more deeply, and share more truthfully. I hope The Stelladaur Series ignites the magic of your imagination as a means of self-discovery and creative renewal." S. L. Whyte lives in Puget Sound, Washington with her husband.

About the Illustrator

KONOHIKI PLACE says, "I have always enjoyed the creative process. As a young boy living in Hawaii, I spent a lot of of time sculpting and sketching. I especially liked drawing dinosaurs and comic book illustrations. Family members, friends and sometimes strangers encouraged me to develop my artistic skills. Seeing others experience joy from my work inspires me to create over and over again. Now a family man with four young boys, I am amazed by their ability to bring their own interpretations of the world into tangible form through various art mediums. This propels me all the more in my world of art."

52767663R00212

Made in the USA
San Bernardino, CA
29 August 2017